**This Large Print Book carries the
Seal of Approval of N.A.V.H.**

The Byrons of Braebourne
Book #1

Tempted By His Kiss

Tracy Anne Warren

CENTER POINT PUBLISHING
THORNDIKE, MAINE

This Center Point Large Print edition
is published in the year 2009 by arrangement with
Avon Books, an imprint of HarperCollins Publishers.

The text of this Large Print edition is unabridged.
In other aspects, this book may vary
from the original edition.
Printed in the United States of America.
Set in 16-point Times New Roman type.

ISBN: 978-1-60285-502-1

Library of Congress Cataloging-in-Publication Data

Warren, Tracy Anne.
  Tempted by his kiss / Tracy Anne Warren.
    p. cm.
  ISBN 978-1-60285-502-1 (library binding : alk. paper)
  1. Large type books. I. Title.

PS3623.A8665T46 2009
813'.6--dc22

2009014829

Chapter 1

Cade Byron tossed back the whiskey in his glass, then reached for the bottle on the side table next to his armchair. Pouring another hefty dram, he downed the second libation as quickly as the first, the alcohol spreading in a burst of fire over his tongue and throat. Leaning back his head, he closed his eyes and waited for the liquor to do its work. With any luck it would ease the ache in his leg.

Confounded thing, he cursed silently, trying not to think too much about the badly healed wound in his right thigh. *Always acts up when the weather turns wet—or in today's case, icy, since it's snowing outside.*

He supposed he could always take a draught of the laudanum the damn quack had left for him, but he hated the stuff and took care to avoid it. He never felt himself when he used laudanum. The opiate clouded his senses to the point where the world seemed to spin around him like some kind of fantastical, disjointed dream, leaving him listless, stultified, and confused. Hard liquor might be just as destructive in the long run, he realized, but at least it dulled his pain without erasing who he was; and even more important, without robbing him of his sense of control.

He knew all about how it felt to lose control. To be denied free will while one trembled on the brink, a second shy of breaking, of begging, of agreeing to violate one's most sacred oaths in order to make the agony stop.

His stomach tightened, a faint wave of nausea rising with the memories. Shoving them aside, he reached again for the glass and bottle, hand shaking as he poured a double measure of whiskey and drank it down. Warmth and calm stole through him. The sensations were artificial, no doubt, but right now he would take what he was given. If only he could add peace to the equation.

That's all I want, he sighed in his head, peace and quiet and to be left the hell alone.

Which is exactly what he'd told Edward last week when his older brother came for a visit, determined to dislodge him from his exile and return him to the bosom of the family—and in the case of the Byrons, that was a very big bosom indeed.

"You've buried yourself up here like a bear in hibernation," Edward had told him as he paced the study with a long-legged stride. "It's been six months now. Don't you think it's time you rejoined the world?"

"From what I can see, the world appears to be spinning along just fine without me," he replied.

Edward frowned, his black brows granting him a fearsome look. "Well, Mama is not fine. She's worried, especially since you refuse to answer her letters."

Cade raked his fingers through his hair. "I read them. Tell her I've read them, and . . . appreciate them. Give her my love. More than that, I can't offer right now."

"Look, I know what you went through in Portugal—"

"Do you?" Cade asked in an almost expressionless voice.

Edward had the grace to lower his gaze. "I know enough. And because of it, I've given you room. Let you have time to yourself to grieve and heal. But all you seem to be doing is grieving with none of the healing. You look like bloody hell, Cade. Come to Braebourne with me. Be with people again, with family. Come home."

For the tiniest moment, Cade had considered the plea, but just as quickly discarded it. "I am home. This estate is mine, or so I was informed in the reading of Uncle George's will. Now, if that's all, Your Grace, I suggest we go have our dinner before it grows cold."

Cade had known Edward wanted to argue further—and his brother had. But after three futile days that did nothing to change Cade's mind, Edward finally conceded defeat, climbed into his coach and drove away.

Or been driven away, Cade mused, knowing he'd forced his brother out—out of his house, out of his life. Just as he wanted.

And I do, he assured himself. *I want solitude. Solitude and peace.*

Taking up the bottle again, he refilled his glass, the last drops of whiskey draining out in a slow *drip-drip-drip.* Setting the bottle aside, he lifted the glass to his lips.

Just then, the study door opened on a set of well-oiled hinges, a tiny old man with a downy nimbus of white hair slipping into the room. Cade gave him no more than a cursory glance before leaning his head against the high seat back once again and closing his eyes.

"Have Harvey carry in some more wood for the fire, would you, Beaks?" Cade commanded in a low tone. "And bring me another bottle of scotch. This one's ready for the rubbish bin."

"Aye, my lord. Oh, and ye've a visitor here to see ye." With that, the old man shuffled from the room, as silently as if he had never been there at all.

Cade scowled. What had Beaks said? Something about a visitor? *Well, if there is someone fool enough to call on me, they can just take themselves off again.* He reached for the whiskey bottle, cursing under his breath when he remembered it was empty.

A faint rustling came from the direction of the door. Turning his head toward the sound, he caught

8

a shimmer of gray as a woman came into view. She hovered, her fine-boned face and slender form revealed in the low light of the fire. Her hair was the pale blond hue of moon glow, her eyes the soft, silvery blue of a mist-shrouded lake. Dusted pink as new blush roses, the color of her lips and cheeks gleamed against the creamy whiteness of her skin.

For a second he wondered if she was a phantom brought on by too much drink, her ethereal beauty more in keeping with a faerie story than reality. But then she took another few steps forward, a lump of snow sliding off the toe of one of her plain, brown half-boots that proved she was every bit as substantial as he.

Cade's fingers tightened against the glass in his hand. "Who the bloody devil are you?" he demanded.

Meg Amberley pulled her woolen cloak more firmly around her body and fought the urge to retreat. She supposed she couldn't claim she'd had no warning regarding the reception she might receive.

"Master don't want no company," the old servant, who opened the front door, had informed her when she arrived. "Get on yer way now."

But she couldn't "get on her way," not with the snow whirling from the sky in violent, blinding fits. When the wheels of her traveling chaise had nearly skidded from the road less than a half mile

9

back, she'd known they had no choice but to seek shelter. And for good or ill, this was the shelter!

Now that she had managed to gain entrance into the manor house, she needed to secure permission from the owner to remain. Unfortunately, however, it seemed the owner might present a more formidable obstacle than the weather itself. *I've faced worse in my nineteen years*, she reassured herself, *and I will face this man, too*. Of course, it might help if she could actually *see* him.

To her consternation, much of the room lay in heavy shadow, the snowstorm having doused all but a last hint of afternoon light. The ruddy glow emanating from the fireplace wasn't doing much to help matters, its light falling mainly on her while leaving the man before her swathed in darkness. He possessed a distinct advantage, since all she could make out was a hazy outline of his long, masculine body. And his boots—well-worn, finely made boots—which presumably contained a pair of equally long, equally fine, male feet.

Drawing a steadying breath, she caught the earthy odors of leather and burning wood, along with another fragrance that was both sharp and sweet—and alcoholic.

"Well?" he barked in a tone as rough as the liquor he had obviously been drinking.

Meg jumped, then shivered. Really, she thought, a gentleman ought to stand in the presence of a lady. But then, he didn't seem much of a gen-

10

tleman at the moment, in spite of his supposed title.

"Have you a name, girl, or are you mute?"

She raised her chin. "Of course. And I am not mute. I can speak quite clearly."

"Good. Then why do you not answer the question? Your name?"

Frowning, she clasped her gloved hands together. "I'm Meg . . . um . . . Miss Margaret Amberley, that is."

"Well, Meg . . . um . . . Miss Margaret Amberley, why have you intruded on my solitude?"

Her muscles drew taut at his mocking rejoinder, but she pushed aside any affront. "I am come in search of shelter. My . . . um . . . my cousin and I were forced here, you see, since the roads have become far too treacherous for travel."

"Cousin, you say? Where is this cousin?"

"She . . . um . . . preferred to wait without. In your drawing room."

Actually, her "cousin" was only her maid, but as she was journeying alone, she had decided to maintain the pretense of a genteel companion for safety and propriety's sake. Suddenly, she was glad she had done so.

A length of wood crackled in the fireplace before giving a faint pop. "This is a private residence," he informed her in a blunt tone. "I do not offer shelter."

When he said nothing more, she realized their

11

interview was over—or at least that *he* thought it was over. Her lips parted in astonishment. "But surely you cannot expect us to make our way in this weather?"

"There's an inn five miles or so from here, I suggest you try that. Now, where is that deuced Beaks with the new bottle I ordered?"

A raw knot formed in her belly, sudden anxiety loosening any last governance on her tongue. "My lord, I would beg you reconsider. The storm is quite severe and growing worse by the minute. You cannot in all good conscience cast us out!"

"A good conscience is highly overrated, I have found, particularly when it interferes with one's own preferences and pleasures."

She peered at the shadowy outline of his head, his face still indistinct, and wished again that he might have the courtesy of revealing himself. "Allow us to stay the night at least," she said. "My mai—um . . . my cousin and I shall be no trouble at all, I promise."

"You are already trouble."

"But—"

"But nothing. Now, go along would you, young woman, and leave me alone."

Her limbs refused to move, stunned by his heartless refusal. "So you would send us out into the cold? Quite literally consign us to our deaths?"

He gave a snort. "I hardly think you'll perish of a little snow. What is there? An inch? Two?"

"No, my lord. There is half a foot at least and more coming down by the second."

"Half a foot! What nonsense is this? The last I looked there was naught but a dusting."

Up went her eyebrows. "Then a goodly amount of time must have passed since your last glimpse outside."

On a grumbling murmur, he leaned forward, rising tall, then taller still, out of the depths of his high-backed chair. Her lips parted as he moved fully into the light, her hand curling tight against her breast, her heart beating out a rapid tattoo.

Her first impression was one of height and lean, masculine strength, his frame well over six feet, with wide shoulders, a solid chest, and arms and legs that looked as if they must be fashioned of pure, corded muscle. And yet, he seemed too thin, his white linen shirt and fawn breeches hanging loosely on his body, making her wonder if he had recently lost an unintended amount of weight.

The natural tan of his skin carried a faintly wan cast, the vivid forest green of his eyes standing out in stark relief. His hair was disheveled and lay around his head in short, thick chestnut waves, one curl dangling in riotous abandon against a stubborn forehead. The rest of his face held an inward determination and the same masculine strength she had first noted—from the angular planes of his cheekbones to the fine length of his nose and square jaw. His lips added a winsome punctuation to a countenance that held a raw, almost sensual beauty.

He was handsome enough to take her breath, and he did, air racing from her chest in a swift rush. But even as she struggled to recover her equilibrium, she noticed something else, something that made her flinch with a mixture of sympathy and dismay.

He wore no cravat, his shirt collar open at the neck in a way that enabled her to glimpse what she would never have noticed otherwise. There, encircling his throat like some gruesome ribbon, lay a line of scar tissue. The wound's edges were mostly healed, but still new enough to show bits of pink.

His gaze met hers for a long moment, and then, with a dismissive expression, he turned and walked across the room. Or, rather, he limped, his uneven gait startling her yet again.

Halting on the far side of the room, he leaned down to peer out the window before rubbing a pair of fingers against the frost-covered glass. Obviously dissatisfied with the results, he cursed beneath his breath, then unlocked the window and flung it upward. Icy wind blasted into the room, the dark green velvet curtains on either side of the embrasure billowing out like sails at full loft. Snowflakes spit and whizzed, swirling around him as he stuck his head and shoulders out the window.

Is he mad? she wondered, hugging her cloak more tightly around herself. For his part, he seemed oblivious to the cold, the thin material of his shirt fluttering around him as his hair whipped about his skull, leaving it even more tousled than before. He hung there for nearly a minute, braced against the frame while the storm engulfed him in its fury. Then, abruptly, as if he knew he'd reached some limit, he stepped back and straightened, shards of snow and ice glittering in his warm chestnut brown locks.

"You're right," he declared in grim resignation. "There are several inches on the ground. Personally, such would not prevent me from journeying on, but I suppose a lady might find it alarming."

"Anyone with sense would find it alarming!" she retorted, suddenly not caring what he might think. A fresh burst of wind roared inside, threatening to steal what little warmth remained in the room. Shivering, she hurried forward, brushed him out of the way and slammed the window shut, flipping the lock in place to keep out any lingering chill. She glanced up, her eyebrows lifting at the grin riding his face.

"Cold?" he inquired.

She nodded. "As you must surely be."

"I'll thaw out again if Beaks ever brings me that whiskey. So," he said with grudging acceptance, "I suppose you shall be remaining."

"Yes, if I might," she murmured, aware how close he stood, close enough that she could see the snowflakes melting in his hair. She restrained the odd urge to reach up and brush them away, her pulse gathering speed at the thought of touching his hair, of touching him.

Breaking eye contact, he gave a muffled grunt and swung around to stalk toward his chair. "Tell Beaks to find you rooms, you and your cousin. You can stay the night, then be on your way as soon as this storm subsides."

She trembled, unsure if the reaction had anything to do with the temperature. "Th-Thank you, my lord. I am most grateful for your hospitality."

He gave another low-throated grunt, one that carried a touch of irony, as he resumed his seat. Arranging his legs in front of him on a low foot-stool, he leaned his head back and closed his eyes.

Once again she realized she had been dismissed. Shifting on her heels, she started toward the door, but paused abruptly and turned back. "My lord?"

He made no reply.

"Your pardon, my lord," she persisted, "but I just realized our earlier introduction was of a rather one-sided nature. You know my name, but I am afraid I do not know yours."

At length he opened his eyes to half staff, appraising her with a speculative gleam. "It's Byron. Cade Byron."

"Ah. A pleasure, Lord Byron."

"No, not *Lord* Byron. I'm not that blasted poet, you know. Byron is my family name and I'm Lord Cade. Now, is there anything else you require?"

"No, not at present . . . Byron, Cade Byron," she added in repetition of his former mockery of her own name.

His green gaze twinkled in acknowledgment of her riposte, but he didn't break a smile. Closing his eyes again, he settled back against his chair and left Meg to make her own way from the room.

Chapter 2

Cade awakened the next morning to high, soft feminine voices talking in the corridor that led past his bedroom. The only such voices he ever heard in his bachelor household were those of the two housemaids he employed, who came twice a week to clean and do laundry. But they were generally quiet, especially in this section of the house. Actually, he was surprised they were here today at all, given the storm. *Well, they can deuced well leave the dusting and polishing for another day!*

Sitting upright in bed, he groaned against the stab of pain that shot through his skull—the result, no doubt, of too much drink last night. After a moment's pause to let the sensation pass, he reached for his dressing gown, slipping into it as he rose from his bed. Crossing in his bare feet, he twisted the doorknob and wrenched open the door.

He stopped dead at the sight that greeted him, finding not the serving women, but his unexpected houseguests, Meg Amberley and her cousin, whatever her name might be. The cousin's plain brown eyes grew wide, her impish gaze sweeping over him from head to toe before she raised a hand to her mouth and giggled. As for Miss Amberley, she stared, a faint wash of pink smudging her cheeks. Still, she did not look away.

"Good morning, my lord," she said with a pleasant smile. "Are we disturbing you?"

If that isn't the understatement of the century. From the moment he'd laid eyes on her, she'd disturbed and disrupted him. Less than twenty-four hours acquaintance and his life was already at sixes and sevens.

Nonetheless, he couldn't help but enjoy the freshly washed glow of her skin and the luxurious beauty of her guileless blue eyes. Her pale blond hair was arranged in an attractive, feminine knot at the back of her head, her lithesome figure clothed in a black wool day dress whose color in no way diminished her beauty.

He caught a faint whiff of something floral, something distinctly *her*, that made him want to lean closer to test the scent. In his mind's eye he imagined himself pressing his nose to the curve of her neck, and brushing his lips against the skin of her throat to see if her flesh was as dewy soft as it looked. Blood coursed in a ripe downward flow, abruptly heightening his awareness of the fact that he wasn't wearing so much as a stitch of clothing beneath his dressing gown.

God, what am I doing? he chided himself. Woolgathering over some girl he didn't know or want in his house. What was wrong with him? Worse, how could he even think of another woman with Calida barely cold in her grave? His nascent desire withered, his brows drawing together as he shot Meg a look he hoped would encourage her to move along—quickly!

"Please forgive my manners," she offered instead, "and allow me to make you known to my cousin, Miss Amy Jones."

He sent a glance toward the other girl, then inclined his head. "Miss Jones."

The girl giggled and dipped a quick curtsey. She gave no other response, apparently too shy to speak.

"Miss Jones and I were just on our way to breakfast," Miss Amberley explained in a lilting voice. "However, we were not quite certain of the location of the morning room."

"The *dining* room is downstairs in the rear of the house. I do not have a morning room."

"Ah, well, the dining room will do nicely, too." She paused, her gaze subtly moving over what he knew must be his disheveled hair and the night's growth of rough whiskers.

His glower deepened.

"Perhaps once you are more suitably attired, you might care to join us, my lord?"

"I would not."

Her pale eyebrows winged upward on her delicate forehead as if she might be considering a rejoinder for his blunt reply. Then she gave a mild shrug. "As you wish. We shall leave you to your slumber then."

The cousin giggled again, her eyes dancing. Dismissing her, he focused his attention on Meg. "Pray enjoy your repast and have a safe journey when you are once more on your way."

"On our way? Oh, but you obviously have not realized again."

"Realized what?"

"That it is still snowing. There is nothing but white as far as the eye can see, and according to my coachman, the roads are completely impassable. My apologies, but I am afraid we shall have to trespass upon your good graces a while longer."

Swinging around, he walked to a window and pulled back the curtain. "Bloody hell!" Just as she claimed, it was snow, snow everywhere, with more falling by the second.

He turned and came forward again, half expecting to find her puckered up with affront over his swearing—that, or ready to swoon as some ladies might pretend to do. Meg, however, seemed utterly unflustered. In fact, he thought he detected the faintest hint of a smile hovering over her lips.

"Perhaps you might enjoy that breakfast, after all, my lord?" she remarked, her expression all innocence.

He growled low in his throat, not entirely trusting what might come out of his mouth.

She sank into an elegant curtsey, then signaled with a hand for her cousin to do the same. The other girl obeyed, though with far less grace than Meg herself. "Until we meet again, my lord," Meg said. "At nuncheon, perhaps?"

"Good day, Miss Amberley."

Stepping back into his room, he closed the door with a near soundless click. Waiting until he heard the pair of them move off down the corridor, he shucked free of his dressing gown, then climbed back between the now cold sheets. Punching his pillow and grumbling beneath his breath about unwanted house guests and damned cursed snow-storms, he rolled over and closed his eyes. Some minutes passed, though, before he fell back to sleep.

"Will ye be needin' anythin' else, miss?" Meg's maid asked. "If not, I thought I might nip off to me room fer a bit. I'm rather enjoying having fancy digs of me own, even if it is only temporary-like."

Seated in a comfortable armchair before the drawing room fire, Meg glanced up from her embroidery. "Oh, certainly, Amy. Do go on. But don't forget what we discussed."

The girl's forehead wrinkled in momentary puzzlement. "Oh, do ye mean about me stayin' out of his lordship's way and not talkin' to him if

I do 'appen upon him? Well, considering we haven't see him all day long, that shouldn't be hard."

"Yes, he has made himself rather scarce, has he not?" Meg replied. Despite her suggestion that Lord Cade join them for nuncheon, he had failed to put in an appearance at the meal. "Nonetheless," she continued, "you are supposed to be my cousin, and if you start spinning wild lies, he might figure us out."

"Plus, there's me accent. Don't sound like no lady like you, miss. A high-'n'-mighty lord like him might notice such a thing."

"Exactly," Meg agreed, repressing a smile.

Once Amy departed, Meg returned to her stitchery, her thoughts lingering on Lord Cade, as they had with great frequency since her arrival yesterday afternoon. A conversation with the wizened, white-haired Beaks a short while ago had elicited the information that his lordship was indeed awake and once again ensconced inside his book room. Apparently he'd retreated there with a plate of cold meat and a libation, leaving strict instructions that he was not to be disturbed.

Well, I shall be cheerful, despite his less than hospitable nature, she thought as she drew a measured stitch with her needle, the indigo thread gleaming even in the watery afternoon light. If he wished to keep to himself, that was his right. After all, this was his house, his domain, and she was the intruder.

Honestly, though, one would think he could be a tad more accommodating. It wasn't as though she'd had any choice in seeking refuge here. The weather was the weather, and could not be changed—not even for a divinely handsome aristocrat with a temperament fit to infuriate a saint! And so, for however long the storm kept them confined, she and Cade Byron would simply have to make the best of things.

For her own part, she was well used to unexpected circumstances and ever changing locales, having grown up roaming from one port city to another with her mother and naval officer father. After a while, one learned to adapt and appreciate new situations and new people. Some might say such a life was hard, but she had never minded, having been happy and secure in the constancy of her parents' love.

Then, five years ago, everything changed. Her mother, to the astonishment and joy of all, had found herself with child again after years of barrenness. A miracle, everyone agreed. And a blessing. Yet in spite of an easy, uneventful pregnancy, the delivery went badly, mother and baby dying within hours of each other.

Numb with grief, Meg had clung to her father. Another man faced with the prospect of raising a half-grown child alone, especially a girl, would not have been blamed for sending her away to live with relatives. Instead, her father had vowed to keep her close. With the sorrow of her mother and infant brother's passing hanging over them, he knew that he and Meg had more need of each other than ever. And so, despite his love of the sea, Captain Amberley traded his ship for an office, taking a promotion with the Admiralty that allowed them to remain together.

But now Papa was gone, too, and she was on her way to live with a great-aunt whom she had never met. She sighed as she took another stitch, wondering what her elderly relation would be like and how remote her house in Scotland might be. If not for the snowstorm, she might be arriving there even now. Until she could continue her journey, though, she would have to make the best of her situation —and her dealings with her irascible host.

Meg's needle slowed, halting entirely as she thought again about Cade Byron. Tingles rushed over her skin the way they had that morning when she came upon him in the hallway, recalling the sight of him dressed in nothing more than a thin silk robe. No man should have the right to look that good, she mused, especially not first thing in the morning. Darkly powerful and irresistibly delicious, he'd driven the breath straight out of her lungs. Even in his unkempt, just-out-of-bed state—or maybe because of it—he'd been nothing less than gorgeous, with his rich chestnut hair tumbled in wild disarray around his head, rough bristles shadowing the lean angles of his jaw line.

If he looked this amazing injured and weary, she could scarcely imagine how he might appear in the peak of health.

Her thoughts took an abrupt turn at the reminder, and she wondered exactly how he'd come by his limp and the unusual scar on his throat. His servants certainly weren't forthcoming, although she hadn't made much of an effort to pry. Nor had she inquired about the amount of pain he suffered, recalling the empty bottle of spirits at his elbow last night. Having grown up around military men, she'd known her share of those who used alcohol to dull a wide range of injuries and afflictions.

Regardless, she supposed such speculation was none of her business. Just as the man himself was not. She knew she would be doing herself a favor if she didn't dwell on him or his circumstances. After all, her time here would be fleeting, Cade Byron nothing more than an interesting detour on her journey north.

To Meg's amazement, the snow continued unabated, not ceasing fully until the third morning after her arrival. On a day that dawned clear and sunny, a quick glance outside made it plain she would not be leaving anytime soon. Lord Cade obviously realized that as well, the door to his bedchamber slamming shut with an echo that reverberated through the house like a snarled shout of frustration. As usual, she saw nothing of her host, and was left to take her meals alone in the dining room.

On her fourth day of confinement, however, she decided she'd had enough. Despite her initial cheerfulness, she'd grown heartily sick of stitchery. As for her small store of books, she had read them all—twice! She knew there were more books in the house. The trouble was, they were all inside Cade Byron's hallowed book room, where she instinctively understood she was not allowed to trespass.

Well, he would just have to abide her interruption, she decided. He could glower and growl, bluster and yell, but his displeasure would make no difference to her.

Yet as she strode down the hallway where she'd been led by Beaks that very first afternoon, she couldn't help the flutter of nerves that swam inside her belly. Pausing in front of the closed door, she rapped briefly with her knuckles, then turned the knob, deciding if she didn't ask his permission to enter, he couldn't deny it—at least not until after she was already in the room. Chin up, she sailed inside.

A brilliant wash of sunlight flooded the space, the buttery cream walls and rich, cherrywood tones of the furnishings revealed in ways she had not been able to appreciate on that first gloomy afternoon. Gone were the heavy shadows, replaced by light that made even the deepest corners of the room visible to the eye. She remembered seeing books on that earlier visit, but only now did she realize how many works were contained in the room. Bound in supple leather, books lined the walls from floor to ceiling, dozens and dozens of them, their varied shapes, thicknesses, and colors creating a mosaic of visual and literary design. Slowing her step, she took an extra moment to survey her surroundings, relishing the lush texture of the Turkey carpet beneath her slippers and the warmth of the fire burning cheerfully in the grate.

Lord Cade was seated in what was obviously *his* chair, a thick leather-bound volume in his lap. His head came up at her intrusion, dark chestnut brows furrowing as he peered at her through a pair of silver, half moon eyeglasses.

So he wears reading spectacles, does he? she mused. She had to admit, the addition in no way diminished his dangerously good looks. If anything, they made him even more attractive—his eyes shining above the lenses with the vibrancy of new spring leaves, his hair once again tousled, with a willful curl dangling over his forehead.

Her pulse gave a hop, her breath growing surprisingly short. Fighting off the reaction, she moved toward the nearest shelf of books. "Never mind me," she called in a breezy voice. "Pray continue your reading and pretend I am not even in the room."

He laid a palm over an open page. "But you *are*

in the room, without so much as a by-your-leave, I might add. What is it you want?"

"A book, my lord. Seeing I am snowbound inside this house, I require some means of occupying myself. I searched the other rooms—well, most of them, at least—and realized my selection is rather limited, what with all the volumes being in here with you. I'll only be a minute or two."

He gave a plainly skeptical snort, scowled at her for a few seconds more, then returned to his reading. Turning her head away as well, she perused the offerings. Powerfully aware of him sitting only a few feet away, she chose a volume with somewhat less than her full attention. Taking the book down, she flipped it open to a random page.

The slaughter of cattle is best done when the beasts are well-fattened at the end of the summer season . . .

Ugh! She recoiled at the topic. Closing the book, she returned it to its place. Her second selection proved little better—this time covering the fascinating subject of crop rotation.

"You'd do better with the shelf on the wall to your right," Cade Byron drawled. "I believe you are in the agriculture section at present."

She shoved the farming treatise back onto its shelf. "You might have said, you know."

"But then I wouldn't have been able to pretend you're not here, would I?"

She waited to see if he might crack a smile. He didn't, although his eyes did glitter with what she surmised to be suppressed amusement. Tossing him a narrow-eyed glare, she moved several feet across the room toward the area he suggested.

These shelves, she discovered, were filled with titles and authors she recognized—Sheridan, Pope, Richardson, and Voltaire, just to name a few. Sliding out a copy of *Candide*, she opened it to discover the work in its original French. She read a few lines and began to smile.

"Better, I take it?" Lord Cade commented.

She glanced over. "Much. Thank you, my lord."

He gave a negligent shrug. "You're welcome."

Turning back, she selected a volume of poetry. Yet even as she examined the book, her mind was taken up with thoughts of the man seated only feet away. That last exchange had actually seemed pleasant. The most civilized of their acquaintance. *Mayhap he is mellowing and has resigned himself to my presence in his house.*

"The way I see it," he remarked, thumbing over a page in his book, "the sooner you choose something, the sooner I'll have my privacy back."

So much for cordial discourse! For a long moment she stared. "You really are a most disagreeable man, do you know that, my lord?"

If she'd expected him to ruffle up over her insult,

29

however, she was quickly disappointed. Looking up, he met her gaze. "That's right. I am disagreeable. So take as many volumes as you like and hurry back to your chair in the drawing room."

She hugged a book to her breasts. "How do you know I have been spending my days in the drawing room?"

He scowled, obviously annoyed with himself over his comment. "Just a guess. Where else would you spend your time?"

But it had not been a guess, she realized. *Has he been inquiring after me?* The notion made her smile. "Well," she mused aloud, "there are other places in which I might have made myself comfortable. My bedchamber, for instance. The room is most excellent."

A mocking light came into his gaze. "I am glad you approve."

"Oh, I do. My feather tick is soft as a cloud. I could lie on it forever. Don't you love lying on a good, comfortable bed?" Abruptly she broke off, realizing what she'd just said, and the suddenly intimate nature of the topic. She hoped he didn't think she was flirting with him. *Come to think of it, am I flirting with him?*

Lord Cade, however, did not rise to the bait. "Again, I am relieved you find the accommodations to your liking."

"How could I not?" she murmured, recovering. "You have a lovely house."

"It suits my purposes."

She paused. "You have a most excellent cook as well. A shame you do not take the opportunity to do his fare justice."

"How so? I am afraid I do not follow."

"Well, I couldn't help but notice over the past few days that you haven't once put in an appearance at a meal. Although I suppose you must eat sometime."

One corner of his mouth turned up. "On occasion."

"Then you should make those occasions more frequent. It's plain that you need plumping up."

His eyes widened behind his spectacles. "Pardon me?"

"You ought to eat more, my lord. You're far too thin for your frame."

"Good Lord, you sound like my mother."

"If I do, then you ought to listen to her. She's clearly a wise woman."

"She is indeed. Wise enough to know I make my own decisions. Now, choose your books and be on your way. Your two minutes elapsed some while ago."

Meg hesitated at the dismissal, then swung around and began studying books in earnest. She selected two volumes of poetry, a novel, and a satire. "Well, I suppose I shall be going," she announced.

He kept reading.

"Thank you for letting me borrow these."

He gave a faint nod but didn't look up.

"Mayhap I shall see you at dinner this evening," she prompted. "Should you decide to take a meal, that is."

He turned a page in his book and made no reply. When the silence became overwhelming, she gave a soft sigh, then made her way from the room.

Cade waited until he heard the door click shut. Only then did he look up, imagining Meg as she walked back to her chair in the drawing room. He knew all about her habits; Beaks and his footman, Harvey, gave him frequent reports.

So Miss Amberley wants me to join her for dinner? Foolish girl doesn't know when she's better off.

Well, he would have his dinner where he always did—right here in this study, on a tray, with a bottle of scotch near at hand. And Miss Amberley could eat alone in the dining room, just as he knew she did each night.

He frowned at the notion, strangely disquieted. Her loneliness was not his concern. After all, he hadn't invited her here, and had no obligation to keep her company.

Still, what would be the harm in sharing a meal?

Brushing aside the thought as nonsense, he resumed his reading. Fifteen minutes passed, however, before he was finally able to concentrate on the words.

Chapter 3

At six-thirty that evening Meg took her now customary seat at the long walnut dining room table. Placing a white linen napkin across her lap, she waited for Harvey to return with the first course. "Potato soup," he'd informed her with a crooked grin before departing for the kitchen.

Glancing idly around the room, she occupied herself by studying the familiar egg-and-dart molding on the ceiling cornice, the cream-and-gold flocked wallpaper, and the elegant, brown velvet curtains. The room possessed a refined, rather masculine atmosphere, one she thought eminently suited to its enigmatic owner.

Linking her palms in her lap, she forced away a sigh. After all, she should be well-used to dining alone by now, seeing as she had done so every night since her arrival. She supposed she might have once again asked Amy to join her, but the girl just wasn't at ease in the formal room, and she hadn't the heart to force the issue.

Briefly, she had toyed with the idea of bringing one of her new books to the table, so she might read while she ate. But the notion went against the rules of proper decorum. And although no one but she and the footman would ever know, she knew her lady mother would have been disappointed had she indulged in such "coarse" behavior.

Soon enough she heard footsteps, her stomach rumbling in silent anticipation of the dish to come. Her eyes widened, however, when she glanced toward the double doors and saw not the footman, but Cade Byron walk slowly inside.

"Good evening, Miss Amberley," he greeted. "My apologies for arriving late."

All she could do was stare, struck by his unassailable masculine beauty, and the fact that for once he was most elegantly and appropriately attired. A pristine white cravat was tied at his throat, and a white shirt and striped fawn waistcoat buttoned across the broad expanse of his chest. A dark blue tailcoat fit his shoulders, emphasizing their powerful shape, and pantaloons, rather than evening breeches, graced his long legs—a sartorial choice that was quite proper given the informal country setting. His cheeks were freshly shaven and his hair neatly combed, although his usual recalcitrant curl had escaped to dangle across his forehead in a most temptingly attractive way.

"My lord," she murmured, somehow finding the strength to unglue her tongue from the inside of her mouth. "I . . . um . . . I did not realize you had decided to join me. Harvey made no mention of it."

"Quite likely because I did not inform him of my intentions," he remarked with a haughty quirk of one brow.

Crossing the room, he moved to the head of the

table, then lowered himself into the chair to her right. His limp, she noticed, seemed less pronounced than it had been on that first evening. Perhaps he is feeling better, she mused, now that the storm has passed. Mayhap the improvement has put him in a more social frame of mind.

The footman entered moments later, a tureen of soup and a ladle borne on an oblong, silver tray. "Why hallo, your lordship. Are ye having dinner with the miss tonight?"

"That I am, Harvey. Another place setting, if you would be so good."

"Right away, your lordship." Placing his burden in front of Lord Cade, the young man went to retrieve a second plate, cutlery, and glassware.

Once the table was properly set and wine poured, Cade leaned forward to do the honors, steam rising in a small burst when he lifted the cover from the tureen. "Plenty for two, I'd say. But then my cook always has a tendency to prepare more than is strictly necessary."

"Excellent. That way you may easily avail yourself of seconds."

He raised a brow, pausing for a moment before taking the ladle in hand and dipping it into the soup. "Are you on about that again? As I advised you earlier, I do as I like."

She waited while he filled and passed a bowl to the servant to set before her. Once he served himself, the footman stepped away. "And I must advise *you* that I shall do the same, my lord," she replied in a soft tone. Dipping her spoon into the fragrant broth, she took a sip. "Hmm, delicious! Do go on before it grows cold."

His lips firmed as if he were contemplating a retort. Instead he took up his own utensil and did as she suggested. "So," he said at length. "Where is your cousin tonight? Why does she not join us?"

Droplets of soup splashed off Meg's spoon, landing luckily back in the bowl rather than on the front of her dress. "Oh, she . . . um . . . wished to take a tray in her room. A bit of a headache."

"How singular."

"What do you mean?"

"Only that I am given to understand she never dines with you. Is she much given to aches and pains?"

"No, not as a rule. She is of a retiring nature, however, and often prefers her own company."

"Curious. She didn't strike me as the retiring sort the morning we met."

"Well, appearances can be deceiving, as they say."

"Indeed." He ate a bit more, then set aside his spoon. Taking up his napkin, he patted his lips, before reaching for his glass of wine. "Although, in this case, you might do us both the favor of ending this ruse of yours. It will not serve, you know."

Her spoon bobbled again. "Excuse me?"

36

"You may cease pretending that Miss Jones is your cousin," he said in a matter-of-fact tone. "We both know very well that she is not."

"Of course she's my cousin!" Meg defended on a sputter. "Why would you think otherwise?"

He tossed her a speaking glance. "Mainly because she's been down in my kitchen chatting up my staff for the past two days. The young woman comes from Wiltshire, I believe, and doesn't sound anything like a lady ought, or so Beaks informs me."

Meg cursed silently beneath her breath and carefully laid down her spoon. "She has a bit of an accent, I admit."

"And a loose tongue to go with it."

Meg held steady for another moment, then let her shoulders droop in defeat. "I should have known she wouldn't be able to resist going below-stairs. I warned her not to talk to *you*, but didn't think I'd have to say anything about not fraternizing with your servants."

His lips twitched with humor. "Well, she's given you away, I am afraid."

"So, it would appear," she sighed. "I apologize for deceiving you, my lord, but such precautions seemed prudent at the time. Amy is my maid-servant, you see."

"Ah." He sipped his wine.

"A friend of the family was supposed to travel with me, but her son came down ill on the morning of my departure. Seeing that my aunt had already sent a coach to collect me and there was no one else willing to make such a long trip, I decided that taking Amy would suffice. When we were forced to seek shelter here, I . . . um . . . thought it best not to reveal my actual situation."

"And so you should not," he told her in a gruff voice. "Have you no other relations who might have accompanied you? No brothers or uncles?"

She shook her head. "No. I am an only child and both of my parents are deceased. There is no one now, except for my great-aunt, that is. She has agreed to take me in, but could not make the trip herself. At sixty-five, she is far too old to journey long distances."

"She ought to have sent a man."

"Oh, she did. John Coachman has seen after Amy and me quite well at the inns."

Lord Cade arched a brow. "And what of here? I have seen little of him here."

"What do you mean, my lord?"

Taking up the wine decanter, he added an inch to her glass before refilling his own. "I mean that you are, for all intents and purposes, alone with me. Aside from the obvious impropriety, there is the matter of your safety."

Her brows knit in puzzlement. "What about my safety? I have been most comfortable."

"And so you have. But what if I were another kind of man? What if I were the sort to have taken advantage of our unusual situation? You must realize, Miss Amberley, that had I wished, I might have done almost anything to you by now."

A startled laugh escaped her lips. "Are you saying you might have murdered me in my bed? Do not be ridiculous, my lord."

"I wasn't thinking about murder, but beds would definitely have been involved."

Her eyes widened, her heart giving a tremendous thump. The treacherous organ beat even faster at the notion of him in her room. In her bed. Kissing her, touching her, doing all sorts of dark, sinful things of which she could only speculate. She shivered, abruptly glad he couldn't read her mind.

He laughed, dimples she had never noticed before appearing in his cheeks. "I see I have shocked you," he said. "Pray do not be alarmed, since I have no such designs upon your person, lovely though it may be. I am merely pointing out the uncertain nature of your circumstances. When you travel on, I shall send one of my own men to accompany you."

"Thank you, my lord. That is very good of you."

He gave a negligent shrug, his gaze turning toward the doorway. "Ah, here comes our next course. Unless I have put you off your food, that is? Perhaps I should not have inflicted my company upon you, after all."

Forcing her still-speeding pulse to calm, she

met his gaze. "No, I am glad you are here, and it is no infliction."

"Despite my being a most disagreeable man?" he inquired with a gentle tease.

The corners of her lips turned up. "Yes, even in spite of that." Suddenly, she could not look away, sinking helplessly into the vibrant green depths of his eyes. But then she remembered herself and forced her gaze aside. "Oh, look," she said on a shaky breath. "Roast chicken, onion tart, and carrots. Cook has outdone himself."

Quietly agreeing, Lord Cade took up a knife and began to carve.

The rest of the meal passed pleasantly, the pair of them confining their conversation to interesting yet far less provocative topics.

As Cade ate, he watched Meg, enjoying the sparkle in her intelligent blue eyes and the expressive way she used her hands when she strove to make a point. To his surprise, he ate a great deal more than usual, truly enjoying the food as he had not in far too long.

He didn't know why he'd decided to indulge her. Even now he could be in his study, savoring his books and his privacy. *Boredom, perhaps?* Though he didn't consider himself bored. *Loneliness, maybe?* Though he had never minded being alone. Yet tonight he found himself relaxing, even forgetting; the sorrows of the past months set at bay for this brief while.

And then the meal was over, dessert and tea served and consumed, a glass of port poured for himself. Turning to assist her from her chair, he prepared to bid her a good-night.

"Are you weary, my lord?" she asked, rising in an elegant sweep.

He arched a brow. "Not as such, no. Why do you ask?"

"I was just wondering if you might join me in a game?"

"A game? My apologies, but I'm afraid I am not much given to such pursuits these days."

"But surely you play chess. I could not help but notice the board in your study."

"You are correct," he said, realizing he'd been fairly caught. "Still, the hour is advanced . . ."

"It is only half past eight. Surely even you do not retire quite so early?"

Actually, he retired late as a rule. The later the better, he found, since he often had trouble sleeping unless he went to his bed in a state of near exhaustion. Drink helped, and if he imbibed enough, he could sometimes sleep deeply, the dreams temporarily quieted.

He studied Meg's hopeful expression. For a moment he considered accepting her invitation, but then ruthlessly pushed the impulse aside. He'd already spent more than enough time in her company tonight as it was. "Be that as it may, I have other matters which require my attention this evening."

She lay a hand against the back of her chair. "What 'other' matters? Perhaps I might be of assistance. If you are planning to review accounts, I am told I have a keen eye for figures as well as a neat hand with a quill."

Accounts! he thought. Persistent minx. "No, not accounts," he admitted.

"Research then?" she ventured, her lake blue eyes gleaming with obvious mischief. "That must be the reason you lock yourself away in your book room for hours at a time. Because you are doing research."

His mouth twitched, threatening to turn into a smile. "No, I am not doing research, either."

"Then what, my lord? Surely now that you have emerged from your solitude, you cannot mean to retreat into it again so soon."

That was exactly what he meant to do. He should have guessed that if he gave her an inch, she would demand a mile.

"Because if that is the case," she argued further, "then I must urge you to continue mending your ways. Besides, what is one little game of chess? Surely you can spare a few minutes tonight regardless of your pressing schedule."

"Minutes can sometimes turn into hours while playing chess."

"But no doubt that will not be so in this case. Unless you are worried I might best you?"

This time he did smile, his grin one of confident

certainty. "No insult meant, Miss Amberley, but I am quite an experienced player."

"Then you should have no hesitation. Give me an hour's entertainment, and if I lose, I promise I shall not intrude upon your solitude again for the remainder of my stay."

He considered her proposal, curiously tempted.

Before he could respond, she held up a finger. "If, on the other hand, *I* should win, then you must promise to act more the proper host."

"Which would entail . . . ?"

"Oh, attendance at meals. The noon meal as well as the evening. I shall grant you leave to forgo breakfast, so as not to interfere with your slumber."

"How magnanimous," he said, setting a casual hand against the dining table. "What more?"

"As host, you would need to provide some sort of entertainment. My needs are simple. Cards or charades in the evening should suffice."

"I have no quarrel with cards, but I must tell you, I draw the line at charades. Crambo is out as well."

A smile broke over her winsome face. "Very well, no charades or crambo, then. So, my lord, have we a wager?"

He hesitated, diverted by her ploy in spite of him-self. "We might. Although I must tell you I had no idea you were so enamored of my companionship."

Her smile widened. "I am finding that when one's choice of society is as limited as mine is at present, one can learn to like almost anyone. Even you, my lord."

A laugh rumbled past his lips, her outrageous remark eliciting amusement rather than offense. He thought he caught a faint glimmer of relief in her gaze, as though she'd wondered, after she spoke, if she might perhaps have gone too far.

She thrust out a hand. "Do we have a deal?"

His amusement only increased at her rather unorthodox gesture, since as a rule ladies did not shake hands. Hesitating a scant moment more, he enfolded her palm inside his own.

Immediate pleasure tingled over his flesh at the contact, her hand soft and delicate and extraordinarily feminine. Tiny, as well, her palm barely a fraction of the size of his own—so small that without care he knew he could crush the fragile bones inside with no more than a squeeze. He was careful and tender, though, aware of his height and strength as he towered high above her.

Gazing down, he met the suddenly rapt expression in her eyes. Without thinking, he tightened the contact between them, the tips of his fingers brushing idly against the silky texture of her skin as he pulled her a fraction closer. She trembled but did not resist, subtly swaying toward him, near enough now for the skirts of her gown to brush against his pantaloon leg. Her lips parted—pink and pretty and sweetly kissable. He bent his head and stared at her luscious, strawberry-hued mouth, wondering if her flesh would taste as good as it looked.

She trembled again, her eyelids drooping with reciprocal interest. Abruptly, he blinked and gave his head an almost imperceptible shake, as if he were emerging from a haze.

What in the blazes? Surely I wasn't about to kiss her? And God knows what else besides!

Desire pulsed through him, his flesh thickening with unmistakable arousal. He was way out of bounds, he knew. Margaret Amberley was a guest in his house, and as such under his protection. Crossing that line, even with a kiss, would be a violation of her trust—and make him little better than the sort of scoundrel he'd warned her against earlier. Then, too, there was his oath to another woman. One whose young life may have been extinguished, but was not forgotten.

As if Meg had suddenly turned into a leper, he dropped her hand. Pivoting on his heel, he started toward the door.

"My lord," she called. "You . . . you did not give me your answer."

Answer? What answer? Then he remembered—the chess game. Christ, he cursed to himself, did she still want to play that bloody game? But of course she did, having not been privy to the prurient direction of his thoughts.

Momentarily, he considered refusing, telling her there would be no chess game tonight or any other. But then he remembered her offer. *What had she said?* If she lost, she would promise not to infringe upon his solitude again for the remainder of her stay. He had to admit he liked the idea of that, and its simplicity, since he knew instinctively that she was a woman of her word.

Slowly, he turned back. "Yes, we have a deal. Pray lead the way if you would be so good." With a sweeping gesture of his arm, he allowed her to pass.

Like candy from a baby, he mused, as he trailed after her to his book room. Thirty minutes from now he'd be handing her a defeat. And putting an end to any further unwanted bouts of temptation.

"Checkmate, my lord," Meg declared in a soft voice nearly an hour and a half later.

Lord Cade's forehead gathered into a series of lines. "What! But—"

"It was your rook, you see. Once I captured that, the next three moves were virtually assured to be mine."

As she watched, he scowled harder and stared at the board, running his fingers through his already disheveled hair. His cravat sat slightly askew around his neck as well, the result of having given the linen several hard tugs during the last few minutes of the match. Until now, his attitude had been one of relaxed overconfidence, nursing his tumbler of whiskey while he monitored the progress of the game with a far too casual eye.

"I am afraid there is no way out," she told him. "Although I must say you made a valiant attempt to rescue yourself there at the last."

Silence fell, his gaze glued to the board as he studied it for some fleeting avenue of escape. At length he reached out, took up his glass of whiskey and swallowed the contents in a single gulp. Setting the tumbler down with a snap, he met her eyes. "Your game, Miss Amberley. And bravo, you are indeed a masterful player."

Warmth poured through her at his praise. "Thank you, my lord."

He shrugged. "It is nothing but the truth. Had I known precisely how good you are, I would have paid a great deal more attention to the game from the start."

"I rather imagine you would have," she said in a mild tone.

He grumbled something unintelligible beneath his breath before recovering his composure. "No chance, I suppose, that I could talk you into a best two-out-of-three on that wager of ours?"

Her lips tilted upward as she shook her head, forcing herself not to laugh at his expression of resigned chagrin.

"Very well. Seeing that I am a man of my word, I will honor our agreement." Reaching for a nearby crystal decanter, he refilled his tumbler. "Since you have now won the right to be entertained each evening, I suggest we have another match tomorrow."

Her smile increased. "It will by my pleasure, my lord."

"And your downfall," he stated. "I warn you now I shall not be so easy to defeat next time."

"I look forward to the challenge."

He huffed low in his throat. "So, where in the world did you learn to play like that?"

Taking up a pawn, she began to straighten the beautifully carved black and white ivory pieces. "My father taught me. We had a game nearly every night for the past few years, and quite often during his shore leave in the days before that."

"Shore leave? Was he a sailor?"

She sent him a quick glance. "Yes, a career officer in the Royal Navy."

A faint pause ensued. "You mentioned at dinner that your parents are both deceased. Was he lost at sea?"

She moved a black knight to his side of the board. "No. Although a part of me always thought that is how he would die, leading his men and his ship in battle. But he sailed for years without serious incident. He was even in the thick of things at Trafalgar and came through without so much as a scratch. Ironic, that he passed away from something as mundane as a heart seizure."

Lines settled anew on Lord Cade's forehead. "How long ago did he pass?"

She swallowed, shuffling more pieces around in a clipped, almost automatic fashion. "Five months. As you may have noticed, I am still wearing mourning colors."

"And your mother?"

"Four years last June." She gazed toward him and forced a weak smile. "Pray do not worry that I shall burst into a messy fit of girlish weeping. I am well used to the circumstances by now." With all the chess pieces in their proper places, she began centering each one precisely inside its square.

Lord Cade's large hand came down and stopped her. She trembled, just as she had at his earlier touch, enjoying the comfort of his strength far more than she knew she ought.

"No one ever gets used to it," he said. "I know. I've lost people myself, including my own inestimable father when I was barely older than you. You have no need to dissemble with me."

She lifted her gaze to his. "Thank you, my lord."

Suddenly, as though only then realizing he was holding her hand, he drew away.

"My lord?" she ventured after a moment.

"Yes?"

"Since I have told you a few rather personal details about myself, I was wondering if I might ask the same of you? Excuse my boldness, but how did you injure your leg?" As for the scar on his throat, she didn't quite have the nerve to inquire about that—not yet, at least.

He paused and took a drink. "In Portugal, in the war."

"Oh, I didn't realize you are a soldier."

"I'm not. At least not anymore. A broken femur from a bullet through the thigh has a way of getting a man cashiered out."

"You were wounded in battle, then?"

"No."

"But—"

"I was an advanced scout, a reconnaissance officer for Wellesley."

"A spy, you mean?"

His lips twisted. "That isn't a term we generally prefer to use, but I suppose it's as good as any."

"What happened?"

"An unfortunate encounter with the French." A shuttered expression lowered abruptly over his features. "Now, isn't it time you were retiring?"

His tone, as well as his words, told her she would get no more from him on that subject tonight. Sliding back her chair, she prepared to rise. Before she did, Cade lifted the whiskey decanter and filled his glass yet again.

"Do you not think you have had enough, my lord?" she ventured in a gentle voice.

He gave her a measured stare. "No." Deliberately, he tossed back the portion in his glass, then reached to pour another.

"I realize it is none of my business, but—"

"You're right," he interrupted. "It's not."

"I only thought that if you are in pain from your leg, there are other remedies—"

"What makes you think it's my leg? Maybe I just like to drink."

"Oh, I . . . I just assumed—"

"Well, stop assuming and go to bed. You can plague me afresh tomorrow." He looked away; clearly she was dismissed.

She held back a sigh, wishing she could rewind the past few minutes and restore their earlier conviviality. Still, she had wanted to know about him, and now she did, at least a little. Although to her frustration, his answers left her even more curious than before. Resigned for now, she stood.

"As you will, then, my lord. I bid you goodnight."

He responded with a sound somewhere between a grunt and a growl, then drank another dram from his glass.

She made her way to the door. Just before she passed through, she glanced back and saw that Cade had transferred his glass to his left hand and was using his right to rub his damaged thigh in a quiet circle, as if he were indeed in pain. In that instant, though, she realized it was far more than his leg that hurt him.

Resisting the urge to turn back and offer comfort she knew he would refuse, she left the room.

Chapter 4

The following day Cade very nearly skipped nuncheon with Meg. But after his conscience prodded him several times, he walked across his bedchamber and reached for one of the starched cravats he so rarely wore these days.

When he'd asked for a neck cloth last night, his batman had been delighted—Knox apparently bored with so little to do. Not like when they'd been on the Continent, making shift as circumstances required. But those times were gone, along with so much else from his former life in the military.

Blasted thing, he cursed to himself as he ruined one long, linen rectangle and reached for another. If not for his inconvenient houseguest, he could have gone downstairs in shirtsleeves and pantaloons. Then again, if not for Miss Amberley, he wouldn't have to dress for a meal at all. Nevertheless, a promise was a promise, and she'd won their wager fair and square.

Of course that doesn't mean I shall enjoy sharing the meal with her, he reassured himself. Or talking to her, either.

Yet in spite of his glum prognostications, the meal proved pleasant. As the minutes passed he found himself relaxing, Meg showing herself to be an amusing conversationalist with a knack for light banter. She was careful, he noted, not to bring up any of last night's uncomfortable queries, and he made sure not to provide ammunition with which to tempt her.

Dinner that evening went well, too—wretched neck cloth notwithstanding—and then it was once again time for the entertainment portion of his pledge.

"So, your lordship," Meg ventured, as Harvey cleared the dessert plates and poured a last round of beverages before withdrawing. "What shall we play tonight? Piquet or speculation perhaps? I'll grant it's not quite as lively with only two, but I suspect we can manage nonetheless."

Swallowing a mouthful of port, he regarded her over the glass's edge for a moment before setting it down. "Chess," he pronounced. "As I recall, you owe me a rematch."

Her pink lips rounded in a circle of surprise. "Indeed, you are right. Chess it is, then, my lord."

"Don't look so confident. I shall not let you off lightly tonight, since I'm on to you now."

She laughed. "I stand forewarned. Mayhap I should have a draught of spirits to soothe my anxious nerves."

"Stick with your tea, Miss Amberley. You'll need your wits about you."

But he was the one who should have followed that bit of advice, finding he required every ounce of his concentration to achieve a defeat.

Achieve it he did, however, sliding his queen into place to capture her king nearly two hours later. "Checkmate," he said in a quiet voice that failed to mask his pleasure.

"And so it is. Congratulations, your lordship."

He nodded and reached for his tumbler, quaffing the whiskey that had been sitting untouched at his elbow for nearly the whole of the match. "You nearly had me," he admitted. "You're a clever and engaging adversary."

"As are you," she said, giving him a faint smile as she began straightening the board the way she had the night before. "Of course, I shall now be forced to demand another game, so that I may reclaim my victory. At this rate, we may never have that hand of cards."

"Chess suits me fine."

"We could have a match after nuncheon tomorrow."

He paused. "As I recall, I promised to entertain you in the *evenings*, not the whole of the day."

She hesitated, then shrugged. "As you prefer. Evenings, it is."

He watched as she finished arranging the board before leaning back in her chair. With her delicate hands clasped in her lap, she studied the fire.

"Fine," he said before he'd even fully formed his next thought. "Tomorrow after nuncheon. We could eat here if you'd like, so we don't have to delay our play."

Her head came up, undisguised delight dancing in her gaze. "What an excellent notion!" she declared. "I'll ask Cook to make us up something simple. Do you like Welsh rarebit?"

She looked so young and pretty in that moment, a picture of carefree, guileless joy. An odd sensation formed inside his chest, an unsettling reaction that he ruthlessly pushed away. "Yes," he said in a gruff tone. "Serve whatever you like. Now, it's late. You should go."

Her gaze went to the mantel clock. "Ah yes, you are right. Well then, I shall bid you a goodnight, my lord."

Nodding his reply, he poured himself another scotch.

And so it went for the next few days, she and Lord Cade meeting for meals, conversation, games of chess—and even cards. They proved challenging opponents and surprisingly agreeable companions. The back and forth was exciting, leaving her—and apparently Lord Cade as well—eager for each new encounter.

What shall we do today? she wondered as she sat in front of her dressing table mirror, tidying her hair in preparation for the midday meal. In spite of being housebound, she found she didn't mind the confinement. Lord Cade might be moody and difficult, even infuriating at times. But he was also unexpectedly generous and fair-minded, never begrudging in his praise of her talents, or dismissive of either her intellect or her opinion.

Many men thought a woman should be pretty and biddable, and that she ought never to dare a comment on anything more complex than which trimmings to buy for her next hat, or the best accompaniments to serve with supper. Yet Lord Cade apparently felt otherwise, encouraging her to speak her mind, even when he held an opposing point of view.

With him, she was free to say whatever she wished, their conversational forays running the gambit from art and literature to history and phi-losophy. They even debated politics, Meg pleased to discover a mutual preference for the Whig method of governing. One thing was certain—she was never bored. And she did not believe Lord Cade to be either. He'd certainly appeared to enjoy himself last night.

She smiled inwardly as she remembered the laughter she'd coaxed out of him with stories about a pair of her father's more colorful officers and their antics, as well as a few tales of her own life as a navy man's daughter.

In those fleeting moments, Cade's whole face had changed, lines of pain and fatigue melting away beneath the humor. She'd watched as a glimpse of another man emerged—a lighter, more easygoing self, which made her wonder about the person he'd been before he was wounded in the war.

And then he'd smiled, sending her pulse into a dangerous rhythm, her breath catching as a pair of dimples appeared in his cheeks. She'd wanted to stroke one, reach out and trace a fingertip across the long, beautiful groove. Just the idea turned her all warm and shivery inside, and she'd had to glance away. When she looked again, the old Cade was back, his usual serious expression making her question she'd ever seen anything else.

She wished she could get him to smile again, smile more, but time, she knew, was growing short. The weather was moderating; the great drifts of snow giving way to sunshine and shovels and horse-drawn plows. Another day or two and she would once again be on her way. She should be glad to resume her journey and her life.

And I will be, she assured herself, when the time comes.

Leaning forward, she smoothed her hair one last time and straightened the lace fichu at her neck. Noticing the pale cast to her cheeks, she pinched them to add a bit of color. Abruptly, she fell still.

Gracious, am I preening? For Cade Byron?

No, she decided. She was merely trying to look presentable, no more than she would under any circumstance. *I like him, nothing more.* Cade Byron was a fascinating, dynamic man, to be sure, but she knew there could never be anything between them. Such ideas would only lead to discontent and unhappiness. And Lord knows she'd had enough sorrow in recent years without deliberately courting more. Instead, she would enjoy the remainder of her time with Lord Cade, then travel on. Once she departed, she would forget him, just as, she was sure, he would forget her. With a sigh, she stood and crossed to the door.

"What would you say to a walk?" Cade suggested after nuncheon was concluded. "Harvey tells me the paths around the house are cleared, and if you're anything like me, you could do with a bit of fresh air."

Meg glanced up in surprise. "Oh, but your leg . . . are you sure—"

"My leg is fine," Caid said. "I'm not a cripple, you know."

"No, of course, you are not. I only meant that the ground may be slick in places and—" She broke off, then gave him a deliberate smile to ease the tension. "A walk would be most welcome, thank you. Pray allow me to retrieve my cloak and we shall be on our way."

When she came down the stairs five minutes later, it was to discover him dressed in a heavy, many-caped black wool greatcoat, a beaver top hat on his head. He held an elegant cane in one gloved hand, the solid gold knob on top fashioned in the shape of a fox. A pair of rich emerald eyes winked out of the metal, their shade reminding her of Lord Cade's own unique gaze.

"Ready?" he asked.

She gave a nod, a fluttering sensation curling inside her belly. "Yes."

Despite the crisp sunshine and buoyant blue sky, a frosty chill hung in the air as they walked. She shivered and huddled deeper inside her mantle.

"Cold?" he inquired. "We can go back if you wish."

She shook her head and cast him a glance from beneath her bonnet. "I am fine. It's only that I'm not used to the cold weather. It's what comes, I suppose, of being acclimated to warmer climes."

"What do you mean? I can think of nowhere in England that does not take a chill come winter, not even along the coastline."

"True. But until two months ago I was living in Gibraltar, where it's warm and sunny all year round."

He paused and angled his head in obvious surprise. "Were you indeed? Well, having been there myself, I can understand your difficulty adapting to this weather."

"So you were in Gibraltar, too. When, might I ask?"

"Last year, but only for a couple of short weeks while I was awaiting orders."

A curious sensation spread through her at the realization that they had both been in such a distant locale at the same time. What would it have been like to have known him then? she wondered.

"Odd to imagine we might have met there," he observed, his words mirroring her thoughts. "Still, I suppose the likelihood was never great, despite our being in the same city."

She gestured with a gloved hand. "Yes, but far more probable, I should think, than the chance that we might encounter each other here in the wilds of England. And in the midst of a snowstorm no less. Fate is a very peculiar creature."

He cast her an appraising glance. "Ah, so you believe in Fate, do you? Destinies and tales foretold and all such mystical folderol? But then I should not be surprised to discover that you are of a romantic nature."

"I have never considered myself to be terribly romantic, but neither do I believe such matters are all nonsense, as you say. There is often more at work in situations than mere happenstance. A greater purpose, if you will."

He stopped and leaned toward her. "Is there indeed? And what greater purpose, do you suppose, led you to my doorstep?"

She hesitated, catching her lower lip between her teeth as she considered. "I could not say for sure. Mayhap I was set in your path to test you."

"Test me how?" he asked, his words a low, sleek drawl.

"By encouraging you to try a new routine, for one thing."

"You've certainly done that."

"And by coaxing you out of a measure of your reserve."

His dark brows drew close. "I am not reserved. I merely appreciate my privacy."

"And maybe by reminding you that your face will not crack if you smile every now and again," she chided, softening her remark with a gentle grin.

"Oh, so you have come to teach me to smile, have you? And what of yourself, Miss Amberley? What have you learned over these past two weeks?"

She startled at the question. "What have *I* learned?"

"Of course. If Fate is working its hand, mayhap it hoped to test you as well."

"I cannot think how."

"Can you not?"

Just then the wind whipped hard, tugging a strand of her hair free of its moorings despite the protection of her bonnet. To her surprise, Lord Cade reached up and caught the errant lock between his thumb and forefinger. With a touch as gentle as a whisper, he slowly tucked the strand behind her ear.

As he did, the edge of one gloved finger glided over the curve of her cheek, leaving what felt like a line of fire in its wake. In that moment, air seemed to still inside her chest, the quick beat of her heart chasing the last vestiges of cold from her body. She trembled, her lips parting as she waited in anticipation, though for what, she wasn't entirely sure.

Cade felt his muscles tighten, his gaze roving over her face before lowering to lips that looked as soft and succulent as a peach, ripe for the plucking. And ripe she was—fresh and lovely and undeniably innocent, despite her efforts to don a more worldly guise.

In that moment, he lost himself, sinking deep into the translucent blue of her eyes, her cheeks flushed pink with cold, and perhaps something more. Maintaining an easy grip on his cane, he wrapped his hands around her arms—though whether to push her away or pull her nearer, even he didn't know. Then, as if every sane, sensible thought in his head turned to ash, he bent and took her lips.

She gasped, then sighed against him, the breathy little sound making his blood beat hot and thick in his temples, and much, much lower, where it pooled like a fist between his thighs. Her mouth tasted divine, honey sweet and rich as silk, her cool lips warming instantly beneath the insistence of his own. Giving his hunger free reign, he eased his tongue into the satiny heat of her untutored mouth and began to play.

She whimpered and trembled, as if she hadn't known men and women did such things together. Despite her innocence, though, she stood willing, even eager, allowing him to explore in whatever way he wished. Drawing her closer, he slanted his mouth to take more, his senses awash in vibrant, vivid pleasure. He reveled in their embrace, an idle awareness running through him that made him wonder if she had ever been kissed before.

Am I her first?

The question jarred him, triggering some small shred of conscience and bringing him back to his surroundings. He pulled away, dragging in a draught of icy air that hit him like a slap after the moist, delicious warmth of Meg's mouth. As rapidly as their embrace had begun, it ended, Cade setting her away from him with a quick, firm dismissal. Dropping his hands, he took a step away, surprised to find his cane still clutched inside his grip. As for Meg, she stared at him, her eyes hazy with pleasure, her lips red and swollen. She looked like a woman who had been well and thoroughly kissed—which was precisely what she was.

Hell and damnation, he cursed silently, glad that there had been no inconvenient witnesses there to view their folly.

Meg swayed on her feet, her senses abuzz as if she'd been caught in the middle of a summer lightning storm; ironic, considering she was standing on a shoveled path, in a chill wind, with white fields of snow stretching around her as far as the eye could see. Yet she felt nothing of the cold, her body scorched inside by the fire of Lord Cade's passionate kiss.

Naively, she'd thought she had known what it was to be kissed, having once slipped into the garden at a ball to share a stolen embrace with a young officer. But now she knew what a fraud that kiss had been, what a dull and pale imitation of the real thing.

Mercy, I can scarcely catch my breath, she thought, her lips throbbing from his touch; his dark, delectable flavor lingering like some kind of sinful confection on her tongue. She trembled and wished he would kiss her again despite the impropriety of such a brazen act. But one glance at the frosty reserve in his eyes was enough to dissuade her.

Abruptly, he glanced away. "You must be freezing. I believe we would do well to return to the house." Rather than offer his arm, he turned and left her to make her own way. He began the return journey at a quick, almost clipped pace, his cane tapping out a soft rhythm against the snow-packed walkway.

She followed in silence, wondering at his mood, and at what she could only surmise to be his anger. Confusion rose inside her, and yet she said nothing. She knew naught what to say.

Rounding a last curve in the path that led to the front steps, he strode even faster, his limping gait momentarily forgotten in his obvious eagerness to once again be indoors.

Suddenly he skidded forward, as his cane

struck a dark, nearly invisible patch of ice. Fighting to maintain his balance, his arms flashed out, wheeling in an instinctive attempt to save himself. But it was already too late, his large body flying up before crashing down onto the hard, unforgiving ground.

Meg cried out and hurried forward. "Cade! My lord! Oh, are you all right?"

He groaned, his features tight with noticeable pain. Reaching down, she offered a hand, but he brushed her assistance aside. "I am fine," he said between clenched teeth. Slowly, he levered himself into a sitting position.

Wanting to help him, but knowing he would refuse her aid, Meg stepped back, holding her tongue as he struggled to regain his feet. When he was standing once more, he smacked a hard hand against a large patch of snow on his coat, then turned toward the house. Leaning heavily on his cane, he advanced inside.

Meg slipped into the foyer after him, watching in concern as he divested himself of his coat, then made his way down the hall to his book room. The door slammed, the sound echoing through the house.

With a sigh, she walked up the stairs to her bedchamber, knowing there would be no further welcome from him that afternoon.

Chapter 5

Seated at the dinner table that evening, Cade drained the whiskey from his tumbler, then set down the glass to pour himself another. Ignoring the look of concerned disapproval on Meg's face, he raised the crystal decanter he'd had Harvey place near his elbow at the start of the meal and refilled his glass.

From her chair at his right, Meg used her knife and fork to cut a piece of meat. "The venison is delicious, my lord. You really ought to give it a try."

Most likely she was right, but he just couldn't bring himself to eat. During the first course, he'd made an effort with the soup, but after three bites gave up, his stomach roiling. Alcohol was all he wanted . . . something, anything, to deaden the painful, piercing ache in his thigh. His earlier fall had badly aggravated his leg injury and now he was paying the price.

Of all the stupid, careless things to do. First, he'd kissed Meg Amberley—a monumental mistake in itself—and then was so preoccupied in the aftermath he'd scarcely paid attention to his surroundings as he made his way back to the house. One second he'd been walking, the next he was on the ground, agony stabbing through him like the thrust of a jagged knife.

Later, in his bedroom, he had soaked in a tub of steaming water. The heat alleviated a few minor muscle aches but did little to staunch the misery that gripped his abused thigh. Letting his batman help him into a robe, he'd nearly taken to his bed. Instead, he forced himself to dress and go downstairs, determined not to act the invalid, especially in front of Meg.

So here he was, drinking his dinner and glaring at her while she did her best to eat and carry on some semblance of a conversation. He should do them both a favor and take himself off, he thought. *God knows I'm not fit company for man nor beast tonight—and certainly not for a lady.*

He didn't blame her for the kiss or the fall—both were his own doing. Nonetheless, today showed him that he needed to put some distance between the two of them. He and Meg—Miss Amberley, he corrected himself—had been spending far too much time together lately and that needed to end. The roads were nearly clear and she would be going on her way soon. As for him, he needed to get back to his life—such as that life might be. Their parting would be for the best, for them both. Draining his glass, he set it down with a hard thump.

Meg startled at the sound, her gaze flying toward his, her fork poised in midair.

"I am sure you have endured more than enough of my sour humor this eve," he declared in a firm voice. "If you will excuse me, I shall bid you a good-night."

"But, my lord, you . . . surely you might stay long enough to eat at least a little of your meal. You have scarcely touched your dinner."

"Which is as I choose. If I wanted food, I would eat it," he said in a clipped tone, pushing aside any twinges of guilt at the wounded look that came into her eyes at his rebuff.

"As you wish. I had only thought to help—"

"Well, don't." Pitching his napkin onto the table, he pushed to his feet, pain biting like a pair of sharp teeth into his thigh. He forced down a moan, his knuckles white as he gripped the chair arms. Taking up his cane, he limped toward the door, refusing to glance back to see if she was watching, as he knew she must be.

Once in the hall, he made slow progress to the staircase. At the base, he clutched a palm around the smooth mahogany of the newel post and gazed upward, the journey seeming a long way tonight. For a moment he considered going to his book room to spend the night in his reading chair. But he'd tried that once before and knew no true rest would come from the attempt. Although considering the level of his present discomfort, he doubted he would be able to rest even in his own bed.

He could always take a dose of laudanum, he thought, then recoiled at the idea—alcohol his preferred anesthetic. But he'd used liquor long enough to realize it wasn't going to do the trick tonight. Without the stronger drug, he knew he was in for a long, painful, sleepless night. Still, maybe he could manage without.

But the climb to the top of the stairs left his skin clammy with perspiration, the whiskey he'd imbibed lurching sickeningly in his stomach. Reaching his bedchamber, he made it just in time to grab a chamber pot and toss up the decanter of alcohol he'd drunk.

Shaking afterward, he let his batman come to his aid, helping him to strip off his clothes and bathe. He washed the sweat from his face and body, then used a toothbrush to scrub the foul taste from his mouth before settling naked into his bed.

The ache in his leg continued unabated.

A hour later he rose to find the laudanum, taking a full dose before limping back to ease between the softness of his sheets. With a sigh, he went to sleep.

Cade tossed against the pillows, caught like prey in an invisible web as the nightmare came upon him. . .

A fist struck him, pain exploding inside his skull, but he scarcely felt the blow; one of dozens he'd endured over the past several hours. Or was it days? He honestly didn't know anymore, the endless rounds of punches having long ago merged into a constant haze of agony.

He sagged against the ropes that bound him to a hard wooden chair, his arms behind his back, his legs half numb after being confined in one position for so long. At least the numbness helped dull the pain from the bullet wound in his right thigh.

He'd been shot earlier trying to escape, but the French soldiers had captured him again and dragged him here to this barn—the Portuguese farmer who owned the land having already been dispatched with callous efficiency. Not wanting him to bleed to death—at least not until they had the information they wanted—his captors had called in a surgeon to dig the lead ball out of his leg.

He'd passed out during the ordeal, only to be shocked awake by a bucketful of cold water in the face, finding his leg bandaged and his big frame bound to the chair. The metallic scent of blood hung inside his nostrils, his eyes so swollen he could barely see, the split skin on his cheek oozing a slow line of blood.

"Give us the names of your contacts!" demanded one of his interrogators in French. "Tell us how many others are working with you and if Wellesley plans to go north or south!"

He cracked open one eye, then licked a few drops of blood off his bruised lips. "I can't understand a word you're saying. I told you. *Je ne parle pas français.*"

The answer earned him a fresh blow, since his

captors knew very well that he spoke French as well as Spanish, Portuguese, and Italian. His head snapped back, pain reverberating between his temples.

There was a hushed conversation, and then one of the men moved to stand at his back.

"Who are your contacts? Who is working with you? Where does Wellesley march next? Tell us, *anglais*! Tell us now or suffer the consequences!"

"Suffering is right," he muttered. "There's a dreadful stench in here. Do the stalls need cleaning, or is it you I smell?"

He waited for the fist, but the blow didn't land.

His interrogator spat out a vivid Gallic curse. "I've had enough of this. Proceed."

A second later the man behind him moved, arms flashing next to Cade's head as he wrapped something around his neck, then gave a quick, hard yank. Cade jerked, his whole body growing taut as his air was abruptly cut off, his lungs straining for breath. Pain seared the skin around his neck, the garrote biting deep into his flesh. Kicking and twisting, he fought to be free, fought for the use of his arms and hands as black spots danced in his head. Helpless, he waited for death.

In the next instant, the garrote was gone, air rushing into his aching lungs. He gagged and coughed, his body convulsed in agony as warm, wet droplets splashed onto his pantaloon legs, spreading over the cloth in round scarlet dots.

Even with his impaired vision, he knew they were blood—his blood. *Good Christ, had the bastard used a wire?*

A fist hit him while he was still forming his next thought, while he was still gasping for breath. "Now you will talk!"

"Oh, but he won't," declared a smooth voice as someone new entered the barn.

Straw crackled beneath even footfalls, Cade sensing rather than seeing the man who had spoken.

"You're only wasting your time," the man continued in mellifluent French. "He won't talk like this and you'll only end up killing him. What good will that do?"

"Monsieur Le Renard," breathed the chief interrogator in respectful tones. "We did not know to expect you tonight."

"It is good I came, seeing how badly you are botching this matter."

"We are making progress. He will break soon."

"Doubtful. Men like Byron don't break easily. They require other means of persuasion." Stepping close, the stranger bent down so that his lips were next to Cade's ears. "Do you not, Byron?" he mocked in perfect, unaccented English. So perfect, in fact, the voice could have been one he might hear in a Society drawing room in London. And how did this "Le Renard" know his name? His real name, and not the alias he had been using while spying for Wellesley here in Portugal?

A shiver ran down his spine.

"Bring in my little surprise," Le Renard said, switching back to French.

A shuffling sound filled the space, followed by hysterical sobbing. The crack of a slap reverberated on the air and a woman's cry of pain just after.

Hard fingers grabbed hold of Cade's hair and jerked up his head. "Look who I've brought to see you. Your little friend from the village. Or is she more than a friend? Did I not hear some mention of wedding bells?"

No! Forcing his eyes to focus, Cade stared across at the girl being held by another pair of soldiers. *Calida!* Her face was bruised, her straight dark hair hanging in tangles around her shoulders, the bodice of her gown torn, with one sleeve all but ripped away. Their gazes met, her beautiful brown eyes swimming with tears that streamed over her cheeks.

"Let her go!" Cade shouted—or tried to shout, his abused voice coming out as nothing more than a raw whisper.

"Oh, I think not. Go on, my dear," Le Renard coaxed, in Portuguese this time. "Remember what we discussed?"

"Madre de Dios," she cried. "What have they done to you? Cade, they killed Mama and Papa! They came to the house and took us all! He s-said if you t-tell them . . . what they want to k-know . . . th-they'll stop. Please make them stop."

"Yes, Lord Cade," Le Renard said, in flowing, aristocratic English. "Tell us, and, of course, I will let you go."

But Cade knew he was lying. Once he gave up his secrets, he was as good as dead. And Calida, too. There had to be a way to save her, though, something he could do.

"All right. I . . . I might have a name," Cade panted, working his mind around a likely fabrication. "Let her go and I'll give it to you."

"I think not. The name first."

Cade hesitated, but could see no means of delaying. "Rodriguez. Pablo Rodriguez."

A silence followed. "Tsk tsk. I'm disappointed in you. As you well know, that name was compromised months ago." Le Renard sighed. "I can see this is going to take a while. In the meantime, my men could do with some sport. Boys, who wants to be first?"

Cade strained against his bonds. "Don't! No!"

Calida screamed as one of the men fell upon her, dragging her to the earthen floor and shoving her skirts high.

Le Renard's hand tightened in Cade's hair, jerking up his head again, his fingers coming down to pry Cade's swollen eyelids wide. "Watch closely. I don't want you to miss any of the fun."

"No! Calida, no!" Cade screamed.

Chapter 6

$\mathcal{M}$ eg slipped out of Cade's darkened study, a book tucked under the crook of her arm. Lifting her candle high, she made her way back up the stairs, the house silent around her. Despite the late hour, she hadn't been able to sleep, climbing out of her bed to creep downstairs in her nightgown and robe to find something to read.

After the disastrous evening meal, she couldn't help but worry about Lord Cade. Though he would have denied it, he'd obviously been in a great deal of pain, his large body visibly tense, a faint white line of strain etched across his upper lip. Then, of course, there had been his drinking, as he downed one glass of whiskey after another. It was a wonder he was able to navigate his way out of the room and up the stairs to his bedchamber, especially considering that he'd barely touched his meal.

Alone after his departure, she hadn't done much better, picking disinterestedly at her food until finally she gave up the pretense and stood to bid the footman an early night.

In her bedroom, Amy helped her disrobe, then brought her a cup of hot milk to aid her slumber. But she couldn't rest, her mind filled with thoughts of Lord Cade, his fall, and most power-fully of all, their kiss.

Even now she could recall the delicious sensation of his lips moving against her own, and the undeniable beauty of their embrace. But once their kiss ended, he'd made his feelings plain, quite literally turning his back on her and walking away. She knew he would be glad to see her go, and by rights, she ought to feel the same. Instead, she was roaming the night-darkened halls of his house, sleepless and concerned.

Passing the door to his bedchamber, her footsteps slowed, her imagination conjuring up images of him lying amid the sheets, his handsome features deeply relaxed in sleep. Forcing her feet onward, she continued toward her bedchamber when she heard a muffled shout.

She stopped and turned back, the candle flame flickering at her abrupt movements, reflected shadows dancing on the walls. It was Lord Cade, and he called out again with another hoarse cry, then a groan as if he were in pain. Without considering her actions, she hurried to his door and turned the knob.

The room lay in darkness except for the ruddy glow of the logs burning in the fireplace, his large bed swathed in heavy shadows. Closing the door behind her, she moved forward. Despite the low light, she could see him shifting restlessly against the mattress, his head rolling on his pillow as though at war with some invisible enemy.

He wasn't awake and in pain, as she at first feared, but instead caught inside a nightmare, his distress palpable as he thrashed and groaned. A low guttural cry came from his lips. "No! No, don't! Stop!"

Without pausing, she crossed to him. "My lord," she said in a soft voice. "Lord Cade, wake up. You are having a nightmare. My lord, can you hear me?"

Instead he rolled his head, his strong masculine features contorted with misery, his mind clearly too caught inside his phantom world to heed her words.

"Lord Cade," she tried again, raising her voice. "You are dreaming and need to wake up. You are having a nightmare. Cade, wake up! Wake up now!"

But he didn't awaken. Moaning and muttering, his limbs shifted in uneasy frustration. Setting her book and candlestick onto his night table, she caught sight of a bottle of laudanum and the spoon that lay beside it. Eyeing the drug, she realized he must have taken a dose; no doubt the reason he was sleeping so deeply.

He groaned, his facial muscles stretched tight as his lips moved in an indecipherable plea. She studied him in the low light, tracing the chiseled angle of his jaw and the way his short, dark eyelashes fanned against his cheekbones. Even in his distress he was undeniably handsome, the powerful shape of his long-limbed body delineated beneath his bedclothes, capturing her gaze.

I ought not to notice, she thought. But notice she did, her pulse hammering at the sight of his broad chest with its appealing thatch of dark, curling hair. And if his chest was bare, what about the rest of him?

I should leave, she admonished herself, aware of the impropriety. But how could she abandon him when he was so clearly in need? In his drugged state, he might cause himself all manner of harm. Besides, if she left now, she knew she wouldn't get a wink of rest for worrying over him.

Bending low, Meg laid a palm against his shoulder, then jerked away in surprise at the heat radiating from his flesh—his body as toasty as a stove. She didn't believe he was feverish, though, but simply possessed a naturally hot-blooded constitution. Intending to wake him, she gave his body a firm, no-nonsense shake.

He groaned and mumbled something, but still did not rouse.

"Lord Cade. Can you hear me?"

He thrashed, growing even more seriously agitated as he shifted against the sheets. "Stop!" he called out.

Moving to soothe him, she slid her fingers over the warm skin and hard muscle of his shoulder, then down his arm and across his chest. Her nipples tightened beneath her nightgown, her body thrumming at the sensations. To her relief, her touch seemed to finally calm him, his breathing growing more even, his mutterings ceasing until, abruptly, he turned quiet.

Encouraged, she continued her caresses, stroking him in a slow, gliding rhythm. As she did, her gaze drifted toward the scar that stood out in stark clarity against the taut column of his neck. Unable to restrain her curiosity, she touched him there, quivering as she traced a single fingertip across the wound.

A hard hand clamped around her wrist, flattening her palm against his chest. Crying out, she tried to pull away, but he held on, imprisoning her as firmly as an iron manacle.

His eyes popped opened and locked on hers, his gaze intensely green, even in the diminished light.

"My lord," she murmured. "I'm sorry to wake you, but you were dreaming."

He frowned. "Dreaming?" he repeated, his words strangely slurred.

"Yes. You were having a terrible nightmare. But now that you are awake, you can . . . you can let me go."

He stared at her, his gaze oddly unfocused, as if he wasn't fully conscious.

"My lord? You *are* awake, are you not?"

Once again she tugged against his grip. But he held firm, his fingers tightening even more to hold her in place.

"Lord Cade, *wake up*! It's Meg—Meg Amberley.

79

You were having a nightmare, but you seem better now."

Or does he? she wondered, noticing the confusion clouding his gaze. Clearly he was still in the grip of the sedative, conscious but not fully cognizant of himself or his surroundings.

Remembering how her touch had calmed him for a time, she eased onto the bed, then reached out with her free hand to stroke his shoulder. He relaxed, but made no effort to release her. Instead he stared, studying her, his gaze roving over her face before moving downward to survey her body with undisguised interest.

Her nipples tightened at his bold perusal, her cheeks warming with embarrassment and something else that made her breath grow shallow. A second wave of heat followed hard on the heels of the first when she noticed that her robe was hanging open. The tie at her waist had come loose, providing him with an unobstructed view of the white lawn nightgown she wore underneath.

She reached to cover herself, but he moved first, his hand finding her breast with unerring accuracy. Cupping her flesh, he traced her feminine shape with an astonishing boldness. She shuddered as he brushed his thumb over her nipple, need sizzling through her.

"Delightful," he murmured. Giving her breast a gentle squeeze, he resumed his leisurely exploration.

She gasped, her body frozen in place as her eyelids fell to half-mast. Even if he'd released her, she knew she would not have been able to flee. The pleasure was simply too great, unspeakable bliss ricocheting through her system.

Drifting in a light haze, she made no attempt to stop him as he unfastened the buttons on her nightgown. Pushing the cloth down over her shoulder, he exposed her bare breast, her stomach clenching as his naked hand closed over her. She whimpered as he played upon her, her eyelids sliding closed against the fierce wash of delight.

They flashed open, though, when he gave an unexpected tug and toppled her across his chest. His fingers speared upward into her hair, popping loose the ribbon that had confined her locks in a neat tail at her neck. Her long, straight tresses swung free, cascading down in a flaxen curtain that framed both their faces. Cradling her head, he leaned up and captured her mouth in a kiss that drove all thought from her mind.

Fire shot through her limbs, a moan erupting from her throat as he traced his tongue over her trembling lips. The moment her mouth opened, he took advantage, delving inside to stroke her with a wet, velvety glide that made her quake. He urged her to follow his lead, tempting her to match his kisses with ardent, avid ones of her own. She clung, yielding completely as he kissed her with a dark, undeniable need she was helpless to resist.

Neither could she resist his touch as his hands roamed over her body in bold, sweeping forays.

A hunger she barely comprehended rose inside her, blood racing in great throbbing beats through her system. An ache formed between her legs, making her shift with restless, wanton abandon.

Cade turned abruptly, rolling her onto her back so his weight pressed her deep into the feather tick. Burying his lips against her throat, he kissed her long and slow before roving lower, scattering caresses wherever he went. Sliding open the bodice of her nightdress, he palmed her breasts again, stroking each one in turn in ways that soon had her panting.

Then he moved lower still, her back arching as his mouth closed in hot, wet bliss over one tender peak. He suckled upon her, laving her with tongue and teeth before transferring his attention to her other breast.

Her hand came up to cup his head, her fingers sliding into the thick silk of his hair. Delirious with passion, she caressed his cheek, a moan echoing from her lips. His hands stroked her, one palm slipping beneath the hem of her nightgown in an upward glide from calf to knee to thigh.

Leaving her breasts, he nuzzled in the curve of her neck. "Hmm, so good," he muttered. "So soft and sweet."

She smiled, swept away by his touch.

The hand beneath her nightgown roamed higher,

brushing over the curls between her legs, touching her with an intimacy she hadn't expected. A hot quiver flooded through her, heart pounding as if it might beat from her chest.

He nuzzled her neck again, scattering kisses. "God, I want you. Oh, sweetheart. Oh, Calida."

Calida!

Meg's eyes shot wide, her body stiffening. Her heart pounded again, only this time not with passion, but instead with pain.

Dear Lord, what am I doing? she cried, her desire withering as abruptly as it had begun. She shoved at him, tears springing to her eyes. "Stop!"

His lips glided over her cheek, his palm stroking across the vulnerable flesh of her lower body.

To her dismay, she felt herself respond again in spite of her outrage. Shivering, she used both hands to give him another hard shove. "No!" she declared. Despite his greater size, desperation lent her the strength to push him off.

"What?" Catching himself on one elbow, he shook his head and blinked, his confusion plain.

She cringed. My God, even now he's not truly awake, she realized. The drugs were still clouding his mind so that he didn't know what he was doing! Shame curled in a greasy ball inside her belly. Trembling, she pressed her fist against her lips to keep from weeping.

Springing off the bed, she flew to the door, her hand slipping on the knob as she tried to turn it.

Cheeks wet with tears, she twisted again and managed to wrench it open. She hurried out, yanking the door closed behind her, then fled down the hall to her bedroom.

Cade squinted against the morning light, groaning as he rolled onto his side and fought to reclaim his slumber. His leg twinged at the movement, though, a dull throb bringing him further awake. The pain receded quickly enough, but as he lay amid the warm sheets, he realized he was awake for the day whether he wanted to be or not.

Scrubbing a palm over the rough growth of whiskers on his jaw, he yawned and turned again onto his back, his feather pillow pleasantly soft beneath his head.

Lord, what a night, he mused, curving an arm over his head. He couldn't remember them all, but he'd had some of the wildest, most vivid dreams of his life. No doubt an effect of the laudanum. The opiate might help with his pain, but it also tended to bring out unwanted, often unpleasant, reactions. Even now his mind felt fuzzy, his body relaxed but not yet fully his own.

Not surprisingly, the night terrors had come—the unspeakable memories he wished he could forget. In time, he supposed the worst of them would fade, though God knows, he didn't deserve them to. Because of him, Calida and her family had died. He'd been stupid and arrogant, assuming he'd outwitted the French and escaped the detection of their scouts, despite rumors they'd been seen in the area.

But Calida had been expecting him to come to her, and there'd been no way to send her word to explain his absence. He'd worried she would think he had abandoned her, as soldiers on foreign shores so often did. And then there was the simple truth that he had just wanted to be with her.

For his hubris, she had paid with her life.

Absently, he raised a hand to his throat to trace the thin line of scar tissue that lay there courtesy of a Frenchman's garrote. He fingered the mark, a curious impression rising of someone else stroking the spot—of a woman trailing her fingertips along the scar. But that could not have happened, he knew, seeing that no woman had ever touched him there.

Since his return to England, he'd been with only one female, a London lightskirt an army friend had thought might cheer him up. He'd taken her to prove he still could, to see if it might be possible to bury his pain in nameless female flesh. But he'd taken no satisfaction from the encounter, scrubbing himself afterward in a hot bath, feeling empty and unclean.

A whore could never replace Calida. He wasn't sure any woman could, though he supposed even his guilt wouldn't be enough to keep him celibate for long. He certainly still had needs, his body reminding him with annoying regularity exactly what it was missing.

A new image flashed in his mind, the sensation of a pink-tipped breast, of his hand cupping its rounded fullness as he fondled the sweet, womanly flesh. And lips. There had been a pair of luscious female lips—trembling and eager and oddly innocent for such a strongly erotic fantasy. He remembered a woman's hair, too—long, satiny strands as pale as moonlight that fanned down around his face as she lay above him; her little hands caressing his chest, her kisses as delicious as nectar stolen from the bees. He closed his eyes, hunger taking him, as his erect shaft tented the sheet that lay over him.

Lord, what a dream. For that's what it had to be; his mind playing tricks with memories of a drug-inspired sex fantasy. To his chagrin, he suddenly realized the identity of the woman he'd cast in the role of his lover.

Meg Amberley.

And it had been Meg, her soft moans sighing in his ears, her graceful limbs shifting against his as he touched her lithesome body—kissing, stroking, and caressing her as he would never have let himself do in real life. And yet it all seemed so incredibly vivid. The way she'd called out to him while he was caught inside his nightmare. How she'd soothed and comforted him as she rubbed his shoulders and chest. How he'd awakened ravenous with the need to touch her and take her.

Yet the dream had ended abruptly, its conclusion hovering infuriatingly out of reach, like a puzzle with a single missing piece. A niggling twinge ran through him.

Shaking off the reaction, he flung back the covers and slowly shifted his legs over the side of the mattress. A large purple bruise stained his hip from yesterday's fall, a minor misery compared to the others he routinely endured. Preparing to gain his feet, he caught sight of a book and a guttered candle on his night table.

I don't remember setting those there.

The niggling twinge returned, growing tenfold.

Rubbing a hand over his jaw, he stared. As he did, he caught sight of something else—a thin length of blue coiled amid his sheets. Momentarily, he froze. Then, with unsteady fingers, he reached out and picked it up.

A hair ribbon! He brought the silk to his nose and caught the faintest hint of flowers and femininity on its surface.

Meg!

Quite suddenly he knew his dream had been no dream at all.

Chapter 7

"*I* understand the roads may still be treacherous in places, but nevertheless I wish to leave," Meg told her coachman as they stood together in the front hall.

The brawny man frowned. "I think ye'd be wise to wait another day or two, miss, else we end up stranded, after all." A knot of apprehension formed in her throat, but she swallowed it down. "Be that as it may, we have imposed on our host's hospitality far too long and must depart. I wish to be gone within the half hour. Please prepare the coach. The luggage is ready to be carried down at your convenience."

Actually, the luggage had been ready since dawn. At the first hint of daylight, she had risen from her bed and begun to pack. After fleeing Cade's bedchamber a few hours earlier, she'd been unable to sleep, her mind and emotions spinning in agonizing circles that refused to let her rest. Her nerves were in a jumble, but she knew one thing for sure—she must leave!

Pinning the coachman with a grim eye, she donned her most autocratic expression, mimicking one she'd seen her father use on disobedient sailors.

Seconds later the servant cleared his throat. "Yes, miss. I'll see to the horses directly."

"What is this about horses?" demanded a low, masculine voice from the landing above.

Cade.

Meg's heart jolted. Somehow, she'd hoped she might be able to depart before he rose from his bed—a bed he probably didn't even remember she'd been in last night. She cringed at the memory, grateful her back was turned so he couldn't see her distress. Drawing a steadying breath, she smoothed her features, then forced herself to turn while he walked down the stairs.

He looked tired, though gorgeous as usual, with his chestnut hair waving around his face, a faint pallor on his freshly shaven cheeks. She couldn't help but remember the way those cheeks had felt, roughened with bristles, as he dropped fervid kisses on her lips and caressed her bare skin with skillful, knowing hands. Glancing up, she struggled valiantly against a rising blush that threatened to turn her cheeks as red as an adulterer's scarlet A.

"As I asked," he said, drawing to a halt at the base of the stairs, "why are you and your coachman discussing horses so early in the morning?"

Meg squared her shoulders. "Because I am leaving. The roads are reasonably clear, and it is well past time I resumed my journey."

His jaw tightened. "But you cannot leave. At least not until we've had a chance to talk."

She studied the toe of one scuffed black leather half-boot. "I cannot imagine what more there is to say."

He leaned close, his voice dropping to a whisper. "Can you not? Not even after your visit to my room last night?"

Her gaze shot to his, the blush she'd suppressed earlier spreading over her cheeks. So he does remember, she realized, her belly clenching at the knowledge.

"If you still wish to run away after our interview," he continued, "you are free to do so. But first, we shall talk."

Before she could regain her voice, Cade turned toward the servant. "Leave the horses to their hay for now. Miss Amberley will call for you later."

The coachman nodded, then strode away.

Meg turned on Cade the moment the other man was gone. "You have no right to command my servant."

"As I recall, he is your aunt's servant. Now, come into the parlor where we can be private. Please."

She nearly refused, but decided a confrontation with him could not be avoided. *Dear Lord, he remembers,* she thought again, wishing she could sink into the ground.

Instead she sank down onto the drawing room sofa as soon as she was able, leaving Cade to close the door behind them. Smoothing the skirt of her black kerseymere gown, she folded her hands in her lap and waited, her pulse hammering out a staccato beat. She sensed more than saw him approach, his halting footsteps muffled against the thick Turkey carpet.

Rather than taking a seat, Cade went to the fireplace, then bent to add a fresh log. Sparks flew upward as the wood popped, the red and orange flames licking like greedy tongues in the wide brick grate. She expected him to begin, but he remained silent, leaning an arm against the mantelpiece as he gazed into the fire.

"I should think you would be glad to see me go, my lord," she said, breaking the silence. "After all, you have never attempted to conceal your wish to be rid of my company."

He turned at her words. "It has never been a case of your company . . ."

She raised a brow in a speaking gesture.

"Well, not your company specifically," he amended, "but rather, company in general. I have no desire for houseguests, as you well know, and my opinion has naught to do with you personally." He raked his fingers through his already disheveled hair, then lowered a hand to his waistcoat pocket. Slowly, he drew forth a familiar length of blue.

Her lips parted on an involuntary gasp.

Crossing, he held out the silken strand. "It would appear," he said in a quiet tone, "that you are deserving of an apology."

She shook her head and fixed her gaze on the floor. "There is no need."

"Apparently there is, if finding this in my bed is any indication."

The knot inside her stomach tightened another inch, a shiver going through her when he laid the ribbon across the hands she held clenched on her lap. Slowly, she twined a pair of fingers around the length, smoothing the silk with her thumb.

He paced a few short steps before lowering himself into the armchair directly opposite her. "Forgive me, but I fear I must ask just how far matters progressed between us last night. It would seem my memory is frustratingly incomplete and I can recall only scattered bits and pieces."

Her fingers tightened on the ribbon. *How does he expect me to answer? Surely he isn't looking for a minute by minute account?*

"Did I take your maidenhead?" he demanded in a soft yet straightforward voice.

A flush burst over her skin, her gaze flying upward. "No!"

"No?" he repeated, apparently unconvinced. "So you are still a virgin?"

"Yes!" she stated in an emphatic tone. She might not know much about coupling, but she felt sure there was more to it than kissing and touching, however pleasurably intimate those acts might have been. Her body tingled at the memory. "Yes," she repeated. "I am still chaste." At least chaste in the way he means, she decided.

His shoulders lowered, tension visibly pouring out of him. "Thank God," he murmured under his breath.

Her lips thinned, fingers rolling the ribbon into a ball. She supposed he was right to be relieved, she thought, giving the wadded silk a squeeze. But did he have to be so vastly pleased about it?

"Well then," she stated, "if that is all . . ."

His scowl returned. "Of course it's not *all*. Just because I didn't take your innocence doesn't mean nothing of import occurred. There is still the matter of you being in my bed—" He broke off for a moment. "Speaking of which, how *did* you come to be in my bed, since I distinctly remember falling asleep alone?"

Fresh blood reawakened the blush in her cheeks. "You were dreaming."

"Dreaming?"

"Having a nightmare, actually. I was passing in the corridor after going downstairs for a book. On my return, I heard you cry out. I thought you were in distress, so I came into your room to help. And I . . . well . . . I . . ."

A glint she couldn't quite interpret danced in his eyes. "Yes?"

"I tried to awaken you, but you were not your usual self."

"No, I rather doubt I was, considering the draught of laudanum I had taken."

"Yes, so I realized. You were thrashing and visibly upset and I . . . well, I don't know exactly how, but matters got rather out of hand."

"I see." The sober cast returned to his face. "I didn't harm you, did I?"

"Oh no, not at all, my lord. You . . . well, what occurred was not your fault. You weren't fully conscious, and I suppose it was wrong of me to come into your room. I only thought to help—"

"Of course, I understand. However, that does nothing to mitigate the seriousness of the situation."

"What do you mean?"

He raked a hand through his hair. "I mean that were I any kind of gentleman, I would offer for you this instant."

"Offer for me?" she repeated, her words trailing off. "You mean as in marriage?"

"Exactly. Despite my incapacity, I took advantage of you last night, and you have every right to demand I do the honorable thing."

She twined the hair ribbon around her fingers. "Do I?"

"Yes. Thankfully, though, your innocence is still intact, and since neither of us has any wish to marry the other, I see no point in consigning us both to a lifetime of misery, trapped inside a union we do not want."

Her gaze lowered to her boots. "I suppose not."

"Nonetheless, I owe you something more than a mere apology."

A chill settled inside her. "No, my lord. No harm has been done, so let us forget the entire incident ever happened."

"Yes, but—"

"You owe me nothing," she said in a resolute voice.

Rising, Meg crossed to the fireplace. Slowly, she opened her palm and stared at the hair ribbon inside before casting the blue silk into the flames. She watched as it curled, flaming red for a brief instant before crumbling into ash. Only then did she turn to face him. "If we are finished, my lord, I believe I will send for my coachman and maid."

He stood. "You need not go—"

"I am afraid I must. Thank you for your hospitality. This has been one of the most . . . interesting fortnights I have ever spent."

He tapped the end of his cane against the floor as though searching for the right thing to say. "Meg—"

"I bid you good day, my lord."

Before she could depart, a knock sounded at the door. Beaks slipped inside. "Yer pardon, yer lordship . . . miss, but the squire's here to see ye."

Cade frowned, his jaw clenching with instant irritation. *The squire? Hell and damnation, what does he want? Though come to it, what does he ever want?*

"Inform him I am not receiving," Cade said, "and send him away."

The servant shuffled his feet. "Tried, but ye know how he is."

"Well, try again." Cade cast a glance in Meg's direction. "He cannot find her—"

"Hallo, Byron. Came by to see if you had survived the storm, what?" a man called from the doorway. Short, round-bellied, with a head of graying hair, he came to a halt just inside the doorway; his gaze homing in on Meg like a hound

95

locating a fox. "Ho now, and who do we have here?" The squire's lips curved upward as he shot a grin toward Cade, brass buttons winking on his blue and yellow striped waistcoat. "Regular Venus De Milo, what? Don't say you've had this beauty tucked up here with you this whole time, Byron, or I shall be deuced put out. Introduce us, my dear boy, or name your seconds."

Cade suppressed a growl, wishing he actually *could* name his seconds and put a bullet through the interfering old fool. But he supposed if he killed his nearest neighbor, someone was bound to take offense. Damn and blast, though, he cursed silently, why did the busybody have to pick today to make one of his unwanted social calls?

"Ludgate," he said, taking a protective step toward Meg. "I wasn't expecting you."

"Sure you weren't, what with the roads being what they are. Frightful storm, eh? Can't remember worse, least not since I was a lad—and I'd appreciate it if we don't speak of how long ago that was, what?" He chuckled to himself, laying a palm over his belly. "M'tenants dug me out with shovels and stamina. Couldn't stand another day's captivity. I mean, deuced awful being confined, like to drive a man mad." He paused, shooting another inquiring glance between Cade and Meg. "But then you were obviously not lacking for companionship during the recent foul weather. So, are you going to do me the honor, or shall I be forced to shame myself and the lady both by effecting introductions on m'own?"

Cade stifled another growl, wishing he had the luxury of grabbing the other man by the scruff of the neck and dragging him from the house. But that, he knew, would do absolutely no good. Matters had progressed too far already—the dye having been cast, as the old saying went.

Moving to Meg's side, Cade took her hand and gave it a warning squeeze. "Squire Ludgate, permit me to make you acquainted with Miss Margaret Amberley. My fiancée."

"Fiancée!" the squire declared, his booming voice luckily masking Meg's own squeak of astonishment.

Before she had a chance to say a word, Cade slipped an arm around her waist and hugged her close, brushing a kiss against her cheek. "Smile and play along," he whispered into her ear.

Her spine was rigid, tension radiating from her frame in a way that made him wonder if she might object regardless of his admonition. Their gazes met and held for a long moment before she gave a subtle nod of agreement. Only then did he straighten to his full height and turn again toward the squire.

"That's right," Cade said, keeping an arm around Meg just in case she decided to object, after all. "Miss Amberley and I are to be married. You have the honor of being the first in the neighborhood to wish us happy."

"Well, this is excellent news. Congratulations, my boy. Capital! Simply capital!" chortled the older man.

Striding forward, he grasped Cade's hand and gave it a hearty shake before making Meg a bow. "A pleasure to meet you, m'dear. And may I offer my most sincere felicitations on your impending nuptials."

She smiled and curtsied, managing the maneuver with easy grace despite Cade's hold upon her. "Thank you, sir. It is indeed an honor to make your acquaintance."

"As eloquent as she is beautiful, eh? A fine choice, Byron. Impeccable. Hope you won't take offense, though, if I confess to a fair bit of astonishment. Had no inkling you were in the market for a bride, what with those war wounds of yours and the fact that you don't venture out into Society, leastwise not that any of us local folk can tell."

Ludgate's salt and pepper brows moved together. "Come to it, how did the two of you meet? Must have been before the storm, what? Can't imagine such a fair thing as Miss Amberley dropping in upon you out of the blue and in the middle of a snowstorm no less!" He laughed, his belly jiggling beneath the exertion.

Cade stared, amazed that the old fool had inadvertently stumbled upon the truth. He was deciding on a response when Meg spoke first.

"Actually, I did arrive on the first day of the storm," she volunteered. "Just as the roads were becoming impassable. A rather harrowing experience, I will admit, but then Lord Cade was here, ready to welcome me inside. As for how the two of us met, I believe I will give him the pleasure of that story."

She shot him a look from beneath her lashes, daring him to concoct a satisfactory lie. But he hadn't worked in espionage without learning a few tricks at deceit. It was always best, he knew, to use as much of the truth as possible.

"We met in Gibraltar," Cade began, "when I first landed in the Peninsula. We were introduced at an officers' ball, and after only one dance, I knew she was destined to be mine."

Their eyes met, her lips parting on a soft inhale that gave her a dreamy expression, one that was surprisingly convincing under the circumstances.

"I proposed during those first two weeks," he continued, "but we agreed to keep our understanding to ourselves, since my duty would take me into enemy territory. We corresponded, then I was . . . wounded and sent home. Meg suffered the unfortunate loss of her father not long after. She came to me as soon as she could."

Cade stroked his hand against her arm in a gesture of comfort. "Meg is still in mourning and wishes to wait until the required period is observed before we make our announcement official. I trust, Squire, that you will agree to keep our confidence until that time?"

"Oh, of course, of course," Ludgate puffed, bobbing his head a bit like a pigeon. "Must say the ladies will be swooning over the romance of it all, once the tale is finally told, what?"

"Perhaps so."

Cade studied the other man, not trusting him for an instant. He knew the squire well enough to assume he would be spreading the news of everything he had learned at his first opportunity. Still, perhaps momentary guilt over breaking his word would stay his hand for a day or two, giving himself and Meg a small amount of room in which to devise their next move.

Ludgate, however, apparently wasn't satisfied with every aspect of Cade's explanation, his shrewd gaze focusing suddenly on Meg. "So if your father is deceased, Miss Amberley—my sincere condolences by the way, m'dear—then you must be here with your mother?"

Meg stiffened. "Um, no . . . my mother is also deceased, I . . . I . . ." She cast a glance up at Cade.

"Came with her cousin," Cade inserted with a casual insouciance.

The squire flicked his gaze between them. "Cousin, you say? And where is this cousin? I should be most appreciative of making her acquaintance."

Meg's mouth tightened, a suddenly martial

gleam appearing in her eyes. "She is indisposed and has taken to her bed. A dreadful head cold, you understand. I could try to rouse her, but she is most unwell and not fit for company at present. Terrible chilblains and a cough that started just this morning. I am worried it may be turning into lung fever. Very contagious, you know. Why, you probably ought not stay too long, sir, else you come down with the contagion yourself."

Ludgate's small gray eyes widened with undisguised alarm. "Oh my, that is most distressing news. Most distressing indeed. Pray convey my heartfelt good wishes to your cousin for her speedy recovery, but please do not attempt to disturb her. A woman that ill should certainly keep to her bed."

Meg nodded, her expression appropriately solemn. "Just so. Most kind of you, sir. And I will be sure to send her your regards."

"Yes, yes," he said, already starting to back out of the room. "Congratulations again on your impending nuptials. I fear I should be going, however, as you suggest. I just recalled that I have an appointment with my secretary this afternoon. Correspondence to answer, don't you know. Byron. Miss Amberley, your servant."

He hurried toward the door, practically stumbling in his haste to be gone.

Cade waited until he heard the front door open and close before letting his laughter escape. He wiped a bit of moisture from the corner of his eyes a long minute later. "If only I'd thought to tell him some story of the plague long ago, I might have done without his infernal visits. Maybe I'll have to develop consumption in the near future. That should keep him at bay."

Meg stepped out of his embrace and moved toward the fireplace, crossing her arms over her breasts. "He is an insufferable little toad. I can see why you wish to avoid his company. The Spanish Inquisition could have used him as an interrogator."

Cade sobered. "Yes, he looks benign enough, but he's got the instincts of an attack dog. He knows just how to go for the throat."

"Exactly." She paced a few steps, then stopped and pinned him with a look. "And now, my lord, *I* have a question for *you*."

"And what might that be?"

"As if you don't know. What in the blazes are you about, telling him we're engaged when we most decidedly are not?"

"Oh, but we are, Miss Amberley," he said, resigning himself to his fate. "For the present anyway. Now, why don't you take a seat and I shall endeavor to explain."

"Explain what?"

"My plan to get us out of this fix."

Chapter 8

"You expect me to go to London with you and pretend we are engaged?" Meg asked a couple minutes later from her place on the sofa. "That's preposterous."

Cade had resumed his seat as well, his thumb playing across the fox-shaped head of his cane. "Not at all. It's the only reasonable solution under the circumstance. You can stay with my family and take part in the Season. My younger sister is making her come-out this year, so it will be an easy matter for you to accompany her to the balls and such. Once there, you can search for a likely husband, and when you have located your man, you will jilt me. Despite my distress, I will gallantly step aside and let you marry this other fellow, no harm done."

"*No harm?* This is insane, for more reasons than I can count. Besides, I fail to see the necessity. No," she said, shaking her head. "I shall simply travel on to my aunt's, as I originally planned, and in a few weeks you can tell the squire that our engagement is over. No one else knows, so that will be that."

"That, as you say, will *not* be that. Word of your stay here will spread like wildfire the moment Ludgate decides to open his mouth—which, knowing the squire, won't be more than a couple of days."

"But he promised—"

"He only promised not to mention the engagement. He didn't say anything about concealing your presence in my house. You've been here for over two weeks, a fact you yourself confirmed during our conversation." Cade sighed and spun the cane top in a slow circle. "No, for a prattlebox like Ludgate this is prime fodder. Scruples or no, he'll never let the telling of such a juicy tale slip through his fingers. The stress of keeping such a secret would probably kill him—or else make him explode."

Normally, she would have laughed at his jest—or at least smiled—but somehow she couldn't muster the requisite humor. Not now, not today.

"But how far can the news travel," she argued, "even if he does mention it to one or two people?"

"One or two? By the time he's done, everyone in this county and the next will be talking of little else. Word will spread all the way to London and beyond. I expect even your aunt in Scotland will learn of it eventually."

"Surely not."

He leaned forward, his gaze clear and intensely green. "You must see this is the only way. If you leave here today on your own, your reputation will end up in shreds, whispers and speculation sure to follow wherever you go."

"But my cousin. I am sure the squire will mention that I was not here alone."

"And that argument might hold some weight if Amy were actually your cousin rather than your maid. It won't wash, Meg. People will see through the lie soon enough, then start wondering what else is false about our story, as well as what occurred between us while you were living unchaperoned under my roof. Their conclusions will be base and cruel and bring nothing but unhappiness your way."

Her fingers grew cold at his words as she realized that he just might be right. How could this be happening? she wondered. In less than the span of a single day, how could her entire life have turned so completely on its head?

Was it only yesterday afternoon that Cade had first kissed her while they stood together on the path outside? His touch driving away the cold as he made her forget everything but him.

Was it just last night that she had gone to his room to wake him from his nightmares, only to find herself in his bed and in his embrace, his hands running over her body in ways that still made her go hot and cold with remembered pleasure?

Was it less than an hour ago that she'd stood in the front hall, attempting to secure her coach so she might resume her journey north? So she could flee from actions and emotions that confused and disarmed her?

With Cade Byron out of her life, she'd assumed time and distance would let her forget, both him and her own foolish behavior. But suddenly that no longer seemed possible.

So, what am I to do? she pondered. Should she dig in her heels and try to brave whatever might come her way? Or should she agree to Cade's outrageous proposition and continue this sham engagement of theirs until she could find another man to marry? *And what if there is no other man?* whispered a little voice inside her head.

Yet would there be anyone for her in Scotland, scandal or not, living as she would be in a remote village with an elderly woman? And if the scandal did follow her there, she would indeed be disgraced, ruined so that no respectable man would ever have her for his wife. Heavens, under those circumstances, even her aunt might toss her out.

Given those prospects and possibilities, Cade's offer didn't sound so very dreadful. And he was right that a London Season would afford her a far better chance of finding a suitable husband.

But what of my pride and self-respect? What of my heart?

Cade had certainly made it clear he didn't want her. What was it he had said earlier? That a marriage between them would only consign them both to a lifetime of misery. And, of course, there was the shame of knowing he'd imagined her to be another woman, when they were intimate last night. What further proof did she need of his disinterest in her?

Even so, it's not as if I have feelings for him, she told herself. It isn't as though I love him. Pushing aside such unsettling musings, she returned to the dilemma before her: accept his suggestion or go on her way?

As if aware of her inner struggles, Cade reached out and took her hand. Her pulse gave an extra beat, his touch so very warm against her own chilled flesh, pleasurable in a way that ought to make her hate herself for responding.

"Meg," he said, "let me do this for you. After last night, I owe you far more than a mere apology. And as for today, I cannot in all good conscience allow you to depart, knowing your reputation—your very future—may be in jeopardy. As I said before, a marriage between us is impossible, but that doesn't mean we can't turn circumstances to our favor by using this ruse. We will be hurting no one with this supposed engagement, yet you will gain an opportunity to not only save your reputation, but make a happy match at the same time."

She lowered her gaze to the carpeting, visually tracing the geometric patterns woven into the blue and tan wool. "How can you be so sure I will find this other man?"

"How can you fail? I do not exaggerate when I say you are a stunningly beautiful woman. You shall have no difficulty taking your pick of eager suitors, despite their believing you are already promised to me. All the men in London will be queuing up, clamoring for your attention."

All the men in London except you.

"And what of your family?" she asked. "Will they not feel ill-used by our deception?"

"They will not realize it *is* a deception. This shall be our secret and ours alone."

She lifted her head, her chin set at a faintly defiant tilt. "And when I cast you aside? What then? Will they not despise me for breaking your heart?"

"I shall make sure they understand that I am bruised, but far from broken, and that I support your decision. No resentment will follow from that quarter, I promise." He gave her hand a light squeeze. "So, are we agreed?"

"You are certain about this, my lord?" she questioned. "Are you not afraid I will turn the tables and find a way to force you to the altar?"

His eyes widened, then he grinned. "No, not a bit. If there is one thing I have learned about you, it is that you are an innately honorable person."

An honorable person indeed, she thought wryly. *So honorable I am about to commit the most dreadful fraud of my life.*

Swallowing, she slid her hand out of his grasp and curled it in her lap. "Very well, Lord Cade, I will be your faux fiancée."

Three days later Meg sat opposite Cade inside his eminently comfortable coach-and-four as it traveled south on the turnpike to London. She relaxed against the plush brown velvet squabs, taking in the vehicle's understated luxury, which put her former conveyance to shame. As for her original coach—and coachman—both had journeyed north without her, the coachman entrusted with a letter of explanation for her aunt.

For nearly an hour the day before, Meg had labored over the missive; ruining several pieces of Cade's cream-colored vellum stationary as she struggled to find exactly the right way to inform her aunt that she would not be coming to live with her after all.

In order to protect her reputation, she and Cade had agreed to maintain their fiction about having met in Gibraltar—at least to those of their general acquaintance. Among their immediate family, however, something closer to the truth seemed best.

And so that was what she had written, telling her aunt how she arrived on Cade's doorstep seeking shelter in the midst of a dreadful snowstorm. Confined together over the next two weeks, the pair of them had quite unexpectedly tumbled head-over-heels in love. Then, unable to bear the thought of parting once the snow began to recede, Cade had asked her to be his wife, and she had joyfully said yes. No wedding date was set as yet, so that she might enjoy the thrill of a London Season, but they hoped to be married within the year.

Reviewing the fabrication in her mind, then again on paper, Meg had read and reread the letter to her aunt to make certain she'd made no errors in the telling. She finished by promising to write again once they arrived in Town. With guilt pinching at her for her deceit, she had sealed the missive with wax and given it to her aunt's coachman for safe delivery.

Now, as she gazed through the coach window at the winter-bare fields, she thought of London and trembled. She had visited the great city only twice before, and then for very brief periods of time while her father conducted navy business. She'd been a child then, wide-eyed with wonder at all the people and activities that seemed never to grow completely quiet, no matter the hour of day or night. Those visits had been exciting, memorable, with everything and everyone around her a marvel to behold.

But this trip would be different, since she was different, with no one save Cade upon whom to rely—his, the only familiar face among all the new people she would be meeting. And then there was his family. What would they think of her? Cade seemed to take it for granted that she would be welcomed with open arms, but she wasn't nearly so certain.

She was from a respectable family, true, but had never moved in the lofty circles in which she suspected Cade and his relations traveled. Then there was the modest size of her dowry. Many families—particularly ton families—put great stock in such matters. What if his family disapproved of the "match"? Worse, what if they disapproved of her!

She swallowed and glanced across at Cade, delicately clearing her throat. "So tell me more about your relations, my lord. Considering our supposed engagement, I believe it would be wise for me to know a few details about them."

He frowned and looked up from his reading. His gaze, finding hers over his silver, half-moon spectacles, never failed to send little tingles of awareness whizzing through her system.

"Pardon?" he asked.

"Your family," she prompted, shaking off her reaction. "You said I would be residing with them. Is it your mother and sister with whom I will be living?"

"Yes, and a couple of my other siblings," he offered, laying a finger over the open page of his book. "There's Mama and Mallory. She's the one who'll be making her debut into Society with you."

"And your sister's age?"

"She just turned eighteen." He paused and raised a brow. "Come to think of it, how old are *you*? I suppose that is one of those facts of which *I* ought to have knowledge."

"I am nineteen, due to turn twenty in July."

"July what?"

"The sixth. And you, my lord? When is your birthday?"

"January twenty-eighth, and I just turned thirty." He shifted slightly in his seat. "With you and Mallory nearly the same age, I suspect the pair of you will get on like a set of matched grays. You'll likely be running in tandem in no time at all, assuming you have the least bit of love for shopping."

"I can be coaxed inside the shops every now and again. And does your sister know you are so ungallant as to compare her to a horse? For my own part, I shall say nothing further on the subject."

The corners of his mouth turned up. "My thanks, Miss Amberley, since no offense was meant. As for Mallory, she is well-used to being compared to all manner of unsavory things. It's what comes of having four older brothers, I suppose."

Her lips parted. "Four!"

"That's right. Though last I heard, she's rid of all but one of them on a daily basis, since Jack and Drake have taken bachelor's quarters of their own. You'll only meet those two when they decide to stop by. Edward will be in residence, of course, but then he would be since he's the duke."

"The duke!" she repeated, aware of a breathless band of pressure around her chest.

Cade nodded. "Yes. The Duke of Clybourne. Did I not tell you?"

"No," she gasped. "You did not."

He chuckled. "Don't look so stunned. Ned doesn't bite, at least not much, and he only pulls rank when he's cross. He's not nearly so top lofty as some might imagine."

Cade's brother is a duke! Heavens!

"So there are five of you, then?" she ventured when she once again caught her breath.

"No, eight."

"Eight!"

"Hmm. After Mallory there are the twins, Leo and Lawrence, but they're away at Eton right now, so you'll likely not meet them except during a visit on school holiday."

"And the last?"

A tender smile softened his face. "That would be Esme. She's nine and a delight. I haven't seen much of her these past few years, but she writes me letters. Sends me drawings as well. I have a likeness of every cat, hound, and horse she's ever met, and considering the menagerie she keeps in the country at Clybourne, that's a great many indeed."

"They all sound . . . lovely. Your family, that is."

"Overwhelming, you mean," he remarked. "Don't worry. They'll take you in without a second thought. You'll be part of the general madness and mayhem before you're even aware."

If I am, she thought, I shall have even more reason to feel dreadful in deceiving them. In everything else, she promised herself, she would be truthful, since nothing less would do.

The coach hit a sharp rut, jostling the vehicle despite the excellent quality of its springs. Instinctively, she reached for the coach strap and held on, while across from her Cade did the same.

Moments later the coach righted itself and settled once more into a smooth forward motion. Meg lowered her arm and relaxed against the seat. As she did, she noticed the taut set of Cade's jaw and the pale cast to his coloring. She watched him adjust his long frame on the seat, closing his eyes as he angled his body into what he obviously hoped would be a more comfortable position. His knuckles whitened as they squeezed around the coach strap.

"Is it your leg?" she ventured in a gentle voice.

His eyes snapped open and fixed on her, sharply green. "Just a twinge. I'm fine."

She held her silence for a full minute, the coach wheels humming an easy cadence against the road. "Might you be more comfortable if you propped your leg out full-length against the seat?"

"I shall do as I am for now."

"As you wish, but there is no need to stand on ceremony with me, you know. I believe the two of us passed that point some while ago."

A slight twinkle gleamed in his gaze. "Hmm, I believe you are right on that score. Nevertheless, I will stay as I am."

Folding her hands in her lap, she resumed her study of the scenery slipping past beyond the window. Cade returned to his reading.

Five minutes passed, then ten, Cade shifting every couple of minutes against the seat as if he couldn't find a satisfactory position.

After another five minutes of the same, she knew she'd had all she could stand. "Enough of your stubbornness," she said. "Put your legs up on the seat."

"Miss Amberley, I do not think—"

"You don't need to *think*, just do it."

"I do not believe you have the wherewithal to insist I do anything."

She stared at him for a long moment, realizing with his superior strength that he was quite correct.

"Very well, my lord. Go on suffering if you wish, but do not be surprised if you find you cannot walk across the inn yard at our next stop."

He pinned her with a speculative eye. "Are you certain you are not already acquainted with my mother? The two of you should get along famously."

"If she's had to put up with five more males like you, then she has my profound sympathies."

He laughed and returned to his reading.

Less than a minute later, though, he tucked his book to one side and without a word levered his legs onto the seat. A sigh escaped him as he leaned back.

"Here," she said, reaching for one of the coach blankets. "Tuck this behind you."

Taking the offered bolster, he attempted to do as she suggested, but couldn't quite get it properly arranged.

Ignoring the swaying of the vehicle, she stood and took the blanket in hand once more. "Lean forward, my lord," she told him, folding it in half, then slipping it securely behind his spine. "There. How is that?"

He relaxed into the new arrangement. "Quite comfortable. Thank you, you're a good nurse."

"And you, my lord, are a typical patient."

"I believe I have just been insulted."

Her lips curved. "I believe you are right."

The coach lurched, forcing her to brace a hand against the back of the coach seat, her arm bowed over him. Cade's hands came up at the same instant and clasped her around the waist, steadying her against a possible fall.

Her gaze locked with his own, their faces close enough for her to trace the short fan of his dark lashes and catch the spicy hint of shaving soap that lingered on his cheeks. His eyes lowered, skimming over her mouth in a way that made her lips part beneath the scrutiny of his gaze.

She drew an inaudible breath, aware of his strong hands clasped around her waist; his touch as delicious as it was disturbing. Her body tingled with memories of the night past—of the way it had

116

felt to lie in his arms; to taste the hot, wet intensity of his kisses; to revel beneath the pure pleasure of his caresses.

Her legs trembled and she swayed, his hold the only thing keeping her from tumbling to the floor.

"Are you all right?" he said quietly.

She tried to answer but couldn't form the words. Somehow, she forced a nod. But instead of releasing her, he drew her closer, his gaze focused once more on her mouth.

Suddenly her hand slipped and landed on his chest—the touch of his muscled form, even through his clothing, as shocking as a burn. How easy it would be to let him do as he wished. And what a fool I would be if I let him, she chastised herself, thinking again of the sound of that other woman's name on his lips.

Abruptly she pushed away, shoving against him in her haste to be free. Nearly stumbling, she scrambled backward and dropped into her seat.

"Meg, I—"

"Are you comfortable, my lord? Is the pain in your leg better now?"

His brows drew together. "I am quite at my ease."

"Good." Leaning sideways, she opened the small traveling valise she had ignored until now and drew out her stitchery. Laying the cloth on her lap, she bent her head and took up her needle—her actions a clear dismissal.

For a long moment she felt his gaze on her, fierce

and penetrating, as though he were willing her to look at him. Resisting, she selected a strand of ecru silk and threaded it into her needle. Willing herself not to tremble, she took a first stitch.

He sighed, the sound a mixture of irritation and acceptance. Moments later she heard him take up his book, open it, and settle back to read.

She and Cade said little to each other the remainder of the day, the hours elapsing in slow drips as the coach made its way toward their first overnight stop.

Amy, who was traveling in a separate servants' coach, hurried to attend her the moment they reached the inn, the girl readying a warm bath and a refreshing change of clothes.

Suitably attired, Meg made her way to the private parlor Cade had secured, accepting the chair across from him before lifting her fork to try a bite of dinner.

They spoke of insignificant matters throughout the meal, her appetite sadly lacking despite the excellent quality of the fare. For his part, Cade drank more of his dinner than he ate, pushing at the steak and kidney pie on his plate before calling for one of the servants to see it cleared. He ate most of the apple pudding that was served for dessert, while she contented herself with a small wedge of cheese. Then it was time for bed.

An hour later night poured over her as she lay

alone in the unfamiliar room atop an unfamiliar feather tick, unable to sleep. Ever since that moment earlier in the coach, she hadn't been able to rid herself of a single, nagging question.

Who is Calida?

She puzzled over the matter, twisting it—and her emotions—into knots as she pondered the mystery of her rival. Yet not a rival, since Cade Byron was not her lover or her fiancé, despite current appearances.

The issue was no further resolved in her mind by the time dawn arrived and she rose weary from her bed, having fallen asleep only a handful of hours before. A sponge bath and a quick meal later, she was dressed and in the coach again, back on the road with Cade.

The moment the coach set off, he slid his spectacles onto his nose and opened his book, his cane angled into one corner for easy access. He was seated upright again, his long legs stretched at a comfortable angle across the floor. His coloring looked better, she noticed, yesterday's discomfort having obviously eased during the night. At least one of us got a good night's sleep, she thought with uncharacteristic peevishness.

Studying him for another long minute, she forced herself to glance away. Reaching over, she dug into her traveling case for a book and began to read, the silence broken only by the rhythmic whir of the coach wheels and the occasional buffeting sound the wind made as it struck the side of the vehicle.

Yet try as she might, she could not seem to concentrate on her novel, despite the liveliness of the text. After only a few lines her thoughts would begin to drift away so that she was forced to start again with the sentence she'd finished only moments earlier.

As for Cade, he seemed utterly content, oblivious to the fact that she was seething inside with barely controlled emotion. But then why would he know? Why would he sense her distress when by his own admission he only remembered bits and pieces of the night she'd come to his room?

"Who is Calida?" she asked, the words out of her mouth before she'd even known they had formed on her tongue.

His hands tightened on his book, his head jerking upward from the pages. *"What did you say?"*

The question stuck in her throat, but she forced it out again. "I . . . I asked wh-who Calida is."

"Where did you hear that name?" he said on a harsh rasp.

She shivered at the suddenly stark expression on his face, his eyes turned to fragments of cold green glass. Abruptly, she wished she hadn't asked at all, hadn't felt the need to satisfy her curiosity and assuage her injured sensibilities.

"Well?" he ordered, his quietly spoken demand as fierce as a shout.

Meg jumped. "I—I heard it from *you*. You said it the night we . . . when you . . . when you were having your nightmare."

Some of the ice left his gaze; the bleakness, however, remained. "I see. I suppose I said a great many things that night."

"No, not so many," she hurried to assure him. "A few."

But enough to make me wonder what you suffered, she thought.

Closing his book, he set it on the seat next to his hip. A moment later he pulled off his glasses, neatly folded the earpieces closed, and laid them on top of the book's fine leather binding. Turning his head, he stared out the window.

One minute went by, then two. She didn't think he was going to answer when finally he turned back.

"Calida was a girl I knew in Portugal," he said.

"Oh."

"She was my fiancée."

"Oh!" Her heart kicked inside her chest, the news drawing forth a sharp exhalation. She'd expected him to admit that the woman was his lover. She hadn't expected to hear she was also his beloved.

Does he pine for her still? she wondered. Of course he must, she realized, knowing now why he was so opposed to the notion of marriage.

"Where is she now?" she ventured quietly. "You said 'was.' What happened?"

His gaze met hers. "She's dead. Raped and tortured by the French in hopes of extracting information from me. They murdered her family as well, her parents and two little brothers. The youngest one was six. He couldn't have known anything of value, but they slit his throat just the same."

Meg gasped, pressing a fist against her mouth to hold in the horror.

He touched a pair of fingers to his cravat and the scar they both knew lay beneath. "You must have wondered where I got this. And this, as well," he continued, lowering his hand to his damaged leg. "Courtesy of the same men who brutalized Calida and her family. She died because of me. Was savaged because of me. Now, Miss Amberley, is there anything else you would like to know?"

She shook her head, her pulse racing in her veins, the truth worse than anything she could ever have contemplated. No wonder he couldn't sleep at night. No wonder he tried to dull the pain with liquor and laudanum and quietude. In similar circumstances, she might well have wished to do so, too.

As a woman raised beneath the shelter of her father's protective wing, she had been kept away from such harsh realities despite having grown up among military men. Of course, she'd known brutalities existed, had heard terrible accounts, but Cade's story made her realize just how safe her life had always been, how cosseted and innocent she really was.

Calida, the girl Cade loved, had not been so lucky. Lowering her hands onto her lap, she gazed at him with beseeching eyes. "I am sorry."

He gave her a nod and reached for his spectacles, setting them on his face. "I would rather we not speak of this again."

"Yes, Lord Cade. As you wish."

Picking up his book, he opened it and resumed his reading.

She sighed and wished she could do the same, but knew she would never be able to concentrate on the story she had been trying to read. Instead she gazed out the window at the frozen hills and bare-branched trees that stretched out on either side of the road, both as cold and gray as the day itself.

Suddenly she was very glad Cade had insisted on a temporary engagement rather than acting the honorable gentleman and insisting they wed for propriety's sake. Not that she would have agreed to marry him under such circumstance. But now that she knew the truth, she realized the danger that awaited any woman unwise enough to covet his regard. More than his body had been damaged in his service to his country. It would seem his heart had been lost as well. Perhaps in time it would heal. But what if it did not? What if the wounds were too deep to ever let him love fully again?

Not that I am at risk of such folly, she reassured herself. At best Cade and I are friends. At worst coconspirators in a mutual deception. Once their fraud was complete, they would each be able to walk away, free and unencumbered.

As for their night together, she would put it from her mind. He barely remembered half of it anyway, and she would find a way to make herself do so as well.

Somehow, in the weeks to come, she promised herself, she would cease this physical attraction she had for Cade and find another man—one who had a whole heart to give. For after all, what woman would want to love a man who might never be able to love her back?

Chapter 9

"Cade, you're home!" came a feminine shout as he walked into the family drawing room of Clybourne House four days later. Planting his cane on the Aubusson carpet, he braced himself for the impact as his sister flung herself headlong into his arms. He returned her exuberant hug and kiss, wavering on his feet for a moment.

"Oh, stars!" Mallory said, keeping her hands on his coat sleeves to steady him as she pulled back. "I didn't think about your leg. I haven't hurt you, have I? I would never forgive myself if I had."

Cade shook his head and gave her a wink. "Not to worry, Pell-Mell. You weigh barely more than a feather, so I'm in no danger of injury."

She smiled, relief plain in her lively aquamarine eyes. "We had your note but did not know quite when you'd arrive. Mama has arranged a special dinner for this evening and asked Cook to prepare all your favorite dishes. I saw the fishmonger arrive this morning with shrimps. Yum."

She paused, but only long enough to take a breath before continuing. "How was your trip? Long and dull, I suppose. Such journeys are always tedious by the second day, are they not? And what is this about you bringing a surprise? It's very bad of you to drop something like that into a letter and leave everyone in suspense. I've been wondering if—Oh!"

She broke off and stared past his shoulder toward the room's double doors. "My pardon. I did not realize we had company. Why did you not say?"

"I was going to do so, but someone wouldn't stop talking."

Mallory shot him a fulminating look that made him smile. He turned to see Meg, who stood just inside the doorway, then motioned her forward.

Despite being simply attired in a mourning gown of gray wool, Meg looked anything but plain, her complexion glowing with healthy color, her ash blond hair pinned into a neat chignon that framed her beautiful features. Her gaze met his as she stopped beside him, discomfort she was doing her best to hide visible in her lake blue eyes.

She's nervous about putting on this act of ours, Cade thought, but everything will be fine. Taking her hand, he gave it a reassuring squeeze.

"Meg, allow me to introduce you to my sister. Mallory, this is Miss Margaret Am—"

"Cade!"

They all turned as an elegant woman swept into the room, the hem of her peach silk skirts whispering around her ankles. "Croft just informed me of your arrival, else I would have been here sooner," she said as she came up to Cade. Opening her arms, she drew him close. "Oh, it is so good to have you here."

"I have missed you, too, Mama," he replied, bending to dust a kiss over her soft cheek. Her brown hair bore a few extra strands of silver in it, he noticed, added since the last time he had seen her. Otherwise, the gentle oval of her face and clear green eyes were the same as he remembered from his youth.

"If you did," she remarked in a light scold, "you ought to have come to Braebourne with your brother when he came to collect you. But you've always had that stubborn streak of your father's. It is a dominant trait among all the Byron men, I have discovered."

"Well, what is it they say of us, Mama?" Cade remarked. "That we Byrons are all rakes, madmen,

126

or rogues. So I suppose it is only natural I would refuse to do the expected."

Before he could step back, she laid a palm against his cheek and studied his face. "You look better. Still too thin and pale for my liking, but much improved from when you were last home."

She lowered her hand and glanced across at Meg. "Now, before this lovely young woman—whoever she may be—decides that Byrons are also unforgivably rude, I believe you should effect introductions."

He moved again to Meg's side. "With pleasure. Mama, Mallory, allow me to present Miss—"

"I thought I heard a racket in the house," a new voice—masculine this time—interrupted. "But I figured it was Drake or Jack come to stir up some new round of havoc or other. Fancy my surprise at finding *you* here."

Cade looked across at his older brother. "You had my letter. I know, since Mallory told me."

"We did, but I figured it must be a ruse. The last time we met, I believe you vowed nothing but a rocket would blast you out of that northern clime of yours." Edward's keen gaze fixed briefly on Meg. "I see your rocket arrived—and a vastly pretty munition she is, too."

A grin spread over Cade's face as he stepped forward and met Edward for a brotherly, back-slapping hug.

"So, who is she?" Edward murmured as they

eased apart, a gleam of undisguised curiosity in his shrewd, dark blue eyes.

"You shall see," Cade whispered back.

Of all the family members he and Meg would have the most trouble convincing of their lies, Cade knew it was Edward. His brother had taken top honors at both Eton and Oxford, and was a formidable presence in both Society and the House of Lords. As Cade had long ago learned, not much got by his brother, the duke.

Returning to Meg's side for a third time, Cade once again took her hand. A faint tremble went through her, nerves he felt certain no one but himself could see.

"Shall we try this again? Meg, allow me to present my sister, Lady Mallory Byron; my mother, the Dowager Duchess of Clybourne; and my brother Edward, the Duke of Clybourne. Everyone, this is Miss Margaret Amberley, my fiancée!"

A heavy silence descended. Despite the lull, Meg drew a steadying breath, bent her knees and dropped into a curtsey, as good manners dictated. As she did, she was fully aware of the collection of stunned, goggle-eyed looks Cade's family members were casting her way.

Staring at the toes of her brown leather half-boots, she rallied her determination, knowing if she and Cade had any hope of perpetrating their deception, this was the time. If they could convince his family, they should have no difficulty convincing Society as well.

Straightening her spine, she lifted her chin and affected what she hoped was an expression of pleasant yet quiet confidence.

"Fiancée, did you say?" repeated his mother, her green eyes moving between her and Cade. "But how did this occur? Where in the world did you meet? Surely not in Northumberland? There hasn't been time."

The duke folded his arms over his chest, his figure tall and imposing, as he waited for a response. He raised one of his dark brows in an arrogant gesture that reminded her forcefully of Cade at his worst. *What had he said about his brother not biting?*

Cade laid a hand on her waist. Gratefully, she leaned against his supporting strength.

"Meg and I met under the most unusual of circumstances," he stated. "She was traveling north and got caught in a snowstorm. She came to the manor in search of shelter and we ended up snowbound together. By the time the weather cleared enough for her to depart, I could no longer let her go. She completely stole my heart. And I stole hers as well—or so she tells me."

Glancing up at Cade, she met his gaze, startled to see his eyes filled with emotion—so intense she might have believed his words herself had she not known them for the falsehood they were.

"Is that not right, sweetheart?" he urged, tugging her against him.

"Yes," she said softly, unable to look away. "Yes, he has quite swept me off my feet."

"Oh, how incredibly romantic!" Mallory sighed, clasping her hands against her breasts. "And how wonderful that I am to have a new sister. You promised us a surprise, Cade, and what a splendid one this is!" Hurrying forward, she rushed to envelop each of them in a jubilant embrace.

Meg returned the young woman's heartfelt hug, guilt curdling like sour milk in her belly. The sensation only grew stronger when Cade's mother approached, a warm smile on her lips.

"My daughter is right," she said, leaning over to press a welcoming kiss against Meg's cheek. "This is happy news indeed, even if it may be unexpected. After the worry Cade's given me these past few months, it's such a relief to see his health improving and a smile on his face again. Obviously, I have you to thank for that, my dear. And for coaxing him out of his exile. We feared for a time that he might never rejoin the family. You have my lasting gratitude for bringing him back to us all."

"I was only in Northumberland, Mama," Cade remarked. "Hardly at world's end."

"You might as well have been in Timbuktu for all that we heard or saw of you," the dowager retorted, a martial glint sparkling in her eyes. "And after Edward's visit . . . well, I told myself you simply needed time—to heal and adjust. I can see now that what you really needed was the influence and affection of this lovely young woman."

She smiled again at Meg, visibly calming as her ruffled maternal feathers smoothed once more. "And now we shall have the delight of a wedding to plan. You must tell me about your parents, my dear, so I may write and invite them for a visit. I am sure we will have much to say to each other."

A wave of melancholy swept through Meg as she thought of her mother and father and the fact that when she did eventually marry, neither one of them would be at her wedding.

"About that, Mama . . ." Cade began. "There's no need to write—"

"Of course there is. Unless you mean to say that they are on their way already?"

"No, ma'am, they are not."

"Well then, they must come." She paused as a new thought apparently occurred. "Oh, pray do not tell me you have yet to secure her father's consent? Margaret will need it, you know, since she is obviously not of age. What are you, child? Nineteen? Twenty?"

"Nineteen, Your Grace," Meg confirmed.

"Just as I thought," the dowager said with a nod. "Her parents must be advised, though I can scarcely imagine them refusing to ally themselves with one of the best families in England, particularly given the nature of your introduction to one another. Neither of you could help being snow-bound together, of course, and I am sure Cade acted the gentleman at all times, but the fact remains that Society might look askance should circumstances become known. Unless Margaret was traveling with a relation. Perhaps even her mother?"

"No, her maid," Cade said. "But there will be no difficulty."

The dowager made a humming noise in her throat. "Well, we shall make sure there is not, since I have sufficient influence. Still, a united front is always best. Her family must come to London and I will host a ball."

"That is quite impossible," Cade said.

"I fail to see why—"

"Forgive the interruption, Your Grace," Meg said in a quiet but firm voice. "But what Lord Cade is trying to say is that both of my parents are deceased. I have no male relations who wish to claim me, and my elderly great-aunt, with whom I was lately planning to reside, will most certainly be happy to see me wed.

"I should probably also tell you that my father was an admiral in service to His Majesty's Royal Navy, and that my mother was the daughter of a viscount. She was disinherited on her marriage to my father due to the family's disapproval, and no one from their side has ever attempted to make contact again."

Meg drew a breath and linked her hands together. "So, you see, the only prohibition to a union between myself and Lord Cade would be from you or a member of your family. I hope you will not decide to retract your consent now that you have heard more about me."

For a long moment silence hung once more in the room. Then Cade's mother came forward and took Meg's hand.

"Retract my consent?" the dowager said. "Heavens child, what kind of ogress would I have to be to do such a thing? How long ago did you lose your parents?"

"My father died five months ago. My mother passed a few years earlier."

Lines of sorrow creased the older woman's still beautiful face. "You poor dear, to suffer such dreadful losses at so young an age. I grieve with you."

"Thank you, Your Grace," Meg said, a reawakened sense of guilt giving her a nasty pinch.

She didn't know precisely from where her impassioned speech about herself had come. Perhaps unintentionally she had been trying to give his family a reason to take a dislike to her and end this sham engagement between herself and Cade. Yet apparently she had succeeded instead in solidifying her acceptance as Cade's intended bride.

She could still tell them everything, she knew. It

wasn't too late. But even as she mustered the determination to confess the truth, the words stuck in her throat; aware that once she spoke them, her last hope of salvaging her reputation and future would be gone.

"I ought to have realized from your attire that you are in mourning," the dowager continued, obviously attributing the distress that Meg knew must be showing on her face to sadness over her parents' deaths. "After all, what pretty young woman would wear gray unless necessity required? But as much as your devotion does you credit, you must give yourself leave to wear brighter shades again soon. Surely your papa would not wish it otherwise?"

"No, Your Grace. I know he would not."

"Good. And enough of such formalities. We are to be mother and daughter now. You must call me Ava, or Mama if you like. No more 'Your Grace.'"

"Yes, Your Grace. I mean, Ava."

The dowager smiled.

"In fact, since you have brought up the idea of Meg coming out of mourning," Cade said, "I was thinking that she could join Mallory when she makes her entrance into Society. Obviously, Meg would not be a typical debutante, since she will already be engaged, but it would be nice if she could enjoy at least one Season before she marries."

"Oh, what a lovely idea!" Mallory agreed with alacrity. "I've been a little nervous about my come-out. I would feel so much better if I had another girl with whom to share all the excitement. Please say yes."

Meg stared at Cade's sister. Why does she have to be so nice? she thought. Why do they all have to be so nice? Except his brother, she realized, who hadn't said a word since she'd told them about her false engagement.

Turning her attention back to Mallory, she nodded. "If you're sure you wouldn't mind sharing with me, then yes, I would be delighted."

"Forgive me, dear," the dowager said to her. "With all this talk, I quite forgot how weary you must be from your journey. Why don't I show you to your room. I am sure the housekeeper has prepared something by now."

"Thank you," Meg replied. "That would be most welcome."

"Cade," his mother said, turning to him. "You will have your old room, of course."

"Of course," he said.

Old room? Does that mean he will be living here? She had assumed he would have his own establishment in Town. A quiver went through her at the thought of Cade being only just down the corridor. *How far away will he be staying?*

"If everything is settled for now," the duke said, finally reentering the conversation, "I should like a word with Cade."

As Meg watched, Cade glanced at his brother,

the two locking gazes to exchange a silent message of some sort. What that message might be sent a frisson of worry through her. Then Cade's brother turned and strode toward her.

"Miss Amberley . . ." he said, stopping before her. ". . . Meg, if I might. Allow me to extend my felicitations on your impending nuptials. Welcome to the family."

For a moment she thought she detected a faintly mocking gleam in his deep blue gaze. But then he blinked and it was gone. "Thank you, Your Grace," she said. "You are most kind."

He smiled, his lips moving into a handsome upturn that once again reminded her of Cade. He said nothing more.

Mallory claimed her arm a moment later and steered her toward the door, launching into a description of the court dress for which she had just been fitted. The dowager gave them both an indulgent look, then led the way from the room.

Ten minutes later Cade sank into one of the comfortable brown leather wing chairs positioned before the fireplace in Edward's study. With a grateful sigh, he stretched out his legs, enjoying the relaxed, masculine nature of the room. On the air drifted the scents of leather, ink, and foolscap, the sweet-sharp tang of alcohol joining the mix as his brother poured draughts of brandy into a pair of fine, mouth-blown Italian snifters.

Crossing, Edward handed him one of the glasses. Cade accepted with an appreciative nod and took a drink, noting the excellent taste and quality of the beverage. "French?" he inquired.

"Of course," Edward said as he took his own seat.

Cade's lips curved in a wry grin, deciding it best not to inquire where his brother had come by the contraband liquor. Edward might be a firm supporter of the war effort, but he was also a gentleman with a certain set of standards to maintain. War or not, he drew the line at drinking bad spirits.

"So," Edward began in a casual tone. "Now that you're comfortably settled, perhaps you'd care to tell me just what it is you think you're about?"

Cade's fingers tightened on the stem of his glass. *Damnation. I should have known I couldn't slip anything past Ned.* Still, he reminded himself, Edward didn't have more than his suspicions—not yet anyway. He owed it to himself and Meg to try and brazen it out, even if the odds of success were slimmer than the chance of finding hair on a goose.

"What do you mean?" He yawned, raising a supposedly negligent hand to cover his mouth. "I'm afraid I do not follow."

"Of course you 'follow,' " Edward retorted, giving him a hard-eyed stare. "Don't try to cozen me, brother. That faerie story you spun for us all upstairs may fool Mama and Mallory, but it won't wash with me. Miss Amberley is a beautiful

137

young woman, but I do not for an instant believe you have tumbled headlong in love with her. In lust, perhaps, but love . . ."

Cade set his snifter onto a side table. "And why could I not have fallen in love? Meg is a wonderful girl, sweet and charming and amusing. Smart, too. She plays a damned fine game of chess, I'll tell you. She's bested me more than once already, and looks like an angel while she's doing it."

His brother regarded him over his brandy glass. "Has she indeed? I can see you like her a great deal. But what of Calida?"

A muscle ticked in Cade's jaw. Glancing away, he gazed at the blaze burning in the grate. "What of her? She is dead."

"Yes. And although the rest of the family never realized that you loved her and planned to make her your bride, I did. I also know how much you've mourned her loss. Now, you expect me to believe you are besotted with this new young woman after a mere three weeks acquaintance?"

Taking up his glass, Cade drained the liquor inside. "That's right."

"Why are you marrying her, Cade? And I want the truth this time."

"I have given it to you."

Edward bit out a blistering curse. "Like hell you have. Stop lying. You never used to keep things from me, not even as boys."

Looking up, Cade met his gaze. "In case you hadn't noticed, we're not boys any longer."

"No, but we *are* still brothers, and that should count for something, perhaps everything. Did you compromise her? And I don't mean by letting her take up temporary residence in your house because of inclement weather."

Cade sighed in his head, suddenly weary of the game of trying to deceive his brother. Edward was right. They *had* always told each other everything, no matter how foolish or base it might make them appear. To protect Meg, he'd been willing to attempt the deception, but continuing now would risk angering Edward—perhaps even alienating him—and that he would not do.

"All right, yes," he admitted, rubbing his knuckles over his temple. "I compromised her—well, at least I sort of compromised her."

Edward scowled. "How do you 'sort of compromise' a woman?"

"By taking advantage of her when you're half delirious from drink and laudanum, then not quite completing the act. She's still a virgin . . . so in my book that counts as 'sort of.' "

The duke quirked a brow. "And so, to do the honorable thing, you have agreed to marry her."

"Well . . . that falls under the 'sort of' category, too." He shifted in his chair. "You see, we're not actually engaged."

"You're not?"

He shook his head. "No. That is to say, we are engaged as far as Society is concerned, or will appear to be anyway. In reality, though, Meg and I have agreed that our arrangement is of a temporary nature. I've promised to give her a Season here in London, thus providing her with a chance to meet an array of eligible gentlemen. Once she finds a fellow she can love, she'll toss me over and marry him."

"Marry . . . Are the pair of you insane?"

"Not at all. It is a thoroughly sound plan."

Edward huffed out a breath. "It is a thoroughly idiotic plan. What if she doesn't find this fellow with whom she is supposed to fall in love? Worse, what if she changes her mind and decides to hold you to your pledge? You will have no choice but to marry her, secret agreement or no."

"Ironic, Meg said those very things to me, when she was trying to talk me out of proceeding with the idea. But just as I told her, she will have no difficulty finding a man to wed. You've seen her. They'll be prowling around her skirts like cats after a plump mouse, our engagement notwith-standing."

"I suppose they will at that. Her apparent unavailability might even make her more attrac-tive."

"Exactly! As for the other, Meg is an honorable, trustworthy young woman, despite this current ruse of ours. I know she would never deceive me."

"You're sure?"

"I would stake my life on it."

"Nevertheless—"

Cade cut him off with a hand. "No. Look, Ned, I put her in this situation, and it's my responsibility to help her out of it, especially after Ludgate found us together at the house."

"Ludgate? Who is that?"

"A nosy pudding of a man, who I have the misfortune to call neighbor. Quite likely, he's tattled to half the country about us by now. I couldn't very well stand by and let Meg be ruined, so I told him we were engaged. By rights, I ought to be the one to marry her after what happened between us. But . . . well, that seems a deuced poor reason to wed, not when other arrangements can be made that suit us better. I figure with you and Mama here in Town to look after her, she'll do fine. I shall stay for a few days and get her settled, then take myself off back north."

His brother arched a brow. "Leave? But you can't leave."

"Why can I not?"

"First of all, because you and Miss Amberley are supposed to be wildly in love, remember? I don't think even the veriest simpleton would believe your tale of devotion if you desert her after less than a week."

"Desert her? Now, that's rather harsh—"

"Society won't think it is, especially if word

gets 'round that the two of you were alone together in Northumberland. They will see your departure as a tacit repudiation of your promise to her, and she'll be as good as ruined. Matters will be dodgy enough at first, even with you at her side. Dance attendance on her and even the highest sticklers will unbend and call the pair of you romantic. Run off back to your estate and you might as well toss her to the wolves."

Cade felt lines crease his forehead.

"No," Edward declared in lowering tones. "If you intend to put this cockeyed plan in motion, you will have to stay for the duration of the Season. Or at least until she finds her future husband and jilts your sorry hide."

Bloody hell! Ned was right. For some idiotic reason, he'd been telling himself that once Meg was settled with his family in London, he would be free to return home and pursue his own plans and desires—alone. But his much coveted solitude would have to wait once again while he saw to her. He'd made Meg a promise and could not abandon her now.

"Very well, then, I shall stay and see to it that Meg finds a husband," Cade declared. Picking up his glass, he held it out. "Now, I believe I could do with a refill."

"Why does your brother keep looking at me that way?" Meg whispered to Cade that evening as they took seats on the sofa in the music room after dinner.

"What way? And which one, since there are three of them now present?"

"The duke," she replied. "He has this . . . I don't know . . . glint in his eye that gives me the distinct impression he knows about us."

Cade paused a long moment. "Perhaps that's because he does."

"What!" she exclaimed, forgetting to keep her voice low.

All other conversation stopped, a cluster of dark heads and brilliantly colored eyes turning her way. Even young Esme, who had been permitted the special treat of coming down from the schoolroom to join the family for dinner, glanced up from where she sat in her youthful yellow gown, quietly sketching with a pencil and paper.

As for the duke, he stood with a negligent elbow propped against the large, ornately carved white marble fireplace mantel. He was sipping a brandy with a casual air—unaware, from all appearances, of the trouble he had just caused.

"Is something amiss, dear?" the dowager questioned, her teaspoon poised motionless over her cup.

Meg's gaze moved around the room, her heart beating so rapidly it was a wonder all of them couldn't hear it, too. "N-No . . . I . . . of course not, Your Grace."

Cade leaned closer and took Meg's hand in his own. "I am afraid the fault is mine, Mama," he said. "I was murmuring things in Meg's ears that are best said in private."

"From her reaction," his mother observed in a gentle tone, "I have the feeling they are things best not said at all—at least not until after the two of you are wed."

Across the room the duke quirked a brow, but said nothing as he drank his brandy.

Smooth as a skipping stone, Cade gave an unrepentant smile and raised Meg's hand to his mouth, pressing a kiss against its back before releasing her. Her skin burned where his lips had been, the sensation only adding to her difficulties as she fought to regain her composure. After his revelation about his brother's knowledge of the situation between them, she desperately wanted to question him further, but realized she would be forced to wait.

"Still can't quite fathom it," remarked Lord John, more familiarly known as Jack—the third son, and younger than Cade by nearly two years. "Our Cade engaged to be married. Somehow, I always figured Ned would be the first to tie the knot, leaving the rest of us a few more years of freedom."

"Don't let me stop you, Jack," the duke commented. "You may take a bride any time you like, with no regard to my matrimonial state."

"You know deuced well I have no interest in being caught inside the parson's mousetrap." Jack remarked. "Pray take no offense, Miss Amberley. I have nothing against marriage in the general sense, only in regard to myself. Obviously, Cade has managed to find himself a true gem of a girl. He is a lucky man."

"Thank you, your lordship," she replied. "And I take no offense, especially given the fact that you are merely expressing an opinion that seems to be almost universally held by the male sex. At least the officers of my acquaintance certainly did. I always noticed that they liked to dance attendance on the ladies well enough, but suggest marriage, and they turned white and wobbly as a blancmange."

Jack laughed, showing straight teeth and dimples that she knew must set women's hearts afluttering wherever he went. Like all the Byron men, he was devastatingly handsome, with dark hair, jewel-toned eyes, a strong jaw, and lips that must surely have been designed by the angels themselves.

Yet as unmistakably attractive as he might be, his looks and flirtatious manners didn't have the power to sway her. Odd as some might surely find the idea, she preferred Cade's more reserved manners and taciturn demeanor. She even liked his caustic remarks—especially when she wasn't on the receiving end of them.

As for his other brother, Drake, she'd been trying to take his measure all evening; the man was cheerful and attentive one moment, then silent and distant the next.

Casting a brief glance across to where he sat in a chair near the fireplace, she watched as he drew out a small writing pad, his tawny brows furrowed as he scribbled furiously upon it. He didn't pause, the pencil moving over the page as if he were afraid he might forget a thought before he managed to transfer it into writing.

"He's solving equations," Cade murmured, having apparently noticed her curiosity. "Drake is a mathematician. Theoretical stuff that I'll never be able to understand. He's always consulting with some set of great minds or other."

"He's an inventor, too," Mallory offered, keeping her voice lowered, as if knowing better than to disturb Drake.

"Indeed," Jack said, his lips twisting in obvious amusement. "You may have noticed the strange, greenish tint to his hands—copper bath to aid in the conductivity of electricity, I am given to understand. At least he didn't come out on the bad end of this particular experiment, seeing he's nearly blown himself up more times than I can count."

"Do not speak of that," interjected the dowager. "Your brother knows better than to blow himself up, and if he comes into my house again with his eyebrows gone, more shall end up missing from him than a bit of hair."

As though he suddenly realized he was the topic of conversation, Drake's head came up. "What's that?" he asked, pencil still poised over the paper. "Are you talking about explosives? There's been some very interesting work in that field lately. Exciting stuff that uses derivatives of gunpowder."

"There shall be no talk of gunpowder, either," the duchess decreed in regal tones. "Mallory, perhaps you could entertain us all with a song?"

Mallory's aquamarine eyes twinkled, but she managed to retain a serious cast to her expression. "Yes, Mama."

"Unless Margaret would care to do so instead," the dowager suggested. "Do you play, dear?"

"Not well, Your Grace . . . I mean, Ava. My mother attempted to teach me, but I am afraid it did not take."

"Ah," the dowager said with polite acceptance.

"I sing, however," Meg said. "I am told I possess some small talent in that regard. Mayhap Lady Mallory might accompany me, if you would like to hear me sing."

The older woman smiled. "Excellent! Yes, of course, we would all like to hear."

Realizing she had been caught in a trap of her own making, Meg rose to her feet and crossed to the pianoforte.

"What shall I play?" Mallory asked, before going on to offer a trio of possible selections.

Meg chose the one whose words she knew best,

then waited as the other young woman arranged the sheet music on the stand and took a seat at the pianoforte.

Nerves simmered in Meg's stomach, her fingers abruptly cold as she prepared herself to perform. She didn't know why she was anxious, since in the past she'd often sung at social gatherings. Yet at those affairs, she'd had no one to impress, no one who would think less of her if she stumbled in some small way.

Not that the Byrons were haughty or unkind. Quite the contrary, since they had welcomed her in with an unhesitating friendliness and a generosity that was frankly surprising, especially given their elevated noble rank. Perhaps therein lay the reason for her apprehension, she thought now. For despite the fact that her very presence here was based on a lie, she quite absurdly wanted them to like her. She longed for them to draw her into their loving, close-knit family, even if she knew her time among them would be fleeting. She'd been so alone since Papa died. So alone until she'd met Cade. . .

Her gaze collided with his forest green eyes, the pull almost electric, as she stood next to the pianoforte. A moment later, his sister played the opening notes of the song with a practiced flourish.

Automatically, Meg drew a deep breath and opened her mouth to sing. Her voice quavered at first, sounding thin and faintly uncertain even to her own ears. Then Cade's lips turned up in an encouraging smile and the tension flowed from her muscles.

From that moment on, the melody flowed outward in an easy cadence, soaring up from her diaphragm to flood the room with lilting song. Confidence filled her, along with a sensation of pleasure. She sang, all the while looking at Cade, her gaze fixed steadily upon his own.

Then the last notes were struck—piano and voice alike blending in a harmonious crescendo that lingered in the room long after their end.

Silence fell, then applause broke out.

"Bravo!" called Jack.

"Wonderful!" declared Drake.

Even the duke clapped with genuine pleasure, as the dowager, Mallory, and little Esme added their approval.

Yet it was Cade whose esteem she truly craved, she realized. Cade, whose opinion was suddenly the only one that mattered.

"Beautiful," he said. "Well done, Meg. Not even the finest of song birds could compare."

Warmth spread through her, an odd shifting sensation forming deep in her center that she couldn't clearly identify nor wholly understand.

"But now if you will all excuse me," he went on, "I fear I must find my bed. It has been a long day and I am in need of rest." He lifted a hand to stifle a yawn.

She blinked, the warmth vanishing as suddenly

as it had come, the spell under which she'd been held shattering like a fragile glass vase.

Silly, she thought. It was naught but a song.

"Yes, it is time Esme sought her slumber as well," said the dowager as she rose to her feet. "Come along, sweetheart, or your governess will be giving us both a scold."

"But Mama!" the girl protested. "I am still drawing. Please, may I have ten minutes more?"

"If I give you ten minutes, you shall soon be wanting twenty. No, you've stayed up well past your usual bedtime as it is. You may take your sketches with you upstairs, however. Now, be a good girl and say your good-nights."

"Yes, Mama." Esme jumped to her feet and ran to give hugs and kisses to her siblings, who all smiled and teased her with obvious affection.

Meg noticed the extra long embrace the girl gave Cade, her thin arms winding around his neck as they exchanged a few quiet words. It was obvious that Esme had missed her older brother a great deal during his absence, and was happy to have him home.

Then Esme turned to her. "Here, this is for you," the girl said, holding out one of the pages on which she'd been drawing.

"Oh, I . . . well, thank you." Meg reached out and took the sketch between her fingers.

Gazing down, her eyes widened. Instead of the typical childish scribble she'd expected, she discovered two well-rendered figures. The style was a bit loose, and still immature with a tendency to distort the proportions. Even so, it was refined enough to have captured remarkably accurate likenesses of her and Cade seated side by side on the sofa. Esme might only be nine years of age, but already she was an exceptional artist, better than many adults would ever hope to be.

"This is . . . extraordinary," Meg said.

"It's you and Cade," the girl offered, clutching a small fist against her yellow wool skirt. "Do you like it?"

"I most certainly do. How could I not? You've drawn Cade and me so perfectly. It's beautiful."

The girl's oval features came alive with a pleased smile. "Good night, Miss Amberley. I'm glad you're going to be my sister."

At a sudden loss for what she knew would never be, Meg settled on the only honest reply she could offer.

"Sweet dreams, Esme."

Flashing another smile, the girl turned and hurried to her mother's side, the pair of them making their way from the room.

The others stood and began to do the same. As Meg moved to follow, she felt a light touch on her shoulder, and glanced up to find Edward Byron towering at her side.

"It's a good likeness," he remarked, nodding at the drawing.

"Um . . . yes, your sister is very talented, Your Grace."

"That she is.

She looked across at Cade, who stood waiting near the door.

"Your secret is safe with me, you know," the duke murmured in a low voice as they strolled forward. "Cade and I spoke earlier about your situation."

Her gaze flew to the duke's. "Did you?"

"Yes. And although I cannot say I entirely approve, I do understand. I must warn you, however, to take care."

She stiffened. "Oh? In what way?"

"In guarding your heart, Miss Amberley. You seem like an amiable young woman, and I would not want you to end up hurt."

The starch eased out of her spine. "My thanks for your concern, Your Grace, but I shall be fine."

"As you say. Well then, I bid you a good evening."

Reaching Cade's side, she gazed up into his inquiring green eyes and felt her pulse beat double. Walking with him as they made their way to their separate bedchambers, she wondered if she had just told the duke yet another lie.

Chapter 10

*O*h, how adorable. She'll take that one as well," Meg heard the Dowager Duchess of Clybourne declare a week later as they stood in consultation with London's most fashionable mantua maker. "In the palest of pink, I believe. Or maybe the stripe?" She paused, tapping a finger against her chin. "Oh, let's do both, what do you say? Yes, yes, a pink and white stripe for the walking dress, and an evening gown in the shell peony. Oh, they will be exquisite with Margaret's fair coloring."

"I agree entirely, Your Grace," said Madame Morelle. "And the pale blue ball gown we discussed will make her eyes sparkle like stars. She will be the envy of every young lady in London."

The two older women smiled conspiratorially while Meg stood mute, having been ejected from all but the most minor decision making over the past twenty minutes.

Twisting her fingers together, she stared at the yard upon yard of stunning fabrics laid out for display—silks and satins, sarcenets, velvets, muslins, and more in a virtual rainbow of hues, patterns, and textures. Beside the material lay laces and ribbons, buttons and feathers, everything a well-dressed lady could possibly hope to use to trim a gown. Rows of fashion babies sat on shelves to display the latest dress designs, while books of watercolor and pencil sketches added still more possibilities.

From Meg's perspective, the dowager seemed to have ordered literally dozens of dresses, so many she had long since lost count of them all. At first she'd tried to voice her opinions and objections, attempting to interject a bit of sensible economy into the conversation. But the dowager and the dressmaker soon shunted her aside and went on as they thought best. Meanwhile, she was rushed away to the back of the shop to have her measurements taken by an assistant.

It was not that she had any objection to the gowns themselves—they were all exquisite, done in a style sure to flatter her figure and complexion. What troubled her was the sheer quantity of clothing the duchess was ordering.

How shall I ever hope to pay for it all? she fretted.

"And oh yes," she heard the dowager say. "She must have at least half a dozen riding habits. Let us look at fabrics again."

A knot twisted in her chest as she wrung her hands. Papa had left her a comfortable dowry, but at this rate there would be nothing left, certainly not enough to tempt a prospective bridegroom.

Turning her head, she glanced at Cade, who sat at his ease on a nearby divan. He had escorted them to the shop, then withdrawn to read a book and sip the glass of Madeira that Madame Morelle had procured for him upon their arrival. As for Mallory, who had come with them as well, she was proving of absolutely no use against her mother, the girl having disappeared with a trio of gowns she was considering having altered.

"I believe you are right. Let us make it an even dozen . . ." thc duchess declared.

"Cade," Meg hisscd as she hurried across to him. "You must put a stop to this."

He glanced up, peering at her over his half-moon spectacles. "Put a stop to what?"

"All this shopping. Your mother is ordering far too many gowns for me."

He raised a single dark eyebrow. "And you find that distrcssing?"

"Of course I do."

One corner of his mouth turned up. "How curious. I believe you must be the only lady of my acquaintance whom I have ever heard complain about buying new clothes."

"If I am the only one to complain," she said, sinking down next to him, "it is because I am the first bearing the brunt of the cost." She hung her head, her voice dropping to a whisper. "Cade, I cannot afford these gowns. You must speak to your mother and explain."

His green eyes widened. "Well, no wonder you are alarmed." Reaching out, he patted her hand. "Do not worry. All the bills will be sent to me. You won't have to pay for a thing."

"Sent to *you*! But I cannot allow you to pay——"

"Of course you can, and you will. Despite being a second son, I am quite wealthy in my own right. I assure you, the expense will not be a problem."

She worried a thumb over a piece of black trim on her sleeve. "The expense is not the issue. Allowing you to buy clothes for me is highly improper."

"I fail to see why. You are my affianced."

"*No, I am not,* in case you have forgotten," she said, careful to keep her voice low. "I cannot permit it."

His jaw tightened with a familiar stubbornness. "And I cannot permit you to be inadequately clothed for the Season. Consider the gowns a present for your future marriage."

"But Cade——"

"But Meg . . ." he replied with gentle mockery before his tone grew serious once again. "I will not be gainsaid in this. Let Mama choose whatever she considers necessary and appropriate for you to wear. As for you, stop worrying and enjoy yourself. And should a particular gown take your fancy, buy it, I shall not complain of the cost."

She made a small huff of protest, then realized the futility of it. I suppose he is right, she thought, knowing that a proper wardrobe was essential for attending the kind of ton parties to which she was already starting to receive invitations. The same held true for the diamond engagement ring he had given her—the gemstone a necessary part of their charade, even if wearing it felt like a mark of deceit. Nevertheless, the honorable part of her balked at the notion of accepting money from Cade, even in the form of clothing. Yet what choice did she have, given the relative smallness of her own pocketbook?

"Very well," she sighed. "I accept, and thank you for your kind generosity. However, there is one item on which I insist bearing the cost myself."

"Oh? And what might that be?" he drawled.

"My wedding gown. I absolutely refuse to allow you to pay for that."

His eyes glittered, a sharp edge springing to life deep within. "On that score," he murmured, "we are in complete accord, since I have no wish to purchase a dress made for the express purpose of joining you forever to another man."

Her lips parted on an unsteady inhale, confusion twining inside her. "Just as I trust I will not be paying for your wedding night trousseau?"

At such a suggestion, she found she couldn't breathe at all. Her gaze locked with his, the room shifting as she lost herself in the rich forest green of his eyes. For a long moment he stared back, his own lips parting on a silent exhale.

Before she knew what he meant to do, he bent and captured her mouth, taking her with a slow, gentle kiss that made her eyelids flutter closed and her mind spin in a dizzying circle. His scent

157

clouded her brain even further, his taste sweet and rich with a lingering tang of the wine he'd been drinking. Then as abruptly as the kiss had begun, it ended.

Her eyes flew wide. "Oh! Wh-Why did you do that?"

"I . . . um . . ." He flicked a sideways glance across the room. ". . . was just keeping up appearances." Leaning down, he set his mouth close to her ear. "We are supposed to be madly in love, remember? No harm giving them a little show."

A show? Turning her head, she saw that he was right. They had attracted an audience, Cade's mother and the mantua maker regarding them with a pair of indulgent smiles before quickly looking away. Meg's skin flushed all the way to her roots, her shoulders drooping at the realization that his kiss had meant nothing. He had only been play-acting.

"Yes, of course," she said, striving to sound as if she'd been in on his plan all along.

"By this time tomorrow," he volunteered, "the tale of how we were caught kissing in Madame Morelle's shop will be all over Town. Particularly since Madame has never been known for her discretion. But it's all to the good. Society will have no doubt of our devotion."

She nodded, suddenly desperate to be away from him. "I just realized that I have been neglecting your sister. She must be in need of assistance with

158

her choices by now. So, if you will pardon me, your lordship, I shall attend her."

Cade stood, gripping his cane hard as he watched her hurry across the room, her dark skirts swaying around her slender hips before she disappeared behind a curtain that led to the fitting rooms beyond.

Resuming his seat, he picked up his book and leafed to the correct page. But as he tried to focus on the words, his thoughts drifted away; the taste of her lips still fresh against his own, the sensory pleasure of their kiss warming his blood even now.

What in the hell was I thinking? he berated himself. Despite his convenient explanation to Meg, he'd had no intention of kissing her—not for show or for any other reason. But there she'd been, sitting next to him looking so pretty and earnest as she shared her concerns over the cost of the gowns his mother was selecting. Everything had been fine—in fact, he'd been rather amused by her prideful worrying—until she mentioned the probable need for a wedding dress.

In the blink of an eye his humor had turned, irritation boiling up inside him along with other dark emotions he had no business feeling. And then he'd been kissing her, without a thought for their surroundings or the consequences of the act.

Thank God he'd come up with a reasonable excuse for his lapse. As for why he'd had the lapse in the first place . . . well, he supposed it was no more than her proximity and the fact that she was a very desirable woman. That was all the kiss had been, he assured himself—a physical act of no real importance. He decided not to dwell on it. Just as he refused to dwell upon the memory of the night she'd lain in his arms and his bed.

I will escort her to the balls and parties, dote upon her like an attentive fiancé, and see to it she is well received in Society. And when we are not in public, I will act like her brother.

Yes, that should serve, though perhaps not entirely, since he supposed Mama and Mallory might find something amiss if he treated Meg with no deeper regard than he did his siblings. He would treat her as . . . a friend. Yes, a friend with whom he shared a unique secret.

After all, is that not what we are already? Friends?

Two weeks later, on a fine evening in late March, Meg alighted from the Duke of Clybourne's resplendent chaise-and-four. Taking Cade's arm, she let him lead her up the steps of the Berkeley Square town house where she was to attend her very first ton ball. Accompanying them was the duke, the dowager duchess, and Lady Mallory, who was buzzing with barely suppressed excitement. As soon as their party entered the main foyer, several liveried footman came forward to take their outer garments.

Meg handed over her pelisse, then brushed her fingertips over her gown, to make sure the dress was straight. Rows of embroidered leaves graced the hem and rounded half sleeves of the garment's sheer white tulle overskirt. The material beneath was fashioned from a length of cornflower blue silk that was gathered under the bust with a darker blue ribbon before falling in a light, frothy glide to the floor. Matching blue silk slippers graced her feet, the shoes just one more part of the massive wardrobe that had been delivered to the duke's Grosvenor Square address only a few days earlier.

With their small group ready, they proceeded up another grand staircase to the ballroom—the atmosphere alive with a profusion of noise and color; the scent of beeswax, perfume, and floor polish drifting on the air.

Never in her life had Meg seen so many elegantly dressed people crowded into so confined a space. It was not that the house was small, rather the guest list was too large.

"What an unspeakable crush," the dowager murmured as they threaded their way farther inside. "No doubt Lady Raybold's reason for holding her entertainment before the Season actually begins. Fewer parties mean more people."

"I only hope my come-out ball will be half so well-attended," Mallory said. "I cannot believe it is next week." Reaching for Meg's gloved hand, she gave her palm an anxious squeeze. "I'm just so glad we shall be sharing the evening together."

Meg sent her a smile. "You are sure you do not mind?

After all, it is your special day. I am not at all averse to stepping aside."

"Don't you dare! I'll need you there to distract people from hearing my knees knock together when we're standing in the receiving line."

Meg laughed and Mallory joined her, the dowager and the men smiling.

"Besides," Mallory continued. "My come-out has to be easier than my presentation to the Queen. I could hardly move in my court dress with that immense train and those ostrich feathers bobbing in my hair. I was sure I would stumble and make a fool of myself right in front of Her Majesty."

"You did splendidly, dear," the duchess said. "Queen Charlotte remarked that you seemed a very sweet child, high praise indeed from her."

"Thank you, Mama. And thank you ever so much for letting me join you tonight."

Ava smiled. "It would have been cruel other-wise, leaving you home by yourself. I suppose I might have insisted you wait for your ball, but since you've already been presented to Her Majesty, I can't see the harm. Anyway, next week is the real start to the Season, and you are certain to make a tremendous splash."

"And Meg, too," Mallory added.

"Yes. And Margaret, too," the duchess agreed with a happy expression.

"I want the evening to be for us both," Mallory continued, giving Meg's hand another squeeze. "Our first official introduction into Society at large."

Meg smiled, touched by her generosity and kindness. Strictly speaking, she supposed that Mallory's come-out ball would be her own official introduction. However, from what she'd experienced over the past several days, Society had already been busy making her acquaintance.

Ever since the notice of her and Cade's engagement appeared in the *Morning Post*, the Clybourne House door knocker had barely stopped sounding. Every day a fresh round of visitors called, each new group seemingly bolder and more inquisitive than the last, all of them eager to be introduced to the future Lady Cade Byron.

Thankfully, Cade made a point of joining her for these visits, taking a seat next to her so he could deflect any questions that grew too personal or intrusive. He had a deft way about him, she'd observed, relying upon a combination of natural charm, humor, and, in extreme cases, a glare that would have sent the devil himself scurrying for cover.

Yet despite his outward displays of devotion and protectiveness, he'd made no further amorous overtures toward her since that day at Madame

Morelle's. He continued to "put on a show," as he'd called it, holding her hand or brushing a light kiss over her cheek as though he were a besotted bridegroom-to-be. But on the few occasions when they were alone together, he withdrew, treating her with pleasant friendliness and a scrupulous politeness that made her long for something more—no matter how foolish it might seem.

Luckily, the Season was here and she would be able to begin searching for a husband in earnest. She only hoped she was fortunate enough to meet a gentleman she truly liked and wished to marry. Cade had made his feelings quite clear on that subject, and she would abide by her promise. Over the next twelve weeks, she vowed, she would find another man to wed and set him free.

After all, that is what I want. Is it not?

Now, with a few murmured words, the dowager moved away to join one of her friends on the far side of the room. Edward excused himself to do the same, leaving Meg and Mallory with Cade.

"Oh, look, there is Jack!" Mallory said as they moved deeper into the room. "Jack!" she called, lifting a hand to give her brother a wave.

From across the room he nodded his acknowledgment, his eyes twinkling with good-natured humor at his exuberant younger sister. Turning away, he spoke to a pair of gentlemen with whom he was quite obviously acquainted, and moments later the trio made their way forward.

"How do you do this evening?" Jack greeted, after the requisite bows and curtsies were exchanged. "Though in your case, imp," he said to Mallory, "I don't believe I need ask. You look fair to bursting with excitement."

"If you don't mind my saying so, Byron, the lady looks exquisite," remarked one of his friends. "Both ladies. I do hope you will introduce us."

Jack quirked a brow. "As you will. Niall Faversham, meet my sister, Lady Mallory. And the lady beside her is Miss Margaret Amberley. Cade, I believe, you know already, though perhaps not the fact that he and Miss Amberley are recently engaged."

"Ah, so *you* are the one stirring up all the talk," Faversham said with a tip of his blond head. "Having now made your acquaintance, I can see why Lord Cade decided to sweep you off your feet. Had I met you earlier, I might have done the same."

Meg laughed. "My thanks, Mr. Faversham . . . I think."

"And this other gentleman is Lord Gresham," Jack continued. "Gresham is an old school chum of mine and is acquainted with all my siblings. Adam, Miss Amberley."

"A pleasure," he said in a deep, rumbling voice. Taking her hand, he made an elegant bow.

"Mine as well," Meg said. "And how are you finding the ball this evening, my lord?"

"I feared it had all the makings of a bore,"

Gresham replied, "but I have to confess it has improved rather dramatically in the past few minutes, now that I have happened upon such clearly delightful company."

He flashed her a roguish grin, his teeth white against his swarthy complexion and head of thick black hair. An undeniably handsome man, she noted. He was tall—taller even than Cade and Jack, who towered well above most of the men in the room.

Like Jack Byron and Mr. Faversham—who possessed a decidedly pleasant countenance in his own right—Lord Gresham must cut quite a swath through the female population, she mused. Yet in spite of the fact that each gentleman had much to recommend him in the way of charm and attractiveness, her heart remained untouched, her pulse continuing to beat at its usual stolid, steady pace.

All that changed a few seconds later when Cade unexpectedly laid his palm against the nape of her neck. The warm strength of his masculine fingers seemed to sear her exposed skin, his touch roaming in an idle, tantalizing glide that made her mouth go dry. Her heart gave a frantic hop, racing wildly as a shudder chased across her flesh. She blinked and prayed no one else had noticed her reaction.

Striving for calm, she tried to ease away, but Cade held her in place, his fingers tightening ever so subtly. Using the fleshy edge of his thumb, he traced an invisible line along the back of her neck up to her hairline, then down again, pausing for a few seconds before repeating the brazen process over again.

Merciful heaven, what does he think he's doing? She wished she could sigh aloud at the enthralling pleasure.

If she didn't know better, she might have imagined he was staking some kind of claim upon her, silently letting the other men know that she was taken. But since he couldn't possibly have such an idea in mind, she supposed he was playacting again, his touch no more than another quiet display of the supposed affection the two of them were pretending to share.

Harsh emotions smoldered like fire within her, making her want to wrench herself free of him. But with everyone looking on, such a response was clearly impossible. Still, it did not mean she was completely without options.

Angling her head slightly, she gave a tiny shrug only he would notice, hoping he might take the hint and remove his wandering fingers. Instead, he skimmed his thumb upward again, then paused to swirl it in a little circle at the base of her skull. She shivered, gooseflesh popping out over her skin.

Suddenly she'd had enough.

"Mr. Faversham," she said, striving for what she hoped was a normal tone of voice. "Do you like to dance?"

His face brightened. "Indeed, I do. In fact, if my eyes don't deceive me, I believe there is a set about to begin."

"I think you are correct. Perhaps you and Lady Mallory might enjoy taking a turn together?"

Faversham's expression brightened even more. "Most assuredly. If the lady is so inclined? Lady Mallory, will you do me the honor?"

Mallory sent Meg a sideways glance, her gaze alive with a combination of surprise and pleased anticipation. "Thank you. That would be lovely." With a smile, she took the arm he held out and the two of them hurried away toward the dance floor.

"And what of you, Miss Amberley?" Lord Gresham inquired. "Do you enjoy dancing?"

"Very much. However, Lord Cade is not so disposed. His war injury, you understand."

Cade's roving thumb stopped, his body stiffening at her back.

"I plan to sit with him on the sidelines and watch the festivities," she explained. "Or perhaps play cards, should a likely game form."

"Lord, love, you make me sound as if I'm in my dotage," Cade remarked in a seemingly light-hearted tone as his hand slid across to her shoulder. His fingers tightened in a brief squeeze that let her know he was aware of her ploy. "I may not be able to take to the floor," he continued, "but that does not mean you need be so deprived. If you wish to dance, my dear Meg, then I have no objection."

She turned, his hand falling away. "If you are certain, darling?"

His jaw tensed, an irritation in his gaze she assumed must come from his defeat in their silent tug-of-war. "Quite certain. Dance with as many men as you like. I assure you, I won't mind."

Lord Gresham cast an interested glance between them, a suppressed twinkle in his warm brown eyes. "If that is the case, then you can start with me, Miss Amberley. Take pity and say you will grant me the pleasure of a dance?"

Meg smiled, then let out a little laugh. "Somehow, I do not think you are the sort who ever lacks for partners, my lord, but I shall be delighted to oblige and stand up with you nevertheless." Stepping forward, she accepted his arm. "Cade . . . Jack . . . behave yourselves while I am gone. I shall be just across the room if you have need of me."

Cade glowered, while Jack grinned and shook his head at her antics.

A measure of her fiery determination faded as she and Lord Gresham took their places for the start of the dance. A large number of other couples were lined up as well, including Mallory and Mr. Faversham, who stood several feet away, deep in conversation.

"Not that I am by any means complaining of your company," Gresham said. "But I would warn you to be careful about teasing that particular tiger."

"Oh, and what tiger might that be?"

"Cade. He's quite besotted with you. I can see why he rushed you into an engagement. I am only surprised you aren't already his wife."

And never will be, she thought. If only he realized the truth, he would surely be astonished.

"Well, we may have rushed at the start, but we're taking our time now," she said, striving to sound natural. "Cade wants to give me a Season."

"Does he? Again, I must count myself surprised. I've known him a long time and have never seen him so possessive of a woman. His patience is a testament to his devotion."

Or rather, his disregard, she corrected silently, her gaze dropping to her shoes. If Cade seemed possessive, it was only further proof of his acting abilities. *Unless he is hoping to tempt other men with the notion that I am a prize worth stealing away.* A prize, she knew, Cade did not want to keep himself.

To her relief, a flourish of notes rang out, signaling the start of the set. Pinning a smile on her lips, she raised her head, took Lord Gresham's hand, and began to dance.

Watching from a far corner of the room, Cade curled his palm over the top of his cane and gave it a vicious squeeze. Luckily, the head was made of solid gold, otherwise he would probably have crushed it. A slash of pain in his hand forced him to relax his grip, his gaze continuing to track Meg's movements as she laughed and cavorted on the dance floor with Adam Gresham.

He took some consolation from the fact that Gresham would not take advantage of her. At least, he assumed he wouldn't, for in spite of Gresham's friendship with the family, he was a wild sort, given to all kinds of ungoverned excesses and worldly vices. Women flocked to him in droves, particularly the married ones who were unhappy in their unions and looking for a means to end their loneliness and appease the sexual desires that weren't being satisfied in their own beds at home.

Innocent girls tossed their caps at him as well, when their mamas weren't looking. And although Gresham generally stepped clear of their lures, he wasn't above a bit of dalliance every now and then. Pleasure in all its forms was always at the top of his must-do list.

Yet he wasn't without honor, and Cade knew he would never poach on another man's territory. If he learned Meg was available, however . . . But no, when and if Gresham ever married, he would need an heiress to repair his depleted fortunes, so Meg was safe from him.

He knew that other men would want her, though. Men who wouldn't mind taking an unexceptional dowry in exchange for her extraordinary beauty and charm. Men with whom she would be dancing and flirting, he thought, his hand tightening again on his cane. Men she would be encouraging with her engaging smile and bewitching blue eyes. Men with whom she might be sneaking off to cajole and kiss.

But was that not what he wanted? What he and Meg had agreed she would do? Of course it was. *I just want to be sure she is protected*, he told himself. To know she has found a man worthy of her trust and affection, who will love her as she deserves to be loved. Which is why he needed to keep her in his sights and make certain she didn't fall prey to unscrupulous scoundrels and rogues.

The set concluded and Gresham offered his arm to escort her from the floor. They had gone no more than ten feet when a rather dandified pair of gentlemen approached, their gestures making it clear they were importuning Gresham for an introduction. Cade watched as Meg smiled and made some remark that drew laughs all around. Moments later the group grew larger still as two more young men came over. Bows and curtsies were exchanged.

A few choice words and he could send them all scurrying, he thought, smiling at the idea of pouncing like a cat into a flock of pigeons. He took a few steps to do just that, then stopped, reminding himself once again that Meg needed to meet eligible suitors if their plan was to succeed.

Thrusting the tip of his cane against the polished

floor with a hard tap, he turned and went in search of a drink. The night was going to be a long one indeed.

Nearly three hours later Meg excused herself from the dancing to escape down a long, crowded hallway and into the relative peace of the ladies' withdrawing room.

A pair of women stood inside, conversing quietly as they tidied their hair and rinsed their hands in the porcelain washbasins provided for the guests' use. Meg glided past to a curtained area arranged to one side where she could take care of her more personal needs. As she moved behind a small screen, she heard the other women depart, leaving the room blessedly quiet.

She paused, taking a moment to savor the sensation of being alone after the constant press of bodies and noise in the ballroom and corridors beyond. Not that she wasn't enjoying the festivities. The dancing was lively and fun, and she had suffered no lack of available partners—standing up for nearly every set so far.

Yet even as she danced and chatted with one gentleman after another, she found herself viscerally aware of Cade. During the interval between sets, he would often come to "check" on her, staying to make sure she had everything she required. Twice he brought her a refreshment—a glass of cool lemonade or punch to ease the dryness from her throat. The remainder of the time he sat in a chair along the ballroom's periphery.

True, he didn't spend every moment watching her—sometimes she would glance over to discover him in conversation with another guest. But far more often he was alone, his deep, forest green gaze trained upon her.

When she had suggested he go to the card room, or find a group of gentlemen with whom he could talk, he refused. Leaning close, he'd whispered in her ear that their affection for one another would hardly look convincing if he abandoned her entirely.

So, at his urging, she had continued to dance. Yet in spite of her best attempts to relax, she could not, her body simmering with the constant knowledge that he sat only a few feet away. But not even Cade could follow her here to the ladies' withdrawing room—although if she tarried too long, she supposed he could send Mallory or the dowager to find her. With that in mind, she went about the business of answering nature's demand.

She was just about to move out from behind the privacy screen when she heard a new pair of women enter the room, their conversation carrying readily to her ears.

". . . Well, I must say it's all proving vastly entertaining watching Lord Cade dance attendance on that new fiancée of his, even though the poor man can't actually dance a step. Such a pity about his leg."

Her companion made a sympathetic murmur of agreement, their skirts rustling as they moved farther inside. From the location of their voices, Meg surmised they had taken seats on the padded benches she'd noticed when she first entered the room.

"He used to dance beautifully, and fence, too. I understand Angelo actually got tears in his eyes when he received news of Byron's injuries. He was overheard to remark that he'd just lost the finest student to ever grace the halls of his academy."

"From what *I* understand," the other woman said in a conspiratorial tone, "Cade Byron's leg is the least of his wounds."

"Oh, how so?"

Yes. What does she mean? Suddenly Meg was glad she hadn't tried to make her presence known.

"My husband has contacts in the military, you know. Word is, Lord Cade was captured somewhere in Portugal and savagely tortured by the French. Not only was he gunshot, he was strangled and beaten to within an inch of his life! They think the French had him for days, though no one knows for sure."

"Dreadful!" the first woman declared with equal measures of shock and fascination.

"Yes. What's more, the heathen frogs pitched him into a drainage ditch when they were through. Apparently they were in a rush to leave, and assumed he was so near death that he couldn't possibly survive. It was a sheer miracle that he did."

"So some of our soldiers found him?"

"No, not at first. He crawled his way out."

Crawled? Meg put a fist over her mouth to muffle her gasp.

"Hmm. Dragged himself out through the mud and offal using a discarded animal bone, or so the reports said. A peasant found him a few yards away and sent for help. Harold told me Byron's face was so battered and swollen he was all but blind. He also says there were bodies in that ditch."

"Whatever do you mean?"

"A local family the French had killed. They flung him in there with them, as if he were already dead."

Meg shuddered and curved an arm around her waist, pressing her fist tighter against her lips. Oh, Cade! she cried inwardly, thinking of what he'd endured. What was it he had told her? That his fiancée was killed by the French. *Dear God, surely one of those bodies had not been Calida's?* With a growing sense of horror, she knew it had been. Brushing a hand over her cheek, she was startled to find it wet with tears.

"He didn't speak for weeks after he was found and sent to hospital, and apparently not for some time after his return to England either," the woman continued with a morbid interest Meg now found sickening. Still, she couldn't help but listen, feeling as if she owed it to Cade to see what was being said about him, no matter how vicious the gossip might be.

"Of course he went to that northern estate of his to hide away like some recluse. He always was a wild sort, doing whatever he liked no matter the consequences. But there's speculation now that his ordeal may have driven him over the edge into madness."

"Surely not!" remarked the other woman. "He seems fine this evening. A touch glowering at times, but then strong men so frequently are."

"True, but appearances can be deceiving. And though I am loath to mention it . . ."

She doesn't sound loath, Meg thought. She sounds delighted. Twisted biddy.

". . . insanity has been known to run in that family."

Insanity?

"Yes," her companion agreed. "Wasn't there a cousin who committed suicide about twenty years ago?"

"Indeed. And a great-uncle they locked away at one of the lesser ducal estates after the deluded fool burned down his own house! I wouldn't be surprised if poor Lord Cade ends up the same way one of these days, just like Mad King George. Tragic."

"Horribly," her companion agreed.

Only by sheer willpower did Meg hold back the indignant snort that rose to her lips. *Ridiculous women!* Cade might have suffered a great deal, but he was in complete control of his faculties. Walking out from behind the screen, she reached for the curtain to reveal herself, but at the last minute stopped, needing somehow to hear the rest.

"And of course there is this hasty engagement of his that has everyone talking. I believe half the guests here tonight came just so they could get a glimpse of his mysterious fiancée. I'll grant Miss Amberley seems a pleasant girl, and lovely enough that one can readily understand the attraction. But she's only an admiral's daughter and has little in the way of fortune. The dowager duchess and the duke surely cannot be pleased."

Whyever not? What is wrong with being an admiral's daughter! Meg's hands curled at her sides.

"Some say Lord Cade compromised her and they are being forced to wed. Others claim their understanding is of long duration, made before his traumatic ordeal, and that they are desperately in love."

"He certainly appears to dote on her."

The other woman made a noise of agreement.

"Well, whatever the truth, it's clear something out of the ordinary prompted the match. Speculation is running rampant, and I understand the betting books are fairly bursting at the seams. Still, given his difficulties, I cannot help but wonder if Miss Amberley may come to regret her choice of husband."

"That's doubtful, not with his wealth and good looks. I mean, which would you rather have? Mad

Cade Byron, or one of the usual crop of deadly dull bores? I think I'd take my chances with Lord Bedlam between my sheets any day."

The two laughed, skirts rustling again as they got to their feet.

A new group of women came in just then, prompting Meg to retreat again behind the screen. She waited until she no longer heard the voices of the women who had been talking about her and Cade, then walked into the anteroom, acknowledging the other ladies there with a faint nod.

Trembling, she washed her hands, her eyes widening when she caught a glimpse of herself in the pier glass—her skin as white as rice paper. Reaching up, she pinched her cheeks to restore some color. Then, with a false smile on her face, she drew a deep breath and returned to the dance.

Chapter 11

Bouquets of flowers arrived at the house the next morning—great vases of hothouse roses and cultivated lilies, with a few nosegays of violets, sweet williams, and forget-me-nots sprinkled in for variety. Color and scent spread through the drawing room like a burst of springtime, beckoning the occupants to draw nearer in order to enjoy the greenery's succulent sweetness.

Most of the blossoms were for Mallory, who exclaimed aloud in surprised delight as she came into the drawing room where the servants had arranged the mass of floral offerings. But a check of the cards revealed that three of the bouquets were intended for Meg.

One was from Mr. Faversham. Another from Mr. Milbank, an older man with whom she had danced an enthusiastic, though toe-crushing reel. And the last had come from Lord Gresham.

He'd sent her roses—two dozen long-stemmed beauties in a spectacular shade of blush pink. His accompanying note was written in strokes of slashing black ink characteristic of his personality.

" 'In appreciation of a memorable evening,' " Cade read aloud from over her shoulder. *"Hmmph."*

Startled, Meg spun about. She hadn't heard him enter the room. Despite his injury, Cade could be as stealthy as a cat when it suited his mood. "Gracious," she said, reacting to the nearness of his large body and the clean scent of starched linen and the soap he must have used to bathe and shave. "I didn't realize you were here."

"That much is apparent," he murmured to her before raising his voice to address the room at large. "I heard all the feminine squeals and thought I'd come investigate. Place looks like a deuced florist shop."

Turning her back to him, Meg took a moment to tuck Gresham's card in among the blooms, gathering her scattered senses as she did.

"You can be so ungallant sometimes, Cade," Mallory remarked in a sisterly scold. "Meg and I do not 'squeal.' Nor does Mama."

"Quite right, dear," agreed the dowager with a smile playing on her lips. "I would assume, however, that your brother's remark stems more from irritation at the notion that his fiancée already has gentlemen vying for the position of cicisbeo than any real effort on his part to liken us all to piglets."

Mallory laughed at her mother's remark, while Meg smiled. She turned in time to see that Cade had not joined in the humor, his brows drawn into a heavy scowl.

His expression cleared moments later, however. "You mistake the matter, Mama. As far as I am concerned, Meg may receive all the posies she likes so long as she remembers to whom it is she is promised."

Meg shot him a glance, her eyebrows furrowing. *Lord, he can certainly lay it on thick when he chooses!* Suddenly annoyed by his game, she crossed again to the flowers that had been sent to her. Deliberately, she picked up the vase containing Lord Gresham's offering.

"Good," she announced, pink roses bobbing their fragrant heads as she walked. "Then you shan't mind if I take this bouquet to my room? I imagine it will look perfect in my window."

A muscle ticked near his eye. "Certainly not.

181

I'll have the servants carry up the rest as well."

She tossed him a saucy smile. "Oh, don't bother, dearest. This one arrangement will suffice. Roses always have been my favorite, you know."

But no, she reminded herself as she sailed from the room with the flowers, he doesn't know. Nor does he care. As she strode down the corridor, she wished she could say she didn't either.

Mallory's come-out ball was held a week later, a grand, glittering event that befit her status as the daughter—and sister—of a duke.

In the days leading up to the ball, Meg marveled at how the town house buzzed with activity. Everywhere around her servants scurried to and fro as they cleaned and polished, dusted and aired, arranged and decorated with a frenzied eye toward perfection. The kitchens hummed as well, the chef outdoing himself when it came to creating an array of gastronomic delights sure to tempt the palate of even the most jaded connoisseur. The cream of London Society would be in attendance, even Prinny, who had sent word that he planned to drop by for the event.

By the time the momentous evening finally arrived, Mallory had developed a dreadful case of nerves. Meg wasn't much better, her stomach doing flip-flops as she let Amy help her into an evening gown of pale pink silk capped by short, belled sleeves and an overskirt of tulle dotted with tiny gold stars.

Now, as Meg stood beside Mallory in the receiving line, she couldn't help but notice how well the other young woman looked, a picture of innocent beauty in a gown of ethereal white. Mallory's dark locks were arranged in an upsweep of soft curls, her only adornment the simple strand of pearls fastened around her slender neck.

On Meg's other side stood Cade, handsome and urbane as he introduced her as his fiancée. In contrast to the easy confidence of his manner, she felt like a fraud—her smile forced, her hands turned to ice beneath her gloves by the time the ordeal was done.

Their duty complete, Edward led his sister out for the first dance. Meg might have accepted the hand of another gentleman and joined in, but decided to remain at Cade's side, knowing he could not take to the floor. With her hand on his arm, they made the rounds, pausing to talk to one guest after another, including an extremely amusing older gentleman with tufts of hair that stuck up like bunny tails on either side of his temples, as well as a younger man who was a friend of Cade's from his days in the army.

As the evening wore on, Meg expected Cade to encourage her to accept the offers of the gentlemen, who approached her for a dance. Instead, he shooed them away with a good-natured wave of his fingers, smiling as he kept her tucked at his side.

By the end of the ball, even she might have believed the fiction that they were in love. Everyone else certainly seemed convinced, guests tossing friendly smiles their way, a few pausing to offer them warm good wishes for their future married life.

The two of them were even written up the next day in the *Times* and *Morning Post,* the columns recounting tales of "young Lady M's glorious come-out ball and Lord C's impetuous love match to the golden-haired beauty who had obviously captured his heart." Cade smiled at the gossip over his toast and eggs, while Meg worried that their act might be getting them in a bit too deep.

Over the next three weeks her concerns did not abate. Amid the never-ending rounds of social calls and entertainments, Meg found herself in a curious situation. Meeting eligible men was easy enough, she discovered; making a real connection with any of them was proving discouragingly hard. How could she invite anything but the most casual regard, with Cade never more than twenty feet away?

In his guise as the attentive fiancé, he escorted her everywherc. To the opera and the theater, to routs and balls and soirees, teas and breakfasts and supper dances. He even accompanied her and

184

Mallory to Almacks, where years before he had apparently sworn never to tread again.

Yet even when he gave her a measure of freedom and withdrew to the card room, as he had lately taken to doing, she couldn't relax, nor could she seem to put him from her mind. When she was with Cade, he was in her thoughts. And when he was absent, he was there as well.

As for Cade himself, he certainly didn't appear to be suffering any such difficulties. When they were alone, he treated her with the same casual affection he showed his little sisters, proving that his loverlike behavior in public was only a mirage. He might like her, she realized, but beyond that he was simply biding his time, waiting for the day she set him free.

And set him free I shall, she vowed, no matter what it may take. Meanwhile, she would just have to try harder. She would find the right man, she vowed. Someone she had yet to meet. Mayhap he was waiting just around the next corner.

And so, as the last of April dawned, she redoubled her efforts, throwing herself into the fray with an enthusiasm that bordered on the relentless.

On Monday she promenaded in the park with Lord Longsworth. Tuesday, she took supper with Mr. Withrow. On Wednesday she went driving in Lord Peacham's high-perch phaeton. Thursday was a group outing to Hyde Park where she let the Earl of Astbury take her rowing on the Serpentine.

Friday and Saturday passed by in a frenzied blur filled with breakfast parties, afternoon teas, and balls where she danced until her feet ached—so tired by the end of the festivities that she fell into bed already half asleep each night.

Perhaps on Sunday she ought to have stayed home to rest, but she rose early to attend church with the family. After services, she was introduced to Lieutenant McCabe, a soft-spoken, rather serious young naval officer, who was home for a few weeks' leave. When he invited her to ride in the park, she readily agreed. His experiences and conversation reminded her so much of her old life that she felt a little heartsick afterward.

He called for her the following morning at ten, both of them having agreed that the park would be far more enjoyable before the fashionable hordes descended later in the afternoon. As for Cade, she explained that his injury did not yet allow him to ride, but that her fiancé had no objection to the outing. Of course, she hadn't bothered to consult with Cade. Why should she, she decided, since his goal was for her to find and marry another man?

Outside on the street in front of Clybourne House, the lieutenant assisted her onto her horse, a lovely dapple gray mare with an easygoing disposition. Seated sidesaddle, Meg took a moment to comfortably arrange the long velveteen skirts of her bishop's blue riding habit with bishop sleeves, the brass buttons on the frogged, military-style front of her bodice winking in the band of sunshine that peaked out from behind a passing cloud. As she watched, the lieutenant mounted his own horse, then cast her an inquiring glance to make sure she was ready. At her nod, the two of them set off.

A surprisingly insistent breeze brushed against her cheeks during the short ride to Hyde Park, the long tails of the stylish, blue-gray chiffon scarf knotted around her tall riding hat sailing outward like streamers. The filmy ends floated even higher after she and Lieutenant McCabe entered the park, urging their mounts to a faster pace.

She let the ground disappear behind her, giving herself over to the spontaneity of the moment. At length each of them slowed, dropping into a leisurely walk side by side.

"That was exactly what I needed," she declared, patting an appreciative hand against the side of her horse's neck. "In the summers when I was a girl, I used to ride by the seashore. I didn't realize how much I had missed it."

"Then I am glad we came here today," McCabe said, his mouth lifting in a smile that displayed a set of overlapping incisors.

"As am I."

She studied him, deciding that he had a pleasing rather than handsome countenance. For one, his nose was far too large and hawkish to ever be deemed attractive, and his long lantern-shaped jaw was not much better. He had a rangy build, carrying himself with the loose-muscled gait of a born seaman. His hair was washtub blond; and his cheeks, tanned from his months at sea, were edged by a pair of neatly maintained side whiskers. Without question, however, the lieutenant's eyes were his best feature, the irises composed of a series of concentric blue and brown rings, intriguing gold flecks scattered in between like stardust.

"I once had the great good fortune of meeting your father, Miss Amberley," he stated as they walked their horses. "I was invited to dine aboard his man-o'-war, when I was no more than a very green midshipman. Despite his generous hospitality, I found myself far too awed to say more than a handful of words." He paused, as if remembering back. "A great man, the admiral, and a fine sailor. I was profoundly saddened to hear of his passing."

Meg swallowed against the sudden tightness in her throat. "Thank you, Lieutenant. My father's loss has been one I have felt most keenly."

"Yes, of course, you have." He cast her an apologetic look. "Pray forgive my clumsy insensitivity. It was not at all my intention to upset you or depress your spirits."

She forced a smile. "You have not. Actually, it's rather nice to talk with someone who knew Papa and remembers what a wonderful man he was. I find I am losing touch with many of my old friends from the navy. I correspond by post with a few, but the longer I stay landlocked, as it were, the more difficult such relationships are to maintain."

He straightened his shoulders, his leather saddle squeaking faintly as he angled himself toward her. "I should be delighted to keep you abreast of all the latest news should you care to write to me. As I am sure you know from your father, life aboard ship can get rather lonely at times, and I would welcome the correspondence. I lost my own parents when I was a boy and have only a few people here in England with whom I keep in touch. It would be a pleasure to make you one of them."

His gaze met hers—an intent gleam of clear attraction shining in his hazel eyes.

Abruptly, his expression changed, his eyelashes lowering to shadow his gaze. "Oh, but forgive me yet again," he said in a thickened voice. "I confess your engagement slipped my mind for a moment, and I did not consider how improper such an offer might appear. In no way did I mean to give offense to either yourself or Lord Cade. Pray accept my pardon, dear lady."

Meg's fingers tightened against her reins, realizing an opportunity was upon her. She sensed that she had only to encourage the lieutenant's interest with a gentle nudge and he might well be persuaded to advance their relationship beyond a casual, friendly acquaintance.

Really, he is perfect for me, she mused.

Interesting, intelligent, and personable, with a shared similarity of experience. She and McCabe had each lived lives revolving around the sea. Both of them had suffered loss and loneliness at an early age and understood what it meant to awaken knowing each new day was a gift to be cherished. In addition, she had felt an instant and honest rapport with the man from the moment they met. A sense of quiet companionship and comfort, the kind one enjoyed when slipping on a warm, familiar old robe.

She barely knew him, but felt sure he would make a caring husband and an excellent father. With the right words and a few, well-chosen looks, she imagined she could encourage him to do more than ask her to share a long-distance correspondence.

All I need do is give him a smile, she thought. Tell him I would be delighted to write to him, and not to worry over my fiancé. Then let nature take its course. Yet even as her lips parted, no sound emerged.

Before she could consider the reason behind her silence, a fat drop of rain fell from the sky and struck her cheek. Seconds later two more raindrops descended, leaving a pair of round, dark patches on the skirt of her riding habit. Only then did she notice the huge black thunderclouds lumbering toward them on the horizon, the earlier breeze whipping up in hard gusts.

"We should head back," the lieutenant said,

glancing over his shoulder at the rapidly darkening sky. "Looks like we're in for a gale."

She nodded and turned her horse around. Beside her, he did the same. Casting another glance at the swiftly approaching storm and the desperate way the leaves appeared to cling to the shivering tree limbs, she could only pray they were in time to outrun it.

In the Clybourne House library, Cade rubbed a hand over his aching thigh and poured himself another draught of whiskey. He downed half in a quick gulp, then filled the glass to the top again before setting the stopper into the crystal decanter with a faint ringing clink.

Bloody leg, he cursed silently. Ever since he'd awakened this morning, he'd known a storm was on its way. Ironic to realize that his injury had turned him into a kind of human barometer, capable of sensing changes in moisture and atmospheric pressure. Perhaps he should lend himself out to the academics in the Royal Navy, he thought sardonically, who tasked themselves with the study and prediction of the weather. Who knew what intriguing information he might be capable of providing to them?

Thinking about the Royal Navy, he scowled, wondering where Meg and that sailor chap she rode off with this morning might be. In his opinion, the man was deuced inconsiderate to have taken her out in the first place, considering the potential for rain. And a worse fool for having failed to return her to the house by now.

Ignoring his limp, which was more aggravated today than it had been in weeks, Cade stalked to the window, his cane thumping forcefully against the polished hardwood floor. Yanking aside the sheer drapery, he stared out across Grosvenor Square. His brows angled into a deeper furrow at sight of the dark, menacing clouds.

As he watched, a handful of gravel-sized rain-drops hit the glass in a loud, staccato splatter. Seconds later thunder rumbled hard enough to rattle the window panes, lightning crackling across the sky in a jagged, flashing arc. A pregnant silence followed as if the entire world were poised on the brink of some cataclysm—as perhaps it was—the sky suddenly splitting open to unleash a virtual wall of water.

Cade cursed and let the curtain fall back into place. He tossed back another swallow of liquor, then thumped across the room, his open book and reading spectacles lying forgotten where he'd left them in the leather-covered armchair before the fireplace.

Perhaps he should call for the chaise and go out after her? he thought. But Hyde Park was only a few blocks away, so by the time the servants brought the coach around, Meg and the lieutenant would surely have returned.

Ignoring the nagging discomfort in his leg, he paced, pausing to swallow the remaining whiskey in his tumbler, then pour himself a refill.

Five minutes later he was on his way out into the hallway to order the chaise, after all, when Croft opened the front door. A blast of cold air erupted inward, bearing Meg in its wake. Her purplish-blue riding habit was plastered to her body, her once fashionable riding hat bent into a soggy, squashy mess, the formally wispy scarf tied around its base shriveled into what looked like a pair of limp, pitiable braids.

Behind her came the lieutenant, water sluicing from his own sodden hat brim to pool in a small lake around his feet. He shivered and flicked water off his frame in a manner reminiscent of a large dog returning from a hunt. A laugh rumbled from the lieutenant's throat, his lips turning upward in a rueful smile as he angled his head to catch Meg's gaze. She laughed in reply, holding her arms out at her sides in a kind of dripping pantomime.

Cade's hand tightened around the top of his cane. "So you're back then, are you?"

Meg swung her head his way, having clearly not noticed his presence until that moment. "Cade!"

The grin fell from the lieutenant's face, his expression sobering abruptly as he also met Cade's gaze.

Cade glared and leaned more powerfully onto his walking stick.

"Uh- hmm." McCabe audibly cleared his throat. "I expect I ought to be on my way before this weather turns any worse."

Looking back at him, Meg shook her head in protest. "How could it possibly be worse than it already is? No, you must stay, since I would not feel right sending you back out now, not with it pouring so hard."

I would, Cade decided.

Seeming to read Cade's thoughts, the lieutenant glanced again at Meg. "Fear not, dear lady, I have been in worse storms than this aboard ship. I've had watches where I had to stand literally soaked through for hours, so a little wetting is no matter."

A tiny pair of lines formed above her nose. "Yes, but—"

"Besides, I could do with a change of attire and have naught here to wear."

"I am sure Cade or the duke would be happy to loan you something of theirs."

Don't count on it, Cade mused.

McCabe hunched his shoulders and kept his gaze fastened on Meg. "Nevertheless," he murmured, "I would do well to return home. My thanks for a most memorable outing, Miss Amberley."

"And mine as well. This is a ride I shall not soon forget. I would still have you remain, but since you insist, I shall bid you a safe trip home."

The lieutenant made her a very proper, formal bow, his wet boots squelching against the tile

194

floor as he turned and strode toward the exit. Cade waited until Croft shut the door behind him, then sent the butler a nod of dismissal. The servant moved away in silence.

Gathering the long, heavy skirt of her sodden riding habit over one arm, Meg swung toward the stairs. "Where do you think you're going?" Cade demanded.

She paused. "Upstairs to my room, of course. In case you had not noticed, I am dripping water all over the foyer, not to mention being cold and soaked through."

Without anticipating his own actions, he let his gaze rove in a long sweep over her body, slowing for several lingering moments as he stared at her breasts. Her nipples, already visible against the wet cloth of her bodice, tightened further beneath his perusal, hardening as if they were an extra set of buttons lodged between the braiding on her jacket.

"Yes," he drawled. "That much is quite apparent." Her pale blue eyes sparked like the centers of a flame, her free arm coming up to cover her bodice.

A niggling twinge of guilt rose inside him over his ungentlemanly behavior, but Cade stubbornly refused to look away. "Well," he said, redirecting the conversation. "It's no more than you deserve for going riding when it was coming on rain."

Her mouth dropped open, the arm holding her

195

gown falling to her side to release the fabric in a great wet plop. "Of all the gall! And it wasn't 'coming on rain' when the lieutenant and I set out. The sky was sunny, with only a few passing clouds."

"I could have told you bad weather was approaching had you taken a moment to ask. But you rushed out of the house so quickly this morning, I didn't even realize you'd gone until Mama and Mallory happened to mention it on their way out to the Oxborns' breakfast party." He paused and flexed his palm against the head of his cane. "Had fun with your lieutenant, then, did you?"

"He isn't *my* lieutenant, but yes, I had a most enjoyable ride."

"Better than your outing in Peacham's phaeton? Or promenading with Lord Longsworth? Or how about your rowing excursion on the Serpentine with Astbury? At least the earl, even if he is a bone-brained macaroni, had the sense not to return you to the house drenched to the skin."

She made a noise deep in her throat, a sound not dissimilar to a growl. "It seems to me you ought to be pleased I am so popular with the gentlemen, considering our arrangement. Now, if you are done with your interrogation . . ."

He thrust out his jaw at a mutinous angle. "I am not."

"Well, *I am*." In a turn-about, she was the one to

sweep her gaze over him this time, her eyes narrowing in clear speculation. "You're foxed, aren't you?"

His brows drew together in a fierce scowl.

"If anyone needs a good soaking—particularly in the region of the head—it's *you*, my lord," she continued. "And a pot or two of strong black coffee as well. Perhaps if you drink enough of *that*, you might be fit company by dinnertime, although I rather doubt it."

"I may have had a couple whiskeys," he admitted, "but believe me, Miss Amberley, I am far from inebriated."

"Just surly then, hmm? Well, you can take your temper out on someone else. As for me, I have had enough and am going to my bedchamber." Gathering the wet hem of her riding habit inside a fist, she marched to the stairs, droplets of water appearing in a damp trail behind her.

"Meg!" he called. "Meg, come back here!"

She didn't miss a step, but kept marching upward at a steady, determined pace, one riser at a time.

"Meg!" he ordered again, his hands turning to fists as he watched her round the landing and disappear from view. Without thinking, he took three limping steps forward before he realized what he was doing and drew to a halt.

Let her go, whispered a voice inside his head. *Stop and simply let her go.* Yet as he stood there, his grip tight on his cane, he found himself wondering why the idea suddenly seemed so hard. Trembling, he forced himself to turn and go back to the library.

Inside, he crossed to the liquor cabinet and reached for the whiskey decanter. As if to prove to himself—and her—that he didn't give a damn what she thought, he splashed a full measure into his tumbler. But as he took up the glass, he made no move to raise it to his lips, studying the amber brew for a long, contemplative moment.

Abruptly, he set the glass on the table, firmly enough to send a few drops of liquor sloshing over the side. Striding to the bellpull, he gave the cord a tug before he had a chance to change his mind.

A footman arrived shortly thereafter.

"Coffee," Cade ordered. "Bring me a pot of hot coffee."

"Right away, my lord."

"And have Cook add some rolls as well, since I missed breakfast this morning." Skipped breakfast, he corrected silently, having opted to partake of a liquid meal instead.

Maybe Meg was right, he mused as he sank down into his chair. Perhaps he should try to take better care of himself. To his amused consternation, Meg was always slipping little tidbits onto his plate at family meals, subtly encouraging him to eat, as if she truly was his fiancée. Sometimes he didn't think she even knew she was doing it. But his mother noticed, he knew, and approved.

She will be sad when Meg finds another man and leaves. Mallory and Esme as well. His sisters had taken a great liking to their new "sibling." Even his brothers approved, including Edward, who sent him speculative glances every now and again, as if wondering whether he didn't want to change his mind about his and Meg's scheme.

Well, I don't, he assured himself. The day Calida died, something died inside him as well, something that would never come back. Whatever he felt for Meg . . . well, it wasn't love.

As for his irritation with all her gentlemen callers, he simply did not approve of her choices, that was all. None of them—especially that damned lieutenant—were good enough. Meg could do better, and he was just looking out for her best interests, as any thoughtful friend would.

Satisfied, he picked up his book and waited for his meal to arrive.

Chapter 12

A hot bath and a warm, dry gown went a long way to soothing Meg's frayed temper over her infuriating encounter with Cade.

Seated in front of a roaring fire with a thick cotton towel over her shoulders, she combed her long wet hair, pausing intermittently to take a sip of the hot tea Amy had brought upstairs for her.

Outside, thunder crashed like cymbals, rain

pounding in an unrelenting drumbeat against the roof tiles and window panes. Given the violence of the storm, she doubted it would end anytime soon.

As the afternoon wore on, she was proven right; Mallory and the dowager returned home with wet shoes and hems to declare that they would not set foot outside until the rain had ceased. With that decision made, plans to attend the theater were canceled, while word was sent to Cook that the family would be dining in that evening, after all.

The rain was still pouring a few hours later when they all gathered around the table for a simple yet delicious meal of boiled chicken, creamed potatoes, carrot pudding, and fresh buttered peas. Cade took his usual seat next to Meg, the two of them sharing friendly greetings for the benefit of the others before falling silent to concentrate on their dinner. As the meal progressed, Meg couldn't help but notice Cade's reserve, nor the fact that he drank only wine and no hard spirits.

A pear tart with a brandied ginger sauce was served for dessert. Afterward, the men agreed to forgo their usual ritual of solitary port and cigars in favor of removing to the sitting room with the ladies.

As Meg sipped a cup of hot tea, she turned her head and caught the set expression and wan cast to Cade's face—an ashen look she had not seen for some while, she realized. A few minutes later he excused himself, murmuring that he planned to retire to his rooms.

Of course, she thought, the storm must be bothering his leg. If she'd cared to pay attention, he'd said as much earlier when he commented on knowing it was going to rain. That had to be the reason why he'd been drinking so early in the day. She ought to have realized it immediately, she mused, but had been too wrapped up in her own difficulties at the time. And then he said all those horrible things to her, and her temper had driven everything else out of her mind.

To her surprise, she realized that he must have taken her words about his intemperance to heart and was abstaining from the whiskey bottle tonight in spite of his pain. Given the circumstances, she wondered if she ought to have a decanter sent to his room. But alcohol was not the answer, nor was laudanum, she reasoned, her cheeks warming faintly as her mind rushed back to that long ago night at his Northumberland estate.

No, she thought, as she offered her own excuses to the others and left the sitting room, perhaps there is another remedy I can provide.

"Are you sure there is nothing else I can get you, my lord?"

"Not at present, thank you, Knox," Cade told his batman as he settled into a well-worn leather wing chair angled near the fireplace in his bedchamber.

The servant's eyebrows twitched above a concerned glance. "As you wish. Good night, then."

"Yes, good night."

Cade waited until the other man closed the door, only then giving himself permission to sigh and rub his knuckles over the nagging ache in his thigh. Resting his head against the high back of his chair, he contemplated the pain and whether he was a fool not to seek out the nearest source of hard liquor. But after his earlier confrontation with Meg, he'd told himself he could do without an alcoholic crutch, and do without it he would—at least for one night.

And a long night it is going to be, he mused. But he'd suffered far worse in the past, and once the storm abated, so too should the ache. Actually, in the last few weeks his condition had shown surprising improvement. He still had painful bouts, and he knew he would always walk with a limp, but the bad days—like today—were gradually becoming fewer. Perhaps in time they would fade to the most infrequent of occasions, such as extremely severe storms. For now, though, he would simply have to endure.

Sliding his spectacles onto his nose, he reached for his book and began to read, hoping the diversion would keep him from forsaking his resolution not to drink. He finished one chapter and was starting another when a knock came at the door.

He sent a scowl toward the portal and the

unknown offender on the other side. Probably Edward, he decided, though why his brother would seek him out tonight, he had no idea.

Muttering under his breath, he marked the page and set his book aside before levering himself to his feet. The knock sounded again.

"Wait a bloody damned minute, will you?" he called as he thumped his way across the room. Turning the knob, he opened the door on a forceful pull, the fresh curse on his tongue dying an abrupt death. "Meg!" he said, his fingers moving to wrap around the edge of the door frame.

"My lord." She met his gaze for a brief instant before glancing away. "I apologize for disturbing you. I . . . um . . . did not anticipate that you might have prepared for bed already."

Dressed in nothing more than his favorite black satin robe, he was well aware how he must appear, including the realization that the scar around his throat was visible. But considering the fact that Meg had seen him, and his scar, in a similar state of dishabille before tonight, he made no attempt to cover himself further. "I decided to retire early," he said in answer to her comment.

"Your leg, of course."

So, she knows, he mused, somehow not at all surprised at her having correctly interpreted the source of his volatile disposition.

"Which is why I brought *this* for you," she continued before he could respond, indicating the covered dish she was holding balanced atop a tray.

He studied the blue and white porcelain tureen, his brows furrowing. "What is it?"

"A poultice for your injured limb. I have been doing a bit of investigating in your brother's library, reading a number of the medical books and treatises on herbal remedies, and I believe this mixture may prove efficacious." She bit the fleshy part of her bottom lip, a move that took his mind in directions it had no business going.

"At least I hope it will help," she told him. "Shall I . . . um . . . bring it inside?"

He raised a brow, then after a long moment pulled the door wider to let her pass.

Her steps quick, she crossed into the room, the skirt of her pale yellow silk evening dress moving in a seductive swirl around her ankles. His gaze fixed for an instant on the curve of her hips and buttocks as she leaned forward to set the tray and its contents onto a table. He raised his eyes only seconds before she turned to face him.

"There," she pronounced, moving a few steps back. "You should use it right away while it is still hot. I would suggest you place a thick towel beneath your leg since the poultice is damp and may leak a bit. From everything I've read, you should place it directly on the area where you are experiencing the most discomfort, then leave it on for twenty minutes to half an hour. Or at least until all the warmth is gone."

Although his leg still hurt, he suddenly wasn't sure if his injured limb was still the part of his body giving him the most discomfort.

Lord, what am I thinking? he considered, giving himself a hard mental shake. And why am I thinking it? It was not as if Meg was doing anything provocative. Then again, she'd never come into his bedroom before and talked about having him place a hot compress on his naked thigh. Unless he counted that one night at his estate, of course. . .

"Yes, all right," he said, his voice like gravel. To distract himself, he moved to the tureen and lifted the lid, a pungent burst of steam wafting upward. "What's in it, anyway? It smells like the brown mash the stable lads use for the horses."

"That's probably because it is that brown mash with several other ingredients added in, such as mustard seed and turmeric. And put that top back on before you ruin it! I got into enough trouble rousing the stable boys and the kitchen staff after hours as it is."

"Did you really?" he asked, rather amazed that she would go to such effort for him, especially considering what had happened between them only that morning. He replaced the lid.

"Well, I should go, so you can try the poultice," she said. "I hope it proves helpful, my lord. I do not like to see you in pain."

An unfathomable sensation burned in his belly. *Dyspepsia, most likely.* "Do you not?"

She shook her head. "No. All creatures deserve ease, even you." Turning, she padded on silent slippers to the door.

"Meg," he called.

She stopped and turned back, lifting an inquiring brow.

"Thank you. You are very kind."

A smile brightened the pale blue of her eyes. "It's nothing. I would have done the same for anyone."

But as he stood gazing at her, he knew she was lying. She had done this for him—and him alone.

"Good night," he said.

"Sweet dreams, Cade." On a whisper of silken skirts she was gone, disappearing like a wraith along the candlelit corridor beyond.

After closing the door, he studied the dish, then shrugged. Even if it did nothing for his pain, the concoction surely couldn't hurt. Limping across into his bathing chamber, he retrieved a thick towel as she had suggested, then moved to his bed to arrange it.

A couple minutes later he stretched out atop the mattress with a very comfortable pile of goose down pillows at his back. Opening the tureen he'd moved to his night table, he lifted out the steaming poultice, then with a cautious breath set it on his bared leg.

Breath hissed between his teeth, the heat nearly as intense as having a shovelful of smoldering coals dumped onto him—or so he imagined. Yet his skin didn't burn, warmth spreading through his thigh in a deep, penetrating wave. As the initial shock faded and his muscles began to relax, the sensation turned from uncomfortable to pleasant, heat radiating further into his damaged flesh. A sigh eased past his lips—only this time from a sense of relief rather than misery.

To his distinct surprise, the merciless ache that had plagued him since first light that morning slowly began to recede. At length he reached down and tugged the coverlet over his other leg and a portion of his torso before reclining again more fully against the ocean of pillows behind him.

Closing his eyes, he gave himself over to the comforting warmth, wondering vaguely if this was how injured horses felt when they received similar treatment—the scents of mash and mustard and the other exotic ingredients Meg had used teasing his nostrils.

Sinking further, he drifted in a state somewhere between wakefulness and sleep, memories and half dreams sliding through his mind without reasoned awareness or control.

A fist struck him, pain exploding in his skull as his head snapped back on his neck. A second blow fell only seconds later, the taste of fresh blood blossoming with a metallic sweetness against his tongue.

"Enough," said a voice, the command silky and

emotionless. "Let's give the major a chance to speak. Surely, he has something to say."

Cade suppressed the need to groan but stayed silent, refusing to give even that much of a response.

"He must want us to play a bit more with his little friend, hmm? I'm sure she has some spark left in her yet. Can you hear her, Byron? Even now she's moaning in eagerness to have another one of these fine soldiers between her legs. Shall we give her another taste of what a real man can do?"

But her moans were those of incoherent agony; even her earlier hysterical weeping had ceased.

"Stop," Cade said through swollen lips. "Stop hurting her." Something burned his eyes, wetness leaving cool trails against his cheeks.

"Are those tears, Byron?" the voice told him in precise, upper-class English. "You can end this, you know. You have only to share the information we require, and I personally guarantee you will both be set free."

But they would not, Cade knew, realizing that the only freedom either of them would ever know again was that of death. It was only a matter of hours now, maybe not even that long, before they both passed into the grave.

Maybe if he'd told them earlier, she would still be whole and untouched. If he'd betrayed his honor and country, they would have left her in peace. But even in his current state of physical and emotional anguish, he knew there was nothing he could have done to save her. He'd condemned her to death by the simple act of knowing her.

His eyelids were forcibly wrenched open as her screams began anew, as the English traitor, whose features he could not see, made him watch.

He began screaming, too.

"Shh," whispered a gentle voice, not the hated one, but another—soothing, familiar, female. Her hand stroked over his hair, along his cheek. He turned into her touch, needing it, needing her.

"Meg?" he whispered.

"Shh," she crooned, feathering her lips over his forehead and temple, rubbing her satiny cheek against the roughness of his own before angling her mouth to meet his. His arms came around her as they kissed, the passion between them as hot and untamed as a tinder set against dry wood.

Impatient, he lifted her so she sat astride him, her arms and legs entwined around his hips. She made no protest at his boldness, pressing her body closer, opening her mouth to accept the dark possession of his kisses and the ravenous ardor of his roving touch.

Yet it wasn't enough. He wanted more.

Reaching for the neckline of her nightgown, he ripped the delicate fabric, silk falling to shreds inside his hands. Tossing the pieces aside, he gorged himself upon the lithe curves of her naked flesh. Cupping her breasts in his palms, he stroked her before moving along the silky length of her back to her finely rounded bottom. He kissed her with wild abandon, wondering if his brain would go blank from a surfeit of pleasure.

Opening his robe, he positioned her for his penetration, spreading her thighs wider to seat her as fully upon himself as she could go. Her breasts bounced, her lips parting on an inhalation of ecstasy as their gazes met. He stared into the lake blue depths of her eyes and shuddered with emotions he didn't dare let himself understand.

"Meg," he murmured.

She smiled and kissed him, stroking his cheeks with the backs of her fingers. "I have a secret, my lord," she whispered. "Do you want to know what it is?"

For a second he thought about saying no, wanting to bury his aching flesh inside her and make everything else, except her, go away.

Instead, he nodded, compelled almost against his will.

"Lieutenant McCabe asked me to marry him. I am going to be his wife!"

Cade came awake with an abrupt start, flailing for a moment inside the mass of pillows scattered around the bed. A light coating of perspiration beaded his skin, a throbbing erection jutting upward from between his legs, poking out from the folds of his robe.

At the same moment, he became aware of something cold and damp lying against his thigh. Glancing down, he found the poultice, the lumpy mass having slid off his leg onto the rumpled towel. Muttering a curse, he picked it up and dropped it into the bowl on his bedside table.

God, he thought, it had all been a dream, nothing more than a dream. As usual, he'd begun with a variation of the old familiar nightmare he'd been having since those terrible days in Portugal. As for the rest . . . Lord, it had all felt so real.

He ran his palm over the empty coverlet as though seeking confirmation that Meg hadn't been there after all. But the cloth was cold, his fantasy nothing more than prurient wishful thinking. Even now he ached, wanting her. Or at least a woman, he told himself.

He'd been celibate too long, that was all, and Meg had been on his mind before he fell asleep. The dream meant nothing—no more real than her phantom declaration about marrying the lieutenant.

His gut tightened at the recollection. Ignoring it, he climbed out of the bed. Shucking off his robe, he tossed it to the foot of the mattress, then yanked back the covers. Slipping between the sheets, he willed himself to sleep. But slumber was a long while coming, even when he realized to his surprise that his thigh had stopped hurting.

Chapter 13

A sennight later Meg curtsied to her partner as another set came to an end, the last notes of the contra dance fading away to leave behind the rhythmic hum of human conversation.

Opening the ivory-hued fan that had been painted with pink roses to match her dress, she waved the silk-covered staves in front of her face. Even that tiny breeze came as a welcome relief, the ballroom packed with so many members of the ton that it was difficult to keep track of who was in attendance and who was not.

Moving off the dance floor, she refused her partner's offer of a cup of punch before politely excusing herself from his company. Once he was gone, she scanned the room in search of Mallory, feeling oddly in need of a friendly, familiar face. Not that she lacked for friends and acquaintances of both sexes these days, but there was something very uplifting about Mallory.

Lady Mallory was one of those rare people blessed with a kind spirit and a happy nature. In all the weeks she had known her, Meg couldn't recall hearing a single cross word pass the young woman's lips. Mallory was sweet and diverting and always a pleasurable companion.

She was also Cade's sister, and with Mallory at her side, it was unlikely that Cade would feel compelled to seek her out and act the attentive fiancé. Not that he was likely to do so at this hour of the evening anyway, she supposed, since he had departed some while ago for the card room. Nevertheless, she wasn't in the mood to don a false smile and pretend to be promised to a man whom she was destined never to wed.

Despite her feelings on that subject, however, she was glad to see that Cade's health was showing signs of improvement. Just this morning his mother had remarked on the hale color in his cheeks and the fact that he'd gained back a share of the much needed weight he lost after his ordeal on the Continent.

His limp remained, of course, but Meg believed he was experiencing less pain overall and most definitely less pain than on the night she'd brought him the poultice. Although he hadn't mentioned her remedy again, she'd been pleased to receive a visit from Knox, who sought her out to inquire about the recipe. With several specific instructions on how to properly measure and heat the concoction, she was gratified and happy to pass on her knowledge.

With Knox looking after him, though, she supposed Cade had little need of her. Though when has Cade ever had need of me? she mused. From the first moment of her arrival in his life, he'd made no effort to conceal his wish to see her gone. She knew he was only biding his time, waiting for the day when he could dust his hands of her and return north to his estate.

Yet despite her continued efforts and a couple of likely prospects—including Lieutenant McCabe, who had called just two days ago to take her strolling in the park—she couldn't seem to make herself put forth enough enthusiasm to actually bring any of her would-be suitors up to scratch. She liked several of them, but as for love . . .

She sighed. I am merely tired, she reassured herself. On the morrow, everything will seem different.

Across the room, a friend motioned for Meg to join her and a group of cronies. But Meg smiled and waved a refusal, not at all in the mood to listen to the usual round of Town gossip and talk of the latest fashions. Walking toward the ballroom's wide, double doors, she resumed her search for Mallory.

Fifteen minutes later, as she made her way into a quiet section of the house, and still hadn't found Mallory, she wondered if perhaps the other girl did not wish to be found. Now that she considered, she'd last seen Mallory dancing with a favorite new beau, Major Hargreaves—a dashing army officer of whom Mallory spoke often.

Meg was about to turn and retrace her steps back to the festivities when she heard a noise from inside a nearby room. Curious, she walked forward, then paused to peer into her hosts' library.

The room was shrouded in near darkness, the only illumination a mellow fire burning in the hearth. Next to the blaze stood a solitary figure—one she immediately recognized as Lord Gresham.

Having obviously heard her as well, he glanced up at her entrance. "Miss Amberley. Good evening."

"My lord."

"Normally, I would make all the usual polite remarks, but I must admit I am rather surprised at finding you here. What brings you into this part of the house?"

"I was about to ask the same of you," she replied. "But it would seem you have beaten me to it."

A smile tugged at his lips. "Well, never let it be said I am so ungallant as to deny a lady first rights at satisfying her curiosity." He swept a hand toward the rows of floor-to-ceiling shelves. "Why, I came in search of a book, of course. What else, since this is a library, after all."

What else indeed, she mused, wondering if she might be interrupting an assignation. He didn't look upset, however, so perhaps he had in fact come here to read. Or more likely he'd stolen off for a few moments respite from the press of the crowd. She had to confess that the shadowy, leather-scented solitude of the room was very pleasant—relaxing after the hubbub of the soiree.

"You aren't lost, are you, Miss Amberley?"

She strolled farther into the room. "No. Actually, I was looking for someone."

He lifted an eyebrow. "Oh? Anyone I know?"

"Yes. As a matter of fact, I was looking for Mallory. You haven't . . . seen her, have you?"

The smile slipped from his mouth, a fierce look crossing his face and shading his eyes. "As it would happen, I have. Lady Mallory and Major Hargreaves were here only a few minutes ago. I believe they have since returned to the ballroom."

Mallory and the major. So, Mallory has been with him. Had Lord Gresham caught them together, here in the library? Alone? If so, Gresham didn't look happy about the discovery. In fact, he looked downright perturbed.

Seconds later, however, his expression cleared, leaving her to wonder if she had glimpsed the emotion on his face at all. The lighting was poor, she decided. She must have been imagining things.

"I should think," he said in an even tone that further belied any strong feelings on his part, "that you would be wanting to return to the dancing as well." Crossing toward her, he held out an arm. "Shall I escort you back?"

In that moment she realized that he was trying to protect her. *Is he worried for my good name?* Contrary to his own scandalous reputation, she found him to be a surprisingly chivalrous man.

"Yes, my lord," she murmured, curving her hand over his sleeve. "I believe you are right and I ought to get back before I am missed."

"Rather too late for that," drawled a familiar voice.

Her gaze flew toward the imposing male figure standing in the doorway. "Cade!"

"Meg," he said in a clipped tone, one she couldn't remember hearing from him before.

"I thought you were playing cards." She pulled her hand from Lord Gresham's sleeve and lowered it to her side. Though why she did so, she couldn't say, since the action spoke of guilt, and she had nothing whatsoever to feel guilty about.

"And I thought you were in the ballroom dancing," Cade remarked, moving farther into the room. "Imagine my surprise when I discovered you were not."

"No, I . . . um . . . decided I needed a respite from the crush of guests. As it happens, though, Lord Gresham and I were just on our way back. Why do we not all return together?"

Cade planted a fist on his hip, his other hand gripped in an intimidating manner around the head of his gold-topped cane. He shot Gresham a look hot enough to scorch metal.

"I think perhaps I ought to be the one to go ahead and let the two of you return at your leisure," Gresham said. After making a brief bow, he steered a path around Cade and walked from the room.

For a long moment the only sound was the quiet snapping of the logs in the grate as wood turned slowly to ash.

"So you've got Gresham in your sights again, have you?" Cade ambled nearer, closing the distance between them. "I rather thought you'd decided on the lieutenant, though I suppose he doesn't move in the same elevated circles, does he? He isn't here tonight, for instance."

Her fingers curled against the folds of her skirt. "Lieutenant McCabe moves in perfectly respectable circles, and the fact that he is not in attendance this evening makes no difference to me."

"Just testing the waters, then, are you? Why else would you have come here with Gresham?"

"I did not come here with him. He was already in the room when I arrived."

"Was he indeed?" Cade said in a deceptively smooth voice. "And why did you wander this way if not to meet him? Surely you hadn't made an assignation with someone else?"

She huffed out an exasperated sigh. "There was no assignation at all, and I must tell you that I resent your inference, my lord."

"Do you? Well, considering the circumstances, it is a presumption anyone might make. The ballroom is some distance away, and you were discovered alone with a man whose reputation for seduction is well-known. Wise mothers make sure not to let their innocent daughters wander off with men like Adam Gresham."

"And what of you? Could someone not make the same assumption at discovering us alone together, even though nothing whatsoever has occurred?"

"No. For one thing, we are engaged."

"Oh, but we're not."

He took another step forward so he stood less than a foot way. "That isn't the point. What matters is that you were alone with him where anyone could have found you. Where *I* found you." He moved forward again.

Meg retreated a step, her path blocked as she came up against the back of the sofa. "So you're worried about looking the cuckold, are you? Resentful of being deceived by your supposed fiancée?"

A growl rumbled low in his throat. "No, I'm worried about you getting hurt, and falling prey to rakes and scoundrels. He's not going to marry you, you know."

"Lord Gresham, you mean? Well, of course I know that. But then neither are you. Now, I believe I shall return to the ballroom. I'm sure I've promised a dance to some gentleman with whom I should make it my business to become better acquainted."

She tried to take a sideways step around him, but his large muscled body prevented her. "Your pardon, Lord Cade," she said, "but pray allow me to pass."

An inscrutable expression crossed his face. "No, I don't believe I will."

"Excuse me?"

Setting his cane aside, he placed his hands against the sofa, imprisoning her in between. "I don't believe I shall excuse you, either."

Before she had time to read his intent and attempt to counter it, his mouth came down upon her own, claiming her with a kiss that literally rocked her back on her heels. For several long, shocked seconds her mind grew dull, her senses caught in an irresistible rush of pleasure.

Resting her hands on his shoulders, she curled her fingers into the warm, pliant wool of his tailored, super-fine coat. Holding on, she let him take her deeper. But something about the contrast of his firm, masculine shoulders against the softness of her skin triggered an inner awareness that nudged her from her haze. Digging in her nails this time, she gave him a little push. "Enough!"

In answer, he turned his head and buried his lips against the curve of her neck, stunning her anew by doing something utterly delectable with his tongue. Suppressing a full body shiver, she willed herself to resist. "Did you hear me? I said stop."

Leaning away, he met her gaze, his eyes the color of grass after a pounding summer rain. "Sound like you mean it and I just might."

"Stop playing with me, Cade."

Sliding a hand upward, he cupped the fullness of one of her breasts. After a brief pause, he gave a gentle squeeze. "Does this feel like I'm playing?"

She couldn't control the shudder that raked her frame. With blood thundering inside her temples, she shook her head.

Gripping her hips, he lifted her off her feet and sat her on the top edge of the sofa. Parting her legs, he stepped between, his palms sliding low to curve around her bottom. "Do you still want me to stop?"

Her toes arched inside her slippers, traitorous need simmering like a fire in her veins. "Yes," she murmured, her refusal sounding frail and faltering even to her own ears.

He stared at her for a long, penetrating moment. "Liar."

Tugging her flush against his body, he crushed her lips to his once more, and dragged forth a ragged moan they both knew to be her surrender. At his urging, she opened her mouth to let his tongue delve inside, accepting his possession with a mindless hunger of her own. Wrapping her arms around his neck, she gave herself over to the pleasure, savoring his taste and his touch.

Meg whimpered as he cradled the back of her head in his hand, angling her face so he could draw even more fully upon her. Time ground down to a slow tick as he led her in a warm, wet dance, her eyelids fluttering closed as she met and matched his every command. Quivering inside his embrace, she let him take her where he willed, his other hand fully occupied as he sent her spinning upward into further layers of delight.

Beginning with her breasts, he caressed her, bringing her nipples to taut, aching peaks as he toyed with her through the thin silk of her gown. When that wasn't enough, he slipped his fingers inside her bodice to find bare flesh, scissoring first one nipple, then the other between the skilled movements of his thumb and forefinger.

She moaned again into his open mouth and instinctively arched against the insistent proof of his arousal, shifting restlessly as her body was claimed by awakening needs that she had no wish to deny.

Groaning low in his throat, Cade kissed her harder, savaging her mouth with an ardor that was as dark as it was seductive. Senses spinning, she gave no thought or complaint when his hand left her breast to stroke the length of her thigh. Nor again when he gathered the material of her dress and slipped beneath her skirts. She quaked at the sensation of his bare hand against her naked skin, his palm gliding high, then higher still along her trembling limb.

His other hand lowered to the small of her back, urging her forward so her legs parted even more. Kissing her all the while, he stroked toward her center, tangling for a few brief seconds in the nest of short curls he found there before slipping a single finger between the tender folds of her femininity. Wet heat dampened his hand, a reaction he seemed to expect and enjoy, the fragrant moisture turning her slick against his touch.

She gasped, the sound muffled against his lips as he tilted her hips a little more to slide deeper, using his fingers, and even the heel of his hand, in ways that drove every rational thought from her brain. Tiny breaths panted from her mouth as he caressed her in the most shockingly delicious manner, her initial embarrassment fading against a compulsive need for more.

Breaking their kiss, he pressed her face against his neck. "Let go," he murmured into her ear. "Let yourself fly."

And after another pair of rapturous, stroking caresses, she did—her entire body shuddering in a great, cataclysmic burst of pleasure that set every nerve and sinew afire. He held her as she shook, her cries muffled against the starched linen of his neck cloth.

She felt him reach for the buttons on his falls, fingers quivering in his hurry to unfasten his breeches. In the distance a clock struck midnight, the chime echoing its sweet music in twelve, evenly spaced beats. Cade froze, his hand falling still.

Biting out a livid curse, he stepped away from her, his lungs working like bellows as he drew in several ragged breaths. "Cover yourself," he ordered, his hands turning to fists at his sides as he fought a silent battle of wills.

For a long moment she couldn't move, her

body still caught up in the blissful aftermath of his touch. Forcing herself out of her daze, she pushed at her skirts—nearly stumbling as she leapt the couple inches off the back of the sofa to the floor. Cade reached out to steady her with a hand at her elbow. As soon as it was clear she wouldn't fall, he let go, turning to make his way across the room.

She shivered, feeling his desertion with a sharpness akin to pain. Hands trembling, she brushed weakly at her skirts, then found her way to a nearby chair. Gratefully, she sank down upon it.

As for Cade, he stood staring into the burning embers, one palm set against the mantel above his bent head. Abruptly, he closed his eyes as though struggling to regain his composure. "Are you capable of returning to the ballroom?" he asked in a brusque tone. "Or do I need to find an excuse for your early departure?"

The ballroom! Dear Lord, she hadn't even considered the festivities still going on only a few rooms away. Heat spread upward into her cheeks, making her wonder if she looked as unsettled as she felt.

"You look fine," he said, as though she'd voiced her thoughts aloud. "Or rather, you will in a few minutes more, once some of the redness fades from your mouth."

Instinctively, she lifted a hand to her lips, only then realizing that Cade's rapacious kisses had left more than a residual tingling behind—her mouth swollen and almost hot.

"You can say you have a headache," he offered. "No one will question you."

Why does he sound so cold? she wondered. Had their passion meant nothing to him? Obviously, he'd remembered himself before matters had gone too far for recall, and put a stop to their embrace while she could still claim to be a virgin. As for herself, she'd had no such self-control, her senses completely abandoned to him.

Shoulders straightening, she drew herself upright. "Pray do not trouble yourself, my lord. I am quite well. Now, if you will excuse me."

"Meg—"

But she couldn't listen anymore. Jumping to her feet, she fled the room.

Cade took a few steps to follow, then forced himself to halt, cursing under his breath as he did. *Hell and damnation.* What was he doing? Thinking? But wasn't that the problem? That he hadn't been thinking?

When he trailed Meg here to the library, he'd intended to separate her from whatever blackguard she had let lead her away from the ball. Yet the instant they were alone, he'd been kissing her himself, craving her with a hunger he knew he hadn't any right to feel. Christ, he was no better than the rakes of whom he warned her. Worse, actually, since he was supposed to be her friend, a brother

225

figure who was looking out for her well-being.

Some brother, he scoffed. He couldn't even blame his behavior on an excess of drink, since he'd had no more than a single glass of wine at dinner, and nothing afterward. Like it or not, the fault was entirely his own. When Meg had asked —or rather, demanded—to be allowed to return to the ballroom, he should have let her go. But the uncomfortable truth was that in those moments, he could no more have allowed her to go than he could have cut off his own arm.

He wanted her, hungered for her with a need that was beginning to border on an addiction. Ever since the night she'd come to his room with her poultice and her good wishes for his improved health, he hadn't been able to get her out of his mind. His dreams were plagued with fantasies of her, most of them so erotic he awakened hard and throbbing, left to beat his fist against the empty sheets in frustration when he realized they had been naught but a chimera. So tonight when she'd been in his arms for real . . .

I need to leave! Go home to Northumberland where everything is calm and quiet and there are no willowy blond temptresses underfoot to drive me mad.

Yet if he left London, he knew he risked putting Meg's reputation in jeopardy by appearing to desert her. Then again, if he stayed, might he not end up doing far worse?

He supposed his best course would be to bed some other woman. There were certainly plenty of willing females wherever he went. Were he so inclined, he knew he could find one tonight at this very ball—some eager widow or discontented wife who would relish a furtive tumble or two. But if he took one of them, word would be sure to get out, and he had no wish to disgrace or embarrass Meg.

No, if he wanted to slake his lust, he'd have to do it with a prostitute. There were discreet houses, of course, with clean, healthy girls of whom he could avail himself. If he had any sense, he would find some excuse and go to one now. Yet in spite of the erection still riding him after his aborted encounter with Meg, the thought held little actual appeal.

On a growl, he dragged his fingers through his hair and battled against his frustration and arousal. As soon as he had himself under control, he decided, he would return to the ballroom and endure the rest of the evening. After that . . . well, he would see.

It took Meg a full twenty minutes inside the ladies' withdrawing room before she could trust herself enough to rejoin the festivities. Even then her body felt strangely unlike her own, an occasional twinge or flutter reminding her of all the places where Cade's hands and lips had so recently been.

Afterward, she was dancing when a fresh quiver took her unawares, causing her to set a foot wrong and stumble. Her partner caught her before she fell, an expression of concern on his face. Tossing him an apologetic smile, she recovered the rhythm and resumed the steps with her usual grace.

She nearly overbalanced again when Cade came into the room a half hour later. He didn't look her way, and after a long, initial glance at him, she did her best not to look at him, either. Somehow she forced herself to talk and laugh and dance, while inside her emotions were in turmoil. *What does Cade mean, kissing me like that? How dare he touch me so intimately, then coolly turn away?*

When the next set drew to a close, she strolled off the dance floor, intending to locate Mallory and the dowager and persuade them to depart. As for Cade . . . he could make his way home with them or not, as he wished. For her part, she needed time alone in her room to collect her thoughts and make some sense of her jumbled feelings.

Just then a rustle of movement and whispering comment rippled like a breeze through the crowd. A latecomer stood at the ballroom entrance, his neatly trimmed, thick blond hair waving around his comely face like a regal, golden crown. Dressed in the requisite black and white that gentlemen wore to formal occasions, he looked a picture of sophisticated gentility and unspoken command.

Meg stared, along with nearly every other person in the room. "Who is that gentleman?" she murmured to her dance partner, who had yet to leave her side.

"Oh, do you not know? Since his return from the Peninsula, the papers have been talking about him without pause."

"Which papers?"

"All of them, I believe. That is Lord Everett, the hero of Corunna. They say he rescued two dozen men from the clutches of the French. Whisked them right out from under the frogs' noses despite a barrage of enemy bullets and cannon fire. Afterward he helped hold off the enemy so the wounded could be loaded onto the troop ships bound for home. I hear he even captured an Imperial French eagle, and is rumored to have stolen secret plans that are aiding Wellesley even as we speak. Apparently, the prince is in thrall over him. So much so he will be awarding Everett a gold cross for valor in a lavish ceremony at court next week."

"It's no wonder if he did all that! Most impressive."

Apparently, everyone else seemed to agree, groups of people making their way forward so they could greet the courageous champion in their midst.

"Shall we say hello?" her dance partner asked as he held out his arm.

Meg hesitated a moment, then accepted his offer with a nod.

• • •

From the side of the room, Cade surveyed the milling throng as a crowd gathered in a widening circle around the tall blond man who had just arrived.

"Everett," he heard someone say as they moved past. Although he'd never met the man, he knew him by reputation. Just as everyone else did, it would seem. If reports were to be believed, the fellow was as brave as the legendary Horatius himself. The ton was certainly showering him with enough adoration to merit such a claim.

Remaining where he stood, Cade sipped a cup of black coffee and watched the fanfare. He caught sight of Meg as she strolled forward on the arm of one of her gentleman admirers. Except for a slight flush that could be attributed to her recent dancing, no one would ever have suspected what the two of them had been doing in the library less than an hour ago. Apparently, she'd had no difficulty regaining her composure. Perhaps she hadn't been as affected as he had assumed.

His fingers tightened against the delicate porcelain as he took a hasty swallow, the liquid nearly hot enough to scald. Placing the cup against the saucer with a ringing click, he set the drink on a nearby table, then moved toward the ballroom doors. In spite of his earlier resolve to stay, he'd decided to call for the coach. Once he arrived at his destination, he would have the vehicle sent back for the ladies. As for the destination itself, well, even he still wasn't sure whether he was returning home this evening or not.

Trying to exit the ballroom proved a challenge, however, since the way was blocked by the crush of Lord Everett's enthusiastic well-wishers. As for the great man himself, he appeared to take the attention in stride, smiling affably as he conversed and shook hands.

As Cade drew nearer, he heard the silky tone of Everett's voice, though his words remained indistinct. His step slowed then, his throat and chest tightening. His breathing grew unexpectedly labored and a line of perspiration broke out across his forehead, his skin itching as if a nest of ants were crawling over him. Like some ghastly phantom, the voice from his nightmares began to whisper inside his head.

You can end this. Just tell me, Byron. Tell me.

Nausea surged like a tempest inside Cade's belly, his hand shaking as he gripped his cane like a lifeline. Swallowing hard, he willed his limbs to carry him forward.

The voice came again as Everett spoke in an otherworldly echo of the remembered whispers ringing inside his head. He squeezed his eyes closed, the scar around his throat throbbing as if he was being garroted all over again.

Tell me and she won't scream anymore!

Someone jostled him as they edged past. Cade

barely noticed, memories flashing in quick succession through his mind.

It's always a delight to form new acquaintances, especially when the lady is so lovely.

Was that the voice? Or Everett? Suddenly he didn't know.

"How do you do, my lord," said a woman in warm, lilting tones. Comforting, familiar tones that wrapped around him like a pair of soothing arms.

Meg.

Cade's eyes popped open.

"The pleasure is all mine," the nightmare voice said, speaking again out of Everett's mouth. As he watched, Everett took Meg's hand and bent over it with a practiced bow.

Not yours. Mine! So take your damned hands off her!

Cade roared aloud as some atavistic beast sprang to life inside him. All conversation ceased, people's mouths dropping open as they turned to stare. But he barely noticed, his attention centered solely on one man.

Everett looked up, his gaze meeting Cade's. In the length of a single second, a silent recognition passed between them, and Cade knew beyond any doubt that a monster stood before him.

"You filthy traitor!" Cade bellowed. Taking three quick, giant steps, he launched himself at the other man.

Women screamed and men shouted, but Cade heard none of it as his hands curved around his enemy's throat. He squeezed, then squeezed harder, wanting to crush the bastard's windpipe so he would never be able to draw breath nor speak again. Everett struggled in his grasp, beating fists against Cade's head and shoulders as the two of them crashed to the floor. The impact sent pain reverberating through Cade's leg, but he barely felt it, too intent on driving his fingers deeper into the other man's neck.

Everett's eyes protruded under the pressure and he gasped for air, twisting in Cade's hold. Prying at Cade's hands he kicked his legs as he tried to break free. But Cade hung on, tenacious as a leech, determined not to let go until the other man had turned into a corpse.

Then suddenly he was being wrenched away, hands reaching down to pull him off Everett. He fought, struggling to maintain his hold, but the men surrounding him proved stronger, his grasp on Everett loosening as he was yanked free. He fought on even after they pulled him off, wrestling them so he could go after Everett once again.

Meanwhile, Everett's concerned friends and admirers reached down to assist him to his feet. Everett's face was mottled with angry color, his lips tinged with the faintest trace of blue. Cade sneered, glad to see he'd done some damage. He only regretted it hadn't been more.

"Let me go, you idiots!" he demanded, but the men who had pulled him off Everett kept a grip on him. "You don't know what you're doing. That man is a traitor and a spy, and he should be arrested for his crimes."

"What nonsense are you spouting, Byron?" one of the gentlemen in the crowd said. "Don't you know who he is? That's Lord Everett."

"Le Renard, you mean," Cade spat, watching the other man for signs of guilt.

There were none, as Everett brushed aside further aid, moving to shrug his coat back into place. With a wince, he tugged at his disheveled cravat as well.

"Whatever name he uses," Cade continued, "he's a blackguard and he knows it. Because of him, countless men have died. And women, too."

"What are you saying, Byron?" another man asked. "He's saved dozen of lives."

"When he wasn't betraying others, you mean."

"Infamy! What proof have you of your accusations?"

What proof? Cade thought. Just the knowledge of my own experience. My own torment.

"You have dishonored Lord Everett and should be called out for this," another man stated. "Choose your seconds, Byron. I shall stand at Everett's side."

"I don't need seconds," Cade replied. "Let go of me and I'll take care of him myself."

"Yes," Everett said with calm authority. "Let him go. Clearly, he is confused."

Cade scowled, a murmur spreading through the crowd.

"Confused how?" someone asked.

"Obviously he believes what he says," Lord Everett explained. "He thinks that I am this . . . who did you say . . . Le Renard?"

"You *are* Le Renard," Cade stated, finally shaking off the restraint of the men around him. As he did, he noticed Meg watching him, pale brows furrowed, blue gaze troubled.

Everett nodded with apparent sympathy. "Is that the Frenchie who tortured you? Who is responsible for your injuries? I've heard they are quite severe."

Cade ground his teeth together. "You should know, since you were there."

Everett gave him a pitying look. "I've been on the front lines, seen battles and the carnage they leave in their wake. I know how easy it is for a man's mind to play tricks on him during wartime. Clearly yours is playing one on you tonight."

"That or drink," someone quipped, eliciting a ripple of nervous laughter.

Cade saw that Meg did not join in, that in fact her expression grew even more concerned. He glanced away and saw other looks, ranging from anger and outrage, to dismay, uncertainty, and even pity. Clearly they believed Everett and saw him as in the wrong; befuddled, deluded, and yes, unstable.

"Don't listen to him!" Cade said. "This man is a clever snake, a French agent who has worked hard to convince the highest levels of command that he is trustworthy. He is a master of deception and he is deceiving you all."

"A French agent! What absurdity," one of the gentlemen said.

"You expect us to believe that the hero of Corunna is a fraud?" another questioned. "That Everett has concealed his true nature, lying to his men and his fellow officers? And what of Wellesley? I suppose you think he has been duped as well?"

Cade paused. He had immense respect for Arthur Wellesley, but all men, even great ones, could be fooled on occasion. "Yes. That's precisely what I'm saying."

Hisses went through the crowd. Everett shook his head, as if to say Cade was a sad case indeed.

"If Lord Everett won't claim satisfaction," declared one of the men, "then I will."

Everett held up a hand. "No. There will be no duel. After all, it would be unworthy to fight a man who was once a brave soldier himself. Obviously, he is mistaken and has lost his way. With time, I am sure his reason will return. Now, why do we not resume the festivities?"

Willpower alone kept Cade from reaching for Everett again, his hands fisted at his sides. As he struggled against his compulsion, Everett turned his back in casual dismissal. Before he did, however, Cade caught the glimmer of triumph in the man's eyes.

Le Renard had won again.

Cade knew he had no choice but to withdraw. Retrieving his cane from the floor, he limped forward. People stepped aside, granting him a wide berth. Still, he wasn't entirely done. As he passed Everett, he deliberately nudged the other man's shoulder and leaned in. "This isn't over," he said in a voice only Everett could hear.

The other man returned his gaze, the faintest of smiles on his mouth as Cade left the ballroom.

Chapter 14

What in the devil were you thinking, attacking Everett like that last night?" Edward asked Cade as they sat in the duke's study the following afternoon. Jack and Drake, who had stopped by for nuncheon, had joined them, and were lounging in nearby chairs.

"Were you foxed?" Edward demanded.

"*No*. Not unless you consider a glass of Madeira and a cup of coffee cause for inebriation."

"So you weren't drunk. What, then?"

Cade stared at his boots. "If you must know, I just reacted. The moment I heard that bastard's voice and realized who he was . . ." His fingers squeezed into a fist against his pantaloon clad thigh. ". . . I wanted to kill him."

"Yes, well, I can understand the impulse, but you might have chosen a more private location than a crowded ballroom to attempt murder. The papers are full of nothing else, while the tale is on the lips of every tongue-wagging scandalmonger for a hundred miles 'round."

"Two hundred, I should imagine," Jack remarked. "You know how fast word travels in the ton."

"Thank you for that sage observation," Edward said, his tone rife with sarcasm.

Jack sent him an unrepentant look, his azure eyes twinkling as he tossed back a mouthful of brandy.

By no means finished with his lecture, Edward returned his attention to Cade. "Were it not for Mama, Mallory, and your fiancée, I wouldn't give a damn if you had strangled him right there in front of everyone. As it is, the ladies are going to have a deuced difficult time showing their faces in public, at least for the immediate future."

Cade scowled, not liking the notion that his actions might have had an adverse impact on three of the most important women in his life. "I didn't think—"

"Yes. So we've established." Edward sighed and rubbed a thumb over the square-cut emerald in his signet ring. "There's already talk at court, you know, about having you banned. Apparently, Prinny is furious. I understand you've cast a pall over his upcoming medal ceremony for Everett."

Cade curled his lip. "Prinny is a bloated fool

who cares more about the cut of his coat and his next fete at Carlton House than he does about the welfare of the nation."

Drake coughed into his hand, while Jack let out a quiet guffaw.

"Yes, well, be that as it may," the duke observed. "That 'fool' could have you thrown in the Tower, or worse, sent to Bedlam. And you'd do well to keep your opinions to yourself on such matters, unless you wish to be accused of treason in addition to attempted murder."

Cade thrust out his jaw. "He can try. Let him do his worst."

"Gratefully, the situation has not reached such dire proportions. Nor, I trust, will it ever. As for Lord Everett, I am equally grateful that he has decided not to press charges against you with the House of Lords or in the courts."

"Charges!" Cade reared up in his seat. "On what grounds?"

"On the grounds that you tried to strangle him in front of five hundred witnesses!"

Cade pounded his fist against the padded arm of his chair. "He's the one who should be up on charges. Blackhearted traitor. Villainous turncoat."

A pronounced silence followed before Edward spoke again, his words quiet and thoughtful. "You are certain it is he? Le Renard?"

Cade fixed his gaze on Edward. "Unquestionably. His is a voice I shall never forget."

239

Edward nodded, then set his bridged fingers beneath his chin. "Interesting. This sheds an entirely new light on certain matters."

"What matters?" Cade knew Edward worked on occasion for the government, but in what capacity, even he wasn't certain.

"Nothing of import," Edward said, brushing aside his own observation. "For now, we need to finish out the Season. After that, we can consider ways to bring Everett to justice."

Tension flowed out of Cade's shoulders as if a huge weight had suddenly been lifted. "So you believe me?"

Edward raised a brow. "Of course I believe you. That was never in doubt."

"We all believe you, Cade," Drake said, finally entering the conversation. "You're our brother, and if you say Everett's the man, then he is, evidence to the contrary or not."

"Bloody well right." Jack thrust out a finger. "That double-dealer can't be allowed to run the streets with impunity. You've got to take this to the ministry and get them to see reason."

Cade ran a thumb over his forehead. "I already have. This morning, in fact, as early as they would agree to see me. Lord Caldwell gave me a polite hearing, then sent me on my way. It was the same at the War Office, the Horse Guards, and the Lord Chamberlain's office. Every one of them listened, then said something to the effect that I was under great duress during my ordeal and that it's only understandable I might have a delayed 'breakdown,' given the torture I'd undergone."

Pausing, he dragged his fingers through his hair. "In other words, they all think I am mad, exactly as that blighter suggested last night. At best, they believe I am confused and leaping to erroneous conclusions. There'll be no help from official quarters, not unless I can obtain better proof than saying I recognize his voice."

"Which is precisely the reason we need to step back and take a more measured approach," Edward stated, meeting Cade's gaze with a penetrating look. "So, regardless of your quite understandable desire for justice and revenge, you are to take no further action against Everett for now. Doing so will only bring more trouble down upon your head and that of the family. So stay the hell away from him, do you hear?"

Cade heard. He just didn't know if he could manage to do as his brother insisted. Simply being aware that Everett was out there made his blood boil. Realizing Everett was being cheered and feted as some great hero—by Prince George and the military establishment, no less—while in actuality being a spy, double dealing for the French, sent his sense of outrage and wrath spiraling to nearly unbearable heights. How many more men would Everett betray? How many lives lost because of his treachery? How many well-laid plans and preparations would he scuttle with his deceit? And all the while, he might be stopped if only people would see the truth.

Bloody imbeciles! he railed in silent fury as he thought of the high-placed gentlemen, who'd dismissed his concerns today. How could they be so blind?

In the end, though, it wouldn't matter whether they were blind or not. One way or another, he vowed to take care of Everett. Calida and her family—and all the others he'd harmed—would be vindicated. If it was the last thing he did on this earth, he would make certain their deaths did not go unanswered.

"So? Are we agreed?" Edward asked, shrewd speculation in his eyes, as though he knew exactly what Cade had been thinking.

Knowing Edward, he probably did. Annoying as it so often was, his older brother had a gift for reading people and being able to discern truth from lies.

Cade inclined his head. "Of course. You have my word that I will not publicly attack that treasonous rat again." *But in private . . . well, nothing will ever force such an assurance from my lips.* As far as he was concerned, if Everett was ever careless enough to be caught alone, he would be fair game. *And I can hardly wait for that day to arrive!*

As quietly as she could, Meg eased away from the study door. Careful to keep her footsteps as light as a ghost's, she resumed her journey to the garden at the rear of the house. Only after she slipped outside and shut the glass-paned door behind her did she give herself permission to breathe normally again. Crossing to a stone bench that was surrounded by fragrant lavender and cheerfully preening white narcissus, she sank down onto its cool surface. Relaxing there, she let pieces of the conversation she had just heard play again in her mind.

The Byron brothers would not have been pleased had they known their words were being overheard. Then again, they oughtn't to have left the door ever so slightly ajar if they wished to maintain their secrecy, she rationalized. And it wasn't as if she had meant to eavesdrop.

After a truly dreadful breakfast party where she, Mallory, and the dowager had done their best to smile and ignore the furtive looks and hushed whispers brought about by last night's melee, the three of them had returned home. By mutual agreement, they went their separate ways—Ava to write letters in her sitting room, Mallory to take a nap in her bedchamber, and Meg for a visit to the garden where she planned to sit and read while savoring the sunshine and warm May breezes.

But as she was passing the duke's study, she heard Cade's deep, throaty voice and stopped, unable to tear herself away despite knowing it was wrong to listen. Now that she had, however, she couldn't regret her actions.

Last night had disturbed her greatly, her dreams afterward a replay of the intense violence that had been unleashed only feet from where she'd been standing in the ballroom. One minute she was conversing with Lord Everett, and the next, Cade was throwing the man to the floor as he tried to choke the life out of him.

She knew that Cade had once been a soldier, and therefore capable of using brute force, but until she'd actually seen it, she hadn't realized how ferocious he could be.

And yet, with her he had never been anything but gentle. She'd seen him drugged and drunken, and still he was always careful and kind; tender, even at his most passionately demanding.

A tingle skimmed over her skin like a pebble across a summer lake, remembered pleasure turning her warm from the inside out. Memories flooded her senses. The way he'd caressed her last night in the library. The way she'd let him, helplessly enthralled by his touch. Now, on the stone bench, she shifted her legs, willing away the ache that sprang to life between her thighs, fighting the sensations that lingered in all the places he'd kissed and stroked.

Dear Lord, he makes me feel so confused! About my own feelings and wishes. About his.

What does he want from me?

What do I want of him?

Yet for all her uncertainty regarding her emotions toward Cade, she suffered no such doubts over his brawl with Everett. She'd heard Cade's accusations, then listened to Everett's denials. She had witnessed people's reactions, and was dismayed by their instant belief that Cade was deluded—or worse, insane. But despite all proof to the contrary, she knew beyond any doubt that Cade believed what he'd said—and even more, that he was right about Everett.

How she knew, she couldn't say, but instinct told her that Cade's memory of his tormentor's voice was as clear and true as the day he'd first heard the man speak. Cade might carry scars—on his body, as well as his mind—but she knew he was as sane as she. Saner perhaps, given all he had endured and overcome. She'd seen what his nightmares did to him, and understood at least a portion of his agonizing loss. For that alone, she knew he would never wrongly accuse a man of crimes he had not committed. As his brothers had stated, if Cade said Everett was a spy and a scoundrel, then that's exactly what he was.

Even more, she knew that Jack Byron was right and that Everett must not be allowed to go free and unpunished. Someone has to stop him! she determined. Cade wanted to, as did his brothers, but after last night's incident, their hands were tied.

But *mine aren't!* she realized. She'd made no promises involving herself, or about finding ways to unmask Everett for the fraud he was. She wasn't sure yet how to prove his guilt to the world, but she was determined to do whatever it might take to help Cade.

"Would you care for a cup of punch, Miss Amberley?"

Meg glanced into the brown, puppy-dog eyes of the young gentleman who had just accompanied her for the last set. He was a friendly sort, if a bit dull-witted. Still, his well-meaning patter and attention was exactly what she needed tonight—giving her an easy opportunity to keep an eye out for Lord Everett.

Despite her resolution made nearly two weeks ago to expose him as a traitor, getting close enough to learn any useful information was turning out to be surprisingly difficult. Not that Everett was hiding himself away. Quite the contrary, in fact, since he seemed to make an appearance at every fete, soiree, and ball in the offing. No, the trouble stemmed not from his lack of accessibility, but rather from an excess of it.

Everywhere he went, people followed. Clusters of gentlemen eager to hear about his battlefield exploits and his opinions on everything from the economy to his choice of tailor. While the ladies —married and unmarried alike—flocked to his side in hopes of attracting some measure of his favorable regard.

Personally, she found the whole thing disgusting.

But she supposed people saw what they wished to see, whether it happened to be the truth or not. Despite her frustration over being unable to proceed with her plan against Everett, the delay had provided at least one benefit.

In the days since Cade's confrontation with Everett, the furor surrounding the incident had thankfully begun to fade from public consciousness. A more tantalizing scandal involving a marquis and the two married ladies with whom he'd been caught in bed—both at the same time—had shifted the attention of the gossip-loving ton.

Nonetheless, there were still those who had taken to calling Cade the "Mad Major"—delighting in offering him slights wherever he went. Stubborn to his core, Cade refused to avoid the unpleasantness and stay home, insisting on escorting her, Mallory, and Ava to their promised entertainments. Since all three ladies had witnessed the fight, there was little required in the way of explanation—and Cade offered virtually none. He did, however, tell each of them how genuinely sorry he was for any personal distress his actions might have caused, then gave his mother a kiss on the cheek that earned him a fierce hug and a single, hastily dashed tear.

His only other concession to the scandal was the fact that, when out in public, he'd started spending more of his time in the company of his brothers. Large and formidable, the Byron men presented a united front that few dared to cross. At the moment, Meg knew they were all ensconced in the card room.

As for the dowager, she was sipping sherry and chatting with a group of her most stalwart friends, while Mallory, also in the ballroom, was dancing with her favorite beau, Major Hargreaves. The radiant smile on her face signaled she wouldn't be leaving his side for some time to come. With all the Byrons otherwise occupied, Meg realized she was in an excellent position to pursue Everett.

She couldn't believe her luck when he strolled outside and onto the terrace—alone. Knowing her moment had finally arrived, she refused her dance partner's offer of punch, then quickly found an excuse to escape him and lose herself in the crowd.

Despite the warmth of the late May night, she shivered as she moved out into the darkness, a faint breeze bringing the contrasting fragrances of roses and cigar smoke to her nostrils. Following the acrid part of the blend, she walked farther away from the sheltering protection of the ball-room. Everett stood a couple yards distant, his blond hair gleaming a few shades lighter against the evening sky.

Fresh tendrils of unease coiled just beneath her skin. He hadn't notice her yet, so it wasn't too late to go back. She had only to turn around and retrace her path. After all, this was the man who had tor-tured Cade. The monster who had ordered the rape and death of an innocent girl and the execution of her entire family. A man who thought nothing of betraying his country and the honor of his name.

Hesitant and suddenly unsure of the wisdom of her plan, her step slowed. Yet I must try to help Cade, she thought, knowing if she failed to make an attempt to aid him, she would forever after feel that she'd let not only Cade down, but herself. Her father hadn't raised her to be a coward, and she refused to be one now.

Besides, what can Everett do to me here with an entire house full of guests only yards away? If he tried something, she would simply scream. Wrapping her sense of resolve around herself like a suit of armor, she strolled forward.

At her approach, he turned his head, a stream of smoke trailing from his lips as he lifted his eyes to meet her gaze.

As if she had only just noticed him, she came to an abrupt halt. "Oh, my lord, I . . . pray beg pardon for the intrusion. I did not realize you were here."

Flicking an ash off the end of his cigar, he lowered the cheroot to his side and bowed. "Please, do not upset yourself . . . Miss Amberley, is it not?"

"Yes. How good of you to remember, my lord." All apparent politeness, she sank into a curtsey. "Well, I . . . um . . . I suppose I should be going."

"You need not leave on my account," he stated in a pleasant voice. "Although I must confess to some surprise at seeing you without a companion.

I rather doubt your fiancé would be pleased to find you in my company."

"No, I . . . am sure he would not." She gave a small grimace, striving to look just the faintest bit embarrassed. "He . . . um . . . he and his brothers are in the card room, you see, and after the last dance, I just had to have some air—"

"Of course. An entirely natural response."

She glanced around, as though checking to see if they were being observed. "Since we do have this opportunity to converse, there is something I have been meaning to say . . ."

"Really?" he said, curiosity clear on a face she might have found handsome had she not known what lurked beneath.

"Yes, but . . ." She gave a quick shake of her head. "I should not. Please forgive me. I ought to go."

"But you cannot go now. Not until you tell me what it is you wish to say."

Appearing to hesitate, she glanced around again before seeming to give in to an irrepressible need. "In no way do I wish to appear disloyal to my fiancé. He has been very good to me, but . . ."

"Yes?"

"What happened the other night between the two of you . . . well, I must apologize for his behavior toward you. I was appalled—shocked, if you must know—as well as mortified. I have never seen anything like that from him. I had no idea he could . . . snap like that and turn so violent.

It was horrible, and I am deeply sorry for any distress it may have caused you."

Surprise lit his eyes. "Do not worry yourself, Miss Amberley. There is nothing to forgive. Major Byron—that is, Lord Cade—endured a very difficult experience during his military service. I have seen other men under similar circumstances who ended up in a far worse way than he has. I am sure with time he shall heal."

She shuffled the toe of one slipper. "Yes, but what if he does not? What he did to you was unpardonable. Here you are, above reproach—a war hero who has received the very highest honors the nation can bestow—and he attacked you! If he could confuse you with this . . . Le Renard he mumbles about, then just think what might happen to the next gentleman he decides has done him wrong. And his brothers . . ."

"Yes?" Everett encouraged with soothing gentleness. "What about the Byrons?"

"They have all taken up for him, refusing to even consider that he might not be as well as he ought."

"They are a close family and very loyal to one another."

"Indeed they are. They have taken me under their wing, and yet . . . I do not always feel completely welcome."

He took one of her hands and gave it a light squeeze. Only by sheer dint of will did she keep herself from yanking it away and wiping it on her skirt. "I understand you are only recently out of mourning," he said in a sympathetic tone.

Needing to collect herself, she lowered her eyes to the ground. "Yes . . . my father passed away a few months ago. And my mother before that."

"How very sad. I am sure you have acquired many friends here in London, but if I might presume, perhaps you could do with one more?"

Her gaze darted to his, then away again, her heart pounding with fear and elation. She hadn't been sure it was going to work, but he seemed to be falling right into her palm. "Who could you mean, my lord?"

"Myself, of course, if you would allow me."

"But Cade—"

"Cade need know nothing of it. It might seem odd, but I feel somehow responsible for you and Lord Cade. Perhaps if we meet on occasion with no one the wiser, I can offer you the occasional bit of counsel."

"That would be most appreciated. Though I am still not certain it would work, what with Cade's volatile nature."

"Surely he doesn't go everywhere with you?"

She paused, worrying a lip between her teeth as if she were considering. "I ride in the mornings and only take a groom."

He smiled. "That sounds perfect. Mayhap I shall take a ride myself, and our paths shall just happen to cross while we are both in the park."

Swallowing her nerves, she smiled back, wondering if she was only imagining the reptilian gleam in his eyes. "Yes. Perhaps we might meet there."

Knowing she had taken all the time she dared, Meg curtsied and said her farewells. Everett gave her an elegant bow in reply.

Turning around, she hurried back to the ballroom. As she went, she couldn't decide if she should feel glad of her success or afraid instead.

Chapter 15

The next week passed in a curious mix of normalcy and furtiveness, as Meg proceeded with her plan against Everett. In the main, her routine followed its usual pattern—if constant rounds of morning calls, afternoon teas, excursions to the park, balls, routs, soirees, and the occasional evening at the theater or opera could be termed "usual." She was so busy some days that she barely had time to change gowns before rushing off to another new social engagement.

With the exception of a brief lull just after the incident between Cade and Lord Everett, she and Mallory had continued to receive a plentiful supply of invitations and callers. Every once in a while she would catch an odd stare or hear the hushed whisper of some sotto voce remark. But as she had learned, the duke and his mother wielded far too much influence for anyone to risk giving her or any of the Byrons the cut direct, especially over what was now being dubbed nothing more than "a lively bout of fisticuffs between gentlemen."

Meg's regular gentlemen callers certainly took scant notice, including Lieutenant McCabe, who stopped by Clybourne House more than once to take her driving or to escort her and Mallory for a stroll in one of the nearby parks. She was grateful for his attention, since she always enjoyed his company. Yet she felt guilty at the same time, as if she were taking advantage of his kindness. Of course, he still believed she was engaged, but *she* knew she was not, and therein lay the difficulty.

With the last full month of the Season upon them, Meg was aware that she ought to be getting on with the matter of securing a marriage proposal—and of all the eligible gentlemen, Lieutenant McCabe seemed the most likely choice. At least she could say she genuinely liked him, and imagined herself capable of spending more than an afternoon in his company without growing bored. But a strong liking seemed to be the limit of her affection for him, especially in light of her reaction to the passionate encounter she'd shared in the library with Cade.

In the three weeks that had passed since that evening, neither she nor Cade mentioned their embrace again. At first she supposed they had both been too wrapped up in the aftermath of his fight with Everett. But as one day melted into the next, and neither of them said a word, broaching the topic seemed to grow more awkward and unlikely.

Besides, what would I say? she argued to herself. It wasn't as if Cade had made further overtures toward her, or in any manner indicated that he felt anything deeper for her than a few fleeting moments of desire. And although he continued to maintain their ruse of being an affianced couple, it seemed to her that he had been going out of his way to make sure the two of them were never alone.

For her own part, she could not forget that night; memories of his touch and kiss remaining startlingly crisp and clear in her mind. Then there were her dreams, both waking and asleep, that plagued her body—and if she was honest, her heart, as well.

Gazing now into her dressing table mirror, she wondered if anyone else had noticed the strain. She supposed not, just as she guessed she ought to be glad for their inattentiveness. Stifling a yawn after another restless night's sleep, she let her maid help her into a riding habit of dark green poplin, a color that was disturbingly reminiscent of Cade's eyes. Brushing the notion aside, she hurriedly finished her toilette, so she could depart for the park before the hour grew too advanced.

Lord Everett would be waiting for her, she

assumed. They never made any actual plans to meet, but he was usually in the park, always happening upon her as if by accident. She would then invite him to join her, the two of them walking their horses side by side while they conversed.

So far she hadn't learned anything remotely useful in her quest to prove he was a spy. But then she supposed he wouldn't be much good at such matters, if he were given to randomly spilling secrets. Another woman might have been discouraged at the initial lack of progress, but Meg remained optimistic. Even careful men made mistakes, she judged. She had only to watch and wait. At some point he would slip. When he did, she planned to be there to catch him.

She left through a rear door that connected the house to the mews and walked toward the stable. The servants knew her routine and had anticipated her wishes; an energetic bay mare stood ready for her use. Climbing into the sidesaddle, she arranged her skirts, then with a nod of thanks set out for Hyde Park.

From his upstairs window, Cade watched Meg ride out of the stable yard. Once she was gone, he let the curtain drop back into place, then turned to take up his morning cup of coffee. Blowing across the inky surface, he took a sip of the steaming brew, his thoughts occupied with Meg.

He wished he could have accompanied her, but

didn't yet trust his leg enough to ride. With continued improvement, he hoped to give it a try one of these days soon. Before his injury, he'd loved riding, and missed it far more than he liked to admit.

Meg was certainly an enthusiastic horsewoman, he knew, rising early so she could enjoy more than the sedate walk she would be forced to endure later in the day. Since coming to London, she had taken up the practice of riding out a few times each week. He knew she missed the occasional day, though, especially if she'd been out exceptionally late attending a ball or other entertainment the evening before.

This past week, however, she had been up and out not long after sunrise each morning, no matter what hour she returned home. He was often awake himself, and unable to keep from watching as she mounted her horse and rode off. There was a determination to her step lately that gave him pause. It was almost as if she were meeting a suitor.

The thought froze him in place.

Is she meeting someone? McCabe perhaps? Or one of the others? With a scowl heavy enough to make his forehead ache, he set down his coffee cup before he broke it.

God knows I've done my best to stay away from her lately. Not daring to trust himself around her again—certainly not alone. After what had happened between them that night in the library, he knew it was imperative he keep her at arm's length.

Of course that was easier said than done, especially since their "engagement" required him to escort her out each night. But with speculation and schemes against Everett taking up a great deal of his attention, he was generally able to distract himself from thoughts of her. Night was the only truly troublesome time, when the house was dark and quiet and his mind had free rein to roam as it pleased. His dreams, over which he had absolutely no control, were a particular problem.

Grumbling low in his throat, he once again considered the notion that Meg had ridden off to an assignation. If so, he supposed he had no right to complain, given their bargain. Perhaps she was even now accepting an offer of marriage, assuring her would-be beau that she would be happy to break her engagement to her fiancé.

Thrusting his feet into a pair of shoes, he stalked across the room as fast as his limp would allow and flung open the door. Five minutes later he was in the stable yard.

He waved over one of the stable boys. "Which groom rides out with Miss Amberley to the park?"

"That would be Brown, milord."

Cade nodded. "Well, when he returns, have him come see me."

A peculiar look crossed the boy's face. "Aye, milord. But the miss didn't take him this morning. Ner y'sterday neither."

"What?" Cade's jaw tightened.

The boy, who apparently decided he'd be better off elsewhere, sprinted away without another word.

An older servant soon appeared, drying his hands on a rag. "Ye wanted to see me, my lord? About the miss?"

"Yes. I understand she rode out alone this morning. Why, may I ask?"

The servant looked uncomfortable. " 'Twas on her orders. Said she were meeting a friend and didn't have no need of me. I tried to talk her out of it, but she wouldn't hear a word."

Cade crossed his arms over his chest. "And just who was this 'friend'?"

"He were a gentleman, milord."

"And does this 'he' have a name?" Cade prepared himself, waiting to hear which one of Meg's suitors had won her favor.

The other man wrinkled his forehead in thought. "If I remember right, I think she called him Everett."

Cade's arms fell to his sides. "What did you say?"

"Aye, that were it. Lord Everett."

More than an hour after her departure, Meg rode into the stable yard with a clattering of horse hooves, dismounted, then hurried into the house.

Her outing had been an immense disappointment, the meeting with Everett proving as fruitless as ever. But at least I made the attempt, she consoled herself, rallying at the thought that she would have another chance to try again. Perhaps the next time would do the trick!

Flushed and in need of a bath to wash the scent of horseflesh from her skin, she raced up the stairs, well aware that she was late getting ready for the promised shopping excursion with Mallory and three of their best female friends. Rounding the corner of the landing, she started down the corridor to her bedchamber.

Ahead of her, Cade emerged from the shadows, stepping into her path with his cane set at a pugnacious angle against the blue and brown Axminster hall runner. The expression on his face was menacing enough to make her halt in her tracks, his dark brows lowered in a glower that made gooseflesh pop out all over her arms.

She shook off the reaction, telling herself she was just being silly.

"So," he said on a near growl. "You're back."

"I . . . Yes, I was riding."

Even in the dim light, his eyes glinted, brittle as diamond-sharp shards of broken glass. Whatever is the matter with him? she wondered. The weather was sunny and warm, with no storms on the horizon, but mayhap his leg was hurting him again nonetheless. Had he done something to aggravate it?

She was about to ask when the dowager came bustling down the hall in a flurry of lilac silk.

"Good morning! Good morning!" Ava called, a wide smile on her attractive face. "How are both of you, dears? Slept well, I hope? Margaret, you have returned from your ride, I see."

"Yes, ma'am," Meg answered, aware of the sudden frustration rolling off Cade like a rough ocean current.

"I hope you don't mind," Ava continued, addressing her. "But I have decided to accompany you and Mallory and your friends on your shopping excursion this morning."

"Oh, of course, Your Grace," Meg said. "We would be pleased to have you join us."

The dowager smiled. "Thank you. You are very sweet. And not to worry, I shall only go as far as the fan makers. To my deep regret, the fan that matches my gown for tonight's ball has come to a rather tragic end. Edward's new puppy, it seems, wandered into my rooms and decided to use it as a teething chew. The poor lovely thing is quite beyond salvation. The fan, that is. Neddy's naughty puppy continues in excellent health."

Meg hid a smile, particularly at hearing the duke referred to as Neddy. "I am most sorry for its loss. Definitely, you must come and buy another."

"Exactly." Ava looked between her and Cade, a small frown crinkling her forehead. "Cade, are you well? You look as though you just ate a lemon. You are not in pain again, are you?"

Meg waited with interest to hear his response.

"No," he said. "I am quite well in that regard, Mama. I merely wish to speak with Meg."

"All right, if you are sure. But as for this talk, you shall just have to save it for later. Margaret needs to run along and change or else she will be frightfully late. Misses Milbank and Throckly will be here any minute."

"But—" Cade began.

"No buts. You two can converse when we return. Now go on, Meg dear. Hurry along." Ava made shooing motions with her hands, leaving Meg with no other recourse but to obey.

She cast one last glance at Cade, who looked even more furious than before, if that were possible. Wondering again what was wrong and why he wanted to speak with her, she hesitated. But the dowager shooed her again, and neither she nor Cade had any chance of overruling her. With mixed feelings of interest and trepidation, Meg continued to her bedchamber.

The hour had just turned one o'clock when Meg accepted a footman's assistance and stepped down from the coach. Entering the town house along with Mallory, Edward, and Ava, she repressed a yawn as she shed her cloak, weary and in need of her bed after another very long day. In fact, she realized, this would be the first opportunity she'd had to stop for more than two minutes in a row, ever since awakening this morning for her ride in the park. Or rather *yesterday* morning, she corrected, thinking again of how rapidly the past several hours had flown by.

Making her way up the staircase, she bid everyone a fond good-night, the dowager pausing to give her a motherly kiss on the cheek before continuing on to her rooms, the others sharing sleepy smiles as they parted to seek their own rest as well.

As for Cade, he had not accompanied them to tonight's ball, sending word that he would be otherwise engaged. Otherwise engaged doing what? she pondered. Was he in pain and stubbornly refusing to admit as much? Or was it something else?

Tiny lines formed between Meg's brows as she considered the question. Only then did she remember his wish to speak with her, realizing that the hectic pace of the day had driven the matter completely out of her mind. *Well, it is far too late to talk now*, she decided as she let herself into her bedchamber. The morning would have to be soon enough.

Yawning, she went straight through to her dressing room, where she found her equally sleepy maid waiting to help her out of her evening gown and stays. With relief, she soon slipped into a thin, white lawn nightgown and summer-weight robe of sheer, pale pink silk.

Moving into the small yet luxuriously modern attached bathing room, she washed her face and hands, then scrubbed her teeth with a tooth powder that tasted like cinnamon and cloves. After drinking half a glass of cool water, she wished Amy a good-night, then sent the drowsy young woman off to her own bed.

Blowing out a pair of candles, Meg padded on slippered feet into her bedchamber and across to the waiting comfort of her feather mattress and soft linen sheets. She was just leaning over to pull the covers down a few inches farther when she caught sight of a large, shadow-draped figure seated in a chair on the far side of the room, the gold buckles on his black leather shoes winking at her like a pair of cat's eyes.

She whirled on a harsh gasp, her heart pounding so hard it sounded like thunder in her ears. Instinctively, she grabbed for the nearest weapon, her fingers curving around the heavy silver candlestick on her night table. Lifting it high, she prepared to defend herself, then the light from the still burning taper revealed what she hadn't seen before—or rather, *who* she hadn't seen.

"Cade! Lord have mercy, is that you?" A full-body tremor ran through her. "You nearly scared the life out of me."

"Did I? My apologies for terrifying you," he

drawled in a quiet voice that didn't sound all that sorry. "I wasn't sure how best to announce myself."

"A simple hello might have sufficed," she said, careful to keep her voice low. Fingers trembling, she returned the candlestick to her night table, relieved when she didn't send the lighted bees-wax taper toppling to the floor.

As she straightened, she noticed Cade's appearance as he sprawled in the chair. His dark hair was tousled, as if he'd been dragging his fingers through it. And he'd taken off his cravat, leaving his neck bare, his scar just barely visible. He reminded her of a sleekly muscled panther that had been patiently lying in wait for its prey.

Placing a fist between her breasts, she strove for calm. "What are you doing here? For that matter, how did you get in? Surely my maid didn't let you inside?"

"No indeed. She would have been most shocked, I suspect. Actually, I came through the hidden panel on the other side of the highboy."

Her brow wrinkled in surprise. "What hidden panel? I've never noticed one."

"You aren't supposed to. That's why it's hidden. One of my less trusting ancestors had them put in nearly all of the rooms when the town house was built. My brothers and I spent our childhood locating the passages and pass-throughs, though I believe only Edward and I know them all."

"But where do they lead?"

"Back along the servants' staircases, for the most part, and a couple run down into the cellar. Fortunately, the one in here is accessed through the family dining room, and no one uses that room at night. At least not *this* late at night."

Her pulse finally slowing, the tension slid out of the taut muscles in her shoulders. "And why are you here so late?"

"I want to talk. Remember, I told you that this morning."

"Yes, but surely it can wait a few hours more? I . . . I'm tired."

Actually, she wasn't tired, at least not anymore. The fright of discovering him in her bedroom had driven away all earlier feelings of sleepiness. Even so, she didn't think this was a good time to talk. For one thing, Cade wasn't acting like himself tonight. For another, she was standing there in her nightgown. Becoming suddenly aware of her state of undress, she drew the edges of her robe closer together, her pulse speeding up again, but not out of fear this time.

"Tired or not, I refuse to wait any longer," he stated. "I've been waiting all damned day and my patience is worn thin."

"Is it your leg?"

"No, it isn't my bloody leg!" he snapped. "Now, I want answers, and I expect the truth. How long have you been meeting him?"

"What?" She blinked, taken aback by the sudden change of subject.

"Has he recruited you or is it something else?"

"*Recruited me?* I don't understand."

Moving faster than she'd imagined he could, Cade shot out of his chair and took three large steps toward her, instantly covering the distance separating them.

"Are you working for him? Are you feeding him information when you ride out for your little early morning tête-à-têtes? What are you telling him?"

Abruptly, everything came clear. *He's found out about Everett! Oh, mercy, he knows!* Her heart leapt into yet another crazy rhythm.

His gaze bored into hers. "That's right, I've found out about your clandestine association," he said, having apparently read the truth in her eyes. "So tell me, Miss Amberley, just how deep have you gone? Who have you betrayed? Besides me, that is."

His accusations shook her out of her momentary paralysis. "I've betrayed no one!" she declared. "Most assuredly not you."

He laughed, the sound hollow and harsh. "Please give me some credit. Men like Everett don't waste their time conducting secret rendezvouses unless they believe there is something to be gained. So what is he getting?"

"Nothing!"

Cade's expression turned cold. *"What is he get-*

ting?" he demanded as he enunciated each word, the question all the more chilling for his quiet, careful tone.

"Well, it isn't information. All we've done is ride. And talk."

"About what?"

"A great deal of inconsequential nonsense, for the most part. It's been sadly disappointing."

Cade scowled. "What in the blazes is that supposed to mean?"

"It means that he isn't the one trying to get information out of *me*. I've been trying to get information out of *him*. Do you really think I would be so foolish as to consort with a man of his stamp unless I had my own motivation? He's a snake. Anyone with two eyes can see that."

"Then a great many people in the ton are blind."

"You'll get no argument on that score from me."

He paused to consider her words. "So you aren't in league with him?"

"No. No more than you are insane. And I think you owe me an apology, my lord. I may be many things, but a traitor is not one of them." She drew a deep breath. "I heard what you said about him that night, and I believe you. I am merely trying to help."

He gave her a long stare. "What do you mean, 'help'? Surely you aren't saying that you have been *deliberately* inviting that scoundrel's attentions in some ill-conceived attempt to prove his guilt?"

"And your veracity," she replied, warming to the topic with a nod of her head. "It's an excellent plan. After all, he doesn't know me, so why would he suspect me of ulterior motives?"

He tapped a set of knuckles against his pantaloon-clad thigh, his scowl as fierce as ever. "Why, indeed? Mayhap because he's heard *we are engaged*?"

She made a dismissive noise. "That's of no matter. I've confided in him—with great distress, mind you—that I think you're loose a few screws on the subject of your war service, and that he's very forbearing about the whole thing considering how you tried to murder him and all. A flattering comment here, an awestruck question about his heroics there, and he preens like a peacock. I've rarely met such a self-absorbed narcissist."

A muscle flexed in Cade's jaw. "That self-absorbed narcissist is a master strategist and not to be underestimated, whatever facade you imagine he projects. He's dangerous, *extremely* dangerous, and you are to stay away from him, starting now!"

"But I'm making progress. It may not look like it on the surface, but I am convinced I'm on the brink of uncovering a vital clue."

Cade's eyes flashed. "The only *clue* you'll be uncovering is how to navigate your way in and out of the ballroom at the next party you attend. You will leave this alone, Meg, do you hear?"

She glanced away, brushing her fingertips over the turned back sheets. "Perhaps."

Abruptly, he caught hold of her shoulders and gave her a little shake. Her gaze flew up to meet his. "There is no 'perhaps' about it. You are done playing this game with him. From now on you will have no further contact with Everett."

"But he'll know something is amiss if I suddenly stop meeting him. What shall I say?"

"Nothing. You are to cease speaking to him completely. If he approaches you, tell him the Mad Major found out and won't let you see him anymore."

"But Cade—"

He shook his head. "But Cade nothing. This is not negotiable. You are out of the espionage business."

She raised her chin. "I don't believe that is for you to decide. Besides, a couple minutes ago you were accusing me of passing information to him."

"A couple minutes ago I didn't realize just how foolhardy you could be. And stubborn."

"No more than you." She paused, unable to help but notice his towering height and lean strength as he stood with barely an inch separating them. He continued to hold her inside his grasp, his fingers around her arms, with no more than the sheer material of her night attire between his flesh and hers. All at once her breath grew shallow, her body growing warm beneath his touch.

270

"That's different," he defended.

"I don't see how," she said. "I know what he is."

His fingers flexed against her arms. "You have no idea what he is, or the barbarous depths to which he will sink in order to gain his own ends. I once had no choice but to stand by and watch him torment and kill a young woman."

Calida, she realized, seeing the anguish in his expression. Had he loved her so much? Did he love her still?

"I won't stand by and let him do the same again," he continued in a gruff, implacable tone.

"To me, you mean?" she asked, shocked by the notion. "He wouldn't. He *couldn't*, not here in London. There are people everywhere. I am perfectly safe."

He gazed steadily into her eyes, his own burning with a glittering intensity. "Crowds do not ensure protection. But you *will* be safe because you're going to stay away from him. I want your promise."

He inched closer, near enough for her to catch the scent of his skin; an appealing mix of clean, male sweat and the lingering fragrance of the sandalwood soap he preferred. She drew a breath and found more—a subtle quality that was Cade himself. The discovery made her quiver deep inside, then again, as she fought the urge to lean forward and press her nose against the side of his neck.

Her nightgown and robe whispered around her

legs as she moved backward, her calves coming to rest against the satin-covered mattress behind her. "I . . . I won't go riding with him anymore. I promise that he and I will not be alone together again."

His thumbs stroked the upper curve of her arms. "It makes me ill to think you've been alone with him at all. How could you put yourself in his power?"

"I didn't . . . I . . ." But even as she spoke she realized that in a way she had done that very thing by agreeing to meet Everett in the park at such an early hour, when very few people were around. And lately she had gone there without a groom. Perhaps she'd been overconfident and unwise. Yet still, nothing untoward had occurred.

As if he were once more reading her mind, he gave her a light, scolding shake. "To think what might have happened. He could have done anything he wanted with no one there to stop him. The very idea makes my blood run cold."

Releasing his grip on one of her shoulders, he slid his palm up and around the side of her neck. "I don't know what I'd like to do more . . ." he said, drawing the edge of his thumb along the underside of her jaw.

Her pulse resumed its earlier crazy dance, her heart hammering in such swift, hard strokes that she knew he must surely feel the heavy beat of it throbbing under her skin.

". . . throttle you," he murmured, his fingers playing over her throat, "or . . ."

A dizzy wave swept over her. "Or what?"

He stared into her eyes, the seconds stretching one into the next. Slowly, his gaze roved lower, gliding over her nose and cheeks, then downward to linger like a whispered sigh against her mouth.

Her lips parted on a breathless inhale.

"Or this," he answered.

And then he showed her, bending his head to capture her mouth in a kiss that was half reprimand, half seduction. She made no demurral, as his lips pressed demandingly against hers, accepting his touch as though it were the most natural thing in the world. As if he came to her bedchamber every night and stood just so, kissing her with a ravenous passion and the promise of more to come.

Tipping his head to one side, he changed the angle of the kiss and urged her to follow his lead. His other palm came up to cup her face and hold her steady for his delectation, pressing her lips open to accept an even deeper embrace. Her head swam, her muscles turning waxen as his tongue glided inside to tease and tempt her.

And tempt her he did, driving away the remnants of her earlier caution and sense of propriety, to replace both with hot, heedless pleasure. Needing to touch him, she curved her arms around him

273

and slipped one palm beneath his silk waistcoat to find his thin cotton shirt and the warm, muscular strength of his back underneath.

Cade shivered, the simple touch of her small hands against him enough to turn him stiff and aching with arousal. From the instant his lips touched hers, he'd known it was a mistake and that he was in too deep before he'd even begun. He wanted her, had been wanting her for an interminable span of days . . . weeks . . . months now.

He hadn't come here this evening with seduction in mind, but rather, with condemnation and contempt. When he'd learned of her clandestine meetings with Everett, he'd been consumed with rage and, yes, betrayal—her apparent deceit enough to drive out every honest belief he had ever held about her. What else could it be? he'd asked himself. Either she was a traitor beguiling him with her wiles, as she worked some plan against him. Or worse, she was a fool who'd allowed Everett to manipulate her and draw her into his web. The thought that she might even have let Everett touch her had driven him wild, so that he'd been pacing like a caged beast tonight while waiting for her to return home.

But she had shattered all his assumptions, turning the tables on him in such a way that he'd had no choice but to accept the truth. He felt ashamed now to have doubted her, especially knowing she'd accepted his word against Everett with no proof at all. She believed him. How he reveled to hear her swear her trust in him. How he quaked to realize the danger in which she had placed herself for him.

Then he'd simply had to have a taste of her, just one small sip before he cut himself off from the source. Like strong spirits, she was another intoxicant he knew he needed to give up for his own good—and for hers. But even as he told himself to release her, he couldn't, the hot satin of her mouth too delicious to resist, the glide of her tongue like a benediction for his soul.

Just one more minute, he told himself. *Just one last kiss.*

Deepening their embrace, he kissed her harder, trying to wring every last ounce of pleasure out of the moment. She hummed low in her throat and returned his ardor, arching against him with a sinuous slide that nearly dropped him to his knees. Her beautiful, pale hair flowed around her shoulders like a sleek curtain. Tangling his fingers into her tresses, he stroked the golden length, then turned his face into its fragrant softness. Breathing in the heady scents of honey and woman, he closed his eyes and fought his hunger.

And what a hunger it was, the ache to have her riding him more powerful than ever. He trembled and struggled to make himself relinquish her. But her sweet little palms began to rove over him, one hand gliding up over his shoulders and the back of his neck before she threaded her fingers into his hair.

Abruptly, he raised his head and began to move away, tapping into some unknown reserve of strength. But Meg hardly seemed to notice his resistance, her cheeks flushed, her lips moist and rosy from his kisses, the silvery blue of her eyes hazy with undisguised passion.

God help me, he thought.

Reaching up, she brushed aside the edge of his unbuttoned shirt collar to reveal the scar encircling his throat. He tensed, for the first time truly caring what she saw, and whether it repulsed her. He was about to withdraw when she prevented him with a single, delicate touch. Using only the tip of her finger, she traced the shape and path of the mark from one side to the other.

"Does it hurt?" she asked softly.

"No," he croaked, his voice so thick and rough he scarcely recognized it as his own. "Not any-more."

"But it must have hurt when it happened. It must have been agony."

He didn't answer; he couldn't, particularly not after she leaned forward and replaced her finger-tip with her lips, kissing him there with a tender-ness that proved his complete undoing. Air squeezed like a bellows from his lungs, blood running hot and thick to pool in his groin.

His senses scattered as he felt the last vestiges of

his conscience drift away like so much faerie dust, his need for her far greater than his resolve. Spearing his fingers up into her hair, he twined the skeins around his wrist and tugged her face up, plundering her mouth in a fiery assault that left her gasping and clinging. Using his tongue to skillful effect, he made passionate forays between her lips that were alternately fast and frenzied, then slow and sultry, keeping them both poised on a needle's edge of passionate madness.

Maybe I am mad, he thought as he broke their kiss long enough to slide her robe from her shoulders. *Mad to want her so. Insane to take what I have no right to possess.* The thought slowed him for an instant as he moved to open the brief row of buttons on her nightgown, pausing while he slipped the first one free of its mooring.

Bending, he pressed his lips against her jaw and neck, scattering kisses over her skin before he moved to catch her earlobe between his teeth. He blew softly against her and felt her answering shiver. "Make me stop," he entreated. "Send me away."

Meg swayed, his words coming as if from a distance even though she stood inside his arms. Giddy with desire, she could barely think, needing his mouth on hers again, his hands caressing her skin.

Send him away? she pondered. Why would she do that? How could she, when she wanted him more than her next breath? More even than her life? How could she let him go when she loved him? And suddenly, in that instant, she knew the truth of the thought, the strength of the emotion.

Oh, heavens, how could I not have known before? How could I not have realized that I love Cade Byron?

Wanting only to be with him, as close as she could manage regardless of the risks, she turned her face and kissed his cheek, his mouth. "Don't stop," she whispered. "Don't leave me."

Something fiery and fierce burned in his eyes, turning them as bright as molten green glass. Then he gave her no further time to think, his hands working open the placket of buttons on her nightgown, nearly tearing them off in his haste. Shoving the loosened cloth down over her shoulders, he cupped her naked breasts in his hands, fondling her with a touch that bordered on the reverent. He made circles with his thumbs, rousing the tips to taut peaks before he leaned down to take her in his mouth.

She gasped against the pleasure as he kissed and licked and suckled, keen desire rising to settle between her legs, together with an aching emptiness that begged to be filled and appeased. Raking his teeth over her, she cried out, his tongue darting out to soothe her tormented flesh. Long moments later he raised his head and claimed her mouth again in a fervid mating, his hips arching against her own in a way that left her in no doubt of the intensity of his arousal. Then, as though he'd had all he could endure for the moment, he urged her backward onto the bed.

Quivering from the series of hot and cold chills racing over her body, she complied, stretching out across the sheets, her head sideways next to the pillows rather than on them. Dazedly, she watched as he tore at his waistcoat, a pair of buttons flying free to bounce across the floor. He seemed not to care in the least as he stripped off the garment, his shirt coming next, then his shoes, which he toed off with a pair of soft thumps.

She waited in a welter of expectation, a part of her eager to see what lay inside his pantaloons, the rest unsure, fearing her reaction should the sight prove intimidating. After all, he was a large man. What if he was more than she anticipated? What if she wasn't enough?

But he granted her no further time for such uncertain musings, leaving his pantaloons safely fastened as he set the knee of his good leg on the bed and stretched himself beside her. Arching over her, he feasted on her mouth, drawing her fast and deep into a realm where nothing mattered except the astonishing beauty of his embrace. She moaned against his lips, the sound reverberating like a delicious purr inside their joined mouths. He smiled and kissed her harder, deeper, drawing forth everything she had and more.

All the while, his hands stayed busy, trailing

over her skin with long, gliding strokes that made her body grow hot and moist, her limbs shifting in restless need against his own. He captured one of her legs, stilling her for a moment so he could fit his own between hers. Sliding upward, he insinuated his thigh against the part of her that ached the most, then rubbed, her nightgown bunched between her flesh in a way that only increased her craving.

Abandoning her mouth, he dappled kisses over her face and neck, across her collarbone and shoulders, before scattering a tantalizing line of them between her breasts. Burying his face against her, he reached up to caress one rounded globe with his hand, while he paid homage to the other with teeth and tongue and lips. At length he switched one for the other.

Not to be left out, she caressed him as well, eliciting a groan, then a shudder when she traced the broad shape of his arms and shoulders, then down the long, powerful line of his back. She gloried in the sensations, delighting in her exploration as she discovered firm, corded muscle covered by smooth, supple skin. Growing bolder, she let her fingers glide low, then lower still, pausing to slip underneath the edge of his waistband. She played her fingers along the dip at the base of his spine, her touch drawing a ragged moan from his throat.

With an uncontrolled movement, he ground his erection against her hip, then angled his thigh higher and harder between her legs. She writhed in response, broken sighs escaping her lips as he widened his mouth to suckle more intensely against her breast, his clever hands cupping and stroking her in ways that increased her delight still more. Growing nearly insensible under his ministrations, time floated away like a ribbon caught in a breeze, her senses spinning out of control.

Without warning, he levered himself away, a rush of cool air flowing over her at the loss of his warmth. Reaching down, he seized her nightgown and yanked it off over her head, baring her fully to his gaze.

With a reflexive sense of modesty, she moved her hands to cover herself. But he stayed her with a touch, urging her to relax and leave her arms at her sides. "You are so beautiful," he murmured, the expression in his eyes one of pure admiration. "I've imagined you like this, but my dreams failed to do you justice."

Laying a large, gentle palm against her stomach, he smoothed his touch over her body in a way that sent her pulse into a wild, dangerous skid. He roamed over her hips and thighs, trailing downward to circle her knees and caress her calves, even her ankles. She was trembling by the time he retraced his path, a loud gasp rattling from her lips when he stroked the soft length of her inner thighs—up and around, then up and around again. With a quiet pause, he let his hand come to rest just below the triangle of blond curls that concealed her most tender flesh.

"Cade?" she said in a strained tone.

"Close your eyes," he commanded. "Close your eyes and let me please you."

"But you have . . . you do."

"Good. Then let me please you more." Parting her, he eased a finger inside and began to stroke.

She arched, inadvertently driving him even farther inside. Her body responded, sending down a rush of wetness that made his caresses that much easier, that much more inviting. As he'd asked, she let her eyelids flutter closed, her head rolling against the sheets, while need coiled hot as a brand through her belly and between her legs. Unable to govern her reaction, her breath came in fast, little pants, her legs parting as he continued his deep inner massage.

Leaning up, he caught her mouth in a slow, ravishing kiss, tangling his tongue with hers in an imitation of what he was doing to her below. She gave a muffled cry when he added another finger, filling her in a way that drove her right to the edge. A few strokes later a swirling flick of his thumb sent her hurtling over, her fingers clenching in his hair as she shook with release.

But he wasn't done, stoking her desire with deep, open-mouthed kisses that made her moan, his fingers building her need once more so that she could do nothing but yearn, held utterly in his thrall until he finally took mercy and sent her flying yet again.

Dazed and drifting, she sensed him working open his falls, her ears picking up the quiet sound of him peeling off his pantaloons and tossing them to the floor. She discovered she was right when she felt the delicious, hair-roughened slide of his naked legs against her own. His chest was covered with a mouth-watering expanse of hair as well; dark, crisp curls of which she only then took full note. But she had no time to appreciate the sight, her attention diverted by the erection he'd revealed to her curious gaze.

Her eyes widened, her throat growing dry, as she realized how large he was—even bigger than she had imagined, his arousal jutting out at a thick, insistent angle. His flesh twitched as if it craved her attention, but she had no chance to overcome her inhibitions and touch him before he loomed up and over her.

Spreading her legs farther apart, he fit his long body in between, his hips touching hers, his erection brushing across her belly. Holding most of his weight on his arms, he reached down to position himself against her, then slowly pushed himself inside.

She met his gaze, his eyes glittering with undisguised hunger, a warm flush staining the crest of his cheeks as though he'd been holding himself back until now. And she realized that he had, taking care to see to her pleasure before seeking his own. Curving her arms around his shoulders, she forced herself to relax and allow his intrusion, his shaft stretching her to the point of discomfort.

He kissed her while he thrust gently, soothing her with his lips and tongue as he worked to join their bodies. Each push brought him deeper inside, until with one last, firm thrust, he took full possession. She cried out against a stab of pain, the sound caught inside his mouth as he apologized with tender kisses and calming caresses.

Smoothing her hair away from her face, he skimmed his lips over her cheeks and temple. "I'm sorry," he said, unsatisfied desire, mingled with compassion, turning his voice into little more than a rasp. "It can't be helped this first time. Stay still for a moment and the pain will ease."

And he was right, she discovered, her inner muscles adjusting to his invasion in a surprisingly short time, especially after he used a hand to coax her to wrap her legs around his waist.

The movement drove him deeper, his jaw flexing with barely repressed need. Suddenly, his restraint broke and he drew partially out of her body, only to come surging back seconds later. Slanting his mouth over hers, he kissed her with a dark rapacious hunger, tangling his tongue with hers as he pumped faster and harder, each new thrust taking him deeper, his every touch a catalyst designed to spark her desire.

And spark her hunger he did, passion claiming

her with the force of a storm. Need ripped through her in a rough, sultry wave that made her writhe and shake in its grip. Catching Cade's rhythm, she tried to match his sensuous moves with her own, arching up to meet him as he drove himself at a relentless pace.

Reaching between them, he stroked her with his fingers—first her breasts, then lower down where she ached with an intensity that made her want to weep. Inflamed and yearning everywhere he touched, she feared she might expire if she didn't find relief soon, his name a prayer on her lips. And then, just when she thought she could take no more, he thrust harder and deeper inside, his hand angling her hips to take all of him and more.

She flew apart then, senses spinning out of control as ecstasy crashed over and through her in a blissful torrent. She wailed out her pleasure, Cade smothering the sound with his lips as she clung to him like a lifeline. Quivering and quaking, she sailed on a rapturous haze, her mind all but ceasing to function beneath the delicious aftermath.

Coming back to herself, she realized that he was still stroking inside her, thrusting in a kind of mindless frenzy as he sought his own satisfaction. Breaking their kiss, Cade buried his face in her neck, breath sighing from his lips in ragged draughts as he plunged in and out.

Abruptly, he stilled, his whole body shaking as he poured himself inside her in violent, shuddering spurts, one fist curled into the sheets next to her head as he claimed his release. He collapsed against her then, his cheek pressed to hers with an intimacy she found shattering. Stroking his hair, she kissed his damp temple, in that moment loving him all the more.

After a time, he levered himself away and rolled onto his back, taking care to position her so she would not be lying against his injured leg. Tugging her across his chest, he cradled her close, then fell asleep almost instantly.

A minute later, with his comforting scent in her nose and his warmth surrounding her like a blanket, she closed her eyes and did the same.

Chapter 16

Gentle sunlight was filtering through the curtains when Meg awakened early the next morning. Stretching out a hand, she searched for Cade, but instead of warm male flesh, she found only an expanse of cool, linen sheet. Her eyes popped fully open to stare at the empty space where he had lain, a faint dent visible on her spare pillow.

Swallowing down her disappointment, she called herself a simpleton for having expected, even in passing, that he might still be here with her. Of course he'd needed to leave, she realized, well aware that the servants rose at daybreak to begin their daily tasks, yawning sleepy good-mornings to each other as they roamed the house like a small army of industrious ants. Letting the servants catch her and Cade together would be highly unwise—even a staff as circumspect as the Duke of Clybourne's. Obviously, Cade wanted to protect her reputation, and for that she should be grateful.

Whatever time he left, it was clear he'd taken care not to wake her. Then again, she'd been slumbering so deeply she probably wouldn't have heard him even if he had stomped around and clapped his hands. As it was, she'd barely gotten more than a couple hours rest all night.

Lord, he wore me out, she thought. But deliciously so.

Warmth stole into her cheeks as she remembered the night just past and the way Cade had made love to her. She'd fleetingly considered such matters before, wondering vaguely what it might be like to lie with a man. But nothing had prepared her for the reality, nor for the pleasure—the intense, bone-deep rapture that even now seemed to resonate in her body and blood.

She supposed she ought to regret the loss of her virginity, but she could not. How could she, when she had given herself to the man she loved? And love him she did, the knowledge shining inside her with the brilliance of a star.

But what of Cade?

A little frown settled between her brows at the thought.

He'd said nothing to her last night, had spoken no words of devotion, made no promises to turn their engagement from a game of pretend into the truth.

But he will, she assured herself. He just hadn't had time to declare himself. *When we see each other next, he'll draw me aside somewhere private, take me in his arms, and confess his love.*

But what if he didn't? What if he couldn't because he was still in love with a dead woman? She knew he'd suffered watching Calida die, and grieved deeply over her loss. Was it too soon to think he might be able to move forward? That he might be able to love again?

Love me?

What if last night had been nothing more than a physical release for him, with none of the emotional attachment? Having grown up surrounded by naval officers and sailors, she wasn't so naive that she didn't realize how men could be. That they were entirely capable of seeking pleasure with a woman without the necessity of love. Had last night been no more than an impulse for Cade? Had he lain with her but was even now regretting it?

Refusing to let herself consider such a possibility, she tossed back the covers and started to swing her legs out of bed. But the smear of blood between her thighs made her pause, that and the fact that she was stark naked. Suddenly she felt vulnerable, unused to sleeping without clothing.

As for the blood, she couldn't very well strip the sheets and replace them herself. Hopefully her maid would assume the few drops on the sheets were from her monthly rather than from the loss of her virginity during a night of torrid passion.

Seeing her nightgown and robe lying neatly at the foot of the bed, she realized that Cade must have put them there for her before departing. Thankful, she reached for the garments, then rose to pad across to the bathing chamber.

Several minutes later she returned to the bedroom, refreshed after a sponge bath. Clad once again in her nightgown and robe, she was contemplating whether to crawl back into bed for another hour's sleep when something winked at her from beneath a chair. Curious, she crossed and bent to retrieve the tiny object.

It was a gold button, she realized, as she studied the small metallic circle in her outstretched palm—Cade's gold button, torn off his waistcoat last night. A memory came to her of more than one sailing free as he stripped off his clothes, flashes of the way he looked naked turning her warm all over again.

A search of the carpet, however, revealed nothing further. Perhaps he'd found the other button and taken it with him. Gazing at the bit of gold, she studied the pineapple design embossed into its surface, rubbing her thumb over the faint ridges. She supposed she should give it back to him, but instead moved to her dressing table and laid it down next to the drawing propped there.

The picture was the one his little sister, Esme, had done of her and Cade all those weeks ago. When she originally set the sketch there, she'd told herself it was because it was a gift from a very delightful girl with a great deal of native talent. But she knew better now, knew she'd displayed it because the drawing contained a likeness of Cade. Running her finger in a gentle stroke over the paper, she closed her eyes and let herself dream.

Cade rose early and rang for Knox, wanting to dress and be out of the house before everyone else was awake and insisting he join them for breakfast.

But even after the servant had come and gone, and Cade stood carefully groomed and attired in fawn pantaloons and a dark blue coat, he didn't leave, guilt chaffing him like an angry rash.

God, what a cad I am, he thought, sinking down into a nearby chair. He had completely lost his head last night. One touch, a kiss, and every ounce of caution, reason, and yes, honor, had flown straight up the chimney stack like so much ash.

He supposed he had the excuse of remaining celibate far too long, since he'd never gotten around to visiting one of the city's brothels and availing himself of a convenient lightskirt or two.

Perhaps if he had, he might have possessed the strength to resist Meg's bewitching spell last eve. Then again, considering the depth of his hunger for her, he rather doubted anything could have stopped him, except Meg herself.

He remembered how he'd tried to convince her to send him away, practically begging her to deny him. Instead she'd welcomed him into her arms, and then her bed and her body.

Another man might have set at least a portion of the blame on Meg's doorstep, but he knew the fault was not hers. No, as she so amply proved with the loss of her virginity, she'd been an innocent, unaware of the implications or the consequences of her actions. He'd been the experienced partner, and as such, responsible for what passed between them. If he were any sort of gentleman, he would go to her now and offer her marriage in truth rather than their current sham engagement.

Confound it, though, he cursed, disarranging the hair he'd so carefully brushed only minutes ago by raking his fingers through it. He no more wished to be married now than he had when he left Northumberland! In that regard, nothing had changed. Calida's memory still haunted him, as did the circumstances of her death. Although he supposed lately he spent a great deal more time thinking about Meg than he did the sweet, happy girl he had once loved and promised to marry.

Calida hadn't been dead a year. What kind of

man was he to forget her so soon? What kind of fickle creature was he to mourn one woman yet be avidly lusting after another? Apparently, the kind who compromises trusting young virgins living under his protection, he berated himself, as a double-edged stab of guilt twisted in his gut.

But Calida was dead and he could do nothing for her. As for Meg . . . well, she deserved far better than he was capable of offering. She deserved a man who could love her with his whole heart, not some battle-scarred ex-soldier who was rumored to be mad. One who had relied on alcohol and reclusiveness to blot out his physical pain and dull his unhappiness.

How easy it would be for him to sink back into that life. From day to day he worried that he might. Whenever his leg ached, the temptation returned. Whenever the nightmares came, he found himself reaching for a drink. But he didn't, because of Meg. *Yet, even sober, look what I've done.*

He'd taken her innocence, but that didn't mean he had to destroy her life.

Of course, he might have done that already, since many men would balk at the prospect of marrying a girl who was no longer a virgin. Then again, none of her prospective suitors would know unless she told them, and any man who truly loved her would surely forgive. A man like Lieutenant McCabe perhaps, he thought, squeezing his hands into fists. McCabe would be good to her. He would be kind. Frankly, he didn't understand why Meg hadn't brought McCabe up to scratch by now, since anyone could see the fellow adored her.

Cade shot to his feet and stalked to the window. Staring out blindly, he fought the sudden fury churning in his blood, half crazed by the idea of some other man lying with Meg, claiming her body and making her his own. Closing his eyes, he laid his forehead against the glass. *I am not for her. As much as I crave her, I will bring her nothing but sorrow.*

And if the lieutenant, or some other man, refused to take her? Well then, he would step up and do the right thing, whether he was wrong for her or not. If necessary, he would marry her. He would not see her ruined and shunned. But until that time came, he would leave things as they stood. He would also stay the hell away from her. *I must, for both our sakes,* he silently resolved.

Yet it wouldn't be easy. Now that he'd had her and knew how exquisite she felt moving under him, her gentle warmth clasping him tight as a glove, he knew that putting her aside would be yet another torment. *But I shall manage . . . I hope.*

With a rueful grimace, he glanced down at the rampant erection tenting the front of his pantaloons. *Christ, just the thought of her makes me randy as a goat.* If he weren't trying to stay away from her, he'd go to her room now and take her all over again.

Gazing into the stable yard, he watched the activity below, striving to regain his equilibrium. At least she'd done as he asked, and hadn't ridden out to meet Everett this morning. Impetuous girl. To think that she was trying to spy on Le Renard so she could unmask him . . . to think she would do such a brave, foolish thing—for him.

But he was the one who needed to take care of Everett. He'd set one man on his trail already, but the idiot had obviously been outwitted, since he hadn't taken note of Everett riding in the park with Meg. A huge lapse that had gotten the man sacked. Cade knew someone else, someone thoroughly reliable, who could trail a cat without the creature knowing. Now, when Lord Everett made a move, he would know. When the traitorous blackguard made a mistake, he would be there to catch him.

Another glance down confirmed that he'd regained enough control over his lust to make him presentable in company. Preferring not to encounter Meg, he went to retrieve his cane. Taking it in hand, he headed for the door and the coach waiting for him outside.

"Is Cade not coming with us?" Meg asked Mallory that evening while they stood in the foyer waiting for the others to join them.

The other girl turned as she finished drawing on her white gloves. "No, he said he had another engagement. I thought you knew."

294

"Oh, I . . . of course. It must have slipped my mind." She hid her dismay by smoothing an imaginary wrinkle from the skirt of her pale peach silk evening gown. "Ah, well, he never really enjoys the opera anyway."

Mallory chuckled. "Cade says he'd rather hear owls screech in a barn than listen to the current flock of sopranos. I, for one, cannot agree. I love the opera."

Meg sent her a teasing glance. "Do you, now? I wonder, though, if a measure of your admiration might be due to the anticipated presence of a certain gentleman. I understand Major Hargreaves plans to attend the opera tonight."

"Really?" Mallory said with supposed nonchalance. "I had no idea."

Meg caught her eye and the two of them laughed.

Before she could quiz Mallory further about the state of her relationship with the major, Edward joined them. A few moments later Ava strolled down the stairs, looking every inch the duchess in a gown of vibrant ruby satin. Crossing the marble-tiled expanse, she accepted her pelisse from a waiting footman.

"If you ladies are ready," the duke said, "I believe we should be going."

An hour later Meg sat in the Clybourne box, listening with only half an ear to the performers on stage. Despite the smile on her face, her spirits were far from buoyant. Why, she wondered again, did Cade not join us tonight? Even more, why had she seen nothing of him all day?

After ringing for her maid to help her dress that morning, she'd calmed her nervous excitement, then gone to breakfast, fully expecting to see him. But he never appeared. Over hot tea, flaky scones, and eggs, she learned that he'd called for his carriage quite early and departed for some unknown destination. It had taken all her fortitude to act as if the news came as no great surprise, nor that she felt disappointment.

The rest of the day had flown by, her schedule as full as ever. Nevertheless, a part of her continued to hope he would arrive at whatever function she might be attending. Once there, he would quietly pull her aside so they could talk.

But again he did not arrive.

He is simply busy, she assured herself as a new tenor burst into song on the stage. Perhaps he is planning to come to my room again tonight, so we can talk then. Pleasurable tingles skimmed over her skin at the idea, her smile turning dreamy.

When the interval arrived, she and the others left their box to mingle with friends and acquaintances in the candlelit corridor. As predicted, Major Hargreaves appeared at Mallory's side, the girl making no effort to conceal her delight at being in his company. The duke was drawn off to talk politics with a pair of serious-minded older gentlemen, while Ava turned away to chat with a group of friends she had apparently known since girlhood.

Sipping from a small glass of cordial, Meg discovered herself momentarily alone in spite of the heavy crowd. A faint touch at her elbow drew her glance, her eyes widening at the sight of the tall man with gleaming blond hair and a dazzling white smile standing at her side. Her heart gave a leap, but not in a pleasant way.

"Miss Amberley, what good fortune to find you here," Lord Everett said, making a gracious bow. "When I espied you across the room, I could not help but come say hello."

"Oh, why yes, hello, my lord. I . . . did not realize you would be here this evening."

"If I am not mistaken, half the ton is here tonight. I must say I am relieved to find you one of their number."

She glanced down at her slippered feet, striving to keep her voice steady. "Oh, how so?"

"I was in the park this morning. When you failed to arrive for your ride, I wondered if you might be unwell."

Drawing a bracing inhale, she forced herself to meet his gaze. "I am quite well. I merely overslept this morning, that is all."

"Ah." He smiled again and leaned an inch closer, lowering his voice. "Then I shall look forward to crossing paths with you on the morrow, I trust."

The liquor in her glass swirled upward along the sides but luckily did not spill. *What to tell him?*

The truth seemed best, she decided, or at least what needed to pass for the truth. "Actually I . . . I shan't be there. My riding days are done, I fear."

He raised a curious brow. "Why? What has occurred?"

"My fiancé." She sighed, as though the admission pained her. After all the careful groundwork she had laid, there seemed no reason to scuttle her entire plan. She'd promised Cade to stay away from Everett, and she would. But that didn't mean she couldn't leave enough subterfuge in place to take advantage of a slip on Everett's part should he make one in the future.

She swept her lashes downward. "Lord Cade learned of our meetings and does not approve."

"I am sure he does not," Everett replied with an unmistakable hint of sarcasm.

"So you see, my lord, why it is now impossible for us to meet each other again. I do hope you understand. In fact, I probably ought not to be conversing with you now in the sight of so many others."

"But, of course, dear lady. Pray distress yourself no further. I shall take my leave."

"Thank you, my lord. You are very good." She added a shy smile to cover her true opinion of his character, feeling a fraud herself for her own deceit.

He bowed. "And should we happen upon one another again, I promise to exercise better discretion."

A shiver moved over Meg's spine like the touch of a ghostly hand. What does he mean by that? she mused.

With the faintest of nods, she watched him disappear back into the crowd. Exhaling, she raised the cordial to her lips and downed the contents in two quick swallows, the liquor spreading through her stomach with a calming warmth. She relaxed further when she scanned the throng and saw that all three of the Byrons were apparently still immersed in their own conversations and seemed not to have noticed hers.

A moment later, though, a new gentleman appeared at her elbow. To her relief, she saw it was Lord Gresham. This time when she smiled, the reaction was genuine. "My lord," she began. "How do you do?"

He cast her an appraising look. "Forgive the question, Miss Amberley, but might I ask the same of you? Are you entirely well? You look a bit pale."

"Oh, I . . . it is nothing. And I am very well."

Gresham frowned and glanced out over the crowd. "I could not help but notice you conversing with Lord Everett a few moments ago. Did he say something to trouble you?"

"No. We . . . um . . . were merely discussing the singers and the Society in attendance tonight."

Gresham paused before seeming to accept her answer. "It is not my place to offer advice, but you may want to exercise caution in your dealings with that particular gentleman. I do not believe Lord Cade would be pleased to see you together."

"No, he would not," she confessed. "And I hope you won't find it necessary to apprise him of the encounter. I assure you it is not an acquaintance I wish to pursue." And she realized she did not, suddenly glad that Cade had demanded she steer clear of Everett. The man was like a cobra— graceful but deadly, and best left alone.

Gresham nodded, apparently satisfied by her response. "Of course, since there is nothing to tell. Where is his lordship tonight, by the way?"

She paused, wishing she knew the answer. "Cade could not attend. He . . . um . . . he . . ."

"Couldn't stand the thought of listening to opera?"

A laugh escaped her. "Exactly. You have caught him out."

"Well, please send him my regards. Matters of a personal nature take me to my estate. I leave tomorrow."

"Oh, we shall all be sorry to see you go. Safe travels, my lord."

"Thank you. Until we meet again, Miss Amberley." He bowed over her hand. As he straightened, his gaze moved briefly to Mallory, who stood in rapt conversation with Major Hargreaves. Then he looked away.

With a smile, he turned and was gone.

As Meg handed her empty glass to a passing footman, a small chime was rung to alert everyone that the interval was over. Ava, Edward, and Mallory joined her, and together they made their way back to their box.

Hours later Meg lay in bed, a single candle burning on her night table. Curled on her side beneath the covers, she waited for Cade, hoping to hear the click of the hidden panel open in the wall, wishing for the pleasure of him sliding beneath the sheets with her.

But as the hours advanced and the candle turned into a mass of drips, she remained alone. With eyelids growing heavy, weariness finally overpowered her. Murmuring Cade's name, she fell into a restless sleep.

Chapter 17

"Are you certain you do not wish to come with us?" Mallory asked three afternoons later. "Lucinda Pettigrew's garden party might be just the thing to chase away your headache. The day is so lovely, surely all that fresh air and sunshine would do you good."

Meg glanced up from where she sat on the drawing room sofa and mustered a smile. "You are such a dear to ask. But really, I would much rather stay here with my stitchery and be quiet. I may even take a nap." After the last few days, she mused, I need a nap. Anything to escape my doldrums. "Do go on and don't worry about me. I shall be perfectly content here alone for a few hours."

A frown moved over Mallory's pretty dark brows. "Mayhap I should send a footman 'round to find Cade. I am sure he would want to be here with you, if he knew you were not feeling well."

I wouldn't be so sure of that, Meg thought, considering how little she'd seen of Cade lately. Since their night together—which felt like an eon ago, though it had only been four days—he'd put in as few appearances as necessary.

As duty required, he arrived each evening to escort her and Mallory to whatever function they had promised to attend. Once there, he would disappear into the card room while she was left to dance and mingle. During the day, he was always otherwise engaged, busy with his brothers and cronies, or immersed in matters concerning his estate. On the surface, nothing had changed, since their social schedules had always been extraordinarily full. And yet, in her heart, she knew things were not the same. Cade was avoiding her.

At first she'd given him the benefit of the doubt, but even with the frenzied pace of their lives, she knew he could have found time to speak with her had he wished. He certainly could have come to her bedchamber again, but each night passed without him, leaving her to awaken alone.

Not that I wish him to visit, she told herself. *Not anymore!*

Heavy lines formed across her forehead, a twinge of real pain arrowing through her scalp. "It's only a touch of the headache," she said. "Nothing over which to be alarmed, and certainly not worth dragging Cade away from his activities. Speaking of which, you're going to be late for your own activity if you do not depart. Enjoy yourself and promise you will not fret about me."

Mallory cast her one last look of concern before her expression cleared. "Very well, if you insist. And I shall bring you a slice of cake. I hear the Pettigrew's pastry chef makes the most divine confections."

Meg smiled. "I shall look forward to your return."

After Mallory and Ava departed, the house grew quiet, the duke having left directly after breakfast and Cade even earlier than that. Taking up her embroidery, she selected a length of green silk thread and applied it to her needle.

Sewing with a calm she wished she truly felt, she watched as a leaf slowly began to take shape on the cloth. She was beginning a second one when a faint tap sounded at the door.

"Your pardon, miss," Croft announced from the threshold, "but Lieutenant McCabe is here and wishes to see you. Shall I show him in?"

"Yes, please do."

Once the butler had withdrawn, Meg laid her embroidery inside her sewing basket, then stood and smoothed the skirt of her gown. A few moments later the lieutenant strode into the room, bringing with him an elusive hint of the sea, even though he couldn't possibly have been anywhere near the water.

"Miss Amberley," he said, losing no time as he crossed to bow over her hand. "I beg your pardon for the intrusion, since I understand you are unwell, but I had to come. I trust you are not too indisposed to receive me."

"No, not at all. It is only a headache, and not so very bad a one at that. Will you have a seat?"

"I thank you, but no." He paced a few steps, agitated in a way she had not seen him before. "I have only a limited amount of time at my disposal, which is why I could not wait until later to call." He stopped and turned to face her, meeting her gaze. "I received news only this morning that I have been recalled. My ship is being put into service immediately and I must report to Portsmouth without delay. I ship out within the week."

Instinctively, she moved toward him. "Oh, what untoward news. I suppose it is only to be expected, though, considering the state of the war. I bid you a safe journey and an even safer voyage. I want you to know that I have grown to appreciate our acquaintance and am very sorry to see you go."

Again his gaze caught and lingered on hers. "I shall be sorry as well. These past weeks have been some of the most cherished of my life, your friendship more valuable to me than I can express."

"And yours to me."

He glanced away for a moment as though caught in some silent struggle, then reached for her hand. "Forgive me, Miss Amberley," he said, clasping her palm inside his own. "I know I have no right to speak. In fact, some might brand me as a scoundrel for doing so, but I can be silent no longer. I must tell you of my deep regard for you. Of my love."

She stiffened. "Lieutenant!"

"I know you are already promised. I know it is wrong for me to say these things when you are to be another man's wife, but I could not leave without telling you, without making some attempt to make you mine. If my feelings are unwelcome, you have only to tell me now and I shall never trouble you with them again. But if I might somehow hope? If I might convince you to come away with me, I would marry you as soon as you would allow. Miss Amberley . . . Meg . . . I love you. Please say you feel the same and that you will make me the happiest of men by becoming my wife."

Her pulse thudded in a painful beat. Of all the things she had imagined he might say, she'd never expected this. Some time ago she had toyed with the possibility of winning a proposal from him, but never seriously entertained the idea, never dreamt she might truly be able to engage his affections—certainly not without really trying.

Yet here he stood, an agony of love and longing visible on his earnest face, along with a hope he could not hide. Guilt wrapped around her heart like a mighty fist, squeezing until she thought she might actually faint. But she was not so lucky, the seconds ticking past while he waited for her response.

He wants to marry me, she marveled. All I need do is say yes and I can be free of Cade, just as he obviously still wishes.

If the last few days had proven anything to her, it was that Cade had no more desire than ever for their engagement to be real. Put in that doleful light, it seemed she would be a fool to refuse the lieutenant.

Yet what of her virginity? Or rather, the lack thereof, now that Cade had ruined her in truth? To her further shame, she suspected the lieutenant would not object. He would likely be quietly angry, even hurt, but in the end she sensed he would forgive her. But what of her? How could she accept him under such circumstances? How could she not?

For a long moment she stared into his kind, forthright eyes. Tell him yes! she thought. Do the sensible thing and accept.

She opened her mouth, unsure until the last second what she might say. "I hold you in great esteem and affection, Lieutenant. However, my feelings go no deeper than friendship. My heart and love belong to Lord Cade. I am sorry if I have done anything to lead you to think otherwise. Please forgive me, since it was never my intention to cause you distress."

He released her hand, silent as he gathered his composure. "No, forgive me," he said in a thick voice. "I should not have presumed nor spoken of my feelings. Please do me the great favor of forgetting this conversation ever occurred."

"Lieutenant—"

He gave a clipped bow. "There is much to be done before my departure, so I must take my leave of you now. I wish you good fortune in your forthcoming marriage. May you be blessed with health and happiness all the days of your life."

Her throat grew tight. "I wish the same for you. Stay safe and do not take foolish chances."

His mouth turned up in a sad smile. "Good-bye, Miss Amberley."

"Good-bye." She watched him stride out the door, knowing she would probably never see him again. She knew also that she had likely just tossed away her last, best hope of ever being wed. But how could she have done otherwise when she loved another man?

Cade walked into the town house enjoying the sense of hushed tranquility inside as he exchanged a quiet greeting with one of the footmen. He'd returned home early, knowing he would have the house to himself for a few brief hours. This morning Edward had told him he was going to Kew to consult with an agricultural expert about a new variety of oats he was thinking about introducing on the Clybourne lands, while Mama had mentioned that she and "the girls" were engaged to attend an alfresco party.

Moving toward the stairs, he debated whether to read one of the new books he'd purchased yesterday at Hatchard's in the library or outside in the garden. Just then a forceful thudding of boots resounded across the landing above. Glancing up, his eyes widened as he watched Lieutenant McCabe hurry down the stairs, the other man pausing only long enough to offer a polite hello before striding out through the front door.

Cade pinned the butler with a look once the lieutenant was gone. "Is the family at home, after all, then?"

Croft met his gaze with an inscrutable expression. "No, my lord. Only Miss Amberley. When last I saw her, she was in the drawing room."

Turning on his heel, Cade took the stairs as fast as his gait would allow. Stomping down the hallway, he made straight for the drawing room, closing the door behind him so the conversation he intended to have with her would remain private. For a second he thought the room was empty, but then he saw her, standing at the window, staring out.

Having obviously heard his entrance, she glanced in his direction. "Cade. What are you doing home?"

He crossed the soft wool carpet. "I might ask the same of you, madam. Are you not supposed to be at a party this afternoon?"

She shrugged. "I felt unwell and decided not to attend."

"Unwell or were you awaiting a visitor? What did McCabe want?"

Her back stiffened. Slowly she turned to face him. "The lieutenant stopped by to inform me that his ship has been returned to service and he with it. He has orders to set sail within the week."

Cade tapped his fingers against his good leg, a sense of relief he had no right to feel moving through him. "Came to say good-bye, did he?"

"Yes. He also asked me to marry him."

His relief shattered like so much glass. For a long moment he could not speak. "And what did you answer?" His gut gave a sharp squeeze, tight as the fist now clenched against his thigh.

She glanced away. "If I had any sense, I would have said yes."

For a second he didn't understand. "Would have? So you did not?"

She met his gaze, her silvery blue eyes brimming with barely suppressed emotion. "No. Now, as I mentioned, I am not feeling well. I am going to my room."

She turned to brush past him, but he caught her by the arm. "Meg, why did you refuse him?"

"That, my lord, is my own concern and none of yours. Pray, release me."

"He would have been an excellent choice. I always thought you liked him."

"I did. I do. But why do you care? Or are you worried I plan to force a commitment from you? Do not be concerned, my lord. You are entirely free. I have no intention of coercing a man who does not want me. Who obviously cannot even bear to have me in his bed."

Hunger flared to life at the reminder of their night together, his other hand coming up to hold her secure. "Is that what you think? That I do not *want* you?"

Her lashes lowered in a downward sweep. "I no longer know what to think."

Pulling her close, he pressed himself against her so she had no choice but to feel the rigid length of his arousal. A small gasp escaped her parted lips, her eyes darting to his.

"As you can tell," he said on a low growl, "desire is not the problem. In fact, it's been killing me trying to stay away from you these past few days. I've done my best, but you seem to have a gift for making me forget all my good intentions."

Bending his head, he took her lips in a kiss that

was ravenous and unyielding. With a demanding sweep of his tongue, he plunged into the lush, wet warmth of her mouth, drawing upon her with a sweet suction that made his brain buzz and his hunger spike to feverish heights. Sliding his hands low, he cupped her buttocks and fit her closer, bumping against her in a way that left no doubt as to his needs.

He knew he should set her away, but just as before, he could not, more powerfully intoxicated by her than he'd ever been on liquor or laudanum, even on his most inebriated days. Remembering the satiny slide of her skin and the brazen pleasure of her small, untutored hands moving on him, he craved more, consumed by the need to touch her bare flesh and sheath himself inside her body once again.

Moving with unerring skill, he went to work on the buttons at the back of her gown, opening them one by one by one. He half groaned, half growled at the delay when he parted the sides of her dress to encounter her stays beneath. Forcing himself to go slowly so he didn't tangle the laces, he loosened each eyelet in turn until the material sagged around her slender frame. Sliding a palm under her chemise, he stroked her naked skin, deepening their kiss with a yearning that was dark and raw and devastating.

Meg shivered, her body engulfed in fire as he played his palms over her spine and back, his kisses leading her toward a rapture from which she knew there could be no return. What little remained of her thinking brain warned her to push him away, to rebuff him as he lately had been rebuffing her. Yet even at further risk to her heart and the complete abasement of her pride, she could not bring herself to deny him, or herself.

I love him, she thought, for good or ill. For always.

Senses sizzling, she gave herself into his keeping, oblivious to everything but the majesty of his touch. A quiver of intense longing pierced her as he arched her over his arm and shoved her bodice down, breaking their kiss to take the tip of one of her breasts in his mouth.

Her eyes slid closed at the enervating pleasure, a low moan keening in her throat. She tried to raise her hands, wanting to cradle his head and sift her fingers through his dark, silky hair, but her sleeves imprisoned her arms at her sides. As if he sensed her dilemma and secretly delighted in it, he tightened his hold. Angling her just so, he raked her with his teeth, then soothed her with his tongue, pausing on occasion to blow a cool stream of air across her nipples that made her tense and twist in his grasp.

An insistent yearning ached between her thighs, begging to be appeased. Yet she refused to be held completely at his mercy. Acting on blind instinct, she moved her hand in search of whatever flesh she could find. The hard width of his muscular thigh came to her first, flexing beneath her wandering fingers as he moaned against her breast. But she wasn't done. Roaming sideways, she located his shaft, pausing to explore its shape and size as the rampant flesh strained hot and hard against the fabric of his pantaloons. He jerked against her hand as she cupped him, his mouth drawing harder against her breast.

Then suddenly she was being danced backward; one foot, two feet, three, until she was tumbled down onto a waiting chaise. She bounced against the goose down cushions, the short fall driving a bit of the air from her lungs. Cade drove out the rest seconds later, leaving her gasping as he tossed up her skirts and spread her legs wide.

She expected him to take her. Instead he lowered himself to his knees, apparently unhindered by his wounded thigh, and buried his face between her legs. She squirmed as he kissed her where she had never thought a person could be kissed, bucking her hips to be free as his marauding tongue licked and stroked. Reaching up, he caged her hips inside his hands and held her still, compelling her to accept this most intimate of caresses.

With a gliding lick he swirled his tongue around a bit of flesh so sensitive she feared she wouldn't be able to endure the sensations. The fight went out of her, the pleasure exquisitely, painfully, intense. Helpless, she could only do as Cade and her body commanded, each demanding more in their turn. Angling forward, she pressed herself toward him rather than away, a move in which he seemed to delight as he increased his ministrations. What should have been an embarrassing flood of moisture poured from her womanly core. But again he seemed to approve, lapping at her with an appreciative enjoyment that reminded her of the time she'd watched him eat a sweet, fancy ice at a party. Apparently, she was the dessert this time.

Rolling her head, she buried her face against a throw pillow and let him build her pleasure even higher. Then suddenly, just when she thought she couldn't stand another moment, he did something with his teeth and tongue that made her scream. She shook, the sound gratefully muffled against the mass of feathers and silk.

Before she had any chance to recover, he lifted his head and dragged her ruthlessly forward so her bottom was balanced on the edge of the chaise. Only dimly aware of his movements, she watched in a daze as he unfastened his falls with impatient hands, shoving the cloth aside to free his eager shaft. Then he was plunging into her, seating himself to the hilt with a pair of solid, forceful thrusts.

This time there was no pain, only a wonderful sense of fullness, a tantalizing stretching that made her want more. Sliding his palms under her legs and bottom, he held her wide for his penetration, pumping into her with long, steady strokes, punctuated by shallower ones that turned her wild. Leaning up, she curled a hand behind his head and bent him down for a rapacious kiss whose fierceness surprised even her. Taking her mouth with an almost savage hunger, he thrust harder, pushing even deeper inside her.

She came on a stunning, shuddering peak, ecstasy filling her in a glorious surge that was shining and shimmering and bright. She rode the wave while Cade claimed his own release, his fists clenched into the cushions on both sides of her head as he shook.

They lay there panting and replete in the aftermath, their flesh still joined as he dropped gentle, lingering kisses on her mouth, cheeks, and temples. Skimming back her tousled hair, Cade buried his lips against her neck and breathed in the honeyed fragrance of her skin. He smiled and nuzzled her, not ready yet for them to part.

In fact, he was already half hard again just thinking about how much she had pleased him. With very little effort, he knew he could easily take her again. Sliding his palms over her thighs, he was toying with the idea of encouraging her to hook her ankles over his shoulders this time when he heard a faint sound. Voices in the hallway. Familiar, feminine voices that were moving slowly his way.

"Christ!" he cursed, springing to his feet in a move that caused a jolt of pain to spear through his leg. Ignoring the discomfort, he yanked his pantaloons into place and fastened a pair of buttons, then pulled Meg up and after him. Her eyes were wide as she clutched her loosened dress and stays to her chest in a desperate attempt to keep herself at least partly clothed. Hurrying her forward, he pulled her across to the far wall.

"Cade, what are you doing?" she whispered.

"Saving us both a great deal of embarrassment."

Tapping a fist hard against a spot just above the gleaming blue chair rail that ran the length of the room, he hoped he was in time. A hidden panel in the wall creaked open and he dragged Meg through. He sealed it behind them only seconds before the main door to the drawing room was pushed wide, the voices of his mother and sister becoming audible as they entered the room.

". . . and that's when Daphne Throckly told me not to eat the oysters," said Mallory, her voice muffled as it passed through the wall.

Swathed in an almost stygian darkness, Cade held Meg inside his arms, his back braced against the unfinished wood that lined the passageway. With one small fist curled into the fabric of her sagging bodice, she leaned her head against his shoulder.

"Well, I am only relieved neither of us consumed any of the shellfish," the dowager remarked from the other side of the panel. "Poor Lucinda Pettigrew will have a dreadful time living this down. I'm sure the dear woman had no idea her oysters had gone off. In all my years, I cannot recall ever seeing quite so many people become ill at the same time."

"It was a remarkable sight," Mallory agreed with a tinge of horrified amazement. "I was going to tell Meg how glad she should be that she stayed home, but she isn't here. Obviously Croft was mistaken in thinking she was still in the drawing room. Mayhap she has retired to her room to rest because of her headache. Should I check on her, do you think?"

Meg stiffened in his hold and made a small sound. Stroking a reassuring palm over her back, he pressed a kiss to her temple to urge her silence. She settled her forehead against his cravat and quieted.

"If she took to her bed, she must be sleeping," Ava said. "If she's anything like your grandmother when she had one of her megrims, I expect you would do well not to wake her for a while yet."

Mallory paused. "Yes, you're right, of course. Truth be told, I could do with a nap myself."

"And I wouldn't mind a warm bath."

Moments later the room grew quiet as the pair departed. Cade stood with Meg, neither speaking as they waited to make certain they were alone again.

"What shall I do if Mallory changes her mind and decides to check on me, after all?" she whispered.

317

"Tell her you went outside to read and didn't hear her and Mama arrive home."

She paused for a moment in consideration. "That might work, I guess. I suppose you have a lot of experience at this sort of thing."

"At what?" he inquired, humor in his voice. "Hiding in the passageways after a bout of passionate lovemaking?"

"Yes."

"No. At least never here at home." Before she had a chance to question him further, he bent to claim her mouth, locating her sweet lips with unerring precision despite the darkness. Long, long moments later he raised his head and traced his hands over the lithe curve of her back, caressing a length of bare skin with his fingertips. "I suppose I ought to help you dress."

"I suppose you ought," she agreed. "Do you think it's safe for us to go back into the drawing room?"

"I wouldn't, not until we're both more suitably attired. I believe I can manage by touch alone."

Meg stood quiescent as he adjusted her stays and tightened the laces, feeling the gentle shiver that ran through her as he fastened her back into her clothes. Once finished, he released her to retuck his shirt and check to make sure his falls were buttoned the right way.

"Could we go out through the passageway? Where does this one lead?" she inquired.

"To a guest bedroom, so I don't think that's such a good idea, not with the two of us together. Stay here. I'll go first."

Listening again, he waited a moment more before popping open the false doorway. Stepping through, he glanced around before signaling for Meg. "It's clear."

She emerged, blinking against the afternoon light. "How do I look?" she asked as she walked forward.

Thoroughly ravished, he thought, her eyes extremely blue in her flushed face, her lips swollen and rouged with color. "Beautiful," he said with complete sincerity. Reaching out, he smoothed a few escaped tendrils of pale hair. "Hurry on to your room and no one will ever know you weren't there this entire time."

"All right."

But instead of leaving, she hesitated, looking a little lost of a sudden. A glance at the doorway showed it was empty. Stepping close, he gathered her to him for a quick, hard kiss. "Go on," he commanded. "I'll see you later."

Eyes shining an even brighter blue, she nodded. Whirling, she raced from the room. A long minute passed before he followed.

Chapter 18

$\mathscr{I}$f there's naught else, miss, I'll be off to bed now."

"Oh, yes, do go on. Good night and sleep well," Meg told her maid. Having received permission to retire, the young woman dipped her knees in a respectful curtsey and departed.

Meg crossed to her bed, took off the ecru silk robe that matched her nightgown, then climbed in. With a sigh, she relaxed against the soft sheets and plump feather pillows, then let her mind drift.

After leaving Cade that afternoon, she'd gone straight to her bedchamber, grateful not to encounter Mallory or the dowager along the way. Once inside the room, she'd taken the pins from her hair, stripped off her gown, and lay down on the bed in her stays and chemise, her body still aglow from the intense pleasure of Cade's lovemaking. She'd closed her eyes with thoughts and emotions ebbing through her like an unrelenting tide.

To her great surprise, she'd awakened more than two hours later to a soft tapping at the door. Mallory slipped inside a moment later to check on her and share news of the garden party, the details of which Meg was compelled to pretend she knew nothing about. Her friend also wanted to know if she felt well enough to attend the musical evening for which they were promised.

Briefly she had considered the idea of saying no and remaining home, but decided she needed company more than solitude. She also wanted to see Cade and make certain she could be in the same room with him and not turn the color of a boiled beet, as memories of their torrid afternoon together flickered through her mind. He'd made love to her once before, but not like today.

Somehow she'd muddled through—no one appearing to notice anything untoward, despite the looks that must surely have passed between her and Cade when he arrived to escort all of them out for the evening. Then again, to his family and the rest of the world, they were an engaged couple, so a few warm, lingering looks were only to be expected.

The evening had passed at a slow drip, her earlier malady giving her the perfect excuse for a few moments of inattentiveness here and there. Then finally it was time to come home, Cade large and silent where he sat across from her in the coach. He bid her a pleasant good-night at the top of the stairs, much as he always did, then strode away in the direction of his rooms.

Now, as she lay in bed, her brows drew together at the remembrance. But this time she refused to dwell on all the permutations and possibilities of Cade's enigmatic behavior. Her heart, she decided, couldn't take the speculation. Leaning over, she blew out her bedside candle, then settled back to sleep.

She was drifting off when a creaking sound in the far wall brought her eyelids open. Light from a candle created a gentle amber glow as Cade came through the open panel. He shut it behind him, then approached the bed.

For a long moment he said nothing, shadows flickering over the hard planes of his face as he met her eyes, his tall body garbed in a heavy, black dressing gown, thin leather slippers on his feet. "I shouldn't be here," he said quietly.

"Probably not," she murmured in a velvety whisper.

"I'll go."

"If that's what you want." She lay there, refusing to invite him this time, but equally incapable of turning him away. As she watched, his gaze roved over her recumbent form, pausing to study her face before tracing the long sweep of her hair where it trailed across her pillow. Her pulse beat a thick rhythm in her throat, yet she stayed still and silent.

Seconds flowed past before he moved, taking three steps forward to set the candlestick he held on the night table. His fingers went to the tie at his waist, freeing the cloth from his body. Laying the garment aside, he revealed his lean-muscled frame, naked and unquestionably aroused.

Tossing back the covers, he joined her between the sheets, heat and hunger radiating from him like a fever. Her lips parted as he leaned over to plunder her mouth, his tongue moving inside for a moist, sultry kiss that made her toes curl and her body weep with desire. Letting her eyelids slide closed, she gave herself over to the magic of his embrace.

But he soon broke their kiss, as though he were compelled to speak, easing his fingers into her hair to cradle her head. "Meg, no matter what happens, I want you to know you're not to worry."

Worry?

"You are safe with me."

Safe? A fist squeezed inside her chest.

"I'll take care of you. I'll do what's—"

She laid her fingers over his lips to stop the last word.

Right.

He'd been about to say right. He was talking about duty. The thought made her go cold.

"Don't," she said.

"But—"

"No. I don't want any promises, not now. Not tonight." *Not ever, if they're made without love.* "Just kiss me."

"But Meg—"

"Kiss me or I'll have to make you get out of this bed. And I don't want to do that."

His fingers tensed against her cheek. "All right, but it changes nothing."

It changes everything, she thought, knowing that as long as he didn't say he did not love her, she could still go on believing there was hope.

Even if it was a fool's dream, she would think what she must, since anything else was intolerable.

He stared into her eyes, clearly warring with the need to say more. But then his expression gentled, his fingers caressing her skin as his thumb moved to graze the full curve of her lower lip in a way that made the breath catch in her lungs.

Without thinking, she slid her tongue forward and licked around the tip of his thumb, sucking against the fleshy digit for a moment before catching it between her teeth in a painless bite.

Hunger flared hot in his eyes, which glittered like a pair of emeralds, while the skin along his jaw grew taut with undisguised need. Yanking his thumb free, he cupped her face between his hands and crushed her mouth to his. She whimpered as he ravished her mouth, meeting the insistent pressure with fervid, frenzied kisses of her own. His tongue thrust and swirled, tangling against hers in languorous strokes that made her quake with longing. Her senses spun in a dizzying maelstrom, intoxicated by his every touch and temptation as he drew her deeper beneath his spell.

His hands soon left her face to glide lower, wandering over her neck and shoulders and breasts. Scattering kisses in their wake, he made her arch with pleasure, her core aching in tandem to the pulls from his lips as he paused to suckle the tips of her breasts through the silken bodice of her nightgown.

After a time he reached for the hem of her gown. "You won't be needing this," he declared on a growl before he dragged the silk up and over her head. Casting it aside, he buried his face between her bare breasts, pushing her flesh together with his hands so he could feast some more.

She reached for him as well, running her palms over what seemed like yards of hard muscle and warm skin, learning his shape and texture and which touches pleased him the most. She caressed his chest, eliciting an appreciative murmur when she paused to flick her nails over the tiny male nipples she found hidden in the whorls of hair growing there. She earned a groan as she skimmed her fingertips over the flat plane of his stomach and again as she caressed his thighs and the lean curve of his firm buttocks.

But she drew the keenest response when she grew daring enough to take his erection in her palm, a long moan of bliss pouring from his throat as she stroked the satiny hot length of his rigid shaft. She sensed his restraint as he let her explore, her caresses causing him to grow so thick and stiff inside her small fist that she could barely hold him.

Finally, when he could obviously stand no more, he snatched her hand away. But instead of parting her legs to push himself inside her, he rolled onto his back and pulled her over him.

"My leg is sore," he told her, clasping her thighs

to settle her astride his hips. "I thought you could ride me tonight."

Her eyes widened, her lips parting on a stunned breath as his wide palms raised her up, then angled her so he could thrust himself inside.

"That's right," he urged, showing her how to accept him in this new position. "Take me in. Take me deep."

And she did, obeying him implicitly, following his every demand and direction as he taught her each delicious, sinuous move. Her hair fell forward in a pale circle, framing her face and his as he leaned up to take her lips in a series of wild, rapacious kisses.

Surrendering completely, she clung as he surged up into her, driving himself impossibly deep. She moaned, her body burning like white hot ash, need enslaving her as she fell into a dazed, relentless rhythm.

When she tired, he took command, pushing her farther and faster than she imagined she could go until finally she broke on a long, tormented cry. Bliss roared through her, everything she was, given over to the ecstasy of the man and the moment. Collapsing over him, she lay drained and dreamy as he thrust into her with relentless intensity. He took his own release seconds later, his rough shout captured against a pillow.

Then they were still, lungs heaving for air, bodies relaxed and replete. Words of love rose to her lips, but she held silent, forcing herself to let the comfort of his embrace be enough. She waited in silence, wanting him to say he felt more for her than simple desire, but he stroked her hair instead, soothing her until she fell into an exhausted slumber upon him.

Cade took her again just before dawn, kissing and caressing her so she awakened fully aroused, her body slick and ready for his possession. Her eyes opened, throaty little whimpers coming from her mouth as he lodged himself inside her with one solid thrust. Her arms and legs wrapped tight as he pumped within her, pacing himself to make sure she reached her peak before he claimed his own.

After they both climaxed, he buried his face against her neck and waited for the world to right itself. Kissing her gently, he smiled when he realized she was already asleep.

Easing himself away, he lay an arm over his face and thought about the past twenty-four hours. Making love to her again had been a mistake, a temptation to which he should never have succumbed. But he had, and despite all the reasons why it was wrong, he could not make himself regret it. He'd wanted her and so he'd claimed her, craving her with a hunger he could no longer control.

As he'd tried to tell her, he planned to do what was right. He *would* marry her, if need be. And considering the number of times he'd taken her now—and selfishly planned to take her again— there very definitely might be a need. Even now she could be carrying his child, and if she was, they would wed whether she wished it or not. He would never stand aside and allow another man to raise his child. He would never let someone else claim what was his. But if their time together ended and she wasn't pregnant, well, he would leave the choice up to Meg. She'd turned down McCabe, but perhaps there was still someone else she preferred.

Then again, he wasn't sure any longer that he could watch her walk away. Just the idea of her with another man made him want to set his fist through the nearest wall. For so many reasons, she would be better off with someone else, but he wasn't certain anymore that such considerations mattered.

Still, a few last weeks of the Season remained. While they were in London, he would make no firm decisions. She'd told him tonight that a declaration on his part wasn't necessary and that she wanted no promises. For now he would make none, and expect none from her as well.

Pressing another kiss to her sleep-warmed lips, he sat up and reached for his robe. Letting the servants find them together would do her reputation no good and only serve to bind her irrevocably to him. Locating a flint, he lit what remained of the last night's candle and then, with a last look at Meg, went to the hidden panel and stepped inside.

Chapter 19

Two weeks later Cade sat in a rough tavern in an even rougher part of London, a place none of his acquaintance would ever think to visit. People who came here liked their privacy, preferring not to draw attention to either themselves or their questionable—and quite likely unlawful—activities. In keeping with his surroundings, he had taken care to dress for the occasion in his plainest, most well-worn set of clothes. He'd also found a seat in a dimly lit corner of the room where he could keep an eye on the door and also make sure his conversation was not being overheard.

Ignoring the scent of old onions, stale cigar smoke, and flat beer, he glanced across the scarred wooden table at the man who'd joined him there only moments ago. With a medium build, thinning brown hair, and unremarkable features, Thelonious Ferrick made the perfect informant since, like the tavern itself, people rarely noticed much about him.

As Cade watched, Ferrick drew his dingy white shirt cuff out from under his coat and used it to wipe the rim of his ale glass. Blowing at a sad tuft of foam, the older man took a sip of the brew that resembled dark Thames sludge more than alcohol. Cade had no difficulty resisting the urge to drink, although he'd bought what he suspected was a well-watered whiskey in order to appease the tavern owner's preference for paying customers.

"So what have you discovered?" Cade asked, pushing his glass with its set of greasy finger smudges another inch away from him.

"Nothin' much so far, milord. I've been on 'im like a terrier after a rat, but he's keepin' 'is nose clean from what I can tell. Sticks with the toffs and to his fancy digs and parties. Pretty borin' stuff—not that I'm complaining, mind ye."

"No, of course not."

Ferrick scratched his bulbous nose. "Thing is, if he's passin' the goods off to another toff at one of them high-tone parties, I can't get in ter see much of anythin'. Seems ye'd have an easier time doin' that yerself, considerin' ye've got an invite to them dances and all."

"Quite true, but Everett would never be fool enough to make contact at an entertainment at which I am also present. He's far too aware that I am watching and waiting for a chance to catch him out."

Considering Everett's arrogance, though, Cade wouldn't put it past him to try something. The man would love to slip information past him, right under his very nose, as it were. Which is why Cade had taken the extra precaution of asking Adam Gresham to keep his eyes open for any unusual action on Everett's part. Before family obligations had drawn Gresham back to his estate, he'd agreed to watch for any suspicious activity. After a while Gresham became convinced that Everett would not make a move in the open but choose instead to meet his contact at some secret location.

Cade was inclined to agree. Still, he wasn't about to underestimate Everett or his ruthless determination to gain his objectives. The man had to show his hand sometime, and when he did, Cade would be ready to expose him for the traitor he was.

"Jest as you say, yer lordship," Ferrick agreed, drinking more of the swill in his glass. "Shall I keep on 'im then?"

"Most definitely. I trust that little maid in his town house is still feeding you information?"

A crooked smile curled over Ferrick's lips. "Oh, Janey, aye. She's a right handful, with a tongue that's good for more than talkin', if ye knows what I mean. Though she does love to babble afterwards."

"Yes, well, if Everett so much as changes the color of his chamber pot, I want to know."

"Aye, and so ye will."

Cade nodded. "Send me a note by the means we agreed, should you learn anything new. Otherwise, I think it's best if we don't meet again for a while. I'm not the only one who can hire watchers."

He'd taken precautions today to make sure he hadn't been followed. Then again, even good spies could be outwitted on occasion. To his everlasting shame and misery, he had the scars to prove it.

Rising to his feet, he tossed down a coin, which he knew Ferrick would pocket. Without another word he left the tavern.

"Which one do you like best, Meg?" Mallory asked from her perch on the padded stool in front of her dressing table. "The pearl and diamond teardrop or the gold and aquamarine cross? The cross is somewhat plain, I suppose, but seems to go well with so many of my gowns. I just cannot decide."

Meg forced aside her wandering thoughts to focus on the question, a frown puckering her eyebrows as she looked between the two items in Mallory's hands. "The pearls, I believe." She frowned harder. "No, the cross. Yes, definitely the cross, since you're wearing the cream satin tonight. It will be simple and elegant without being overdone."

"Major Hargreaves likes the cross. He's complimented me over it on more than one occasion. He says it matches my eyes."

"Well, in that case, why did you even bother to ask?"

She and Mallory traded smiles before hers fell from her face.

"Is everything all right?" Mallory asked, laying the necklaces aside.

Meg forced another smile. "Yes, of course. What could be wrong?" *What indeed? If only everything could be as easy as choosing the right jewelry for a gown.* But lately nothing seemed easy, the uncertainty of her situation dragging on her like a leaden weight.

"Because if there is something you'd like to talk about, I would be more than happy to listen," Mallory added, her interest clearly genuine, and meant in the spirit of kindness and friendship.

Meg gazed at her for a long moment, sorely tempted to confide. What a relief it would be, she thought, to unburden herself, to share her secrets and concerns, her fears and worries, instead of keeping them all bottled up inside. But as much as she longed to let the words flow unchecked, she knew she couldn't, not when all her difficulties centered around Mallory's dearly loved brother Cade. She could only imagine how round Mallory's eyes would get if she told her the truth.

Cade comes to my bedroom each night and makes the most intense, passionate love to me. I know it's a terrible risk and that I should turn him away, but I cannot. I love him too much. I continue to hope he feels the same, but I worry that he does not, since he never says the words. I've told myself to live each day as it comes and not trouble about the future. Yet this limbo in which I am living preys upon my mind and stabs at my heart. Oh, and one more thing . . . Cade and I aren't actually engaged!

No, telling Mallory was completely out of the question. Just as it was equally impossible for her to reveal her feelings to Cade. In her mind, she'd told him a thousand times, but if she were to actually do so, she feared what he might say. Worse, she was terrified what he might *not* say.

And so she held her silence, sacrificing her pride and her principles for another chance to be in his arms. Though in all honesty, being his lover was far from a hardship, and was a circumstance over which she had no regrets. She cherished those hours in the dark and the quiet when he held her close, his kisses and caresses building her passion, his possession slaking her needs.

Afterward, as they lay together with sleep hovering just out of reach, she knew no greater pleasure or peace, able to forget for that brief span that there was anyone but the two of them in all the world.

Come morning, though, she always awakened alone, the side of the bed where he'd lain grown cold to the touch. She knew he left in order to preserve her good name. Even so, she could never seem to banish the feeling of loss she experienced at his absence.

As for her days, they continued in a normal if frenetic pattern. Nothing was different—not on the surface anyway. Which is why she was sitting here in Mallory's bedchamber discussing what clothes and jewelry both of them planned to wear at this evening's ball.

Thinking again of Mallory's offer to listen, Meg

gave her a genuine smile. "You're sweet to ask," she said, "but really, there's nothing to tell. I am a little tired from dancing so late last night, is all."

And from staying up afterward with Cade, while he introduced her to yet another new sexual position. Her blood burned at the remembered ecstasy.

"Well, if you are sure," Mallory said.

"I am," she affirmed, using the moment to shake off all thoughts of Cade. "Now, which gown do you think I should wear? The primrose satin or the white silk with the embroidered, Greek key design?"

Several hours later Meg slipped out of the crowded ballroom, the music and sound of chattering voices dimming by a full octave as she left the room behind. The air grew cooler as well as she made her way down the staircase, through a nearby corridor, and into an unoccupied portion of the house. The change came as a welcome respite after the warmth and closeness of too many bodies packed into too confined a space.

Spying a conveniently located chair, which stood partially hidden on the other side of a huge, potted fig tree, she moved down a long hallway to claim the seat. Whoever placed this chair here is a genius, she decided as she sank down upon it. After she did, she realized that her presence in the hall was concealed by the plant's mass of luxurious green leaves—especially since she'd decided

335

to wear an evening gown of spring green sarcenet, rather than one of the other two dresses she had been considering earlier.

Five minutes, she told herself, and then she would go back to the festivities. Five minutes away from the constant small talk and thinly veiled innuendos of all the people who were forever speculating about one bit of gossip or another.

Actually, she was growing weary of the Season, especially now that Lieutenant McCabe and Lord Gresham were no longer around to amuse her with their keen observations and wry wit. Not that the lieutenant would likely have wished to have anything to do with her now, considering her refusal of his offer. And though she did not regret her decision, she nevertheless missed his company.

She could have sought out Cade or one of his brothers, she knew, but a peek into one of the adjoining salons had revealed the men deep in debate about politics and the war. Mallory, on the other hand, was enjoying the supper dance with her major, to no one's great surprise, while Ava was busy playing cards with a set of her friends.

A couple more hours, Meg thought, *and I can go home. A couple more hours* and she could be alone again with Cade. Closing her eyes, she let herself dream.

A minute or so later she heard a door open at the other end of the hallway. Glancing toward the sound, she watched as a man exited some unknown room. Her brows rose when she realized it was Lord Everett, his golden hair and lean physique unmistakable even from a distance. She held still while he paused to scan his surroundings, his gaze moving past the potted fig tree with no evidence that he had noticed her presence behind it. Apparently satisfied, he turned and walked on silent feet down the corridor toward the rear of the town house.

Where is he going? she wondered. And more important, why? Without giving herself more than a few seconds to consider, she rose to her feet to follow.

Cade would be furious if he knew what she was doing, she realized, but she couldn't in all good conscience sit idly by while Everett might be committing some infamous deed. Of course, he could just as easily be indulging in an assignation with a lady, but her instincts told her otherwise. And if she was right and he was passing secrets to the French, well, wouldn't it be brilliant if she could catch him at it? Not that she dared let him see her, since doing so would be idiotic on her part, as well as dangerous. But if she could witness him together with his contact, perhaps it would be enough proof for Cade to not only clear his name, but capture a pair of traitors.

Moving with as much stealth as she could muster, she crept after Everett, her thin slippers skipping over the polished marble floor in a soundless whisper. When he stopped ahead, she pressed herself into a well-shadowed niche in case he turned around to look behind him. To her relief, he opened a door to the last room in the corridor and, without glancing back, went inside.

Meg cast a look over her shoulder to make certain she wasn't being followed herself. The hallway, however, was blessedly empty. Luckily, it was also swathed in heavy pools of shadow where candlelight from the party did not reach. Careful to stay inside those darkened areas, she continued toward her goal. Edging as close to the door as she dared, she stopped and pressed her back to the wall, her heart thudding against her ribs in an anxious beat. Striving for calm, she listened.

For a long moment she heard only silence, as though Everett were in the room alone. But then it came, a deep, sibilant murmur from another man. Sliding another inch forward, she strained her ears to hear more.

". . . far too risky and I won't take a chance like this again."

". . . but what better place? . . . never be suspected," Everett drawled.

A lengthy pause ensued.

"So what do you have for me?" Everett asked.

To her immense frustration, she wasn't able to hear the other man's reply, their voices growing indistinct again, as though they had moved farther into the room. Ignoring the obvious risk, she left her place against the wall and eased closer. As she did, she noticed that she could see a portion of the room through the narrow space that ran along the edge of the door frame between the hinges. Through it, she could see Everett standing in the center of a dimly lit library, his body angled to the side, in order to face his compatriot. As for the mystery man, he remained tantalizingly out of sight, only his shoulder and one arm visible, his face obscured by shadows.

As she watched, he extended a hand with a small piece of vellum held inside his grasp. Reaching out, Everett accepted the missive and paused to scan the contents. "You're certain of this information?"

"Only as certain as my source. Gaining his corroboration might prove rather difficult, however, seeing that he's dead."

A gasp rose in her throat, which she only just managed to silence by pressing a fist against her lips. Trembling, she listened as Everett gave a soft laugh, a chill running over her skin like the stroke of some ghostly hand. If she'd ever harbored even a sliver of doubt regarding his guilt, she certainly had none now. In her estimation, he was as wholly without conscience or remorse as his companion apparently was.

Abruptly, Everett grew quiet and turned his head in her direction. Angling deeper into the shadows, she pressed her fist tighter against her lips and tried not to so much as breathe. Whispering a silent prayer in her head, she beseeched whatever god might be listening not to let Everett see her through the crack in the door.

After a long moment he relaxed and glanced away, focusing his attention once more on the note in his hand. "Excellent work," he pronounced as he slipped the paper into the inner breast pocket of his coat.

"I am glad you approve," the stranger replied in a low, silky voice, a hint of sarcasm in his tone. "I dare remain no longer. Unless there is something else of an urgent nature, I shall be going."

His words ought to have been her cue to flee, to turn and hurry on soundless feet back to the safety and shelter of the crowded ballroom. Instead, some instinct held her in place, her body motionless as she huddled on the other side of the door.

She tensed when the stranger strode forward to leave. But instead of moving in her direction, he advanced toward a pair of French doors on the far side of the room. As he passed her vantage point, she tried to get a glimpse of his features, but his profile proved indistinguishable in the dimly lit room. She was left with nothing more than a general impression of a moderately tall man with dark hair and a medium build. He could have been almost anyone.

A light June breeze blew the sheer curtains inside as he opened the doors. Without stopping to glance back, he stepped over the threshold and was gone.

Everett, remaining in the room, shut and locked the doors behind him. Then he reached into his coat pocket and withdrew the note he'd been given. Opening it, he took a moment to study the contents. Striding to the fireplace, he paused before the barely smoldering ashes in the hearth, crushed the paper in his fist and tossed it into the grate with a flick of his wrist.

Knowing she dare not wait a second longer, Meg ran. Halfway down the hall, she saw a partially open door to her left that she hadn't previously noticed. Without giving herself a second to think, she darted toward it and dashed inside, immediately swallowed by the room's shielding darkness. Slipping even deeper into the shadows, she waited, her heartbeat drumming so loudly in her ears she feared Everett would surely hear it as he passed.

Then his footsteps sounded, echoing ever so softly against the marble tiles. She closed her eyes and willed herself not to make a peep, a tight, asphyxiating sensation forming in her throat, as though an invisible hand were cutting off her air.

His footfalls grew closer, then drew even with the room. Biting the inside of her lip, she waited to see if they would stop and turn to come inside. But instead his footsteps continued on down the hallway, their sound diminishing.

Meg sagged with relief, the chemise under her stays damp with perspiration. She stood in the darkness for a full five minutes more, not completely trusting that he was gone. Only then did she inch toward the door. Peering around with a cautious eye, she scanned the hallway and found it empty and silent again. Moving out into the corridor, she started in the direction of the ballroom, then suddenly stopped.

The note, she thought. What was written in that note?

Whatever it was, Everett had obviously committed the message to memory, since he'd thrown the missive into the fireplace. It was probably ash by now, but what if it wasn't? There had barely been a fire in the grate. Was it possible enough of the message remained that she could retrieve it? Or a portion of it, at least?

Worrying the tip of a fingernail between her teeth, she considered her options and knew she could not let the opportunity pass. *I've come this far, I might as well see it through.* Spinning on the balls of her feet, she raced toward the room at the end of the hall.

The hour was just past two when Cade pressed the latch that controlled the hidden panel leading to Meg's bedchamber. Easing open the false door, he moved into the room, the flame of his candle flickering as he closed the panel behind him.

Usually she waited for him in the darkness, but tonight she had not extinguished her bedside candle. Nor was she in bed. Instead she sat near the fireplace in a wing chair, the same one in which he himself had sat on the night he first visited her here. How long ago that all seemed now.

He crossed to the night table and set down his candlestick. Turning back, he noticed the pensive expression on her face. "Why are you not already abed?" he questioned in a soft voice.

"I'm not tired."

"Even more reason for you to be in bed." He held out a hand. "Come, and I'll see if I can help wear you out a bit."

She said nothing and did not smile, nor did she make an effort to do as he suggested.

"What is it?" he asked, his arm dropping to his side.

"Nothing, I . . . actually there is something, but . . ."

"But what?"

She rubbed a palm over her rose-hued dressing gown, then looked up and met his gaze. "Promise you will not get angry."

His brows furrowed. "And why would I have cause to be angry?"

"Just promise and I shall tell you."

He crossed his arms over his chest. "Meg—"

"Promise. And swear you won't yell, either. I do not want the whole house descending upon us."

"I am always careful about that. Though I must point out, the same cannot always be said of you."

A pretty wash of color spread over her cheeks.

"Nevertheless," she continued, "I would have your word as a gentleman."

A muscled tightened in his jaw. What was this all about? he wondered with a sudden uncomfortable tug in his gut. "Very well. You have my word that I will not yell. I will also do my utmost to curb any anger that may arise. Now, what is it?"

"This," she said. Reaching into her pocket, she drew out a heavily creased piece of writing paper, faint whorls of brown and black along the edges and center as if the vellum had been partially burned.

He stared for a long moment. "A note? Why would I yell at you over a note?"

Her gaze fell, the fingers of her free hand pleating and unpleating the silken skirt of her dressing gown. "Because it's not just any note. It . . ."

"Yes?" he drawled encouragingly.

"It was meant for Lord Everett, but he threw it in the fireplace, so I plucked it out."

"You did what!" he bellowed.

"You said you wouldn't yell."

He fisted his hands at his sides and wished that he'd never made such an idiotic promise. Drawing a deep, calming breath, he forced himself to speak in a quiet, modulated tone. "What do you mean the note was for Lord Everett?"

"He had a secret rendezvous with one of his spy contacts tonight where he received this missive."

A vein throbbed in his temple as he strove for control. "And how would you know that?"

"Because I followed him and eavesdropped on the conversation."

"You did what!"

She sent him a reproving look. "You're yelling again, and in case you don't realize it, you are starting to repeat yourself."

His hands opened and closed at his sides. Careful to keep his voice lowered, he asked his next question in deliberate tones. "Just so I am certain I understand, you trailed Everett out of the ballroom—"

"No, not out of it," she interrupted. "I was already in the corridor downstairs from the ballroom, enjoying a quiet moment to myself, when he entered the hallway. I saw him disappear into one of the unoccupied rooms at the far end of the house and knew immediately that he was up to no good."

"That blackguard is never up to anything good, a fact of which you are fully aware." He thrust his hands into his robe pockets and paced a few steps. "Why did you not go back to the ballroom? Why did you not come and find me?"

Tiny lines puckered the usually smooth surface of her forehead. "There wasn't time to find you. As for the other, well, I could not stand aside and let whatever he was up to go unobserved."

"You certainly could have, and *should* have. You promised me you would have nothing more to do with the man."

"And I have not," she defended, twisting her

fingers together in her lap. "Well, except once when he approached me at the opera—"

A muscle twitched in his cheek. "He sought you out?"

"Yes, one evening a few weeks ago, when you were not in attendance. I told him I wanted nothing more to do with him, and he has abided by my wishes. I have not spoken so much as a word to the man since that night."

"Why did you not tell me this sooner?"

"For the same reason I wish I did not feel compelled to tell you about tonight, since I knew how you would react. But there is this note, and I thought it vital that I pass along what I learned."

"And what is that exactly?" he bit out, doing his best not to raise his voice. "Did Everett see you?"

"Of course not."

"How can you be sure?"

An expression of affront crossed her face. "I took great care not to get caught."

"But you might have been seen anyway. Do you know the kind of risk you took? Did you even stop to think what might have occurred if he'd found you listening in on him?"

A faint shudder ran through her. "Of course I did. But it all worked out fine and he and the man he met have no idea I saw them."

Cade paced again and raked his fingers through his hair, wanting to rail at her for putting herself in such terrible jeopardy. He wanted to drag her to her feet and give her a long hard shake, scare her enough that she would never, ever consider doing something so fool-hardy ever again. They'd been through this once before, and he'd thought the matter resolved. Apparently, he was mistaken.

Not trusting himself within two feet of her at the moment, he walked over to the bed and sat down. "So who was this other man?" he asked in a strangely flat tone.

Tension eased visibly from her shoulders now that it seemed he would no longer upbraid her for her actions. "I don't know. He stayed in the shadows the whole time, so I could not see his face. He sounded English, though, and of the nobility."

"And the note? How did you obtain it?"

"Oh, well, all the details aren't necessary, but after Everett threw it in the fireplace and returned to the ball, I went back to the room."

His lips firmed. "Naturally."

"We're lucky the note wasn't destroyed, considering it was lying in the grate. But the coals had burned so low there wasn't enough heat to ignite the paper . . . well, not much," she added, holding up the partially seared slip of vellum.

He repressed the urge to show his teeth. "And what does the note say?"

"Here," she said, rising and coming forward. "Maybe you should read it for yourself."

Pausing for a moment, he leaned forward to accept it. The sorely abused piece of paper crackled softly between his fingers as he unfolded it along one crease.

Sunday
Midnight
Steybridge Lodge

A dark, looping signature was affixed at the bottom, the scrawl completely indecipherable.

"It's not much," she said, "but I thought it might be important. A meeting place perhaps."

"Perhaps." Folding it in half again, he tucked the note into his pocket. He decided not to tell her that Steybridge Lodge was a bankrupted estate that had recently been sold on the auction block to an anonymous bidder. Could the new owner be Everett, or did it now belong to someone else entirely? Some other spy? Some new traitor?

"Sunday is tomorrow," she continued. "Could it mean midnight tomorrow? Or rather today, since it's morning already."

"I am not sure yet what it means, and you are done speculating on such matters."

"But Cade—"

" 'But Cade' nothing. I gave you my word, now I want yours. You will not engage in any further attempts to eavesdrop or spy on Everett or anyone else with whom he might meet. And in the future, if he so much as looks at you, you are to find me immediately and stick by my side like a burr."

"A burr, hmm? That might prove a bit too close for comfort."

He yanked her against him, one arm locking behind her legs as she stood between his spread thighs. "This isn't funny, Meg. You could have been hurt. Your promise, please."

She sobered instantly. "You're right and you have my word. I will never trail Everett again." Reaching up, she brushed her fingers through his hair. "Actually, it was a rather frightening experience."

"As well it should have been." Inhaling, he worked to throw off the worst of his anger. "It's late. We should go to bed."

"Yes, we should." Sliding her hand over his cheek, she caressed him. "Are you still in the mood to wear me out a bit?"

Blood rushed straight to his loins, his arousal springing instantly to life—aching and urgent. Any further conversation about the note and her retrieval of it could wait until later, he decided. Pressing his face against her breasts, he breathed in her sweet, feminine warmth. Wanting more, he clasped her buttocks in his palms and kneaded her pliant flesh. Then, without giving her any warning, he leaned backward across the bed and toppled her across him.

As they fell she cried out, bouncing against his

erection, which was pressed to her stomach like a steel rod. "I guess you are still in the mood," she murmured, shimmying against him.

Capturing her mouth with his, he proceeded to show her exactly how much.

Chapter 20

*C*ade drew her aside the next morning after breakfast, delaying her departure until everyone else had left. A nod to the servants had them shuffling out and closing the door behind them.

"I wanted you to know not to expect me tonight," he told her in a quiet voice. "So do not wait up."

Meg turned and set a hand on his sleeve. "You're going after him, then?"

"I am going to see if there is anything to the message you foolishly risked life and limb to retrieve. There's a very great chance Sunday midnight is another Sunday midnight. It could also be a code for something else entirely."

She felt lines form across the bridge of her nose. "Do you believe it's a code?"

He caught her hand and pressed it flat against his chest. "Whatever it is, don't worry. I shall return by morning. You'll barely know I was away."

"Away where? I assume you are familiar with the location in the note?"

He grew silent for a long minute, as if deciding

whether to respond. "I've never been to Steybridge Lodge, but the property is in Kent. And that is all I plan to say on the subject."

Realizing there was no use attempting to pry further, she moved on to another concern. "Are the duke or any of your brothers going with you?"

"No," he said, releasing her hand to take a step away. "Nor is there need for them to bother. I plan to do nothing more than a simple reconnoiter, then I will be on the road back to London once more."

So he is going alone, she realized, her stomach churning with anxiety. Suddenly she found herself awash in regret, wishing she'd never taken the note out of the fireplace or shown it to Cade. With typical male arrogance, he assumed he could do everything himself. But what if he could not? What if he were wrong?

"Perhaps you ought to—"

"Let me handle this, Meg," he interrupted. "I only told you about my plans because I knew you would fret and do something potentially foolish."

"I take umbrage at that characterization, my lord. I may act rashly on occasion, but I am never foolish."

He smiled. "I intended no insult, only a dose of well-deserved caution." Abruptly, he sobered. "Speaking of which, I want your promise you will go to the party tonight with Mama and Mallory, dance and enjoy yourself, as usual, and then come straight home. Is that fully understood?"

"Completely," she agreed.

Of course, just because she went to the party didn't mean she had to remain the entire time. Nor did his requirements stipulate that she stay home once she returned for the evening. Possibilities raced through her mind, though at the moment she didn't know which of them she might act upon, if any. Striving not to let her thoughts show, she gave him what she hoped was a concerned yet compliant smile.

Cade pinned her with an assessing look that made her wonder if he knew she wasn't nearly as acquiescent as she seemed. But then he nodded in apparent satisfaction and seemed to dismiss his qualms.

After a glance at the closed breakfast room door, he drew her into his arms and gave her a slow kiss. "I will say good-night to you now, since we will most likely both be too busy today to do more than share hellos in passing. I shall see you tomorrow morning, or earlier should I return in time."

"Until tomorrow. Promise you'll be careful," she said.

"I wouldn't think of being anything else."

Contrary to what he'd implied to Meg, Cade knew he wouldn't be without an ally at Steybridge Lodge. Although he'd made no effort to contact the man, given the lack of time, he knew Thelonious Ferrick would find his way there. After all, Ferrick's task was to follow Everett, and Cade trusted that's exactly what he would do.

He supposed he could have remained in London and let Ferrick report on what he discovered. But now that Everett was finally coming out into the open again, Cade wanted to be there to take advantage. He also wanted to find out who Everett was meeting and, if possible, what secrets were being passed between them.

He'd been honest when he told Meg that he planned no more than a simple reconnoiter—at least for now. But if matters turned in his favor tonight, he was prepared to act. With any luck, perhaps he would catch not one, but two spies in the act. Then again, if the note proved to be nothing more than an interesting tease and Everett failed to appear, Cade knew he would find himself alone in the Kentish countryside with a long, dark ride home. Either way, he decided, the journey was worth a few hours of his time.

Late that afternoon, while the other ladies were having a lie-down before rising to dress for dinner and that night's ball, Meg decided to go outside to the mews. Before leaving the house, she checked with one of the servants to make sure Cade was absent, since she was all too aware—after one of her midnight conversations with him—that his bedchamber possessed an excellent view of the stable yard. One of the horses whickered a soft greeting as she moved into the stable's shaded interior, the air ripe with the scent of hay and horseflesh. Not long after her entrance, her usual groom approached, giving his cap a respectful tug.

"Hallo, miss."

"Good afternoon, Brown. And how are you?"

"I'm well, miss, and thank you for asking. Can I be helpin' ye with some'at?" he inquired, giving her a curious look, since she didn't generally venture out to the stables at that time of day.

"Actually, you can. I was wondering if you could tell me if Lord Cade has ordered his carriage for tonight?"

He took off his cap to scratch his head before setting it back in place. "I wouldn't rightly know, since his lordship usually deals directly with the head groom. But I do remember hearing some mention about havin' his curricle made ready for the evening."

"Was a particular time discussed?"

Brown arched a shaggy brow. "'Round ten, I think I heard."

She smiled. "Thank you. Now, I have a bit of a favor."

The man shuffled a foot, looking uncomfortable. "Favor, miss? An wot would that be?"

"Nothing much. I am just wondering if you could see to it that my mare is saddled and ready by, say . . . half past nine tonight?"

"Well certainly, miss."

"And I would like you to leave her in her stall. I shall come get her when I am ready." Reaching into her pocket, she withdrew a gold guinea—as much money as she knew the man likely earned in a fortnight. "You won't say anything about my request, will you? Most especially not to Lord Cade."

His eyes strayed to the coin. After a moment's hesitation, he scooped it out of her palm and into his own pocket. "No, miss. Don't know nothin' about such things. Following his lordship, is ye?" he added with a wink.

"Perhaps."

"Aye, well, the horse'll be ready by nine. They'll miss me at cards in the tack room if I saddle 'er any later."

"Nine it is, then."

Leaving the party early proved far easier than Meg had anticipated. Drawing the duchess and Mallory aside not long after their arrival, she explained that she had a dreadful headache and wished to go home.

"You do look rather pale," Mallory remarked.

Do I? Meg wondered. If her cheeks were markedly pale, she could only assume it was the result of the nerves that had been gnawing at her all afternoon and evening.

"I hope you are not coming down with a summer cold or some such," Ava added, laying a motherly hand across Meg's forehead. "No fever at least."

"Oh, I do not think it is anything serious," Meg said. "Just another of my megrims that shall pass soon enough."

Mallory nodded. "We shall go home, then—"

"Oh no, I would feel even more dreadful knowing I had ruined the evening for you both. You must stay and enjoy yourselves. I shall take the coach home, then have it sent back for you."

Another minute's persuasion was needed before she was able to convince them to remain at the party, but finally the deed was managed. She also convinced them that they did not need to look in on her upon their return.

"It will be late when you arrive," she declared, "and I plan to go straight to bed. I am sure all I require is a sound night's sleep. I shall see both of you in the morning."

With everything settled, she soon found herself inside the family coach traveling back to Clybourne House.

Once there, she had to playact for her maid as well, allowing Amy to assist her out of her evening gown and into night attire. With the minutes ticking past at an alarming rate, Meg hurried the girl out, then stripped off her clothes to don one of her old black day dresses and her most service-able pair of boots.

A last-minute flash of inspiration had her tucking her pillows underneath the coverlet in the shape of what she hoped would resemble her sleeping body should one of the ladies decide to check on her after all. Then, after snuffing out her bedside candle, it was time to go.

Until she stood out in the hallway, however, she hadn't considered that she might have the terrible misfortune of encountering Cade on his way to his carriage. In fact, she was hurrying down a back staircase that led to the mews when she heard his voice echoing somewhere above her in the house. Hurrying faster, she somehow succeeded in making her way to the stable and into the stall with her mare—which she found saddled and ready, exactly as promised—without discovery.

Minutes later she heard Cade speaking again, this time with one of the grooms as he climbed into his curricle. Knowing she dare not wait more than a minute after his departure, for fear of losing him after he reached the first tollgate out of the city, she led her horse from the stall, mounted at the stable block, and set off.

A few minutes before midnight, Cade parked his curricle along a secluded lane about a half mile away from Steybridge Lodge. Leaving his horse happily munching on a feed bag, he set off through an area of woodland, which an earlier survey of the property had shown would be his best means of accessing the estate without notice. He was careful to keep his footsteps silent against the loamy ground, glad he had his cane to assist not only in crossing the uneven terrain, but also to aid in his potential defense.

He'd had the new cane especially commissioned a few weeks ago, its hollow interior housing a sword blade honed to a lethal sharpness. Not that he anticipated having to use it, but one never knew.

The moon was high and full, crickets chirping out a rhythmic tune in the warm night air. As he drew within sight of the property, he noticed a sense of abandonment and disuse, despite the single light that shined within the house. With the possible exception of a caretaker, the place looked as though it was still not lived in, despite its new owner. A perfect location, he mused, for a clandestine meeting between traitors.

He chose a sheltered spot with an excellent view of the lodge and prepared to wait and watch. Five minutes passed. Then ten. Then twenty. There was no movement anywhere, no indication that anyone else was around. Maybe the time and day in the note had been erroneous. Perhaps there was no scheduled rendezvous here, after all.

He was about to turn away when a feeling crept over him that made his gut tighten and the fine hairs on the back of his neck stand up. As he watched, a fresh source of light flared abruptly on the drive leading to the house. A man, obviously a servant, moved into view with a lantern held high before him. Behind him came another man, the stride of the second both arrogant and familiar.

Everett!

Cade's hand tightened on his cane, ready to draw his weapon and fight. Yet a glance behind him showed he was still alone, no enemy at his back. Scowling, he watched as Everett stopped, the other man's boots crunching against the gravel as he turned to face the woods.

"I know you're out there, Byron," Everett called. "I've been waiting all evening for you to arrive."

Cade said nothing. *Does he truly know I'm here or is he only guessing?* he wondered.

"You've chosen a good spot there in the woods," Everett continued. "It's the one I would have picked had I been in your shoes."

Where is Ferrick? Cade wondered. Was the other man there, listening as well? If they could only locate each other, the two of them could work to take down Everett. Assuming they could justify taking him down, since it appeared Everett was not meeting a contact tonight, after all. At least not one Cade had seen.

"Tsk, tsk," Everett said in a taunting voice. "You really should be more cooperative, you know, considering I have something you may want returned."

Something I want? What could that be? His senses warned him that Everett was attempting to lead him into a trap, but perhaps the scoundrel was only goading him for his own twisted purposes.

"Not curious then, hmm?" Everett remarked in

a conversational tone. "I'm sure there are those who would be very disappointed to hear of your indifference. Your man, for instance."

Damn. Ferrick.

"That's right. I found him skulking around about an hour since. He's a wily bastard, and strong. He put up a good fight, but it didn't do him any good in the end."

Cade leaned against a tree at his side and pressed his fist hard against the rough bark.

"He isn't dead, if that's what you're wondering. Though he may be by morning, considering the crack he took to his skull. He certainly won't be rushing to your aid, or his own, anytime soon."

Cade knew he could try going after Ferrick, but chances were good he would only get himself caught in the process. His best option, he decided, was to go back to the city for his brothers, then return for Ferrick. With any luck, they wouldn't be too late to save the man—assuming Everett didn't kill him in the meantime.

Everett sighed loudly. "You really are tedious, do you know that, Byron? Do you not want to know what else I have? I'm sure you'll regret passing up the chance to see."

The squirming sensation returned, writhing in his belly like a nest of vipers. *Other than Ferrick, what could the blackguard possibly have that would lure me out?*

Everett moved then, dragging another person out

into the glow cast by the lantern. It was a woman, her black skirts swinging as she nearly stumbled, her pale blond hair gleaming like moonlight.

Meg!

Cade's heart nearly stopped.

"Shall I dispose of her, then?" Everett inquired.

Abruptly, Meg broke free of her captor's hold, ripping the gag out of her mouth. "Don't do it, Cade!" she cried. "Don't come out! If you're there, go away. Go away now!"

She tried to run, but made it no more than three steps before Everett caught her around the waist and dragged her back. He raised his other hand and held it to her head, revealing the pistol held inside his grip.

"So what is it to be?" Everett demanded, his voice no longer as calm as before. "Your freedom or her death?"

Without even pausing to consider, Cade left the shelter of the woods.

Chapter 21

A fearsome ache rose in Meg's chest as she watched Cade emerge from his concealment, her misery so intense she barely felt the hard, metallic press of Everett's pistol barrel where it rested against her temple.

How could I have been so stupid as to follow Cade and then let myself get caught? she berated herself. Because of her actions, Cade was in even graver danger than before.

She still didn't know how she'd been discovered. One minute she'd been sneaking along the grounds parallel to the drive, her feet silent against the grassy lawn, then suddenly Everett appeared. He was on her before she even knew he was there, taking her completely unawares. She hadn't even had time to scream before he wrapped his smothering palm over her mouth and nose. And now she was being used as bait to lure Cade to whatever fate Everett had planned.

"Stop," Everett ordered Cade when he was a few yards away.

Cade stopped.

"My man will see what weapons you have concealed on your person."

With a nod, the servant hurried forward. Patting Cade down, he removed a pair of knives from the inside of his coat and another from his right boot. He confiscated his cane as well, twisting at the top with a paw-sized fist to see if it could be opened. The gold head and fine ebony shaft remained solidly secure. "Wot about this? Shall I take it as well?"

"You can," Cade said. "But I can't vouchsafe for being able to walk steadily without it."

The corner of Everett's mouth turned up. "That's right. Bit of cripple, aren't you? Terrible, the suffering that can happen to a man during wartime."

For a long second he studied the cane in the servant's hand. "Let him keep it," he said. "I doubt he'll find it very handy at stopping a bullet."

With a smirk, the servant tossed the cane toward Cade, who had to limp a few steps to one side and bend to retrieve it out of the grass.

"Inside," Everett ordered, using the gun to motion Cade to precede him into the house. Meg cried out as Everett gave her arm a painful yank that demanded she move along next to him at a hurried clip.

The wood-paneled foyer was dark and shabby, she noticed as they entered the lodge, the air musty with dust and disuse. Spiders had been at work weaving cobwebs high in the corners of what must once have been an attractive hall. But financial ruin had stripped the place of much of its beauty and possessions. Only a few pieces of furniture still remained, including a single hard-back chair in the entry and a threadbare sofa that loomed large in the shadows of an adjoining room.

Sensing danger, a rodent squeaked and scurried off as quickly as its tiny feet would take it, disappearing into a crack along the baseboard with a last whip of its tail.

Meg shuddered and glanced away while the servant lit a brace of candles. The increased illumination did little to improve their surroundings, the interior turning even more forbidding.

Everett motioned Cade toward the chair. For a

moment he looked as if he might resist, but a glance at the gun Everett was still pointing her way obviously changed his mind. Moving with a more pronounced limp than he had shown for a while, Cade crossed the room, pausing to lean his cane against the nearby wall before taking a seat. At the servant's urging, Cade placed his hands around the tall back of the chair so his wrists could be tied together using a stout length of rope. Nearly finished, the man gave a last, hard tug that made Cade's muscles visibly tense against the strain.

"Go," Everett told the servant. "I'll call when I have need of you again." Whatever sort of need that might prove to be, Meg decided, it was probably best not to know.

With Cade now under his control, Everett relaxed, satisfaction rolling off him like an inexpensive cologne. "I must say that matters are working out even better than I had anticipated. When I set up my little deceit in the library, I had no idea how splendidly it would turn out."

"What do you mean?" Meg asked in surprise. "What deceit?"

"Oh, do you not realize, my dear? I knew you were there last night at the ball, listening in on things that were really none of your concern."

"But I—"

"Was so quiet? So stealthy? You were, I suppose, for an amateur, but I am well-versed in issues of subterfuge and deception. It is, after all, what I do

364

best. And I must say you fell right in line with my plan, coming back to retrieve the false note I had planted."

Her mouth dropped open. *"False?* But how could it have been false, when I saw you take it from that other man? When I watched you toss it into the fire?"

"And so you did, but the thought obviously never occurred to you that it was not the *same* note, that the real one was tucked safely inside my pocket."

"How could you know I would come back and collect the other?"

Everett shrugged. "I didn't, but it was a gamble worth attempting. I knew if you did retrieve the note, you'd run straight to Byron, babbling to him about your astonishing find. I also knew that once Byron was aware of a potential rendezvous point, he wouldn't be able to pass up an opportunity to investigate, in hopes of catching me out. I really must thank you for your assistance, my dear Miss Amberley, for leading him exactly where I wanted."

Nausea rolled in her stomach, guilt adding a bitter aftertaste. *Dear Lord, why did I not listen to Cade?* He'd warned her about Everett time and again, but she thought she had everything under control. She thought she could help. Knowing Cade had to be disgusted by her actions, she lowered her gaze to the floor, unable to stand the derision she knew must be visible in his eyes.

"You did surprise me, however," Everett continued. "When I set my trap, I never expected to catch both of you in it. My intended target was Byron alone. Since our first encounter in London, he's caused me nothing but trouble, disturbing all my skillfully laid plans. I had the perfect cover until he started in with his accusations. Because of him, I've had to lie low and do nothing, while I watched valuable opportunities slip past for fear of detection. It's taken me weeks to repair the damage he has caused among those whose trust was once implicit. I've been wanting to put an end to the situation for some while, and the opportunity has finally arrived."

"What do you mean, 'put an end to'?" she asked.

"Exactly what you imagine, my dear. I'm going to kill Byron, of course. My men were supposed to have finished him off all those months ago on the Continent, but they were careless, like underlings so often are, and made mistakes. Which leaves it to me to see the deed done properly this time."

"Dear God," she murmured, her breath growing faint.

Everett angled his head to cast her a tender, almost regretful look. "A shame I will have to kill you now, too. You truly are a most unusual female, full of fire and determination—qualities I admire in a woman. You really ought to have stayed home, you know."

She gasped and jerked within his hold, but he held her steady, his gun unwavering.

"Oh, don't act so astonished." Everett made a tsking sound. "You must realize I cannot possibly set you free now. You have heard far, far too much and would run straight to Clybourne and others with your incriminating tales."

"I wouldn't. If you let Cade and me go, I would promise not to tell—"

A laugh escaped Everett, his chest booming with unconcealed amusement. "Oh, the wit. Truly, it is a pity to extinguish such a brilliant light. And such a pretty one, too." He continued chuckling to himself.

"And just exactly how do you plan to do away with us both?" Cade demanded, abruptly joining the conversation. "I would think our deaths might prove rather problematic to explain, even for you."

The laughter fell away from Everett, his face hardening. "I've already thought of that as well. I'm going to say that you murdered Miss Amberley in a fit of jealous rage before you turned the gun on yourself."

"And why would I have done that?"

"Because everyone knows you're insane, of course."

Cade strained against his bonds and wished he were free to use his fists to wipe the smug expression off Everett's face. *The bastard will be surprised when I do just that,* he reassured himself. *Only a few minutes more and the whole game will change.*

Luckily for him and Meg, Everett still didn't know how to enlist the services of infallible minions. For though the servant had readily enough discovered most of his cache of weapons, he'd failed to find the small shiv he'd secreted in the cuff of one of his shirtsleeves.

And while Everett had been boasting and complaining, Cade had been busy repositioning his hands so he could work the blade through the cloth and down into his palms. He'd had to repress any display of triumph and hope once the task was successfully accomplished. Now it was only a matter of keeping the blade properly angled while he cut through the thick width of hemp.

Luckily again, Everett enjoyed taunting his victims, as Cade well knew. So while he worked on loosening his bonds, he knew it was essential to play along with his captor, to keep Everett talking so he wouldn't notice the shift of muscles in his arms and hands as he strained to free himself.

"No one will believe you," Cade declared as he sawed steadily at the rope. "Certainly not my family."

"I very much doubt that your family will sway anyone's opinion," Everett remarked. "Not after everyone reads the note."

"What note? I assume you don't mean the one that brought us here."

"Not at all, though even if that one's found, it is of no importance. After all, it provides nothing of a suspect nature, but merely lists a time, date, and place. No, I am referring to the note you wrote Miss Amberley tonight, telling her of your plans to confront me here and see justice served."

"But Cade didn't write me a note," Meg interjected.

"Oh, but he will," Everett said with smooth assurance. "In fact, it fits in much better than my original story. How I came here to oversee repairs, and despite the deplorable condition of the place, resolved to stay overnight for an early morning meeting with the architect. How Cade tracked me down here at this property and, in his maddened rage, tried to kill me."

"How convenient," Cade said, continuing his subtle motions with the blade.

"Yes, it is. The architect really will be here at first light—another witness to my distress."

"Distress, hmm?"

"Oh, yes. 'I am just sick over what happened,'" Everett said, playing a part as he obviously pictured the scene. "'I was about to close the house up for the night when Cade Byron burst in upon me, ranting about plots and secret meetings and how he must have revenge for what was done to him. I attempted to reason with him, but he was so deep in his delusions, there was no getting through. I had no choice but to fight back out of self-defense.'"

"As I said," Cade told him, "no one will believe you."

"I beg to differ. For one, my servants will confirm everything I say, acting as direct witnesses who saw and heard it all. Then there is Miss Amberley herself. You see, she was quite understandably distraught over that wild, rambling note you left her, and resolved to come after you. She hoped to stop you and get you the help you so desperately required."

"Why didn't she go to my family, or a friend? Why would she have come alone without seeking assistance?"

Everett paused, clearly considering the question. "Well, I suppose I don't know, women being foolish and fallible in their haste. I would think it was because she wanted to protect you and your reputation, seeing that it was already tarnished, even among your closest relations. Perhaps she feared you would be sent to Bedlam, from where they say no one ever returns whole. But I digress."

"My apologies," Cade said with mock politeness as he felt the shiv sink deeper into the rope. "Pray continue. I must admit I am curious to hear the rest."

Everett smiled.

Beside him, Cade saw the expression of incredulous horror on Meg's face. He did his best not to dwell on what she must be feeling, concentrating instead on working the blade.

"Upon receiving the note," Everett went on, "Miss Amberley followed you here, discovering us locked in a heated argument. In your delusion, you assumed she had come to save *me*, since you had recently learned that the two of us were meeting alone for early-morning rides in the park. You did know about that, I presume?"

Cade's jaw flexed. "Yes. Meg told me."

"Good. Then it goes to my story, which is that you conceived a terrible jealousy and turned your fury upon her. Despite my attempts to save her, you shot and killed poor Miss Amberley. Then you attacked me. We wrestled for the second pistol you brought, and in the scuffle you, too, were shot, soon dying of your wound. Absolutely tragic."

"And you think you will get away with that faerie story?"

"Oh, indeed, I do," Everett boasted. "Your hatred of me is well-known, as is your volatile temperament. You did attack me at a ball, if you will remember?"

"I only wish I'd succeeded in choking the life out of you!"

"Exactly my point about that temper of yours. Frightening!" he chided with mock reproof. "But to return to the subject of the note, I had the excellent fortune of obtaining a sample of your handwriting some while ago. A concerned friend at the War Office showed me the letter you wrote warning them about my activities—very bad form, by the way, dear boy. This particular gentleman was most obliging about allowing me to borrow the letter to show my solicitor. As it happens, I am quite adept at copying, and when I returned the correspondence the next day, I had the sample I required."

He gave a smile that didn't reach his eyes. "With my skill at forgery, not even your family will be able tell whether you wrote the note to Miss Amberley. No doubt, a few will have their suspicions, but there will be nothing anyone can prove. I will walk away free, able to return to my real work of seeing this war won by the right side."

Cade laughed. "You're as deluded as you make me out to be, if you believe all that. Let Meg and me go now, Everett, and I'll ask the Crown to spare your life. Of course, it will be from the inside of a cell, but there is only so much I can do."

"You're nothing if not tenacious, Byron. Almost a shame to see a man of your caliber find his ultimate reward, but alas, your luck has run its course."

Cade continued cutting the rope. Having to pause occasionally to keep Everett from noticing slowed his progress, but he was nearly there, the bonds beginning to loosen. When they did, however, he knew there would still be the gun Everett was holding on Meg. I'll figure something out, he told himself, when the time comes.

"Now, which one of you to kill first?" Everett mused aloud. "You, I suppose, Byron, which would leave me time to play a bit more with

Miss Amberley. But that seems wrong somehow, depriving you of the opportunity to watch."

The blade slipped, cutting into Cade's wrist. Only a quick save kept the shiv from tumbling to the floor. *"What?"*

"Oh, come now, you must know how attractive I find your fiancée. There are no secrets between us now, so I see no reason to conceal my lust. What a waste to send her to her grave untouched, do you not think? I believe it would be an even greater crime than taking her life."

"Let me go, you disgusting animal!" Meg struggled against him, her unexpected resistance momentarily loosening his grip on her. But he caught her again and slapped her hard across her face.

She swayed from the force of the blow, crying out against the pain as she raised a trembling hand to cover her reddened cheek.

"None of that now," he warned. "Unless you want to play rough. With a little persuasion, I could be convinced."

Cade came partly out of his chair, despite the bonds that still held him in place. "Let her go! This is between the two of us, not her."

"But you're wrong. This does involve her now, and I want you to suffer a bit more before you die. Just like in Portugal, I know of no better means of tormenting you and enjoying myself at the same time."

Cade fought the red haze that enveloped him, his blood beating in time to the fury pulsing through his veins. He wanted to leap up and pound his fists into Everett, beat him until there was nothing left of the man but regret and pain. But that reaction was exactly what Everett wanted, he realized, as he struggled to calm himself. Everett wanted to draw his rage and anguish, to revel in his suffering. And he knew that the more he reacted to Everett's provocation, the worse matters would go for Meg. What he needed was a calm head, so he could gain their freedom. In the meantime, he would have to find a way to distract Everett. But how?

"This is nothing like Portugal," Cade declared, working the shiv into the rope again.

Everett paused. "Oh, and how is that? The similarities seem striking enough to draw certain important parallels. For one, you're once again at a disadvantage—all tied up, as it were. For another, I have your woman again, yet another fiancée for you to cry over."

"But it's not the same, since she isn't really my fiancée."

"What!" Everett narrowed his eyes, his attention most definitely caught.

"That's right. Our engagement is a ruse. We've been deceiving everyone this Season, while she looks for another man to marry."

"This is nonsense," Everett scoffed.

"Not at all. Ask her yourself, if you don't believe me. A few months ago Meg was forced to take shelter at my country estate. We were alone for some time, which unfortunately left her compromised. But neither of us wished to marry the other, so we came up with an alternate plan. A Season at my expense in exchange for the opportunity for Meg to find another bridegroom. I've been waiting eagerly for her to make up her mind and jilt me. So despite an admitted affection for her, I am by no means in love with her."

Everett swung his head toward Meg, whose face had drained of color. "Is this true?"

She nodded. "Yes. Everything is as he says."

"So you see, Everett," Cade continued, "my objection to seeing you force yourself on Miss Amberley is the same one I would have were I made to watch you violate any young woman against her will. If your intention is to elicit some sort of personal anguish on my part by assaulting Miss Amberley, you will be sadly disappointed. The sort of feelings you crave are dead in me now. You killed them the day you murdered the only woman I shall ever love."

A soft sound escaped Meg's throat, as though she couldn't quite catch her breath, her eyes vividly blue, almost bruised looking, against her stark white cheeks.

"It doesn't look like Miss Amberley is glad to hear you say that," Everett remarked. "And I am

375

not convinced that a closer relationship doesn't exist between the two of you."

Cade forged on, refusing to let himself dwell on any distress his words might be causing Meg. Surely, he reasoned, she must realize he was doing this to keep Everett from her and buy both of them a bit more time.

"You're right," he admitted. "You've caught us out on that. Meg and I are lovers."

Under Everett's inquiring gaze, a rush of condemning warmth returned to her skin.

"She's an extremely attractive woman, so how's a man to resist when she's living right under his nose?" Cade went on, using a seemingly negligent shrug to cover the snap of the rope finally pulling apart, yet careful to keep his arms together as if he were still confined. "But just because I've enjoyed a tumble or two doesn't mean I want to slip on a parson's noose. After all, why pay for the sweets when I'm already getting the sugar for free?"

Meg gasped in obvious offense. With the sound still reverberating in the room, he reached sideways for his cane and leapt from the chair.

Everett started in shock, completely caught off guard. He brought the pistol up, but not in time, as Cade bounded forward. Lifting the cane high, he slashed it down against Everett's head, grabbing his other hand, as he fought for control of the gun.

Everett bellowed in pain and fury, twisting in an attempt to escape Cade's hold. But Cade drank in the sound, Everett's resistance fortifying his own rage and determination to crush the other man like the low, vile insect he was. Tightening his grip, he squeezed harder, willing bones to break, if that's what was needed to take possession of the gun. He pressed on with relentless force, knowing he couldn't afford to lose his advantage or underestimate the viciousness of his opponent.

Cade raised his walking stick to strike a second blow, but Everett grabbed the cane. The two of them took several staggering steps as they grappled for control of both weapons this time.

Everett lashed out with a savage kick at Cade's weak thigh. Leaping to one side, he managed to take only a glancing blow, avoiding what otherwise would have been a disabling strike. Nonetheless, the kick sent painful reverberations pinging up through his leg, his muscles protesting the strain and abuse. Instead of weakening him, though, the discomfort only increased his ire, his heart hammering out a vengeful beat, as he redoubled his efforts.

He and Everett struggled for a seemingly endless time, muscles bulging, lungs heaving for breath, as each tried to gain supremacy. Suddenly, Cade sensed the other man weakening. With a brutal, almost merciless strength, he wrenched the cane free of Everett's grip and brought it down, aiming for the arm and hand that held the gun.

Everett roared at the blow, his arm trembling, his

fingers reflexively loosening their grip. Cade reached for the weapon, but the barrel popped free of his sweat-slick grasp and flew into the air. For a second he watched as the gun hit the floor, spinning outward in a series of wild circles.

But he didn't have time to consider going after it, as Everett lowered his head and plowed bodily into him. Cade stumbled, fighting to retain his balance and his hold on the cane as he was propelled back. Dimly, he heard Meg scream.

He hit the far wall with a punishing thud, bits of dust drifting over both he and Everett, as they continued to struggle. Again Everett tried to get in a few well-placed kicks, Cade taking more glancing blows that left him aching.

With blood pounding between his temples and desperation fueling his efforts, he reached out and clamped a hand around Everett's neck. The other man's eyes bulged and then he was gasping, his hands clawing to escape Cade's brutal grip. Blood dripped over Cade's fingers as Everett's nails scored his skin, but Cade did not let go. Instead, he squeezed even harder.

Abruptly, Cade shoved Everett to the floor, leaving him sprawled in a heap, the other man gagging and struggling to gain his next breath. While he did, Cade pressed a pair of fingers against the bejeweled eyes on the head of his cane and unsheathed the sword inside with a single, graceful sweep.

Moving quickly, he brought the lethal tip down and laid it against Everett's neck. The man grew still, chest still heaving as he stared up at Cade with undisguised malevolence.

And something else this time.

Fear.

In his mind's eye Cade saw himself driving the blade deep, watching Everett's life slip away as the blood drained from his body. Clearly, this was a man who did not deserve to live. Yet such a fate seemed too easy; no punishment at all, really, for someone who deserved no less than hell. Cade towered above him, his hand unmoving while he weighed his choices.

With a sudden twist of his hand, he drew the blade across Everett's throat from one side to the other. A shallow line of blood blossomed deep scarlet against the material of Everett's ruined cravat, the wound deep enough to scar but not kill.

"Something to remember me by," Cade murmured.

A heavy footfall sounded from the doorway. "Put that down now an' let 'im go!"

Cade looked up and saw Everett's manservant slowly approaching, a gun in his hand, with the muzzle pointed squarely at him.

"Like I said, step off or I'll shoot ye," the servant declared.

Cade heard a rustle of skirts to his right. "And I'll shoot you!" Meg declared. Everett's pistol—

the one abandoned in the fight—was now in her hands.

The servant sneered and took another step forward.

Meg fired. The gun gave a kick, the acrid scent of gunpowder thick in the air.

Across the hall, the servant dropped to his knees and toppled sideways, a red stain spreading across his shoulder.

Cade met her gaze, reading the shock in her silvery blue eyes and pallid cheeks. "Dear heavens!" she said. "Did I kill him?"

He didn't have an opportunity to reply, as the sound of footsteps rang out in the entry. A moment later his brothers—Edward, Jack, and Drake—burst into the room. They stood silent for a long moment as they took in the scene. Everett lay moaning on the floor in pain, Cade's sword still leveled just above his chest. The servant was slumped in an unconscious, bleeding heap, while smoke still curled from the end of the pistol in Meg's hand. Cade could only imagine how the tableau must appear.

"Well, damn," Jack remarked with raised eyebrows. "Looks like you didn't need us, after all. Sorry we missed all the excitement."

Chapter 22

ot that I'm displeased to see you, but why are you here, and more to the point, how did you know where to find us?" Cade asked his brothers.

As he watched, Edward strode forward with his usual smooth, commanding gait. "Obviously, we came to help," his older brother replied. "As for the how, you are not the only one who has been having Everett watched. When my man saw what was happening tonight, he rode immediately to notify me. Jack and Drake were there when word arrived, and insisted on coming along to lend their aid." The duke looked down at Everett's bloodied body with derision. "Though as Jack so aptly observed, you and Miss Amberley do not appear to be much in need of our assistance at the moment."

"Nonetheless, Meg and I are glad to have it," Cade stated.

Edward nodded. "We found your man, by the way. He's suffered a severe beating, but I think he'll pull through. I already had him sent along to the nearest inn to have a physician see to his injuries."

"Again, my thanks." Cade said. "Now, maybe the three of you can help me decide exactly what to do with Everett and his servant. Is he still alive?"

Drake walked over and bent to check. "He's breathing, so I would have to say yes. Did you really shoot him, Meg?"

All eyes turned toward her, where she stood with the gun still clutched in her hand. She said nothing, just stared, her cheeks devoid of color. Only then did Cade realize she must be in a state of shock.

"Watch him, will you?" he said with a glance at his brothers.

Jack stepped forward. "With pleasure."

Handing the sword over to his brother, he crossed to Meg. "Here, let me take that," he urged in a low tone as he gently pried the pistol from her grip.

She relinquished it without resistance, then let him lead her across to the chair in which he'd so recently been tied. She sank down, her eyes lowered to the floor.

"Will you be all right here for a few minutes?" he asked in a voice meant for her ears alone.

"Of course," she said.

"I shan't be long, then we'll go home."

"Yes," she murmured. "Home is exactly where I need to be."

He made no comment to that cryptic reply, but brushed his fingertips over her cheek. She withdrew ever so slightly from his touch, leaning subtly away. He frowned but said nothing, knowing how hard the past few hours had been. With another concerned glance at her, he rejoined his brothers.

Cade told them about the evening and how Everett had plotted to kill both him and Meg. Prudently, he left out as much of Meg's involvement as possible, glossing over their intimate relationship and the fact that she had followed him there against his express wishes—something he planned to discuss with her later, when she was more herself again.

"Given the circumstances," he said as he concluded his tale, "I suppose the most we can pin on Everett is kidnapping and attempted murder. Hopefully, that will be enough to see him imprisoned—and hanged, if we're lucky."

Everett, who had been silent until now, glared up at Cade. "It won't be enough. I'll deny everything, so it will be your word against mine. I have powerful friends who will rally to my side, including Prinny. I won't spend so much as an hour in gaol."

"I wonder if that will be the case, when your friends realize that you have indeed been spying for the French?" Edward mused aloud.

Everett laughed, then stopped abruptly to press a hand against the lacerated skin around his throat, fresh blood seeping into his cravat. "There's no proof," he rasped. "I'm a loyal English citizen."

"That's not what *this* will prove," Edward stated as he crossed the room to retrieve a small leather satchel lying near the door. "You're not the only one who can set a trap, you know."

"What trap?" Everett jeered.

"The one I arranged with the War Office a few weeks ago. I consulted with two of the highest military officials, and together we let certain classified information slip out. Only, that information was false, planted to see if you would take the bait." The duke leaned down as if to share a secret. "The documents I have in this case prove you did."

Everett remained defiant. "I don't see how—"

"No, you don't," Edward interrupted, his contempt clear. "The man to whom you passed this particular bit of intelligence—which includes what would have been vital troop strengths and positions—just happens to have been one of ours. France isn't the only country with double agents, *mon ami.*"

Everett paled—and not due to blood loss from his wound.

"With this evidence, we have enough to put you on trial for treason, and to eventually see you hanged," Edward continued. "My only regret is that we weren't able to trail you to a meeting with your other contact. We know there's someone else, a mole in the organization. We just don't know who."

"Well, I'll never tell," Everett stated. "You won't get a scrap of information out of me."

Edward shrugged. "We'll see how you feel after you've spent a few weeks in a cell. The accommodations are rather lacking in creature comforts."

Everett sighed resignedly, as though the prospect didn't trouble him.

"And if he would like to do the honors, I believe I can convince the ministry to allow Cade to conduct your interrogation. I assure you he would be given free rein on his choice of methods."

A visible shudder went through Everett, the last of his bravado slipping away. In that moment, he looked terrified.

Footsteps sounded near the entrance as a quartet of men came inside—rough, burly fellows who looked to Cade as if they regularly bent iron bars with their bare hands.

"Your escort has arrived, your lordship," Edward announced, gazing down at Everett. "Before I left London, I sent word to have a prison wagon driven this way." He looked at the men. "Take him," he ordered. "And the other one over there. See that he is given medical attention."

Over the past few minutes, Everett's servant had regained consciousness, and now sat clutching his bloody shoulder in obvious agony. He groaned aloud as he stared at his gaolers.

"Aye, Your Grace," stated the eldest of what Cade presumed were a crew of Bow Street Runners. "We'll give both of 'em our finest."

Everett and his accomplice were led out into the night, Lord Everett complaining volubly at being handled by such rabble.

When they were gone, Edward turned to Cade. "I can actually arrange for you to conduct the interrogation, if you would like. Perhaps it would provide you with some much needed recompense for all he put you through."

For a long moment Cade considered the offer, waiting for the familiar, burning need for revenge to sweep through him. Instead, he felt only an odd sense of quiet—of peace.

"No," he finally replied. "Let someone else do it. Tonight I've gained all the recompense I need. It's enough to know that the truth about Everett will finally be out for all to see and hear. I'm done with violence. All I want now is to get on with my life and be a plain, ordinary man."

"There's nothing plain or ordinary about you," Edward remarked. "But I'm glad you're ready to put this behind you."

And I am, Cade realized with a dawning sense of wonder. The time had come for him to make some essential choices—to bury the painful memories that were holding him in the past, so that he could look ahead to the future.

With those thoughts in the forefront of his mind, he turned and gazed at Meg, who sat patiently waiting. As he studied her, he considered the evening just past. Her impetuous decision to ride after him tonight had been reckless in the extreme. And, of course, she had disregarded his express wish that she remain safely at home—a topic about which they would clearly need to speak again.

Yet Meg had been incredibly brave, as well. Calm and resilient under circumstances that would have reduced a great many of his acquaintances—including men—to blubbering fools. But she'd held her own, even at the last, coming to his defense in a way he could only admire. What other woman, he mused, could possibly have done such a thing?

Only my Meg.

And she is my Meg, he realized, a wondering smile tugging at the corners of his mouth. "If you'll excuse me," he murmured to Edward, "I believe I ought to take my fiancée home."

"Yes, of course," his brother replied, a curious glint in his eyes as he glanced between Cade and Meg.

Before Cade could go to her, however, Drake appeared. "Here's your cane," he said, offering the walking stick with its hidden sword. "Interesting mechanism. I took the liberty of inspecting it. Good design, but I could make some improvements, perhaps even add a new feature or two."

New features, hmm? Cade wondered what those might be, well aware that Drake was a marvel when it came to all things mathematical and mechanical. Right now, though, he had other more important matters that required his attention. "Let's talk later."

"Oh," Drake replied, as if he'd just then remembered their circumstances and less than elegant surroundings. "Not the time or place, I suppose. Besides, the delay will allow me to refine a few potential flaws."

Cade hid a smile, then started across to Meg. As he did, he realized that this was also not the time or place to discuss all the things he had to say to her. Early morning was already upon them, and they still had a long drive home before they could seek their rest. Tomorrow would be soon enough to talk, he decided. For now, he would keep his own counsel.

Stopping before her, he held out a hand. "Come. Let us be away from this place."

After a brief pause, she nodded and laid her palm in his.

Despite having arrived home at nearly five in the morning, Meg could not sleep. Lying awake and alone in her bed, she watched the sun grow ever brighter in the morning sky.

Earlier, she and Cade had slipped in through the servants' hall, silent as they made their way upstairs. He escorted her to her door, but did not come inside.

"Sleep well," he whispered. "We shall talk later on." Then he bent, pressed a sexless kiss to her forehead, and disappeared along the corridor to his rooms.

Going inside, she'd stripped down to her chemise, then stretched out atop the coverlet, the room warm in spite of the faint summer breeze drifting through the open window. Closing her eyes, she'd willed herself to find oblivion in slumber.

Instead, her thoughts ran in circles, replaying the events of the night in a continual loop. Shivering, she recalled the sensation of having a loaded gun held to the side of her temple, and considered again the horror of being threatened with rape. But strangely, those were not the events that truly distressed her. No, it was the memory of Cade's words that made her eyes sting and pressure build in her chest, as if a hod full of bricks had been laid on top of her.

Of course, she realized that a great deal of what he'd said to Lord Everett had been done in an effort to distract and delay the man, his words far from sincere. Still, there were phrases that rang with an undeniable truth . . .

Just because I've enjoyed a tumble or two doesn't mean I want to slip on a parson's noose . . .

That statement had come as no particular revelation. Cade had never made any claims of wishing to wed her, not even after they became lovers.

Despite an admitted affection for Miss Amberley, I am by no means in love with her.

She squeezed her eyes closed, willing the memories to cease . . .

You murdered the only woman I shall ever love.

Hot tears slid across her cheeks, the echo of Cade's declaration leaving her numb inside. The sentiment of his words allowed her no hope at all.

At the beginning of this deception of theirs, she had thought to find another man and marry him, had assured herself she could forget Cade Byron and happily go on with her life. But she knew now that she'd only been deluding herself. She loved Cade, had loved him from the first, and no other man would do.

Not now. Not ever.

And even if Cade abided by his promise to "take care" of her by offering to make her his wife, she knew she could not endure the thought of marrying him simply to assuage the dictates of Society and convention. She did not want his pity or his forbearance, she wanted his love. But his heart had been given to another, as she'd been so cruelly reminded tonight, and she needed to accept that truth, however harsh it might be.

So then, what to do?

Brushing at the wetness dampening her cheeks, she considered her options. At length she came to a decision, then rose and rang for her maid.

Chapter 23

*L*ater that afternoon, Cade exited his carriage, his step light in spite of the physical strain he'd put his leg through the night before during his scuffle with Everett. Walking into Clybourne House, he barely felt the residual discomfort, his spirits too buoyant to let an aching muscle or two interfere with his day, or his plans.

He had just returned from Rundell and Bridge,

where he'd spent over an hour selecting what he hoped would be the perfect offering for Meg—a ring chosen expressly to serve as a tangible expression of his love and devotion for her.

After arriving home early that morning, and parting from Meg, he'd lain in his solitary bed attempting to sleep. Instead his mind was crowded with thoughts of her and the undeniable realization of just how much she meant to him.

How could I not have known that I love her? he'd wondered. How could he have been so stubborn and blind all these long weeks, ignoring the truth that had literally been staring him in the face?

It had taken nearly losing her to awaken him to the true depths of his feelings, to make him see that she had become as essential to him as breathing, and that he would, quite simply, be lost without her.

A part of him still believed she would have an easier life with someone else—with a less complicated sort of man, such as her Lieutenant McCabe. But she'd turned the fellow down, and now that he was aware of his own feelings, he wasn't going to give her an opportunity to find someone else. If she would have him, he would marry her today!

In fact, he'd nearly gone to Doctors' Commons to obtain a special license, but stopped himself at the last minute, wondering if she would rather have a more traditional wedding with all the usual rites and trappings. He decided he would leave the details up to her, but first, of course, he needed to ask for her hand—properly this time.

"Have the ladies gone out?" he asked Croft as he moved toward the main staircase. If Meg wasn't in, he would leave word with her maid to let him know the moment she returned.

"Yes, your lordship. Her Grace and Lady Mallory left some while ago. As for Miss Amberley . . ." The butler paused, his brows shifting on his forehead.

"Is she abovestairs?" Cade asked, grinning at the thought of surprising her. "Don't worry. I'll find her."

"But my lord—"

"Still abed, is she?" He rather liked the idea of that, imagining himself finding her warm and sleepy as she lay amid the tumbled sheets.

Waving off the butler's attempts at further explanation, he took the stairs as quickly as he could. He continued down the corridor, a smile riding his lips that he feared must look fatuous. But right now he didn't care; he was in too good a humor.

When he reached her bedchamber, however, he found the door ajar and the room unoccupied. For a moment he stood nonplussed, a fist planted on his hip. Perhaps she was in the drawing room, he considered. Or the music room, where she occasionally went to play the pianoforte. Maybe that was what Croft had been trying to tell him.

He was about to go in search of her when he saw Esme running down the hallway toward him.

"Are you looking for Meg?" she ventured. He turned to greet his sister, her child's skirts swinging around her ankles, her dark curls bouncing in a pretty sweep against her shoulders as she came to an abrupt halt.

"I am," he said. "Have you seen her?"

The small bridge of her nose wrinkled. "She left."

"She went out, you mean? Was it with friends? Or with a gentleman caller, perhaps?" If so, he thought, that is the last drive she will be taking with a member of that male coterie of hers.

Unfashionable as it might seem, he planned to keep her close by his side, monopolizing her time and attention both day and night. Particularly at night, especially after they were wed.

Esme shook her head. "No. She's gone away. I was playing with the puppy—"

"Escaping your governess, you mean?" he said, hiding an amused smile.

The little girl grew slightly pink. "Miss Carson gave me time after nuncheon to rest, but I thought Zeus could do with a walk in the garden. We were on our way there when I noticed Meg coming out of her room. She had on one of her old black gowns and she was carrying a traveling case."

His gut clenched as though he'd just suffered a roundhouse punch. "Did she say where she was going?"

"No. I asked her, but she only said that she had to leave and how sorry she was to be going without a proper farewell. I tried to get her to stay, at least until you or Mama came home, but she wouldn't listen. She gave me a hug, then hurried off down the stairs. I know Croft and one of the footmen did what they could to delay her, but she told them she'd leave on foot unless they called her a hackney cab. She was crying, Cade. What happened to make her cry?"

"I don't know. But not to worry, I'll find her." How, he wasn't sure, since he didn't know why she'd left, let alone where she might be traveling. Surely she hadn't believed all that claptrap he spouted last night when he'd been taunting Everett? Then again, maybe she had.

Meg's maidservant appeared then, eyes wide in her pale face. "Beggin' pardon, your lordship, but Miss Amberley asked me to give these to ye on your return." Lifting her hand, she held out a short stack of letters.

He scowled. "What are you doing here, Amy? Why did you not accompany your mistress?"

The girl trembled. "So ye know, do ye? About her leaving?"

"Yes. I know. My sister just informed me of her departure. So, why was Miss Amberley allowed to leave unaccompanied?" Why, he thought, had she been allowed to leave at all?

"She wouldn't let me go with her. She was all

upset, packing her bag with nothing but her old things. Left all them pretty gowns and shoes and whatnot behind. Said how they weren't really hers and she weren't going ter take 'em."

"Yes, go on."

"Well, when I couldn't change her mind about goin'—an' I tried, I really did—I told her I'd pack my bags, too. But she said no. That I weren't to come, 'cause she didn't have the money, but that she'd send for me after, if everythin' worked out like she hoped."

The ache in his belly increased, panic knotting tight as a sailor's hitch beneath his breastbone. *Good God, she is traveling alone.* And it wasn't as if she was unaware of the potential dangers she faced journeying without so much as a maid for protection. *What is she thinking, doing something so risky?* When he caught up with her—and he would—the two of them were going to have a very serious talk about this proclivity of hers to ignore the need for safety. In the meantime, he just wanted her back.

"Have you any idea where she might have gone?"

The maid shook her head. "Mayhap she says in her letter."

"Yes. Very well, you may go," he said, dismissing the servant. The girl curtsied and moved away.

Impatiently, he shuffled through the correspondence, which included letters addressed to his mother, Mallory, Edward, and himself. Singling out the one with his name inscribed in Meg's neat, feminine hand, he tore it open.

As he did, a diamond ring tumbled free. Her engagement ring—or rather, the ring he'd given her as part of their false engagement. Obviously, she'd decided to return it. Clenching the band inside his palm, he slipped it into his pocket, then opened the letter and began to read.

Clybourne House
June 1809

Dear Lord Cade,

Pray forgive the abrupt nature of my departure, since I admit, with all humility, that it denotes a marked lack of courage on my part. But I find I cannot remain any longer, and know that I would never be able to voice aloud what I shall endeavor to express in this missive.

First, allow me to thank you and your family for your many kindnesses to me over these past months. Recent events, however, have reminded me rather forcefully of the temporary nature of the bargain into which you and I entered prior to our arrival in Town. Given that I have failed to live up to my end of the arrangement, I see no reason to persist in what has become a fruitless endeavor.

Pray do not imagine that I shall importune you further. I want no vows or promises made for honor's sake alone, since such sacrifice would only lead to sorrow for us both, as you so rightly stated at the outset. I, therefore, release you from your pledge and absolve you of any further sense of obligation you may feel toward me. Please know that what we shared was done with no expectations of any sort on my part.

I shall be resuming the journey I was making, when first we met, with the expectation of a generous, familial welcome at its end. Do not worry for either my health or welfare, I shall be well in all regards.

> *Yours sincerely,*
> *Margaret Amberley*

Devil take it! He crushed the page in his hand. *What a heartless scoundrel she must think me. How unhappy she must be to have run away.*

Yet she hadn't said she did not want him, only that she did not wish to be married out of a sense of duty and obligation. Well, he would disabuse her of that notion the instant he caught up to her.

And if she left because she does not love you and does not want to be your wife? whispered a niggling voice.

Well, if that was so, he would just have to press his case and convince her to change her mind.

At least she'd made the search for her easier, since he now knew where she was headed. Glancing up, he found Esme watching him.

"What does it say?" she asked.

"That Meg has gone to her aunt in Scotland. I shall be traveling after her immediately."

A moment later Zeus barked with an excess of puppyish energy as he raced up and down the hall. Cade felt a bit like that himself, full of pent-up anxiety, knowing he had not a moment to waste.

"You had best take your friend there for his walk now, before you're missed in the schoolroom," he told his sister.

"I hope Meg comes back."

"She will," he promised.

She has to, he thought, since anything else would be unbearable.

Chapter 24

Meg leaned a shoulder against the cracked brown leather upholstery of the mail coach and gazed out the window at the passing countryside. The late afternoon sun hung high and strong in the sky, virid patches of tall grass waving between cultivated fields of ripening wheat and corn.

Folding her arms up close to her chest, she did

her best not to notice the occasional press from the elbow of the bony, gap-toothed man wedged in next to her. She'd tried scooting over, but there was no more room to scoot—not with herself and two other passengers crammed onto the same seat. Another equally hampered group sat packed like sausages on the other side.

She wished she'd thought to bring a book. If she had, perhaps a story might have kept her mind occupied. Of course, she would probably have just found herself thinking about Cade again, as she had been doing every two minutes all day.

She would have begun thinking about how much he loved to read, only to move on to consider how handsome he looked in his spectacles. Next, she would have thought about how much she would miss seeing him frown over some passage with which he disagreed, and how empty everything would seem without the chance of hearing his deep, masculine voice as he discussed something of interest. And the way his broad palms looked when he gestured to make a point. And how beautifully formed those hands were. How strong they were when he held her. How glorious they felt sliding over her body at night, when he made love to her . . .

Abruptly, she cut off the thoughts. Such nights were over now, and as for Cade, she would not be seeing him again. If she knew what was good for her, she would do well to erase him from her memory. But how was that to be done when she'd given him her heart? When he was the only man she knew she would ever love?

I did the right thing, she told herself with a firm internal rebuke. She'd chosen the only path possible, since staying would have been utterly insupportable.

So why then did she feel as if some vital part of her had been cut out? Why did she wish she could lay her head down and weep until every last tear inside her had been shed?

But she refused to cry, not here in this cramped coach among all these strangers. Once she reached Scotland, there would be time enough for tears; years and years for her to weep, if that is what it took for her to get over Cade.

Assuming she found welcome with her aunt when she arrived. She had no idea how the old lady would react, and whether she might find herself shown the door again only moments after walking through it.

If her aunt refused to receive her, she would travel south again. She had a few friends from her youth who would take her in—long enough at least for her to find a paid position. Perhaps she could hire out as a governess. Or as a lady's companion, if the other option would not serve. Somehow, she would make her way.

She was still contemplating that lowering notion when she heard several of her fellow passengers exclaim over some commotion taking place on the road outside.

"Wot's he think he's doing?" complained a man in the window seat opposite. "Must be some madman, racin' 'is carriage like that."

"It looks like he's waving, trying to get the coach to stop," said a round-faced woman. "Merciful heavens, you don't think he's a highwayman, do you?"

"Not in that rig, he's not," spoke a third. "Looks like some toff out causing trouble. Probably in his cups and half blind to boot."

"Oh, I hope he's not one of those drunken young lords who's tryin' to win a wager. I heard about some fool who took the reins to a coach-and-four last month. He sent every folk inside to their death with his reckless driving."

"Don't look now, but here he comes on the other side. Tryin' to pass again."

Leaning forward, Meg strained to see who the mad-man might be. Her eyes widened when she recognized the tall, broad-shouldered driver wielding the reins.

Cade!

Slumping low in the seat, she prayed he would not see her. But then, he must know she was inside, she realized, otherwise, why would he be trying to stop the coach? *And come to think of it, why was he here at all?* She'd assumed he might be secretly relieved to read her letter and discover her gone.

No need for any awkward confrontations or recriminations on either side. Maybe his pride was involved, though, and his sense of honor. Well, she wasn't interested in satisfying either one.

Less than a minute later the vehicle began to slow. As it drew to a halt, voices sounded outside, while Cade and the driver engaged in a brief debate. Then suddenly the door was wrenched open on a set of squeaking hinges.

The woman who'd expressed her fear of being set upon by highwaymen drew in an audible breath—all eyes turning toward Cade as he filled the doorway on the side farthest from Meg.

Shrinking down farther in her seat, she tried to make herself as small as possible, in hopes of disappearing within the tight mass of passengers. But Cade's keen, forest-green gaze locked on her with unerring accuracy, pinning her with a steady yet implacable look.

"Meg," he said, holding out his hand in clear expectation of her leaning forward to take it.

Instead, she retained her seat. "You should not have come. I'll thank you to go away, my lord."

"Not until we've talked. *In private*," he added, plainly aware of the small audience watching them, as though they were actors putting on a very interesting play.

"I have nothing to say. Did you not have my letter?"

His jaw stiffened at a familiar angle. "I did, else

I would not have known in which direction to drive after you."

Drat! she cursed to herself. She knew she should never have mentioned her intended destination, but hadn't wanted his family to be concerned.

"It makes no difference," she said, folding her arms tighter against her chest. "I am not coming back, so you may go home and tell everyone I am quite well. Now, you are delaying all these good people, not to mention interfering with the Royal Mail Service's usually punctual schedule."

"The postmaster can levy a fine against me, should he wish. Of course, if you would simply step down, the issue would be resolved."

"As it would if you would just be on your way."

Once again he extended his palm. "Meg, enough."

"Leave the miss alone," said one of the passengers. "Wot d'ye want with her anyway?"

"Yeah. If she don't want ter come wit' ye, I says leave her be," declared another.

"I might," Cade said in a determined tone. "But this woman is my wife, you see, and she has run away. I am retrieving her."

Meg's arms fell to her sides, despite the cramped quarters. "I am not your wife!" She turned to the others. "I am not his wife. He's lying."

"Why would I lie?" he said, showering them all with his most affable smile. "Most men try to deny being married, not the other way around."

The mood among her fellows changed, the gazes shifting toward Meg ranging from disbelieving to suspicious.

"If she is your wife," the bony man next to her demanded, "then where's her ring?"

A murmur of agreement rumbled through the coach interior.

Cade paused for a moment, then thrust a hand into his coat pocket. After a brief search, he held out his palm to reveal the diamond ring she'd returned inside her letter. "Right here," he declared. "She left it behind when she ran off this morning."

The mood shifted again, turning to condemnation this time.

"Well, missus," one of the men announced, "you'd best be gettin' along. You've cost us all half our dinner break at the next inn."

"Indeed you should be going," stated the woman with a disapproving glare. "A wife's place is with her husband."

"But he isn't my husband!" Meg declared, defending herself.

The others would hear none of it, though, and acting in tandem, soon had her maneuvered out of her seat and pushed into Cade's waiting arms. He received her with a gracious smile and lifted her to the ground.

Her traveling valise came hurtling down from where it had been strapped atop the coach, its impact sending up a brown plume of road dust. The coach door was slammed shut moments later and the horses set to. Cade drew her safely back as the coach raced off down the lane.

For a long moment Meg stared after the departing vehicle, her lips parted in astonishment. As soon as the coach vanished, she snapped her mouth closed. With a glare at Cade, she picked up her traveling case and stomped toward the side of the road. Setting down the sturdy piece of luggage, she turned around and took a seat upon it. Cade studied her. "What is this all about?" She crossed her arms. "I am waiting for the next coach, assuming there is a seat available, when it comes through in . . . oh, three hours or so. I only hope they will not charge me again, since I possess limited funds for the fare."

Reaching again into his pocket, he drew out a pair of coins, holding them out as he strolled toward her. "Here. This should more than suffice."

She made no effort to take his offering. "Put that away. I do not want your money."

"Then what is it you *do* want? Why did you run off, Meg?" he asked, his gentle tone working against the righteous sense of anger she'd been nursing in order to hold him at bay.

"I gave my reasons in my letter," she stated.

"Ah, yes, the letter. I found it left rather more questions than answers."

She lowered her gaze to her boots. "If it did, I

am sorry, but it said all I have to say. I am not coming back, Cade, so you might as well get in your carriage and leave me here to wait for the next mail coach."

"I would never leave you." He stopped beside her, his large, booted feet entering her line of sight.

"And what were you thinking," she charged, "telling all those people that I am your wife?"

"Why should I not, when that is what you will be soon enough."

Her breath caught at the base of her throat. "I won't marry you."

"Why not?"

"I will not be wed out of obligation. I told you that."

"And so you did, in your letter. What I want to know is if you will be wed for love?"

"What?" Her gaze flew upward, her eyes widening when they encountered the open, black velvet jeweler's box he was holding. Inside lay a stunning moonstone ring, the pearly blue gem surrounded by a cluster of glittering diamonds set in gold. "What is that?"

"It's yours, if you'll have it. I know it's unusual, but I thought the stone suited you. I went out this morning to buy it."

"You did? Why?"

He reached for her hand and drew her to her feet. "So I could ask you to marry me for real this time. So I could give you a ring that had no taint of falsehood behind it. I love you, Meg. Please make me happy and say you will be my wife."

"But you don't want to marry me."

"Do I not?" He drew her into his arms.

She trembled. "No. And you don't love me. You love Calida, even though she is lost to you forever."

"I see you believed my lies to Everett. Forgive me for that."

"But they weren't lies. Not all of them. You loved her, I know you did." She fixed her eyes on his cravat, afraid to glance up for fear of what she might see.

"Yes, I loved Calida, and I mourned her. But I think a part of my grief came more out of guilt than a true sense of loss. For some while now I've had new feelings. I suppose I didn't want to let myself admit it, didn't want to take the risk. But I can't deny the truth anymore. I have fallen in love again—with you."

Her heart squeezed inside her chest, unable to believe what she was hearing. Her gaze met his and she couldn't look away.

"What I feel for you is nothing compared to what I had with her," he went on. "My emotions are so much deeper, so much stronger than I ever imagined they could be. When I nearly lost you last night, I realized how much I love you and how bleak my life would be without you in it. And when I found you gone today . . . well, I only stayed sane knowing I could come after you and that I had the hope of getting you back. Please take mercy and tell me you'll have me. I don't believe I could bear anything less."

Tears burst from her, a violent sob catching in her throat as she pressed herself against him.

He cradled her and stroked her hair. "*Shh*, don't cry. Don't cry, darling. What is it? Please don't be unhappy. Is it because you don't love me?"

Her head came up and she sniffed. "No. Of course I love you. How could you think otherwise?"

He brushed a thumb over one wet cheek. "Then why the tears?"

"Because I'm happy . . . Really," she added at his bemused look. "You truly love me?

"Yes."

"And you really want to marry me? You're not doing it because you've compromised me?"

"No. Though I must confess that I have definite plans to compromise you again, as soon as we can manage."

"And you're not proposing because it's the right thing to do?"

His lips turned upward in a warm smile. "No. And although marrying you *is* the right thing to do, I'm not doing it out of any sense of duty, but rather because I know we're perfectly suited to each other. I can't imagine another woman of my acquaintance willing to put up with my tempers and moods."

She raised a hand to his cheek. "I love you, even your tempers and moods. So yes, yes, I will marry you."

On a laugh, he slid the ring onto her finger. Then before she had time to do more than glance at it, he tugged her tight against him and crushed her lips to his. Delight flooded her senses, sending her soaring as high and light as a cloud.

Kissing him back, she let him sweep her into a pleasure so intense it made the world fade away, leaving behind only the joy and glory of his embrace. Sliding her arms around his shoulders, she held on and let herself get lost. His touch was such bliss, even the earth began to shake beneath her feet.

A long minute passed before she realized that the effect wasn't solely from the force of their desire, but rather that the road actually was shaking. Male catcalls rang out as a coach thundered into view, hoots and a few ribald comments from the male occupants setting her cheeks afire.

"Give her a good hard tumble, and don't stint on the tongue!"

"Show her what you've got in them breeches of yours!"

The coach raced on past, the men continuing to cheer and tease until the vehicle moved out of sight.

"Well," Cade observed. "They make some interesting suggestions. What do you say we go home and follow up on their advice?"

Meg blushed harder and laughed. "I think, my lord, that sounds like a very fine idea."

Chapter 25

*O*ne month later Meg leafed through the fabric samples spread across the polished surface of the satinwood table in the family drawing room. Selecting two, she turned to Cade. "Which do you like better? The cream or the willow green?"

Seated in a nearby armchair, he raised his head from his book and peered over the top of his spectacles at the swatches she was holding up. "What is this for?"

"The ribbons on the epergnes. I want them to complement the arrangements without conflicting with the flowers."

"I should imagine either would do nicely. Which one do you prefer?"

A tiny frown settled between her pale brows. "The cream, I think."

"The cream it is, then."

"Or the green," she said, vacillating on the subject again. "I am just not sure." Laying down the samples, she picked up a quill and tapped the feathered end against her chin. "And what do you think about the wedding breakfast? Should we serve sliced oranges in champagne or a fresh cherry cordial?"

"You love cherries and they will be in season then, so the cherries, I believe."

"Yes, but I know you are very partial to oranges, as are many of the guests, so perhaps the cherries would be a bad idea."

Marking the page in his book, he set the volume aside, then removed his spectacles and laid them on top. "Meg, come here."

Her brows rose. "Why?" she said with clear suspicion.

He suppressed a smile. "Never mind why. Just come."

Laying down her quill, she crossed the room. As soon as she moved within range, he caught her hand and tugged her down onto his lap, careful to settle her on his good leg. She let out a laugh as he bounced her once and tumbled her forward for a kiss.

Her breathing was far from steady by the time he let her come up for air. "What was that for?" she murmured, a dreamy expression in her soft blue eyes.

"I thought you could do with a distraction from all this wedding planning. It's making you tense. I want you to relax and have fun."

"I *am* having fun," she defended. "Well, most of the time. I just want everything to be perfect."

"It doesn't need to be perfect. It only needs to be what you want. If it were up to me, I would have had you in front of a vicar four weeks ago, and we could even now be lying in our honeymoon bed. But you wanted a big church wedding, so that is what you're going to get. St. George's is confirmed for two weeks from Saturday, and all the invitations have been sent—you have the ink-stained fingers to prove it," he added, holding up one of her smudged hands. Kissing her palm, he folded it inside his own.

"A girl only gets married once," she said. "And I didn't have the heart to disappoint your sisters and your mother. Esme is so excited about being a flower girl, she mentions it now every time I see her. Mallory is thrilled to be my maid of honor. And as for Ava, she actually tears up every now and then over the fact that she's getting to be both the mother of the groom and of the bride."

She paused. "I was deeply touched that she wants to act in my own mother's stead, and she's been truly wonderful, especially considering the short amount of time we have to put everything together."

"Six weeks may be a rush for you, but it's an agony for me," Cade said. "Particularly since I idiotically agreed to stop visiting your room until after the wedding."

She stroked a hand over his chest. "I don't like it any better than you, but since I am not enceinte, it seems the wise thing to do. I don't want our first baby plagued by comments about being conceived too early for a full-term birth."

"Well, be forewarned, my dear, that as soon as that marriage register is signed, it will be my goal to get you with child. I'll be at you morning, noon, and night. Although I hope you don't conceive too soon. I rather fancy the notion of having you all to myself for a while."

Her skin warmed at his comment and she smiled. "I shall look forward to it, especially this winter. I miss having all that lovely heat in my bed at night. You're much nicer than a blanket, you know."

He growled under his breath and gave her another bounce on his knee. "If you aren't careful, I'll break my promise."

"If you keep testing me, I just might let you."

He met her gaze for a long moment, her eyes lambent with a barely restrained desire that mirrored his own. With a sigh, she moved back slightly on his lap. Reluctantly, he allowed her to do so.

He cleared his throat. "Now, as to the original topic of the wedding."

"Yes?"

"From here on, I want you to relax and not worry about the details."

"But—"

"No buts. Choose what you like best, no matter what anyone else may have to say on the matter. If you want tobacco brown ribbons on the epergnes, and liverwurst pudding for breakfast, then that is what we shall have."

She made a face. "No one would want tobacco brown ribbons and liverwurst pudding. *Ugh!*"

"That is not the point. What matters is that this is *your* special day and I want you to have everything *you* want. There is no right or wrong. Only what suits you best. You are the bride, remember? You do what you wish."

"But this is your day, too. I want you to be happy as well."

"I am happy. Happier than I can ever remember being, and I know things are only going to get better after we are wed. Don't you realize by now, sweetheart, that every day with you is my special day?"

A beatific smile spread over her lips. "Oh, Cade. I'm the luckiest woman in the world to have you. I love you so much."

"I love you more. Now, come closer so we can put each other's resolve to the test again."

An effervescent laugh drifted past her lips. He waited for her to snuggle up against him and press her mouth to his. Kissing her back with a deep claiming, he took them both where he knew they most longed to go, pleasure burgeoning in his veins and love in his heart. A love he now knew she returned without conditions or restraint.

Abruptly, he heard a pair of hands give an intrusive clap.

"All right. Enough of that, you two! You'll have plenty of time for such foolery once you are married," his mother declared as she strode into the room. "Now, be a good boy and let Margaret go."

Meg started to slide off his lap, but he held her firm. "Ordinarily, I would, Mama. But you see, that's impossible now."

"Oh, and why is that?"

"Because Meg is mine, and I've decided I'm never, ever letting her go again."

Center Point Publishing
600 Brooks Road ● PO Box 1
Thorndike ME 04986-0001 USA

(207) 568-3717

US & Canada:
1 800 929-9108
www.centerpointlargeprint.com